Salleys Kitchen

a novel

Bruce Wise Weeks

SALLEYS KITCHEN by Bruce Wise Weeks

ISBN-13: 978-0692946671 (Salleys Kitchen)
ISBN-10: 0692946675

Cover Design: Jacob Hunt Chambers, JC Photography & Design

Second Edition

Printed in the United States of America

A Note to the Reader

Please understand my story is a work of fiction. While the tale recalls a few of the events that occurred during my boyhood, the story as a whole is fiction. Any names or characters thought to represent any persons in particular are just coincidental and they do not have reference to any specific individual, family, or community. Those acquainted with me are well aware of my impulsive obsession to spin yarns and those unfamiliar with me soon find all knowledge gleaned may become part of an eclectic hodgepodge of bits and pieces molded and shaped into a story. Never is there any intent to offend or disrespect anyone, any place or anything, in any way. However, I do not apologize for any emotions the historical facts may evoke.

I find great pleasure and understanding in placing imaginary characters among the historical facts and then allowing their voices and actions to play out a story of how the events most likely occurred.

Also, I must offer an explanation for the title being Salleys Kitchen as opposed to Salley's Kitchen. I grew up in the cotton fields with African Americans and loved them with all of my heart. They had a colloquial language that was heavily influenced by the Gullah people from the coast. In a layman's way I have tried to illustrate their actual voice and dialect. Putting an 's' on the end of names of places was part of their voice. They would not say, "That boy is from Salley" rather they would say, "Dat bo bez from Salleys." It was a distinct part of their everyday language as well as mine for a time. To honor and remember my friends of the field, I choose to use Salleys Kitchen as the title of my book. I offer my sincere apologies to all teachers of English grammar.

Dedication

I dedicate this book to Jan Hunt Weeks, my wife and soulmate; the rock upon which my life has been attached for 42 years. Without her by my side, this work would have never been completed. With the greatest humility and gratitude, I acknowledge she is the finest part of everything I am. While I was lost in a world of make-believe, unable to extricate myself, she kept our lives on track, fed me when I forgot to eat and made polite excuses to friends and family while I ignored the world. When I faced a wall, she made quiet comments that penetrated my exclusionary fog and returned me to write. She even reminded me of the title she chose for the story in the years before we were married.

Thank you, Bunk, I love you so much — always have and always will!

Acknowledgments

Thank you to Jacob Hunt Chambers of JC Photography & Design for the original cover concept. His talented eye and interpretive gift are indisputable and radiate from all of his work.

Thank you to my beautiful granddaughter, Aileen, for being the girl in the cotton field. She is my supermodel and well on her way to being a dynamic young woman.

Thank you to my editor, Tamara Trudeau, who saw something in my writing that everyone else overlooked. I am so thankful for our serendipitous friendship and anticipate its evolution with wonderment and excitement as I write into the years to come.

Thank you to my cousin Debbie Weeks for working alongside me during the countless editing sessions and for being my greatest promoter and supporter.

Finally, thank you to my 'friends of the field' who pulled me away from an abyss of hate and prejudice by looking past my color and into my heart.

Chapter One

On the first day of school in fifth grade, after we prayed to Jesus, but before we said the *Pledge of Allegiance,* our teacher told us she had a new flag to show the class. With excitement in her eyes, she said, "We will be entering a new decade with a new president and a new flag."

In my narrow world, I had not faced change very often so her words of a fresh, new flag for the United States of America grabbed my attention. Unrolling it, she explained we had been pledging allegiance to a 48-star flag. With the addition of Alaska and most recently Hawaii officially becoming a state, we would now be pledging to a flag with 50 stars. As Mrs. Poole held the little classroom flag out so everyone could see, we counted each star together and indeed she was right; we had a brand new 50-star flag.

Excited and naïve, this event was to be but the opening salvo in a decade of transformation for me. The new flag would be only one of many things I would encounter for the first time over the next ten chaotic years. Like a gut-wrenching rollercoaster ride, the decade would climb to the heights of the most wonderful events of my life, but it would also plunge downward into an abyss of the most devastating ordeals I would ever face. Enduring such an unrelenting horde of extremes, my life was forever changed.

In 1960, I carried a hoe and chopped my father's cotton, but in 1970, I carried an M16 rifle and fought Gooks for Uncle Sam. At age ten, I knew more about growing cotton than how to talk to a girl; at age twenty, I knew well how to slip through a jungle and silently kill Charlie.

As an innocent preteen in 1962, I watched Andy and Opie and wondered how a boy could be so lucky to have a father like Sheriff Taylor. As a veteran in 1972, I cynically stared at Archie Bunker berating 'the Meathead' and thought him to be so stupidly typical.

As the 60s began, the majestic atmosphere and promise of greatness surrounding the young and handsome new president,

John F. Kennedy, consumed our nation. The words of his inaugural speech gave everyone a sense of excitement at the possibility of a new world that until now we had only dreamed. The decade started with such eager anticipation, but in the second year of his regal administration he was forced to make a speech that slapped our nation with the coldness of reality.

My father yelled during the nightly news, "Shut up and get your ass out of the way! They're about to blow us all to kingdom come and I want to hear about it!"

The new president picked a fight with the communist rebel leader in Cuba, Fidel Castro, triggering the Cuban Missile Crisis. With nuclear Armageddon looming on the horizon, the nation's optimism was quickly fettered. While Russia and the U.S. pointed their doomsday missiles at each other, we were faced with the sobering fact that the leaders of our nations had in their hands the capacity to bring our world to an end. Global nuclear destruction was averted, but a veil of mistrust shaded our country and we watched an Iron Curtain drop as we entered the Cold War. While we were coming to grips with Communism as our new enemy, tragedy fell upon our nation with the suddenness of a guillotine's blade and I cried as the president's beautiful wife, our nation's queen, kneeled to kiss his flag-draped coffin days after an assassin's bullet blew his head into pieces.

On first hearing about the assassination of President Kennedy on my school bus, I couldn't believe the shocking news, but seeing the reactions of people around me, I soon gave it credence. Jumping off the bus running, I flew into the house and asked my mother, "Is President Kennedy dead?"

With the coldness of a morgue attendant, she said, "Yes, somebody shot him in Texas, probably a crazy nigger; they're ruining the whole country!"

Shocked, I could not believe what she said. As I put on my work clothes before heading to the field, the newsman on TV said they had caught a white man named Lee Harvey

Oswald and he was believed to be the President's killer. With a cold biscuit in my mouth, I remember thinking *A black person would not kill the President. She told me that so I would think bad of Wes and Della and the rest of my friends. What makes her hate them so?*

My mother was not a warm and nurturing person. Though she had concern for me, I'm sure it was in deference to what other women in the community might say about her mothering skills.

As a girl from a small cotton mill village in the valley, she had married my father during World War II when men were scarce in her town. I heard her explain her choice of husband to a neighbor lady at a Missionary Meeting one night. She compared herself to one of two men that had to travel through the woods one day and decided upon a competition to keep their journey interesting.

Just for the sport of it, they would see which could pick up the straightest stick. Traveling through the woods, each man would pick up a stick and look it over, only to say, "I can find one much better than that!" then throw it down.

Surprisingly, one of the men found himself without a stick as he looked up to see the end of the wood ahead. Earnestly looking around, he saw none that met his standards, but having reached the end, he picked up the only one that was available. My mother said she saw the end of the woods ahead and had to pick up the only stick available to her — my father.

The seventh child of ten, she was born to the son of a poor English immigrant from Wales. He had worked all of his life in the cotton mill and drank heavily when not working. Having a habit of gambling away most of his earnings, he also became abusive when he drank and would often beat the nearest family member when he arrived home. My mother found safety at the Baptist church and became enamored with its beliefs and sacred rituals. She was baptized in the Holy Spirit and became a devout member as a little girl and carried its idioms in her heart as a young woman.

She met my father through his mother, another child of God, visiting her mill town church during a revival meeting. Mother and son lived on a small plot of land just outside the village and he helped her with their small cottage industry. Dragging her only petted son to the church meeting, he was pushed toward my mother and their association began. He was one of the few men left in the vicinity of the little mill town because his 4F classification deemed him unfit for military service during World War II. Having battled scarlet fever as a child, he had hearing in only one ear and very poor eyesight. With thick glasses and protruding ears, he was bullied throughout his boyhood and his mother had protected him; now with the bullies off at war, he was free to exert his authority. Argumentative and combative, he was often at odds with people in the mill village.

After a long arranged relationship, the couple decided to marry. Each had reason; he wanted to get his nagging mother off his back and she wanted to get away from her alcoholic father's abuse. Having been killed in the trenches during World War I, his father's pension allowed his mother and him to live on a veteran's pension. Before the war, the father had purchased a house and small plot of land because he hated living in a mill house. He paid the mortgage by working in the mill, but his death had dropped that financial responsibility in his wife's lap.

Most frugal, the mother sold eggs from the chickens she kept in a coop attached to an outbuilding near the alley in back. They also sold butter from the milk my father begrudgingly coaxed from their cow every morning. It grazed on a small plot of pasture and was kept at night in the outbuilding. Having saved every penny she made, in addition to her husband's pension, the mother had managed to pay off the mortgage. All of his life she had doted on her son and now she assumed it her responsibility to make arrangements for him to wed.

After they were married, he was goaded into working in the mill like every other person living in and around the village.

This proved to be a trying time for all three, but it was most disagreeable for the son as he soon lost his temper at the mill and hit his supervisor. Fired immediately, it fueled his resentment to new heights. Having been rejected by the military, he hated the sight of the soldiers that the girls swooned over. Having to take a job in the mill so the family could survive had stripped him of his last parcel of dignity and he flamed with anger. In a heated exchange with his mother after he was fired, he told her he hated her, the mill town and his wife and was thinking of walking away from it all. He left the house in a huff and when his wife returned from a visit with her mother, she found his mother dead from a blow to her head. Upon review, it was decided by the authorities that she had passed out and hit her head as she fell. Shortly thereafter, the son sold his mother's house, bought a farm in the middle of nowhere, packed up their belongings and took his wife, cow and chickens to live near a crossroads called Salleys Kitchen.

As a mill town girl, having never spent a day on a farm, she had much to learn about her role as a farmer's wife, but she remained committed to the church which removed any possibility of leaving her husband. Fully self-confidant, she felt she was a rung higher on the social ladder than the ignorant farmers and their wives. However, needing their help, she became friends with them and gradually assimilated. Their first year was hard as she learned to work and harvest a garden in addition to canning and preserving the produce she raised. Becoming a church leader, she found she could intimidate the uneducated pastor and his flock with her knowledge of the scriptures and her high school education. Becoming the undisputed director of worship, with an unquestioned status in the community, she enjoyed the power she gained over them, in the name of Christ.

After that first year she picked up a few pointers from her husband and found that she could use and abuse the black women that had been persuaded to live on their farm. Following his lead, she had her house cleaned by the lady who lived in a shack her husband built on the edge of the farm. Using her assumed authority, she made them plow plant and harvest her garden. In addition, she had them take care of the other daily chores she so abhorred such as feeding the chickens, gathering the eggs, and killing a chicken for dinner. Having dragged the milk cow to the farm, she was forced to milk, but now, she relegated this task to the tenants as well as separating the cream and butter and pasteurizing the milk for drinking. She soon found she had much more time that could be devoted to prayer and her church work.

Having picked up the knack of being a farmer's wife, all was going well for their first five years on the farm, until she missed her menstrual cycle one month and began to feel a little sick in the mornings. Putting it all together, she was horrified. With neither she nor her husband wanting children, she knew he would be livid for he had always said he did not want to look at a snotty nosed brat while he ate his supper. After she confirmed the fact of her pregnancy, she fixed her husband's favorite meal and prepared to dump the news on him. Once he had eaten and was sitting in his chair, she approached him sheepishly and said, "James, I have some surprising news to share with you: I'm pregnant."

He sat glaring at her for a while before he yelled, "Well I'll be a son-of-a-bitch! I knew it! I knew you would screw up all of my hard work!" She admonished him for swearing, but did not dwell on it too severely.

After his first statement he told her, "I don't have the money to waste on getting rid of your mess; besides, the church people around here would run us out of the community if they found out. Crap, I guess we're just going to have to live with this screw up. How in the hell could you have let this happen? I was warned about the 10/20 crap a wife could bring to a marriage, now I've learned the hard way — ten minutes of pleasure and twenty years of pain in the ass! You have just ruined our lives!"

She thought to herself, *You had a lot to do with this, too, and I didn't get any pleasure from you humping on me!*

When it was time for me to be born, he took her to the hospital and dropped her out, then came back four days later and picked her up. He had a scowl on his face the entire trip home. Once home, she found the local midwife and asked which black girl in the community had recently had a baby and had enough milk for two. They located the unfortunate girl and she became my nanny and wet nurse. My father had to drive over early every morning and pick up her and her baby and they stayed until I was put to bed. Hungry at night, I cried until she arrived in the morning. I was weaned onto cow's milk as soon as possible because he hated having the black girl and baby in his house and deplored every trip he made to retrieve them. Once I was weaned, the girl was abandoned and no one came to pick her up. A woman from the field started coming over early before work and changed, fed and dressed me in the mornings until her husband decided he couldn't work for my father anymore and they disappeared in the night.

Della took over after that and pretty much raised me.

In the first year my father worked the land and put in a crop with the equipment that came with the farm. Planting the cotton and plowing the fields, he was able to harvest enough of the white fiber to pay his debts and have a little bit of money left over. Along with the food from his wife's garden, they made a meager living from the farm that year. Quick to see his mistakes, he watched the farmers around him and soon learned the secret of success on a cotton farm lay in manipulating the black people of the community. Cobbling together a shack, he was able to entice one family to live on his farm. From an association with the local storekeeper, he bought debts owed by the black members of the community and was schooled in the centuries-old art of handling 'niggers'. Honing his skills as a tyrant and slave driver, he became much more successful the following year and progressed each year thereafter.

He soon found the more sadistically he treated the blacks working in his field, the more work he could coax from a day's labor. Becoming increasingly demanding, he used, abused, and intimidated his hired help to operate his farm and seemed to enjoy the control and domination it allowed him. As his farming abilities grew, so did his reputation as a slave driver. He became more abusive and drove those laboring in his fields to work harder and do more than the other farmers in the area. Paying his help a paltry amount, he always cheated them on what he owed and gave them verbal abuse if they argued with him. Those in the black community with a choice began to avoid his farm like the plague and the few who worked his fields cursed him under their breath and looked for a way to escape his tyranny.

In church, however, my father could stand before the congregation and pray like a saint. His mother had taught him to pray aloud as a boy and he soon realized the benefits of appearing pious in the church. Using the eloquent prayers of his boyhood, he had everyone in the country church thinking he was a saint. He was often called on to lead the congregation in an opening prayer and as his religious words resonated across the sanctuary, 'Amen' was often repeated by the preacher to reiterate his supplications to God.

Old women would tell my mother, "Your husband prays the most beautiful prayers; he is such a benefit to our church."

She would smile with pride, for church was her favorite place. But as most knew, my old man was equally skilled with vile, vulgar and profane words when he addressed the people that worked in his fields. Vehemently determined to 'keep niggers in their place', he used fear and intimidation to continually oppress those who kept his farm running.

The good ole boys that heard his rants said, "He's got them niggers so scared, they're probably about to piss their nasty pants."

In our community, he was considered a good farmer and an expert at handling 'niggers'.

***

Having just spent my first day in fifth grade, I stepped down off the school bus and saw the hot rod Ford parked in our

13

driveway. It belonged to Luke Cutter, nephew of Boot Cutter, the meanest bootlegger in our community and the most evil person I could imagine. Boot's nephew was not a person who frequented our yard and I knew no reason for his presence, but I figured it meant trouble. He was sitting in his fancy car watching my father chain a fertilizer tank onto the back bed of his old two-ton truck. Walking closer, I saw Wes standing behind my father talking.

Once close enough, I heard Wes say, "Please Misser James, I needs dey money in the worstest ki'na way! Dat man say he gwine cut me bad if I ain'ts pay him. Please Misser James, I's gotta pay him or he gwine hurt me bad."

My father turned around and pushed Wes to the ground and I knew immediately he was drunk. My old man could have never pushed Wes down if he was sober.

Wes got up and staggered over to him and again, began to beg. "Please Misser James, I's needs ta works fo yous and I'lls works has long's you needs me if you's gives me dis money."

Ignoring him, my father continued to chain the tank to the truck. Still begging, Wes put his hand on my father's shoulder to try and get him to turn around and face him. In a flash of rage, my father grabbed the log chain from the truck and swung it at Wes. It wrapped around his head and the hook split his forehead open like a melon. Staggering backward, my ole man kept swinging the chain and hitting Wes' head until it became a bloody pulp. Putting his arms up to protect his head, my father continued swinging the chain and repeatedly hit Wes' ribs and chest area. Finally Wes fell to the ground and the enraged fool stepped close to him and started to kick him in his stomach and groin. Wes was barely conscious and as his face was on the ground, my father stepped on the back of his head and ground his face into the blood stained sand.

Breathing heavily, he backed away as Wes groaned in pain and shook his finger at Wes yelling, "You were lucky this time, but if you ever put your hands on me again I will kill you on the spot!"

Then he spit on Wes and yelled at the bootlegger's boys to come and get him out of the yard. The two greasy-headed louts sitting in the car were laughing as one cleaned the dirt from under his fingernails with what looked like a Bowie knife.

The driver got out of his car laughing and said, "That nigger oughta had knowed better than to put his filthy hand on your shoulder. He got exactly what he deserved. He's damn lucky he ain't dead."

His brother, who had been sitting in the car with him, climbed out and slid the knife in his boot as he snorted and said, "That nigger got a lot worse whupping than we was gonna put on him. He done shit and fell back in it!" Then he laughed outloud.

Luke Cutter, the car owner, gave the final words, "Mr. James, you just gonna had'a take that chain and hook it around his leg and drag him outa yo yard, cause I ain't putting him in my car. That nasty nigger can rot for all I care!"

I was not sure Wes was still alive. In a state of shock, fear and disbelief, I had watched this deacon in the Baptist Church whip an inebriated black man with a log chain in our yard. He beat the man as he begged for money to pay a bootlegger threatening his life. He beat a man who had faithfully toiled in his fields for years and was more of a father to his son than he. He beat the man while other white men watched and laughed. No one ever considered his attack to be illegal in any way and he was assured by the good ole boys that observed the attack, 'the nigger got what was coming to him'. This was not something considered unusual in our community, especially where my father was concerned. It was merely an exercise often needed to keep 'niggers' in their place and show them who was boss. My old man got in his truck and left. The bootlegger's kin got in their car and sped off, too.

Walking over to Wes, I tried to help him roll over. Once on his back he said as he spit blood and tried to sit, "Don't

15

looks at me like dis, James, you shouldn't hada see this. I'lls bees all right, d'eckly. Now go on away froms me!"

I tried to help him up, but he couldn't stand. He told me to go in the house and let him be, but I refused to leave him until he began to yell and told me to go away. I sat and snubbed while watching him from the porch. He collapsed several times crawling out of our driveway and finally tumbled into the ditch by the road. I was horrified and helpless as I saw him struggle to breathe, for I knew if I tried to help him get home, my father would whip me with his belt and Wes knew that, too.

My mother came out on the porch and saw the tears in my eyes. She swatted me in the back of the head and said, "Quit your snubbing! That drunk nigger got what he deserved. Now get inside, change into your work clothes and get to the field."

As I pulled on my old clothes, I saw Sully's old Ford come poking along and stop. He took off his shirt and wrapped it around Wes' head as he lay in the ditch. After a few minutes, he got Wes to his knees and helped him get into his car. Wes didn't come back for over a month. Then one morning he showed up for work and my ole man laid into him like a yard dog. He cursed him and threatened to beat him again. We tried not to smile, because he may have lashed out at us, but we knew he was just shooting off his mouth. Wes was sober now and would have killed him if he had hit him again. After the beating, Wes had scars all over his face, head and arms and he limped when he walked, but he never said a word—just went to work after the tongue lashing. Everyone in the field heard me cursing my old man and wishing him dead. They grumbled in low agreement, but Wes told us to stop talking about what had happened because there was nothing we could do about it now.

Chapter Two

As were most southern white children, I was baptized by total immersion in a smothering concoction of humidity, Holy Ghost preaching, sweet tea, cotton and racial bigotry. Force fed the standards of white supremacy since my earliest recollections, my mother and father, along with the rest of the white people around me, constantly reinforced this ideology as I moved toward manhood.

But unlike most white boys growing up during this time, I matured in a bicultural environment and lived in two separate and very unequal worlds. My mind, my body and my soul were divided among opposing black and white cultures and the black side was by far my real home.

As an infant, I was cared for by two different black ladies, whose names I was told, but I don't remember their person. As a toddler, I was taken to the cotton fields to be watched over and cared for by my father's 'field-hands' so my mother would be free to help him. My early days were spent in the shade, at the end of the long rows of cotton, playing on a burlap cotton sheet. In the morning, Della would knock on the door and wait for my mother to let her in so she could get me out of my crib, change my diaper, and feed me. Then she had to go to the field, so I rode her hip to my play area near her work. She stopped each time she came to my end of the row and checked on me. She taught me to walk, talk, potty and sing. When a little older, after Della worked all day chopping cotton, I would hold her hand as we walked home and she would feed me, wash me and put on my PJs. When I was ready for bed, she was allowed to go home. She always kissed me and made me wave bye-bye. I would then sit with my mother a short while until she tired of me, and then I was put to bed. On Saturdays, Della cleaned our house and took care of me and on Sundays my mother took me to church.

The black women chopping my father's cotton lovingly watched over me until I could follow them up and down the hot sandy furrows. Once old enough to work, I was given a hoe and became a white speck in the wave of black workers progressing across the fields. Though obviously different in color, I was accepted into their humble way of life and never made to feel I didn't belong. Unlike other white boys my age, I saw firsthand the spirit of black culture and the dominating oppression that had smothered their lives as free people from reconstruction to the late 1960s. Soothed by the spiritual songs, comfortable using their Gullah-infused dialect and nourished by soul food, I wore a smile during most of the days I spent in the field. Though often corrected and set straight by my caregivers, I never remember being rebuked or chastised about my color.

On the other hand, I was a silent member of the white ruling class. By default, being Caucasian on sight, I was entitled to all of the rights and privileges attached. When I started school, I didn't talk at first because everything sounded different. My teachers said I had been hanging around with the 'nigras' too long. As did my mother, the teachers corrected, chastised and often whacked me for using the language I learned in the field. I soon learned to speak only when someone spoke to me and gradually got the hang of full time 'white talk'. Out of necessity, I learned to switch personas when I entered the white world and could make the change without any problem, but found it safer to remain mute. I quietly attended the white school and became part of the white church without drawing any attention or criticism with my words or actions.

Believing I had made for myself a comfortable but camouflaged seat upon a post in the fence that separated whites and colored, I felt somewhat secure, but always wary in the white world. I spoke freely in the field, but to avoid ridicule and bullying in the white world, I continued to speak very little and carefully chose my words. For that reason I was considered a shy little boy and never earned the star status in my class. Making plenty of acquaintances in school, I didn't have real friends like in the field. In my 12 years of attending the white school, I never completely let my guard down around my schoolmates. Always on alert, I constantly felt as though I was really black and only masquerading in the white world.

In my first year of school, I thought everyone had to learn how to negotiate two worlds and that I was just not smart enough to master that art. As the school year progressed, the absence of black people became a troubling matter and I could not figure out why this was happening. But I had learned trouble could be cooked up quickly if I became too inquisitive, especially asking white folks too many questions regarding the colored members of our community. For this reason, I constantly felt as if I had misunderstood something or missed some important information that had been given to everyone else. There were just too many things that seemed wrong. The reasons black folks lived a near-destitute lifestyle and had such a hat-in-hand attitude remained a baffling question during my first year of school. The thought of mere skin color giving me such superiority was directly opposed to the lessons taught me in Sunday School. Anyone I asked, white or colored, would not give a straight answer.

After hearing of the way the Jews and Romans treated Jesus during his life, I asked my Sunday School teacher, Mrs. Ester, if Christ was black. Quite offended at my question, she shook her finger in my face and said, "Why would you ask such a crazy question? I'm a good mind to tell your father what you just asked me!"

That scared the bejesus out of me. I sure didn't want my behind striped with his belt for asking an inappropriate question. I also asked Wes once when we were alone at one end of the field, "Why does my daddy cuss you and call you a nigger?"

Without looking me in the eye he continued to chop around the knee-high cotton plants and said, "Now boy, you don't needs to be acksing me thangs like that." After a pause, he added, "And don't be acksing yo daddy thangs like dat, lessen you want yo butt to'e up!"

This was true, for my father needed only the slightest provocation to whip me with his belt. He considered me a field-hand and I was to keep my mouth shut, but he didn't call me a nigger. As we hoed our way down the cotton rows, I gave Wes a 'you ain't being straight with me' scowl for a while and finally he reached across the rows and pulled me over close to him and gingerly grabbed my head with his rough callused hands.

Looking me straight in the eye and smiling, he patiently said, "Boy, don'ts be'a hurri'n to grows up so fass. Being growed up ain't a good thang sum-times." Then he showed me how to make a loud noise by blowing on a green cotton leaf he held between his thumbs.

***

With her yard stick Popeye in hand, my first grade teacher, Ms. Louise, pointed to each word in the flipbook hanging on the three-legged stand. Wanting to retain my place in the bluebird reading group, I tried to concentrate while we round-robin read *The Adventures of Dick and Jane*. I had been demoted to the redbird group once for not knowing my words and I sure didn't want to be put in the blackbird group with the non-readers. Now back among the bluebirds, I tried my utmost to concentrate as we sat in our child-size chairs and formed a semicircle around the tripod. Try as I might though, it was always a struggle for me to follow my bluebird buddies chosen to read aloud and not drift off thinking of things beyond the window.

One morning just before bathroom break, as I listened to Kenny Hall mundanely read out loud, "Look Sally! See Puff run; See Spot run!" The reality that there was not even one colored person around grabbed my thinking once again! I was affronted by the fact there weren't any colored kids in the blackbird group itself or for that matter, not one colored friend of Dick and Jane in the big book. This seemed wrong for I had been open-heartedly bathed in southern Black culture since I could walk. Again trying to give logic to my problem, I had a momentary lapse of attention from the task at hand, and was naturally, at that moment, called on to read. I had no clue where Kenny stopped reading.

Ms. Louise always used her trusted Popeye as a pointer. Popeye was a pulpwood scaling stick that was a little longer, a little wider and double the thickness of a regular yard stick and she used him to point to the words as her students read. He was also used to punish those who didn't pay attention and follow along with the reader.

Pulling her glasses down on her nose, she gave me the stare of doom, then coldly stung the top of my thigh and pointed to the starting point. As I began to read aloud and rub the burning spot on my leg, I kept the 'no coloreds' problem in the back of my mind. Later I asked a grown up high school boy on my school bus, "Why are there no colored people at our school?"

He said, "Niggers ain't supposed to go to school with whites, stupid. It ain't right." I knew better than to offer a follow up question.

Viewing the affairs of the world through the guileless eyes of a young boy often left me bewildered. As I grew older, I wondered even more why there was such a stark difference between my family and the people I loved. I could not understand why my friends had to live in such pitiful houses without even running water inside, while my family had indoor plumbing and a TV. I wanted to know why Albert, Dagger, Della, Puddin and Wes wore such rags and acted so afraid around white people. Most puzzling was the fact that Wes didn't own his own farm, for he could fix anything, grow anything and solve any problem and my father only knew how to yell at people.

I loved Wes and he told me, "Dats ust da way da worl his. You gwine ust ha'va learns to lib wid hit!" I was bewildered, but in deference to my mentor, I took his advice and didn't ask anyone else about this strange situation, but I kept my eyes and ears open in search of the obvious explanation that I had somehow missed. As I grew older I realized it was white people forcing black people to live such pitiful lives and the black people were scared to say anything! It became clearer as I grew older that white people - my own race - were intentionally preventing my friends of the field and black people everywhere from living the lives they wanted to live. Soon it became very obvious that my friends of the field knew they were being wronged and wanted a better life. As the decade of the 60s began, it became crystal clear that white people had decided to do whatever it took to keep all black people scared and helpless to change the status quo. The most hated three-word-combination in the white world became 'Civil Rights Movement'!

The Moses of my day, anointed to lead his people to equality, was a dynamic young black preacher from Atlanta named Martin Luther King, Jr. As a Baptist minister, he acknowledged being led by the same Holy Spirit to which my mother prayed and professed unconditional devotion, but somehow she had a different idea of His will. By the mid-1960s, he had become the nationwide symbol of the Civil Rights Movement. Often criticized by racist whites and impatient blacks, he struggled valiantly to keep his crusade of change nonviolent as he pressed for the release of his people from Jim Crow bondage. Under his leadership, brave disciples used civil disobedience to bring attention to their plight. Their nonviolent actions were met with horrific attacks by white hate groups and local police. We talked in the fields about Dr. King's civil rights movement and I believed him to be a great and powerful leader. All of my friends of the field were devoted to his cause, but said openly that equality with white people probably wouldn't come in their lifetime and especially not Dr. King's lifetime because somebody would soon kill him. I argued that was not a possibility, because the president had been killed and they surely would not let another great man be murdered.

The bloody assaults on Dr. King's marches were dramatically broadcast on our brand new TV in the den and those attacks slowly opened the window of our nation's social conscience in small ways. A few of our national leaders began to peer through that window and found the courage to join the morally correct movement for equal rights. The tide began to show the smallest signs of change and therefore, the efforts to stop the movement increased.

In my world, the background noise was my father cursing and swearing, "Those niggers are ruining our county! I hate every goddamn one of 'em and I'd just as soon kill'em all if I didn't have a crop in the field!"

In reality, I saw a bold determination in the faces of most black people, both young and old. The police turned loose attack dogs on them and beat them with billy clubs before they dragged them away in handcuffs. High pressure fire hoses sent black children hurling through the streets as white crowds threw rocks and bottles and spit upon them. They shouted racial slurs and threatened the freedom fighters, but the courageous blacks took the abuse and continued to demand change.

The ancient hinges on the door of social change squealed in resistance as white thugs tried desperately to stop the movement for equality. The white vigilante group from Reconstruction was revived as the KKK resurfaced to power again and they vehemently attempted to stop the transformation with fear tactics. They bombed black churches and assassinated Civil Rights leaders in a murderous attempt to continue their white supremacy. Politicians shamelessly used their opposition to the equal rights movement to bolster their support among the ruling white population. As the former Governor and Senator from South Carolina, Benjamin C. (Pitchfork) Tillman, and his Redshirts had done in a murderous rage — killing black people at the Hamburg Massacre in 1876 — we saw a mirror image in 1968. Another former Governor and Senator, J. Strom Thurmond, ramped up his white supremacy rhetoric and whipped the less-educated white farmers and ignorant cotton mill workers into a frothing boil as South Carolina Highway Patrolmen killed black students at the Orangeburg Massacre.

"We of the South have never recognized the right of the

Negro to govern white men, and we never will. We have never believed him to be the equal of the white man, and we will not submit to his gratifying his lust on our wives and daughters without lynching him." **Benjamin C. Tillman**

"I want to tell you that there's not enough troops in the Army to force the Southern people to break down segregation and admit the Negro race into our theaters, into our swimming pools, into our homes and into our churches."
Strom Thurmond

In the cotton fields, I could sense the impatience and feel the tension growing among my friends. A few times, when other blacks would join our group in the field, racial barbs would be aimed at me. "Why ya'll let that honky-ass, white-cracker work with ya'll?"

My friends would shake their fists and quickly defend me. "Dat boy ain't got nuthin to do wid dem white folks dat's treatin' you bad. He know what dey doin' and he know hit ain't right, but he 'ust like us's and ain't nuthin he can do 'bout hit short'a being beat half ta death. He ain't yo problem, so yous watch yo mouf and let 'im 'lone or yous'll get some o' dis!"

They protected me and I continued to move between each world, but the guilt of not standing with my friends and the shame of knowing my race was wrong began to occupy a major place in my mind.

Finally, the oppression became too great a cross to bear. Black people all over our nation exploded into a rebellious rage in the latter part of the 1960s. Approaching the mountaintop from which was thought America might finally proclaim with moral certainty, "All Men Are Created Equal", I heard stories and saw cruelty, brutality and murder regularly on the TV in our den. Frustration in the black high-rise ghettos of Newark and Detroit detonated, sending the shrapnel of fear through every middle class white American home 'out there in TV Land'. In the heart of Dixie everyone, white and black, believed it impossible for the two ethnic groups to live side by side in peaceful coexistence, much less in an integrated society.

One Sunday as we left our Sunday school rooms to join the rest of the congregation in the big church for preaching, I sensed something unusual. Entering the sanctuary and heading for my regular seat, I felt an uneasy hum of tension among the flock of farmers and their wives.

Always inquisitive, I studied the crowd for the cause of the unrest and spotted my seat-mate on the school bus across the sanctuary motioning for me to come over. He filled me in on the revelation. Betty's daddy, my father and four other deacons were standing in the foyer of the church to repel any attempt by 'coloreds' (church talk for their everyday word 'niggers') to enter and disrupt the church service. It had been said - and was probably true - that our house of worship was the most likely to refuse entry to any black worshipers. Watching the deacons' actions as they huddled, I saw Betty's daddy check his revolver to make sure it was loaded and ready.

Afterward they stood with their feet apart like the National Guard on TV and I could tell by their actions that the rest of them were packing heat, too. Nothing happened, but the self-righteous and eloquent prayers coming from the mouths of that group of men made me wonder if maybe God hated black people, too.

Traditionally, southern white children were allowed to play and grow up with black children in the rural areas of the South. But upon reaching what was known as 'the age of reasoning', there was an abrupt halt to any childhood friendships or associations. Around the age of ten or twelve, all relationships between the black and white young people were severed and for the rest of their lives these once childhood friends lived in totally separate and unequal worlds. White children were taught of their superiority and to demand subservience from all members of the Negro race in every aspect of their lives. They were urged to have little or no concern for their counterparts in the antiquated and poverty laced black schools across town. Good Southern children were expected to walk in lock step with their parents and display the traditional mantle of complete separation of the races while harboring the hatred and bigotry for blacks they had been religiously taught.

But for me, having lived, loved and blossomed in black culture, the latter part of the 60s became a gut wrenching time of decision. On one hand, I could choose the safe option of silent complicity. To let the everyday voices of hatred and bigotry ring in my ears and hear nothing, to continue drinking from the whites only water fountain as if it were morally right, seemed my only path and I chose it for a time.

On the other hand, I had the option of following the path of virtue—a dastardly direction considered to be public disloyalty to my race, my creed and my Southern heritage. This choice meant having a multitude of abuse and scorn heaped upon me in order to offer freedom and equality to a people that my parents thought of as dark, dirty and inferior. This choice meant I would be rejected by my parents and my white peers at school. I would certainly be denied any opportunity to participate and gain the advantages of the white world. Treated as a pariah, I would face an overwhelming tide of prejudice and hatred that could easily end in my death or worse.

The closer I got to adulthood the more difficult it became to manage my façade of black-whiteness. Though I had been told what to do and what I should think all my life, I knew in my heart what was right and just. Though I never said it or let it linger in my mind, I knew the people of my race were wrong. Trying to imagine what my life would be like if I stood with my friends of the field and told my father he was wrong triggered nightmares. I could see no way out of my mixed up life.

I had never seriously contemplated taking any part in changing the racial status quo and kept well away from anything that could possibly pull me into the out-of-control storm of the Equal Rights Movement. Mind you, I was white and protected by that hue. Even though I felt in my heart it was the right thing to do, I did not have the strength or courage to make such an irrational move.

In the summer before my last year of high school, I walked

through the sandhill cotton rows facing a future in chaos. Most distressing was a feeling of being hopelessly trapped between two worlds that did not understand my despair. During those days of oppressive heat and inner turmoil throughout my last summer at home, this despair would have probably brought about my doom had it not been for two redeeming factors: the acceptance and camaraderie offered to me by my black brothers and sisters in the cotton fields, and long, solitary, Sunday afternoon rides across the South Carolina sandhills on my shiny, solid black gelding, Blackie.

Chapter Three

Having grown to hate the summer routine of my father's small cotton farm, I despised the submissive life he forced upon me. A callous money-grubber, he could not bear the sight of his son sitting idle or off having fun while there were boring and mind-numbing tasks that could be done to improve his farm. On a typical summer day, my father usually offered an after breakfast session of verbal denigration followed by banishment to the fields. After allowing time for the crew to get into the field, he would periodically ride by in his pickup to make sure everyone was working and ensure the endless rows of his money crop were completely free of weeds and grass. This drudgery guaranteed at least eight hours under the blistering sun in humidity so thick it felt like you were breathing steam. Seemingly gallons of perspiration would be siphoned from your body and every part of you would become greasy and wet, forcing rivers of brine to drip from your ears, run down your face and flood into your eyes to sting you blind. As a sunup to sundown overlord, the old man believed idle hands were good for nothing, and he wanted everyone and everything living on his place to make him money. My father was a Sunday church goer, but my mother was in church every time the doors were opened. Therefore, when I was not being chastised by my father and sent to the field, I was attired in my hand-me-down church clothes and sitting near my mother to be exposed to the word of God.

My mother, a Baptist-Pentecostal hybrid, who wore the bright armor of God with righteous indignation, was most certainly a Bible-thumping, pew-jumping, child of God with a sharp tongue that she wielded like a sword. With my pious mother in charge of my person, I was promised a bath, along with a highly starched and ironed shirt held together with a tie around my neck. Over this, I wore a suit coat with pants to match and my Sunday shoes. Upon arriving at church, our initial hour was spent in Sunday school as we studied the word of God and the teachings of His son Jesus. Immediately afterward we moved to the sanctuary for a half hour of preliminary song and prayer, followed by another hour of preaching while sitting on an unforgiving pew. Sunday night was a repeat of the morning routine. On Wednesday night, I didn't have to wear a tie for prayer meeting, a shortened version of Sunday services, but I did have to stay for choir practice afterward. Upon hearing my voice, I was not allowed in the choir, but I had to sit on a pew where I could be seen by my mother and made to behave.

Most Sundays I sat with correct posture and tried to ignore the loud and obnoxious man, missing a front tooth, as he exhorted the lost sheep to come into the fold. With the standard threat of a whipping from my old man's belt, I fought mightily against the Devil and his luring antics aimed at ruining my perfect behavior. His evil surrounded me in the person of my white peers as they winked and signaled me with their hands — trying to lure me into an ass-whipping and a laugh for them.

As an entertaining way of taking my mind away from being guarded and threatened by frequent glances from the all-seeing-eyes of my sanctimonious parents, I focused my attention on Betty in the choir. A hot blonde with legs to match, she always pulled her choir robe above her knees as she sat during the sermon. I had long wondered why girls went to so much trouble to keep anyone from seeing what they had between their legs. *Why didn't they just wear pants and sit comfortably?*

After spending what seemed like an eternity with my eyes fixed on Betty's knees, the snaggle-toothed preacher gave the song director the high sign. Averting my eyes for just an instant to verify the end was in sight and damn! Before I could glance back, Betty and the choir were standing, causing me to swear under my breath, *Damn! Missed again*! The sound of hymnals being snatched from their racks on the back of the pews and Bea's juke-joint beat on the organ combined to drown out the last entreaty for the lost to come home.

Bea was a recent addition to the Lord's Kingdom. Having been saved during a tent revival in a nearby mill village, she had previously sung and played the piano at Shady Lane, a local beer joint. Having had close relationships with a number of male church members, my mother questioned her religious sincerity. Though Bea had no experience playing an organ, she had been pressed into action as the only alternative. The status quo would have been a growing embarrassment. The redheaded dancehall musician had been called upon to replace a talented but promiscuous single young lady that got knocked up.

In this culminating flurry of movement, the sleepy flock aroused as the hymn of invitation was finally upon us. Receiving a nod from the preacher, the pot-gutted song director rose from his seat on the front pew and stepped on stage to the right of the pastor. Positioning his hymnal in his left hand, he adjusted his glasses with his free hand at an angle for his bifocals to work and prepared to lead the congregation in the last song of the service. Bringing his right hand up in front of his face as if to make a karate chop, he bellowed out the first words of the familiar refrain and with gusto swung his hand like he was shooing flies. Struggling to follow Bea's beer joint beat, he led the verses of a seemingly never ending mantra as it fell from the mouths of tone deaf farmers, jittery from the need of a cigarette. Standing to join in the joyful noise, the homely women pulled their girdles back over their bellies and yanked down their bras, while in the back of their minds hoped there was enough water in the pot cooking the roast at home. Underwear wedgies were removed as the caterwauling crowd easily drowned out the dirty words I replaced in the verses here and there where they easily fit.

If anyone had asked, I couldn't have told them whether I hated my father and his fields or my mother and her church the most! Crap, I hated summer!

But long past lay-by time, after the cotton was picked, the dog-days would slowly wane, inevitably producing my favorite season: Fall! The relief of cooler weather was always welcome and with it came a break from the ever-present gnats. But the greatest thing about this pre-winter season was school and the reuniting with those prejudiced and bigoted teenagers I called my 'friends'. For me it was a magical time of relief, even though it meant leaving my friends of the field. Though they spewed racial slurs at will, I was eager to see my white schoolmates, most known since first grade, for they were the most important sources of information from the outside world.

As I moved into the white world for a substantial period of time, I knew there would be none of the spontaneous camaraderie like in the field and I would be forced to switch my persona for it was a much more judgmental world. In my two-world life, I had long associations with other white boys my age and the shift had become a natural transformation. For some this may have seemed difficult, but I had been raised this way and that made the movement just another part of my mixed up life.

Each year, I ached for the end to the long sultry summer and celebrated as the last field of cotton was picked, for my ultimate emancipation was nearing. With great eagerness, I awaited the reappearance of the yellow school bus and the journey it offered away from the farm. Unlike most, I could hardly wait to resume the customary educational routine among my pallid peers.

In my middle teenage years, one particular 'quest for knowledge' took center stage in my thoughts. Before that, I thought girls were interesting, but not something to which I really wanted to devote a lot of time. As my number of years on earth grew, so did my interest in my peers of the female persuasion and consideration of these perplexing and unknown creatures began to dominate more and more of my daily thoughts. Then, in my middle teens, the intrigue, the anatomy and the puzzling actions of the opposite sex began to drive most of my thinking to a fevered pitch. I had often brought up the topic of girls and sex with Wes, but he said that was something I needed to talk about with my daddy. We both knew that wasn't going to happen.

Inevitably, high school pulled me into its chaotic fog of learning and as I navigated through my final public school years, my thoughts of the 'female' reached what I now know as *an Unquenchable Thirst for Knowledge!* My studies were not a hard task and I made good grades, so I focused most of my school time on a frantic search for information about girls. It drove me to seek the company of lads with passionate, worldly parents who drank too much and didn't shut the bedroom door. It led me to hang around with brothers of loose older sisters who liked to sit on the couch in the dark with their boyfriends and rub their quickly expanding crotches. In my shameless search, I needed the hard-to-get information from successful, young men that had made it to third base and carried protection (whatever that was) in their wallet, just in case. My lust for learning of the opposite sex kept me in a state of what Wes referred to as "full of piss and vinegar!"

Having no sisters, the female body was a mysterious enigma to me and the only actual locations that offered a small window of discovery were PE, lunch, Study Hall and the long bus ride home. In these venues I was always assisted by the on-the-spot, color commentary of my closest white pal, Burt. His brother was four years older and quite the ladies' man. But older brothers don't always disseminate the truth and Burt's brother fed him enough misinformation to make him celibate well into his adult years. To say my knowledge of sex was limited would be a gross understatement and therefore every opportunity to learn was of greatest importance to me. Having reached my last year of high school, the final installment of understanding the opposite sex was at hand. My senior year also caused my mother concern for she did not want my post-high school actions to bring embarrassment upon her as she steered her church and labored for the Lord.

Since I was always one to make good grades, my mother decided I should consider a career in the Armed Services. With that in mind, she insisted I go with her on a visit to her cousin in a nearby mill town. Since I had turned 17 the previous summer, she thought it time for her to decide my career path as she had everything else in my life. Her cousin's boy, Joe, having joined the Marines after high school, had returned after three and a half years in Viet Nam. Thinking that my seeing a real soldier might persuade me to enlist, I was forced to join her on this visit. Sitting across from me in his mother's den, the Marine sat very straight in a chair displaying his broad shoulders, chiseled features and bronze tan. Sporting a crewcut, a tee shirt and green fatigue pants he seemed to embody a man. After a chat, he left the den and headed for his hot rod Chevy and I followed.

Noticing his bandage, I asked if he had been shot. In the garage away from our mothers, his polite demeanor vanished and he said, "Fuck yeah I got shot; took off half of my pecker and one of my nuts before it tore out my asshole. That's why I have this bag full of shit hanging off my side."

He pulled his tee shirt up and displayed the yellowish brown bag of fecal matter hanging from the bandage wrapped around his torso. With demons in his eyes, he took a pack of Marlboros from his pocket, pulled one out and stuck it between his lips. Flipping open a shiny metal lighter bearing the Marine Corps emblem, he rolled the flint wheel with his thumb and a flame danced to life. Holding it near the end of the cigarette, he pulled hard on the filter and the tip glowed red as he took a deep draw. After lighting his smoke, he reached through the window of his car and retrieved a half-pint bottle of vodka from the glove box. He blew the smoke up into the air then removed the cap from the bottle and gulped its contents. Afterward, he threw the empty bottle across the street onto the neighbor's driveway. It shattered on the concrete and he laughed, then yelled, "Stop that, you mother fucker!" Standing with my mouth open, he looked at me and said, "Get out of my face, you little piece of shit."

Having often experienced my father's temper, I immediately cowered and quickly ducked back into the house. My mother and her cousin were standing at the window staring out the at the pieces of glass in the neighbor's driveway. My mother's cousin said, "He's got that 'Stop the

War' bumper sticker on his car and he knows it upsets Joey."

My mother hugged her cousin and said, "We should probably be getting back home; I have to fix supper." We did not talk on the way home.

With the chance of my enlisting almost nil, my mother, the church leader, concluded it would reflect well on her and my father if I went to college. I took the test required and had been accepted, so my mother began telling everyone I was going to college - the agricultural college - to learn how to help my father. For me, there was no certainty in this statement, for my parents had broken every promise they ever made me. Having been told I could have a BB gun, I never got one. When I asked to be in the high school marching band, play football and drive to school, each time they said yes only to eventually deny they ever agreed. I was not convinced whatsoever this college thing would come true until I heard them complaining about having to send a check for my tuition. Suddenly it was real, at least for a little while. For years I had had visions of my exodus from the bondage of the farm and now with each passing day my dream came closer to fruition. I was cautiously optimistic outside, but inside, I was delirious with excitement.

***

As I inched toward my freedom I was still forced to contend with my present circumstances. On Saturdays during the school year, reality slapped me in the face, literally, if I wasn't careful. My presence was thought of as that of a runaway slave who had been returned to a seriously ticked-off master. After my mother arranged for me to go to college, it seemed my old man increased his resentment of my being around. There were very few days that he didn't rake me over the coals and belittle me in front of his field hands. One day his meanness got the best of Wes and he spoke up and said in a very humble way, "Now Boss Man, you ain't need to be so hard on him; he's a good boy."

He unleashed on Wes and threatened to hit him. "Don't you ever tell me how to raise my son, you black son of a bitch. I'm

34

half a mind to take a belt to your ass and teach you a lesson."

Wes didn't say anything, but the look on his face made the old man keep his hands by his side as he finished his tirade and left. When we got to the field, Daggar said,

"Yo old man 'bout met his maker. If'n Wes had had to hit him, he just as soon kilt him and run, cause dem udder white men wooda killed Wes for shore."

I shuddered thinking what might have happened. Wes never spoke of the incident and he told Daggar to shut his mouth and get to work.

After that, most of the other folks that gathered each morning to work in my father's fields steered clear until he had finished abusing me both verbally and with an occasional blow to the head. Wes wouldn't come about until he left and only after his departure would the others approach me. Having long learned to put his rants and raves out of my mind, I acted humble within in his sight and earshot. But once he was safely away, I would release the most vile, foul mouth, filthy oaths that would curl the eyebrows of the most seasoned sailor. My major was the opposite sex, but my minor was learning new words to call that man, that piece of rejected afterbirth lying in a pile of cow shit. I never used my best material in mixed company, of course, but once in the field and after the women put distance between us by chopping a good way down the rows, I would let fly the raunchiest expletives in my vernacular. Dagger, Wes, and Albert always whooped and hollered and repeated them as we hoed our way down the rows of cotton. After a few hours of toil in the field, the heat, humidity and long rows would bring silence to our brotherly band. Nevertheless, upon coming to a particularly thick spot of weeds or grass infesting the cotton, inevitably, one of them would flail his hoe at the weeds and break the silence by using some of my patented vulgar cusswords and we would hit the dirt — exhausted but laughing our heads off. This kindred captivity kept me real.

But oh, Sunday afternoon - on those blessed Sabbath days

the entire farm rested as instructed by the Lord. It was a morning of worshiping the Creator, contemplating His grace and an afternoon of getting the hell away from my slave driving parents. As soon as my penitence of church was completed and I gulped down Sunday dinner (lunch, for those who are not from around here), Blackie would be waiting with his head over the pasture fence. His addition to my life was an accidental incident of great fortune.

My father had no cows, but he cut his hay fields to sell the hay every summer and he had bargained to sell some to a man in the next community. Upon arriving in his yard driving a rickety old truck stacked high with bales of Coastal Bermuda hay, the prospective buyer announced he didn't have the money to pay for that many bales. After the greedy seller finished his cussing fit, the buyer offered to trade for the remaining bales of hay. The bargain included some cash, an old hay rake and a big shiny, solid black gelding that he had raised to pull a plow in his garden. Maintaining equipment is an integral part of farming and the hay rake on my father's farm was the exact model offered in the trade. The parts from the old rake would be very useful to him. But the horse was a problem - he didn't want another mouth to feed. I wanted that horse so much it made me short of breath and my heart was racing. He kept sticking his huge black head over the fence and as I rubbed his nose, he seemed to be begging me to take him home. There was nothing my father hated more than having to work in my mother's garden.

Wes smiled at the friendship I quickly made with the coal black horse, then walked over near the rusted old haying equipment, leaned in and spoke in a hushed voice as the old man looked over the hay rake. "Dat rake be 'ust like yourns, Mr. James and we's sho could use dem parts. I cud's plow yo wife's garden wid dat hoss, if'n we's had a plow.

Wes was a master at manipulating my old man. By leading him to ask for the plow in the trade, he knew it would make my old man feel as if he was getting the best end of the deal. The greedy farmer rubbed his chin and finally said, "If you'll throw in the plow, I'll do the deal."

Wes was a genius and if the truth were known, he was the reason for my father's farming success. When the man shook my father's hand and the bargain was struck, elation filled my heart. We unloaded the hay and the old man wanted to load the hay rake first and come back later for Blackie, but Wes and I knew that was a lie. Loading the hay rake, Wes pushed it as far to the front of the truck bed as possible and I prayed there would be room for my horse. Once the plow was loaded there was little room left. Blackie was petrified because he had never been loaded in any vehicle. Jerking on his lead rope, the old man made Blackie rear up and refuse to load. He threw the rope down and said, "To hell with that crazy son-of-a-bitch, just leave him here and we'll call it even.

As disappointment and determination ran together in my soul, Wes picked up the lead rope and told me to get up on the truck bed. With his rough hands, he rubbed Blackie's nose and whispered to him softly, praising his every move. Handing me the lead rope, I urged the mountain of a horse to put his enormous feet up on the back and follow me onto the truck. With Wes pushing him from behind, the big horse and I were able to find just enough space to stand. His former owner handed me an old fertilizer sack and said, "Wrap that around his eyes; what he can't see won't scare him."

Precariously hanging on the tail end of the truck bed, I held the bag and lead rope in one hand, and fearfully grasped the side body with my other hand while continuously whispering praise to Blackie for how well he was acting. The old man's frustration was evidenced in his driving. Honestly, I thought he was trying to throw us off of our tiny spot on the back of his truck. Immediately upon arriving in the sandy yard in front of the barn, I hopped off and removed the burlap sack from his eyes. Encouragingly, I talked to him, urging him to jump off the truck. Putting his trust in his new friend, he reared on his hind legs and leaped toward me. Landing inches away from my bare feet, he nuzzled me with his nose as I patted his muscled neck and beamed with joy. From that moment until his death, I loved every part of that mammoth animal and he was a loyal and loving friend that tried to please me unconditionally.

My Blackie looked forward to Sunday as much as I, for he knew a good brushing and some soothing talk would soon come his way. Anticipating some sweet feed to munch for energy on the long afternoon ride, the huge horse would paw with anticipation. He wanted that soft blanket, small saddle smelling of oil, and 145 lbs. of teenage boy on his back. He, as did I, loved the feel of freedom as we galloped down the sandy driveway and heard the sound of his steel shoes clicking as we crossed the paved road and anonymously slipped through the ankle high Coastal Bermuda grass. Exhilarated and free, we would ride across the sandhills of Salleys Kitchen, disappearing among the ancient sand dunes covered now with tall Longleaf pines and fields of King Cotton.

Chapter Four

Roy Asholee's Store was a unique, latrine-like place that formed the hub of Salleys Kitchen, and was the only store in the community. No matter how unsavory, everyone had to enter it at one time or another. As a young boy isolated from most of the world, it was a place of fascination and intrigue that I entered with wide eyes. Until I started school, it was the only retail store I knew. As for the community, if trouble was brewing, more than likely the fire under the kettle was being stoked there.

A few of the customary items found in most country stores were for sale among its filth, but those ancient provisions only collected dust and occupied space on the shelves. None of the community residents would have ever considered using staples purchased from Asholee's Store. The largest stock and trade of this store was hog meat and assorted hog delicacies. The main cuts of meat: ham, chops, tender loin, streak-a-lean (bacon), sausage and fatback were ever present. Other treats available, in limited quantities after a hog-killing, were: liver pudding, souse meat, tongue, chitlins, hocks, feet, tripe, jowls, rind, cracklings and buckets of lard. From what I noticed, the store also did a fair trade in beer, chewing tobacco, snuff, cigars, cigarettes, nabs, chips and cold Nehi drinks, Coca-Cola and Pepsi.

As the local hot spot, a peculiar group of unsavory men usually sat around on drink crates swilling beer in the hog-wire enclosed front shed of the store where the gas pumps used to be. My mother called them worthless white trash and told me never to speak to them. They were all big gutted and loud mouthed. Most wore white T-shirts under faded bib-overalls, with white socks and worn out brogans. As a former mill-town girl, she detested these men and often spoke of them in disparaging terms in my presence. Generally speaking, the group was made up of cotton mill employees — lint-heads she called them — who worked the second or third shift; however, a good many of them *sucked the sugar tit*. They lived on what working folks called *rocking chair money*: GI disability, Social Security disability, unemployment insurance benefits, welfare and the recently re-instituted food stamp program. They were not church-going men and with no family to support, they typically lived in the home of their aging parents, cashing the elders' Social Security checks and using them as their own. As if dodging chicken droppings in front of the store were not challenging enough, this group of louts formed a gauntlet through which all persons had to pass going in and out of the seedy former filling station. The joys of their fruitless lives were joking with the good ole boys and making lewd comments to black and white females as they passed into the store. Slinging racial epitaphs and making disparaging remarks to any black male passing near, they also grabbed any kid that entered their hangout, just to scare them. Their bad behavior was usual, but they never grabbed me nor did they say anything offensive to my mother or father.

In The Kitchen, my father's reputation and temper were well known. The store bums knew, even when a little tipsy, their safest approach with him was a *Hi-ya-do-'n* and nod with no eye contact. My mother, however, demanded an entirely different protocol, for she was the daughter of an alcoholic and all too aware of the abuse that often accompanies alcohol excess. To disrespect my mother in any way would have not only brought down upon them the vicious wrath of my old man, but that woman of God, that fearless soldier in the Lord's army, would have stopped in her tracks, closed her eyes and prayed out loud to Jesus. With a fire and brimstone voice that recalled prohibition, she would fling fiery arrows of guilt and shame, amplifying her voice to a decibel level that equaled a public-address system. Her supplications in the name of Jesus could humiliate and disgrace the coldest of hearts and send the most ardent of sinners cowering with his tail between his legs like a beaten yard dog. Few of them spoke to her and those who did bowed their heads, tipped their hats and softly said, "Mayum."

At her arrival, there was always a scramble to hide any

alcoholic beverages. She knew well that Roy didn't have a license allowing alcohol consumption in his store, and she would remind the world of that fact in the loudest of ways. Roy never wanted the ABC (Alcohol Beverage Control) men to visit his place; therefore, she was never made to endure the sight of an opened cold beer. In the off chance she was compelled to enter that den of iniquity, they made sure hats covered any open display of alcohol and their brogans were not in her way, as she walked by, ignoring them with her nose in the air.

Roy Asholee and his wife lived in the back of the store where mysterious sounds and smells emanated. He was a short, nasty old man who wore suspenders that framed his gut and made him look pregnant. Always chomping on the stub of a cigar, he seldom shaved and seemed to always have his navel showing and fly open. His usual spot was behind the counter near the huge old cash register that was never used. All of the candy was kept behind that counter so only he could get to it. This meant all candy purchased had to be taken from his grimy hands. My mother forbade me to buy candy from him, but I did when Wes would give me a dime and when she wasn't around, and only if it was in a wrapper. There was a knot hole in the floorboard in front of the counter with a Prince Albert Tobacco can nailed over it. With Prince Albert staring up, the flattened red can caught on your shoe and seemed to always get kicked up. He nailed a new can over the hole all the time, but between kick-up and replacement, I wondered what came in and out of that hole. Cigarettes were sold separately for those who could not afford the whole pack, and he sold single aspirins along with Tums out of the bottle. If needed, a dose of mineral oil was dispensed in a Dixie cup.

Roy was also the local loan shark and he was in cahoots with the farmers. He offered credit to his black clientele, usually in an emergency situation. If a field hand needed a substantial amount of money for food, doctor, or bail bond, Roy would lend them the amount and write it down on a *ticket.* The loan had to be repaid, including whatever interest he felt necessary, in seven days. If the debt was not cleared, he claimed the right to sell the debt to any farmer that might need farm labor. Many day laborers in my father's fields were purchased from the pool of folks who owed Mr. Roy money. After selling the debt, the new owner determined the amount owed him for his services in carrying the debt and he would decide the terms of repayment. Roy had his finger in everyone's business, by hook or crook. In the store, he was the point of sale for most everything, except meat.

There were two outhouses out back a ways from the store, near the woods. Between the smelly latrines and the store was a large pen where pigs were held. A path led from the store to their slop trough. Nearer the store was what Wes called the 'dead pen'. A single pig from the large pen was moved here to be fed a short while before it was slaughtered. A faucet was attached to the back of the store just above an old Gulf oil sign that lay flat on the ground under it. After a time, the pig was coaxed onto to the metal sign with a little food. Here it was shot in the back of the head with Roy's infamous .22 caliber pistol. It always stunned me to watch the pig or hog being killed. With one shot, the pig's life was over.

I had watched the process standing next to Wes a few times and the swiftness with which Roy could end a life was astounding. I often wondered if he realized the power he wielded with his pistol. Always laughing afterward with his mouth agape drooling tobacco juice, he would say "Dat sum-bitch be graveyard dead!" then put the deadly little gun back in his pocket. Never without it, he had a habit of drawing down on anyone who scared him.

After the hogs stopped kicking, their back legs were spread apart with a metal rod and they were pulled up by a pulley hung on the old Gulf sign bracket that had been moved to the back of the store. Once dangling over the orange and white sign, Mrs. Asholee took over quickly cutting the throat then severing the jugular vein so they would bleed out. She was handy with the big knife she wore on her side. Afterwards, their bodies were dipped in a barrel of scalding water, then scraped to remove the hair. Splitting the belly open was a delicate incision, for care had to be taken not to prick the stomach or other organs which would result in the release of putrid gas and fluid, ruining the taste of the meat. The ugly old woman made quick work of it and the entrails were pulled out of the body cavity and dropped into an old galvanized wash tub. Once the head was completely severed, the tongue was cut out, the ears cut off and eyeballs popped out. The eyes were usually given to the awaiting dogs and the ears were ground for souse meat. The rest of the head was put into a large, black, cauldron of boiling water to be cooked until the meat fell from the skull. Head meat and the liver were then cooked together and mixed with rice to make liver pudding. Cooled in long narrow pans, it formed a gray, grainy-like gel that was a favorite of Roy's clientele. With her knife the skull was hacked opened and the brains removed; another delicacy to be sold to some lucky person. The remaining parts of the hog were cut up and further processed to sell in the store. The intestines, however, were special. They were cleaned, washed and beaten, then boiled and cleaned again before being chopped into bite-size pieces. The twice cleaned nuggets were then battered and deep fried. When Roy made up a batch of these delectable treats, known as chitlins, (or chitterlings for those who aren't from around here) his store was abuzz with commerce. The news of the offering blazed through the community like poop through a goose. It was first come, first served, for the intestines of one or two hogs could not satisfy the cravings of all the bowel buffs in our community. Personally, they made me gag. After the fried batter came off in your mouth, a tough, membrane-like piece of gray rubber was left. It was like chewing a piece of bicycle inner tube. The more you chewed it, the bigger it got and if you tried to swallow it whole, it had a tendency to reappear.

There was, however, one overall reason for my continued patronage of that smelly cesspool of a store, and it had nothing to do with pork. The drawing quality for me was the shiny, coal black myna bird that perched on the door separating the living area from the retail part of the store. I was fascinated by its ability to talk. On each visit to the store, I immediately headed to the back, hoping to see the amazing and exotic bird. You could tell this was its favorite perch because of all of the white guano dripping down both sides of the door. Though limited in vocabulary, it mimicked Mrs. Asholee's syrupy mountain brogue perfectly. In fact, if I were not facing the speaker, I could never decide if she or the bird was talking.

Always standing behind the meat cooler, just in front of the bird door, Roy's wife was in charge of any swine related products. The women who worked in the field with me said she was from the Georgia Mountains where her father traded her to her first husband for a hog. They also said she was quick to cut people that tried to steal things out of the store and several people bore scars from encounters with her. She was not a pleasant woman with whom to talk or look upon.

Tall with long, yellowish gray hair which she braided, it was spiraled into a bun and pinned on the back of her head. With hairy ears and the face of a beige prune, I don't think she had a tooth in her head. It was said she killed the last man with whom she lived after he came home drunk, passed out and peed in her bed. Supposedly, she cut his throat and bled him out into a foot tub, then dragged his body to the cemetery and dug his grave. As she was burying him, someone passing saw her shoveling dirt into an open grave, and asked what she was doing. She shot back, "I'm cleaning up a mess!"

Wes told me the man she killed was Roy's cousin. At trial, she was found not guilty by reason of insanity. Roy petitioned for her to be released to his custody and when granted, he was there to pick her up. Bringing her to Salleys Kitchen, he began calling her his wife. Unlike Roy, she was a hog killing expert and a very efficient butcher. She wore a butcher knife on her side within easy reach. Customarily attired in a blood-stained white apron, she wore it over a homespun dress that mercifully fell well below her knees. During cold weather she wore faded denim work pants under the dress and had brogans on her feet. In summer she wore only the dress and had hair on her legs like a man. I was as scared of her as a mad dog foaming at the mouth!

At the bottom of the bird-poop door, holding it open, was a scum-covered brown coffee can where she aimed when spitting her snuff. The excess snuff and saliva gathered in the corners of her mouth and when it drooled down each side of her hairy chin she used the bottom of her apron to wipe it off. She was usually standing behind a yellowish-white meat cooler, near the back of the store with three glass windows across the front; each angled back with a thick black rubber gasket around it. Above, at eye-level for adults, was a counter on which sat the notorious, thumb-heavy scales. Both buyer and seller carefully scrutinized this weighing machine when purchasing meat. Inside the cooler, behind the thick glass, there was usually a bloodied cardboard box. It contained whole dressed chickens harvested from the store yard, some with heads and feet on, others without, but all with liver and gizzards inside. Other items in the smelly cooler were sticks of bologna, pans of fresh ground sausage, souse meat, liver pudding, and other swine-related treats. On top of the cooler, there was a jar of pickled pig feet, a jar of pickled eggs and a jar of small link sausages floating in recycled pickling liquid.

Approaching the meat display or nearing the back of the store, a customary question would be proffered in a back-woodsy drawl through a mouthful of snuff and saliva, "Wat kin I git fer ya's?"

Invariably, the next sound heard was that of her spitting snuff in the general direction of that scum-covered coffee can. The intriguing part for me was deciding who was doing the talking and spitting. Not only could the bird mimic her hickish voice perfectly, but it also never moved its beak. Even more fascinating, it also mimicked the spitting sound and the sound of the spit hitting the can. The bird was most talented — but mean - and could never be approached for fear of having a piece of your ear ripped off. The old woman knew I was fascinated and she always tried to scare me by barking out her warning, "Stay 'shed 'a dat bird, hit'll take-hoff a chuck 'ov yourn eir!"

Wes said she fed it cayenne pepper to make it mean.

Chapter Five

My mother and father had always referred to the vine covered mansion just down the road a piece as the Sullivan Place. The owner and only inhabitant, as far as I knew, was James Anthony Sullivan, V, known as Mr. Sully to the black community but to most all of the white folks he was Ole Sully. It was said that he was the last descendant of the Sullivan family and had never married. He lived in the ancient mansion alone and it seemed, from the outside, to be falling down around him. Wes pointed him out to me one day at Roy Asholee's Store. As we walked in, he was standing, leaning on one of the brick pillars that held up the shed on the front of the store. I saw him writing on a folded newspaper with his eyes as close to the paper as possible and talking to the man sitting on a crate with a bottle of beer in his hand. The fellow holding the beer bottle was staring at us like we had done something wrong. Sully was asking him a question and the guy was ignoring him, just saying, "Uh huh." As we walked by I heard, "It's a four letter word that means hello."

Ole Sully stuck out like a sore thumb among the regulars in The Kitchen. The traditional bib overall look was not his thing. He had on a pair of worn out dress pants and a wrinkled oxford shirt. Hung on the front of the shirt was a pocket-protector with everything except the kitchen sink stuffed in it. The collection of pens and pencils crowded the plastic shield and it stuck out like a boob. His iron gray hair looked unkempt and pointed in all directions and his horn rimmed glasses were so thick, I thought they must be bulletproof. The overloaded shirt was dirty and threadbare with food spills on the front and perspiration stains under his arms and there was little doubt he had slept in it. The button in the middle was missing resulting in an opening that exposed his hairy white chest. His pants hung precariously under his protruding belly and I wondered if he was growing a beard or had an aversion to soap, water and razors.

Ole Sully was a rare individual and he proved it in most

every aspect of his life. The car he drove matched his appearance and doubled as his office where he kept every receipt or important paper he had ever received. They were scattered on the seats, dash and floor of the neglected old Ford sedan, among the empty beer bottles and other trash. While driving on the main paved roads, his top speed was 20 mph as he incessantly worked the *New York Times* crossword puzzle with a pen. Crawling along the backroads of The Kitchen, he used the entire width of the road to travel and zigzagged from ditch to ditch as he filled in the blocks of his puzzle, swerving at the last moment to avoid peril. On the main road, truck drivers hated to get behind him and they had pushed him in the ditch on more than one occasion. Luckily, there were always plenty of farm tractors around and most anyone with a little decency would hook a log chain to his bumper and pull him out. But if he had had one too many of those Country Club Malt Liquors that he drank, it was prudent to just pull the whole kit and caboodle home and unhook him in front of the vine covered house. Ole Sully usually ended up sleeping in the old Fairlane on those occasions, after which, he always came by to say thank you a day or so later.

The weirdest thing was the way he talked. When sober, he seldom spoke, but on rare occasions when he did, he was eloquent with a vocabulary seldom heard in our neck of the woods. His words were not part of a regular beer drinker's vocabulary. It was very intimidating to talk with him, so most people just said, 'Uh-huh' and kept on walking when he spoke to them. Besides, most had no possible idea of an eleven letter word for benevolence that started with an 'm'. Never could I understand why he hung around with that sorry lot of ne'er-do-wells at Roy Asholee's Store. Wes said after a few Pabst Blue Ribbon Beers they didn't care who listened to their thick-tongued gossip, as long as they were white.

Sully was our neighbor and one of few residents of Salleys Kitchen with the intestinal fortitude to speak to my parents whenever he saw them, drunk or sober. He smiled and seemed to enjoy my mother's pity as she persistently witnessed and begged him to give his heart to Jesus. She had been trying to save his soul from eternal hell and damnation for as long as I could remember. As a soldier in the army of the Lord, she had probably quoted every usable scripture verse in the Bible to Sully at one time or another. To compound her frustration, he could quote scripture right back at her and tell her things that sent her home to search her well-worn copy of The Word.

Sully also smiled during my father's tirades, which happened often since their farms bordered. My old man thought he could overstep on anyone's property at will. Sully had been forced to have his land surveyed to determine the actual property lines and sure enough, the old man was plowing 50 feet over on Sullivan property. Recently, Sully had put up fences along the borders, which infuriated my old man.

I heard Sully tell my father on one occasion, "Why James my good man, we must remember the poet's words 'Good fences make good neighbors' and scrutinize their meaning. I should wish it a joint venture and an effort to generate a closer bond." This statement sent the old man into a rage and Sully smiled at him the entire time.

The way my father saw it, that sorry excuse for a man needed to pack up his nasty clothes and get the hell out of The Kitchen. Rumor had it he was running around with a half breed woman and had three or four little bastard children that were drawing welfare, but I had never seen any children. My father constantly berated Sully, saying his tax money was being used to feed those scums of the earth. But I knew of many other men he called his friends in The Kitchen, doing exactly that and he saw them as pillars of the community.

Another reason - and probably the real motive - for my old man's hatred of Sully was his benevolence to black people. The traditional farmers tried to keep the field hands in debt, allowing the white landowners to use the Jim Crow laws to swindle and force them to labor in their fields. All of the white

49

farmers knew if there were any arguments over wages, they could call the deputy sheriff, have the black person arrested for disturbing the peace and haul him or her to jail. After the magistrate, always a local 'good ole boy', pronounced guilt and sentenced the perpetrator to 30 days or $100, the land owner would graciously pay the fine. This forced the black person to work for him until the debt was paid. Refusal meant going back to jail. Sully would invariably loan money to members of the black community to pay off their debts. All he would ask of them was their word for collateral. The records of the loans were kept in the abyss of his car and might as well have not been kept. They would pay him what they could, when they could. It infuriated my father as well as most of the cotton farmers in the area that had used this time honored tradition of legalized slavery since the 1870s. That lunatic, as most referred to him, was certainly not the stereotypical farmer in our Jim Crow world. His racial views were not the only sore spot he rubbed in The Kitchen. Ole Sully had an affinity for 'crop experimentation', like growing the unheard of Kiwi or planting wine grapes or canola or sunflowers, but certainly the most promising was soybeans. Of course most all were a bust at that time because there was no market for the products he produced. The soybean was the first of his nontraditional crops that showed any promise and it only produced a break-even harvest, but that never deterred him and seemed to spur him on even more. These daring forays with crops on the cutting edge of agriculture were the fuel that fed the flames of hatred for most of the ignorant citizens of The Kitchen. His unorthodox methods of farming were innovative and followed the future of agriculture in the South that only he could envision. His farming goal was never set in monetary terms. It was evident that most of his trial forays failed and ended after mistakes and miscalculations, except 'the year of no cotton'. That year he set the entire community on its ear.

***

With a liberal, mind Sully was often intrigued as to 'what

would happen if'… Forming a new planting hypothesis after studying the long range weather forecast for the region, his method deviated greatly from the generally accepted approach. Putting a plow sweep on his cotton planter, he dug a deep rut in front of his seed hopper trying the ridiculous stratagem of planting cotton in a furrow very early in the planting season. This was diametrically opposed to conventional wisdom. Everyone in The Kitchen knew that cotton in the sandhills had to be planted in a flat row just under the edge of the top soil and all farmers in the area knew that it was lunacy to plant cotton early in the spring. Cotton needed warm weather to get it started and the hot, sticky, humid weather of late summer to make it flourish and produce a thousand pounds per acre — the dream of every farmer. But the "scientist" of The Kitchen, as the local county agent referred to him, plowed and planted his way and on his time. The seeds he planted deep in the sandy loam recognized the cool soil temperature and refused to germinate. Thus began the customary name calling ridicule and scorn that followed Sully like a curse. However, it did not seem to bother him at all. He continued to creep down the road in his moving trash can with his crossword puzzle propped on the steering wheel, looking for a hyphenated word that meant unconventional. Seeing that sideways smile across his face and watching his relaxed manner, I wondered if he knew something the rest of us did not.

A month later, when the real, official, and proper planting season arrived, fields were plowed and leveled to perfection, looking as if someone had ironed them flat. Then seeds were carefully placed at precisely the prescribed shallow depth in long, straight rows, but we had not had rain in three weeks. Every farmer 'felt in his bones' rain would come soon for it was late spring and that's when it rained, so they continued planting. But the rain did not come and the weather turned real warm, which produced the curse of a hot, dry planting season. Most of the tiny cotton plants that found enough moisture to sprout withered and soon dried to a crisp, but enough of the tiny plants lived for the planters to hesitate replanting.

Meanwhile, in the furrow, Sully's improperly placed seeds were deep in the topsoil where moisture was abundant. As the warm weather finally made its way down to the deeply planted seeds, they germinated and began to produce roots. They grew downward toward the moisture and established a solid nutrient path which kept them healthy. As the late spring rays of the sun continued to heat and warm the soil, the natural mechanism in each little seed was triggered; they popped off their seed coats and grew toward the sun. Sully's cotton began to pop up forming uniform rows of tiny cotton plants across his fields. But no one took notice because the furrows kept the fledgling plants out of sight. The mini-trench also protected them from the baking heat of the sun, allowing the newly sprouted cotyledons to feed the plants and nourish their growth.

As other farmers delayed, hoping and praying for rain, Sully continued his snail's pace trek up and down the roads trying to think of a seven letter word for eccentric with two sets of double letters.

Finally, the multitude of farmers in The Kitchen decided they could wait no longer. Like an epidemic spreading over the sandhills, farmers began disking under what little of their failed first crop was left. The demand for seed skyrocketed, causing the supply to plummet. As frustration fueled a time sensitive panic, planters emptied their checking and savings accounts and ordered seed from other regions that were not exactly suited for the sandhill growing season. Those that came to this realization last were now in trouble.

Most of the families in Salleys Kitchen had ancestors that had grown cotton since they had first come to the area in the pre-war 1800s. Their oral histories were filled with the stories of devastation during the Civil War and the almost inhuman Reconstruction Period that followed. Most of the men farming now were children of The Great Depression. They had experienced and barely survived the subsistence life forced upon them during those hard times of the 30s and could still feel the pain of those days. Nervously waiting for delivery, nights were long and sleep was short, as fear of impending doom wracked their brains. Constantly thinking of what could happen if they were unable to make the payments on their farms and crop loans, an uneasy tension gripped the community.

For wealthy farmers this was just a bad year, but for dirt poor farmers that scratched from year to year to make ends meet, it spelled disaster. We were not wealthy and if the cotton had to be plowed under, there was no money to buy more seed. My mother knew this all too well. Alone, she began to drive our old station wagon to the church every morning just before dawn, for an 'on her knees at the foot of the throne' talk with the Lord.

As a couple, my parents attended church every Sunday as tradition demanded and though he could have summoned up a most eloquent prayer, my father knew it would be a waste of time for him to pray earnestly. He wasn't getting on his knees for anyone. I never really understood why my mother got up, dressed, and drove down there every morning, when she could have just knelt by her bed and prayed. Sensing things were bad, I didn't hear the usual bragging and talk of making money drifting into my room late at night. There was a loud silence throughout our house as I lay for hours listening to the cry of the rain frogs begging for relief.

During this stressful time, my aunt from Virginia called to say my older cousin had decided he was too old for his BB gun and he was sending it to me. For some unknown reason, my mother did not want me to have that BB gun. Her overt excuse was I was too old for a kid's gun, but I had never been allowed to have one so I wanted to try it out and have the opportunity to brag like all the other boys at school. All week I waited and on Friday I asked the mailman when he thought it would come. He said, "I bet it will be here on Monday." Monday had come and gone and there was no BB gun. Nothing seemed to be going right!

On Tuesday I awoke to the sound of my mother crying. At

first, I thought she might be crying because my old man had yelled at her, but she was like me in that she had grown used to his tirades and would brush them off while asking God to punish him. My mother did not cry very often, so I knew something big had happened. As I lay listening and trying to figure out the cause, the noise of my mother's sobs were joined by another sound. It was my old man cursing.

Something was up and I didn't want to get out of bed and walk into trouble. I was hoping to avoid this situation by pretending to be asleep, but the cursing began to drown out the crying and finally I heard, "I can't fucking believe this!"

That was enough to get me up and pull on my britches. Slowly and cautiously entering the kitchen, my mother was sitting at the table squalling. Quietly I asked, "What's wrong?" She ignored me, so I moved passed her, opening the door and walking out onto the porch. Under the huge elm our station wagon was parked in the sandy driveway with the tailgate down. My old man was walking around and around cussing, then stopping to put his hand in one of four large tubs in the back of the old Ford wagon.

Walking barefoot through the sand, I cautiously approached the tubs and peered in the closest container. They were full of cotton seed. He kept saying, "Son of a bitch!" and walking around in a tight circle at the back of the car. Even more cautiously, I ventured to ask, "Where did you get the seed?" Again, I was ignored and he repeated, "Son of a bitch!"

By this time, as he always did, Wes appeared in the yard and walked up to the tubs grabbing a hand full of seeds and letting them trickled through fingers. He said, "Lord have mercy! Where's yous get 'em?"

Still no answer as my mother came out the door and sat on the steps and tried to stop crying. Through broken sobs and snorts she said, "When… I… came… out… of… the… church, they… were… there!" and she was lost to the sobs and snorts once again.

Suddenly I thought about staring at Betty's knees in church

and all the other sins I had committed. *HOLY CRAP!* I was thinking, it might be time for this lost sheep to come into the fold, but I heard Wes backing the truck up to the tubs and I was jerked from my guilt back to reality. My old man wanted us in the field. Helping Wes move the big tubs from the station wagon to the back of the pickup truck, I rubbed my hand across the outside of one of the containers and noticed it had been numbered with a metal cutting die; they were numbered 1, 3, 4, and 6. Wes smiled when he saw me notice the embossed numbers. That was his, 'I know something but I'm not saying' smile. As I wondered about the numbers on the tubs, Sully came creeping by our house. He was trying to think of a nine letter compound word for 'to seed'.

Wes and I worked all day, eating dust and planting cotton. The old man stood guard over the seed in the pickup and acted like they were gold nuggets. Not taking the time to plow the old crop under, he hurried us from one powdery field to the next planting cotton. After a while, Wes and I were so covered in dust, there was no way to tell who was black and who was white. Once on a stop to fill up the seed hoppers, I asked the old man if there was any talk of rain on the radio.

"Hell" he said, "Them sons of bitches don't know no more than I do. They're just guessing like everybody else. Now both of you get your black asses back on that tractor and keep plantin' until I tell you to stop!"

In the waning daylight, I am sure all you could see was the whites of our eyes and teeth in the middle of a big ole grin. For some reason I felt his words were the biggest compliment he could have ever given me, and Wes knew it, too. He slapped me on the back and it looked like a can of talcum powder had exploded. With smiles on our faces and squinting to see by the dim tractor lights, we planted late into the night and early morning. After finishing the last field, we parked the tractor and planter by the gate and Wes decided to roll a smoke while we waited on the old man to come back and tell us what to do. After he smoked, Wes pulled an old mayonnaise jar of water wrapped in newspaper from one of the cottonseed tubs and we drank it dry. Afterwards, we lay back in the dry parched grass at the edge of the field and watched the stars. The old man never showed and I was so tired. We woke up just as the sun was climbing over the trees. Wes sat up and wiped his eyes then punched me. I sat up and looked around as Wes looked at me.

"Damn yo black ass his dirty!" was his reply. Grinning again, we peed on the dry ground, cranked up the tractor and hauled the planter, along with our dirty asses, back to the house.

Wes was the best hand my father had and the old man made sure he controlled every aspect of Wes' life. He smoked Bugler roll-your-own cigarettes and would give me a rolling paper to practice rolling one with him. I tried to smoke those things a couple of times but they made me cough too much, so if I rolled one I usually let Wes lick it and he put it in his tobacco pack for later.

But Wes had a problem. He was an alcoholic and when he drank, he drank way too much and did stupid things. Also, he drank the rotgut sold around Salleys Kitchen, made from stagnant water in the swamps and corn meal fermented in old DDT barrels left over from spraying the cotton to kill the boll weevil. The corn meal mash was boiled and the steam was distilled through lead car radiators. If you drank it long enough, the alcohol ruined your liver, but the lead content was quicker to drive you insane and Wes had been drinking it since I could remember. He was a perfect gentleman and mentor to me when he was sober, always patient, gentle and perceptive and seemed to love teaching me the tricks of the trade. He had a knack for reading my father's mind and would anticipate what he needed and have it ready before my father could ask. My old man would never admit it, but he depended on Wes' knowledge to run his farm. Without a moment's hesitation, if he was not drinking, I would have put my life in his hands. His problem solving skills were unequalled and the selective breeding of his ancestors had made his frame the envy of any bodybuilder. To me, without alcohol, he was the consummate man's man.

Working for Sully before he worked for my father, it was recognized that both had a problem with booze. Sully told Wes it would be in everyone's best interest if they did not work together. As a little boy, I remember Wes beginning to work with us in the field. While Wes was in the pickup one day, my old man stopped Sully on the road and asked him why he 'ran Wes off'.

Sully rubbed his stubbly chin and said, "Salleys Kitchen may have eventually grown accustomed to our cognitive approach to agriculture, but the injuries attributed to our inability to avoid alcohol foreshadowed doom for everyone."

My old man said, "I don't know what the hell you said, but if he owes you money, you can kiss it goodbye!" I remember Sully laughing like Santa Claus and saying, "Might I inquire if you know a seven letter word for 'ignorant in actions'? My father just drove away.

Together, Wes and Sully formed the cutting edge of innovation and modernization, but their drinking was a powder keg that could have blown the whole place sky high. I think they were afraid of their weaknesses and each feared the possibility of hurting other people. Both seemed to sense an impending nightmare and ultimate fall that might take both to their graves.

Now, the aggravation and helplessness of waiting for rain rekindled memories of the hard times that all planters had faced at one time or another. As children and young men, those difficult times left deep scars from a long, slow healing process. Their recollections of the struggle to survive caused doom to meander through their minds. Those who found seed planted and waited. Those who didn't looked for jobs and other places to live. The worry and heat-fatigue along with the silent resentment felt from the black community permeated the planters and seemed to be nearing a crescendo as tension spread over the community like a layer of volatile gas.

Chapter Six

I had never been bold enough to check out that big old house. Blackie hated the place, balking each time we neared it and I sure wasn't going alone. The closest I had been to the mammoth dwelling was unhooking the chain after Wes pulled Sully home one day at lunch time.

Curious as to why Wes would help him, knowing my father would have tongue-lashed him if he found out, he said, "Mr. Sully be okay, hit's ust dat mos peoples haint understands his way of thanking." Then he told me he didn't want to talk about it anymore.

The year before, during a summer day, I had been lying hidden in the shade of some waist high cotton waiting to jump up and scare Albert and Dagger when they came down the row. As I listened for the sound of the sand scrunching under their feet, I recognized the voices of the women working their way back up the rows. Most days, we worked in two separate groups, male and female. It seemed to be a normal occurrence as we began to toil for the males to lag behind until the females had worked their way down the rows and put at least three quarters of the length of the field between the sexes. Della, Mary, and Puddin had reached the end of the field and were working their way back on new rows. They were talking about Mr. Sully as they approached and I, lying quietly in the sand, eavesdropped on their conversation.

They spoke of him in a reverent way using a tone of voice I had heard them use when they talked about ghosts and haunted graveyards. Haints and spirits were very real to the women folk and they talked in hushed voices, giving due respect as if he were a preacher. For some reason, they didn't want anyone to hear what they were saying about him. I couldn't make out what they were saying because their words were rich in Gullah voice. Mary spit on the ground then dragged the handle of her hoe through the wet spot while saying something. I had seen Della do this all my life when she realized something she said was gossip. She believed it wrong to talk bad about people behind their backs. I always thought it was her way of saying she was sorry she had sinned but the older I got, the more I realized it was not a Christian practice. She called it 'tearing-up the talk' like tearing up a note someone slipped you in study hall. I never understood the deep Gullah talk, but I heard Della tell her she had better quit talking about that man and tear-up that talk just before she did it. When I jumped up and scared them, Della said I almost made her pee on herself. She threatened me with her hoe, but I saw all of them holding back a laugh and I knew she wasn't really mad.

She said, "You done got too old to bees doing mean thangs lak dat! You pert-near growed up; yous needs to stop actin' like yous still a yung'n."

When they calmed down I decided to delve into the Mr. Sully quandary a little further. We were in a field that bordered the Sullivan property and the rows we were on were near the fence between his field and ours. Pulling up a big pigweed, I tossed it over the fence onto his side. Immediately Puddin, who was often inclined to spill the beans, said, "Man, what chew do dat for? He ain't did nuthin to yous."

I shot back, "He won't care; they say he doesn't farm for money anyway."

Before she could stop the words from shooting out of her mouth, she blurted out, "You stupid; dat man do need da money, he got chulin."

As the last word left her lips she was looking as if she had said something she was not supposed to say.
She glanced toward the other females and I fired a couple more questions at her. "He does? Who's their mama?" and followed it up with, "Where do they live?"

The smiles grew on their faces and they refused to speak; just shook their heads at my further questions and started singing one of their ole religious songs, a common practice while we were together in the field. They always sang when they wanted something to go away. It was their remedy for sickness or injury, fatigue or weariness, hunger or thirst, but especially anger and the 'man'. It was some kind of secret language, an antidote passed to them by the old folks. I knew it was a song aimed at me and a tactic the lady-folk often employed when my questions became troubling. While they were singing the old spiritual refrain that I had heard since I was a toddler, they laughed at me with their eyes.

I wondered what was up but I figured I had plenty of time to find out from Wes. I didn't give it another thought until April Fool's Day almost a year later, when the school bus stopped in front of the old mansion. Wondering what was going on, I peered down the sandy driveway through the tunnel of pecan trees. Suddenly, a beautiful, bronze goddess came into view and I almost choked on my saliva. Walking with her eyes down, she held her body erect and her hips swayed ever so slightly from side to side. Wearing a baby-blue mini-skirt, it was wrapped around the top of the most gorgeous pair of legs I had ever seen. My eyes moved up her body, to the dark blue pullover sweater under which her ample breasts, covered by a white turtle neck, slightly bounced. A gold pendant hung from her neck by a matching chain, while on her shoulders danced a bouquet of the shiniest coal black hair that shimmered in the sun as it reached the length of her back. Parted in the middle she had the sides pulled back into a little pony tail that revealed her gold hoop earrings and framed her face like a black glass border. Her facial features were magazine-like with high cheek bones and a wonderful little nose, but most stunning was her smooth, magnificent bronze skin.

In Salleys Kitchen she would not be considered white and one of the boys at the front of the bus said out loud, "Dey's a nigger in that woodpile!" I cringed and prayed they wouldn't say anything like that after she got on the bus.

Moving ever closer, the stunning caramel princess glanced up at the door and flashed a small peek of her sparkling white teeth behind the most luscious and exotic lips I had ever seen. Neither smiling nor frowning, she portrayed a business-like appearance, with a notebook clutched close to her chest and a purse in her right hand. She reached the bus steps just as I was about to drool and deftly switched the bag to her left hand, grabbed the rail and floated onto the bus.

Sitting near the aisle, I was saving a seat for my buddy Burt waiting two stops later; he had an older brother that looked like Elvis and brought girls home to watch TV. Burt always spied on his petting sessions and told me everything. Little did I know Burt was going to be on his own today because once aboard, she surveyed the seats and looked straight at me. I turned away quickly, but the Cher Bono-like angel sauntered down the aisle and stopped beside my seat. I tried to ignore her, but she kept standing and the bus driver was waiting to pull away. I gave in and looked up as if my mother had just caught me peeing in her flowerbed. She never said a word, just lightly bumped my head with her notebook. I moved over and my stomach flipped.

What in the hell just happened?

As the bus took off, I stared out the window to avoid eye contact with her and saw Sully driving down the driveway in his faded old blue Fairlane with a newspaper propped on the steering wheel inches from his eyes, pen at the ready between his fingers. As he approached the stone columns on each side of the mansion's entrance, he was trying to remember a word he had used recently, a nine letter word for 'confuse' with the letter 'z' in it.

Stunned, I sat like a statue as we stopped at Burt's driveway. Without turning my head, I made eye contact with Burt as he walked past looking for a seat. His eyes were saying, *What the hell?* And my eyes were saying, *I don't know!*

I remember little about the rest of the trip, just the bus pulling to a stop at school. Dooney, the driver, was automatically the first one to leave the bus. Most juniors and seniors that could pass the bus driving test drove buses for the monthly pay check of course, but, also among other things, for the perks of getting out five minutes early from the last class of the day and being first off upon arrival in the morning.

As everyone stood up to leave, the goddess sat beside me unperturbed without moving. As I stood and watched everyone filing by, I must have looked like a fellow with bad diarrhea holding a bent nickel in front of a pay toilet. What in the hell was she doing? Soon we were the last ones on the bus except for Betty. Looking agitated, Betty evidently felt she had lost her 'most voluptuous on the bus' title. Walking from the back of the bus in her usual slow swinging gait, she stuck her notebook out and knocked the super model in the back of the head. I'm not talking about a tap; this was an eye-blearing, goose-egg leaving, kathunk on the back of the ole noggin'. Betty may have gotten by with the sucker shot if she had said, 'I'm sorry.' Instead she smiled and snickered as she walked by. In an instant, before my very eyes, the notebook and purse hit the seat between us. Reaching her hand in the pocketbook, she pulled out an object and grabbed Betty by the back of her hair. She snatched her backwards so fast the startled blonde didn't have time to scream. With the moves of a cat, the perfectly dressed, raven-haired paradox threw her prey down on the seat across the aisle. Grabbing a handful of the yellow hair on top of Betty's head with her left hand, she flicked open a long, thin stiletto, with beautiful mother of pearl inlay with her right hand.

Frozen in place, I thought, *Oh my God! She is going to cut her throat!*

Rather quickly, I moved away from the lady-folks and plastered my behind up against the bus window on the opposite side of the bus. I could only imagine the scowl on that lovely fawn face. As plain as day I heard, "If you ever again get close enough for me to get my hands on you, I'll cut your face into string meat. Do you understand me?"

That said, she stepped back and let the horrified blonde flee. Without so much as a hiss, she straightened her sweater and checked her skirt then held out the now closed knife and captured me with her stunning steel blue eyes. "Would you mind keeping this for me until this afternoon?" Obediently, I took the knife and shoved it into my jeans as she gathered her belongings.

Once off the bus, she walked hurriedly over to Dooney, the bus driver. He was smoking a Lucky and talking to some other drivers by the drink machines before homeroom. As I lingered back, I saw her talking to him and taking his hand to make him feel the knot on the back of her head. He must have told her to get lost because she left quickly and made a beeline for the principal's office. Betty, on the other hand, fled into the girl's restroom near the gym, gathering with the female crowd that always smoked there before the bell rang. She kept their attention with the knife story and they helped her fix her ruffled hair. Meanwhile, Miss Congeniality walked into Mr. Rawls' office and I could only wonder what she was saying.

As we sat in homeroom waiting for the garbled announcements to come from the wooden box above the blackboard, the classroom door opened. Everyone turned to see the voice in the box in person and following close behind, yes you guessed it, the knife lady herself. He stood in front of the class and began introducing her.

"Folks, this is Salley Sullivan. She is coming from a private school in Virginia and will be with us for the rest of the term to complete her senior year. I hope you will all welcome her and get to know her today."

He escorted her to an empty desk in the front, but as he pulled it into just the correct position for her, he realized why it was unoccupied: it was broken. Looking to the back of the room where Betty was sitting surrounded by her usual drooling hounds, he called to one of them and said, "Bring your desk up here and let her use it while you take this one to the wood shop to be fixed."

The boy complied as the blonde fumed. Once she was seated, the comb-over-king stepped back up to the blackboard and cleared his throat. We understood he was switching to his official voice for emphasis as he said, "Now students, I want you to know, I will not tolerate any type of hazing or teasing of any new student." Miss Wonderful wore her professional smile and looked intently toward the speaker. "If there's anyone who doesn't believe that, I will be glad to prove it. I think everyone understands; is that correct?"

A couple of 'yes sirs' were offered up as the 'new one' continued to smile on the front row. Then the death knell tolled. "Betty, could I see you in the office right now, please?" The petrified farm girl walked to the front with a red face and exited the room with 'the man'. As a low rumble rose through the classroom my heart and stomach began to spar when the new student looked at me and flashed her innocent smile.

***

Once in the outer office, the 'all business' principal opened the swinging gate and motioned the young lady into his private office. Pointing to a chair in front of his desk, she nervously took the seat, straightened the pleats in her dress and pushed her hair behind her ears. Walking around the desk, Mr. Rawls picked up a pack of Salem cigarettes and stuck one between his lips. He eased down on his well-worn cushion, pulled a matchbook from his shirt pocket and fired up the menthol smoke. The old chair squeaked as the principal leaned back and took a deep drag. With smoke coming out of his mouth and nose, he looked straight at his victim and asked, "Did you hit our new student in the back of the head getting off the bus this morning? Now before you answer, I want you to know I spoke with Dooney and he said she told him about it and I felt the lump on the back of her head. She also said, you said if she told anyone, you would swear she had a knife. She showed me her purse and the only thing in it was pencils, pens and girl things and she didn't have any pockets on her outfit. Now do you want to tell me the truth or do we need to call your parents and get them involved?"

With that he took another hit off of the butt and stuck it in one of the slots in the ash tray on his desk. Mr. Rawls was an equal-opportunity-punishment-principal which meant he had two teenage girls of his own and he didn't give two hoots about male or female; he paddled them all.

When the door of the tiny office opened, a blue haze belched out. The secretary, standing at the counter, had already heard the SMACK – SMACK – SMACK coming from the inner office and she had the hall pass filled out when the two emerged. It read, "TO: bathroom and homeroom / 8:25" with her initials scrawled on the bottom. Keeping her stern face looking forward, she stuck it out to the sobbing girl as she walked through the swinging gate at the end of the counter. Nothing was said until the door closed. The secretary opened her purse and pulled out a compact to check her beehive hairdo. Placing it back in the purse she pulled a cigarette from a pack of Pall Malls and tapped it on her lighter. She lit it and it bobbed up and down between her lips as she said, "Children can sure be cruel sometimes."

***

First impressions mean so much! Watching Salley Sullivan from afar, I kept my distance during the rest of the day. That afternoon I hurried out to the bus and sat by the window hoping Burt would get his ass there soon and sit down before she came; but no, she waltzed onto the bus, spied me and flopped down beside me again. We didn't speak, but before she got off, she put her John Romain purse between us and opened it. I nonchalantly fished her knife from my jeans pocket and dropped it in the leather bag.

***

Each day after that momentous Monday, she claimed the seat beside me on the bus. On Monday, Tuesday and Wednesday, I rode the bus in stone silence with a vicious war taking place in my stomach. Arriving home each afternoon, I worked in the fields but even though I was prodded, I did not mention meeting Salley or the events of that Monday. Tension among my friends in the field seemed to be rising as they sang the old spiritual song I had heard since a small boy. I hummed

65

with them as the apprehension grew among the lowest members of the community. Words were few as we walked down the rows of tiny shriveled cotton plants and wondered what would happen next.

On Thursday after school, we walked the rows and the women sang; all polite conversation vanished. In his usual merciless way, the old man didn't let us start leaving the field until well after six. But in an unusual move, my mother had the pay ready and he begrudgingly doled it out a day early. Standing on the back steps of our house he told all of his field hands not to come back to work until he told them to do so. As he started to walk up the steps, he stopped and out of pure meanness turned and yelled at the group of workers as they stood together under the giant elm in our driveway looking at their shortened pay.

"If it don't rain tonight, you can all just carry your black asses up to Memphis and march with that trouble-making Martin Luther King nigger. See what you can get out of him because I ain't wasting another dime on any of ya!"

They stared at him without saying a word for they had all heard his racial slurs before. My mother had been watching and listening from the jalousie window in the back door. As he turned and walked up the steps into the house, she backed away to let him in and said, "You shouldn't have said that."

As he walked by her into the kitchen he shouted back, "Just shut-up! What the hell do you know about handling niggers, anyway?" He walked through the kitchen and flopped down in an old worn-out wood and leather recliner. As he leaned over to take his boots off, he yelled at me, knowing I was lurking nearby but out of sight, "Turn that damn TV on so I can see the news and weather."

I appeared from the shadows, flipped on the old black and white Philco and tuned it to the news. As it warmed up and started vaguely producing some bluish characters on the screen, the audio announced, "This is a special news bulletin from NBC News: Civil Rights Leader and President of the Southern

Christian Leadership Conference and the NAACP, Dr. Martin Luther King, Jr., has been shot at a Memphis motel. Repeat, Dr. Martin Luther King, Jr. has been shot at a Memphis motel. First reports indicate he appeared dead at the scene, however he was rushed to a nearby hospital and we are awaiting a further report at this time."

I was standing in front of the TV captivated by what was being said when I heard, "Get your ass out from in front of that TV before I come over there and kick you out of the way!"

I jumped to the shadows again and listened as the reporter's features came into focus and he announced, "It has now been confirmed: Dr. Martin Luther King was shot and has been pronounced dead at St. Joseph Hospital at 7:05 PM."

My mother was standing in the doorway between the kitchen and den with her hand over her mouth and her eyes very wide. I heard my father say, "Well I'll be goddamned, they finally got him! They should have got him back when he was in Washington. He's had it coming a long time; a bullet's the only way to handle a loud mouth nigger!"

In the shadows of the adjoining room I remembered the predictions that had been made in the field and felt sick to my stomach.

***

Sully was poking along back to his house and trying to think of a 10 letter word for 'explosive'.

Chapter Seven

It did not rain Thursday night and my BB gun had not come in the mail. At school Friday, I must have heard, "They killed that King nigger, finally; took 'em long enough!" a thousand times. After school Friday, I had to work cleaning out the chicken coop by myself while my old man rode around talking to the other farmers. It was a crappy day altogether.

After the announcement of Dr. King's death, everyone seemed to be waiting for the lid of the pressure cooker to blow off; they only hoped it would not cause them harm. After hearing my parents discuss the brewing racial storm at supper, I walked out to brush Blackie and talk to him. At dark, I went to bed early and read a magazine by flashlight while the old window fan blew a breeze across my sweaty body.

Rising early Saturday morning, my parents were huddled together at the kitchen table, so I grabbed the corn flakes, poured some in a big Bugs Bunny plastic cup, threw in three or four tablespoons of sugar and filled it the rest of the way with milk. As I walked out the door, the yard was uncharacteristically empty, but I saw a slight movement and figured Wes was hanging out in the equipment shed in case the old man needed him for some reason. I made my way over to talk, drinking my corn flakes as I walked. I noticed the old man walking back and forth in the den window pointing and shaking his finger as he cussed and raved at my mother. Out of sight under the shed, I dropped the tailgate of the pickup and sat down to finish the thick, milky gunk that used to be my corn flakes. They were stuck to the bottom of the cup, so I had my head tilted back, my mouth wide open and I was pounding on the bottom of the cup to get the last of the mush to fall into my mouth when I suddenly heard Wes say, "Boy, listen to me!"

I figured he was there somewhere, but I didn't expect him to appear out of nowhere like that. Choking in surprise, I coughed as I pulled the cup away from my mouth. Wes grabbed my arm and again said, "Listen to me!"

I returned, "Damn Wes, you trying to kill me or

something? You can't come up on a fellow in that position and scare 'em. It's dangerous!"

He never smiled and started talking fast. "I could get my black ass kilt for coming over here. Now listen hat what I gwine tell you. Dey's gonna be trouble t'night and I don'ts wants yous in da middle ah hit. Yous keeps yo ass in da house, buts near at da doe and if'n yous smells smoke, yous hit da ground and belly crawl to dat garden fence. Hen you run to da woods and stays put till morning. Yous hair me?"

I asked him what he was talking about but he turned and went around the other side of the cotton trailer. I called to him and told him to come back and tell me what he was talking about. I hopped up from the tailgate and walked over to the other side of the old wagon, but he was nowhere to be seen. Walking back to the house, I slipped into the den to see if I could find out what was going on. As soon as my father saw me, he grabbed my arm and demanded to know where I had been and with whom I had been talking. Startled, I said, "I was just outside sitting on the tailgate of the pickup talking to Wes."

When he heard Wes' name he shook me and said, "What did he say to you?"

Trying to get him to turn me loose, I said, "He said there was going to be trouble."

Immediately the old man increased his grip on my arm and said, "What else did he say? Tell me boy, what else did he say?"

Realizing immediately I had made a mistake, I tried to avoid his questions and just kept saying Wes acted nervous and left. That fool grabbed me by the collar, dragged me out to the pickup and told me to get in. Driving like a maniac, he flew straight to Roy Asholee's Store. The usual crowd was there, including Sully, when he screeched to a stop in front of the hog wire porch and jumped out. As he walked toward the opening he was yelling and pointing his finger at the gathering. "I just had a nigger come to my house and scare my boy."

I started to say, "Hey, he didn't scare me!" but then I

remembered, he did scare me.

The loud mouth continued to roll, "There's going to be trouble at my place tonight and I need some help. If any of you have a hair on your ass, you'll be at my place before dark with something to help me protect my property and family."

As he walked under the shed, Roy Asholee joined him along with the other louts and they all huddled around and started talking. Sitting in the truck, I watched Sully walk by heading to his slow-mobile and heard him talking to himself, "Eleven letter word for misguided."

Late that afternoon, a couple of hours before dark, a train of riffraff driving hot rods and pickups blew into our driveway with a dust storm in tow. My mother made me stay inside while the old man walked out to stop the convoy before they reached the house. As the afternoon sun beamed down, they parked all around the asphalt apron at the end of our driveway and gathered together. An hour later the area where our driveway met the highway turned into the scene of a mob. They covered the small trapezoid shaped piece of blacktop and spilled out onto the main road hollering at the cars going by, waving a Rebel flag, holding a rope noose and acting like white trash. All had seen the looting and rioting on TV and were excited about the prospect of trouble here in 'The Kitchen'.

Two months earlier, just a little ways away in Orangeburg, South Carolina, a group of Highway Patrolmen had killed three black college students and wounded over 20 others during a protest at South Carolina State. There was a news report on TV and all of the white thugs were hamming for the TV camera as they proudly waved a Confederate battle flag and spouted racial slurs. I remember hearing one young man yell as he passed the TV camera, "Kill'em all, kill all dem niggers!"

Everyone thought a showdown was about to take place at the end of our driveway. The mob standing around was a tobacco farmer's dream. They were chewing tobacco, dipping tobacco, smoking pipes, cigars and cigarettes. Tobacco and testosterone seem to be an old-time southern marriage. The

traffic picked up on the farm-to-market road and horns started
to honk as cars and trucks drove by. Frequently, a head would
protrude from a car window and someone would scream "Bust
dem nigger heads!" followed by a rebel yell. All the
malingerers would shake their weapon in the air, whether a
rifle, shotgun, pistol, knife or baseball bat and yell back.

Finally, a Deputy Sheriff's car pulled half way off on the
side of the road, turned his blinking light on, put his radio on
the loud speaker outside the cruiser and got out. He situated his
gun and paraphernalia belt back down under his huge belly, put
his Smokey the Bear hat on his bald head and covered his eyes
with reflector sunglasses. As he started to waddle toward the
crowd, they all welcomed him asking him about his wife's
hysterectomy, about coming to the poker game at the clubhouse
Tuesday and about the new stock car track being built at
Talladega, Alabama. He greeted all with handshakes and pats
on the back.

My old man then broke up the party. "Why'd they send
just one deputy? Them niggers is laying low, figuring to
burn me out and all they send is you?"

The officer smiled and spoke to all of his friends, "Now I'm
here on official business. You all need to break this up and go
home."

The mob protested and a voice from the crowd yelled,
"You might know they'd send a nigger lover out here!"

Now, it didn't matter who you were, to say that to a typical
southern white man at that time was a low blow. The crowd
suddenly quieted and the big ole cop pointed his finger at the
man who yelled the insult. "I ain't no nigger lover and if you're
a mind to say that again, I'm a mind to take this gun and
uniform off and commence to whooping yo ass right here in
this driveway."

The man from the peanut gallery hung his head and said,
"I'm sorry, I oughtn't said it."

With that, two or three of the boys pushed him toward the
policeman and said, "Go shake his hand like a man and tell him

to his face." The over-spoken member of the crowd stepped forward and stuck his hand out and looked the deputy in the face, "Sorry man, I let my mouth overload my ass, I guess. I know you ain't no nigger lover."

With that the crowd chuckled and the big fellow went back to official business. "Now I'm giving you all a warning. You need to break this up and go home."

Turning to waddle back to his car, one of the T-shirted boys yelled, "How many warnings do we get?"

Not turning around the officer of the law shouted back, "As many as you want, I guess!" The mob laughed hysterically and agreed; they knew all along he was an okay feller.

As the sun waned, a lack of beer in the crowd took its toll and the dedicated protectors of white supremacy began to find reasons to leave. At first it just took a quickie lie and the guy could take off, but as the crowd began to get noticeably smaller, it was taking more of an in-depth and complicated lie to beg off. Finally it came down to one man that hated his wife and didn't want to go home, and a bootlegger who had slipped a pint in his overalls, drank it all by himself and passed out against a fence post. When the sun was behind the trees, the drunk woke up and didn't have a way home. The wife hater volunteered to run him home and the big mouth boss man was left all alone.

Now near dark, my mother walked out to try and get him to come in. He scolded her and told her to get back to the house out of danger. She told him he should come into the house with her and eat supper, but as she spoke to him, she saw over his shoulder the first flames. "Oh my Gawd, they've set fire to Willie and Puddin's house!"

***

There were three tenant houses on the farm. If you worked on the place, rent was free; if not, you paid $8 a month and were subject to be thrown out if a good field hand with a family came along. Willie didn't work on our farm; he stuttered and it drove

72

the old man crazy. The first day - and last - that Willie was in the field with us, my father came by in the pickup to bring some plates my mother had fixed for the fieldhands for lunch. As he returned the empty plate, Willie tried to tell him the food was good but he liked the sweet tea best. Willie stuttered so bad that finally the old man yelled, "Gawd almighty boy, if you can't say it, you need to shut the hell up and get away from me!"

Willie didn't say a thing, just backed up and looked at the ground. He was a tall, slender, well-groomed man and usually wore fairly new bib overalls, the dark blue kind that weren't faded. That day he had on a white shirt and was wearing a Sammy Davis Jr. kind of hat. As always, he had very few words to say. When the loud mouth fool left, Willie put his hoe across his shoulder and walked out of the field, back to his house. He never worked for the old man again; instead he sent $4 at the end of the month by Puddin. My mother promptly gave it back to her and said, "The $8 will come out of your next pay."

She protested, "But I's works in the fields for yous!"

My mother was quick and stern with her response. "That doesn't matter; Willie doesn't work for us. If we need that house, both of you will have to move out."

Willie didn't work in the field with us anymore but Puddin talked about him constantly. She told anyone who would listen that Willie had a year and a half of college learning at South Carolina State College. He was presently making arrangements to return to college and finish. She never admitted it, but others said he was working for Mr. Sully. Puddin kept working, but she hated my father almost as much as I did.

***

As the fire moved above the tree line, my mother's screams grew louder and I stood with my feet on the threshold of the door watching in disbelief. The old man came dragging my mother back to the house and dialed 0 for the operator. Screaming in the receiver he said, "Get the fire department and the police out to my place as quick as you can; the niggers is trying to burn me out and I'm going to kill as many as I can! I'm on the Augusta Road just before Roy Asholee's Store. Hell you can probably see the smoke from where you are!"

With that he hung up the phone, grabbed the shotgun leaning beside the door and ran out of the house. I followed him to the door and heard my mother on the porch screaming again, "They've set Mary's house on fire. Oh my God, what did we do to deserve this?"

I thought to myself, *Right, what could you have possibly done to them?*

Suddenly my old man yelled, "Just goddammit, Wes and Della's house is burning, too."

With the sun almost gone, the flames grew and appeared like three bright suns coming over the horizon. All three houses were along the field road on the back side of near a hundred acres of recently replanted cotton. Standing about three quarters of a mile away the roar of the flames, the crackling and popping of the ancient heart pine boards flooded our ears and created an ominous scene on the horizon. As my mother faced the flames, she was so brightly lit I could see the anger in her eyes. The pickup kicked up rooster tails of sand as the madman tore down the driveway. Reaching the main road, he spun the straight drive, six cylinder around and came tearing back to the house. Sliding to a halt, he jumped out with the bird gun and yelled above the sounds of the fire, "Ain't a damn thing I can do about them houses, but I can shore as hell shoot the black son-of-a-bitch that tries to burn this one!"

As his dark figure disappeared around the edge of the house, I waited for the gun battle to begin. While I stood in awe, listening to the eerie sounds of the fire, a faint wail of sirens fought to enter the surreal mixture of noises attacking my ears from all directions. The first strobes of blinking red lights streaked across our house as a deputy's car pulled to an abrupt halt in our driveway. He flipped his radio to an outside speaker and the overpowering scream of the dispatcher's voice combined with the sights and sounds of the fire to move the scene into a dreamlike realm. This time a younger officer opened the cruiser door to climb from under the red strobe light. Walking hurriedly toward me as I stood on the porch, he asked, "Where's your daddy?"

I quickly pointed around the corner of the house and as he neared the edge of the house, I remembered the gun. Stepping around the corner, the young officer flew back like a screen door on a spring and plastered himself to the white boards. Almost instantly the report of a shotgun blasted above all other sounds and bird shot peppered the siding around the corner from the officer's head. The lawman drew his pistol, held it pointed up at the night sky and yelled around the corner, "I'm the deputy sheriff, drop that gun and walk straight forward with your hands over your head!"

After a few tense moments, the old man appeared at the corner of the house with his hands over his head holding the shotgun. The scared cop held the pistol on him and told him to step into the light. When he recognized him, a severe tongue lashing ensued. First the lawman: "You idiot, you almost killed me! What the hell were you thinking? I could have been your boy or your wife. Have you lost what little brain you have?"

Ever the narcissist and always the fool, my old man said, "I thought you were trying to burn my house down; can't you see what's happening to my property? Besides, my wife and boy would have had better sense than to come at me in the dark."

Then the lawman again: "You crazy fool, give me that shotgun and get your ass up on that porch with the rest of your family. If I even think you might leave the porch, I'll cuff you and put you in the back of that cruiser. You understand me?"

The man of the house started to say something and the cop reached to his back to grab his cuffs. That ended the conversation and the old man walked up on the porch with us.

With the bird gun now in his hands, the deputy headed

back to his car. No sooner than reaching his cruiser, the officer faced another and potentially more dangerous situation. The store bums had seen the flames and loaded into a pickup truck with their weapons of choice. They swerved into the yard with two or three of them barely hanging onto the back bed of the truck. Not taking any chances this time, the overwhelmed lawman threw the confiscated shotgun on the backseat of the squad car and grabbed the pump shotgun from the rack near the front seat. Stepping into the beam of the headlights from the truck full of men, he pointed the shotgun at them.

"What the hell you doing pulling a gun on us?" came a shout from the dust cloud.

"I've been shot at once tonight and I don't aim for it to happen again," said the deputy.

Looking at the porch, the mob leader saw my old man and pointed to him. "We just came by to git him and go see who's settin' fires."

To which the young officer replied, "He's not going anywhere tonight, 'cept in the house and to bed, so go home and settle down."

A quick reply shot from the truck, "The hell you say! We figure on showing them niggers just who's boss round these parts! That's right, and we don't want them to forget it. We got a rope for the ones that can't remember who runs this show."

The man behind the wheel shoved the three speed shifter on the steering column up into reverse and snatched his foot off the clutch. Dirt and dust boiled from under the floor boards and the crowd in back lurched forward as the truck sped backwards, then slung around 180 degrees and took off. The patrolman jumped into his car and followed. Both were heading in the direction of the field road with the deputy's red light flashing, the siren screaming and the good ole boys bellowing a Rebel Yell at the top of their voices.

Passing by Willie and Puddin's house, the flames were dying down and the boys in the back with guns fired them in the air as the truck bumped and jerked them around. Willie was standing in the yard with a pine bough in his hand. He had been beating back the flames so they wouldn't get into the nearby woods. Standing up straight to see the parade going by, he couldn't see anything but dust and the red light flashing. As the mob approached the ruins of Mary's house, the yells and gun fire started again. She lived in a small two-room shack and it had burned much faster than the others. Following the field road, the crazy run didn't stop there and with zeal, the gang made straight way for Wes and Della's flaming house. They circled the fire two or three times making a dust cloud that was sucked into the flames' updraft. After all of the bums were covered with gray-white dust, the truck turned for home.

The deputy had stopped at Willie and Puddin's, they guessed because he didn't want to eat any more dust. On the way back by the first fire, the bums pulled up to tell the young patrolman to say hello to their lodge buddy and no hard feelings. When the truck stopped and the dust cleared, they saw him standing with his hand on Puddin's shoulder. She was on her knees holding the lifeless body of Willie in her arms and sobbing uncontrollably.

"Shiiiiiiiiit, why'd you shoot that skinny nigger! Is he the one set the fires? Good 'nuff for his black ass, then!"

Filled with indignation, sorrow, and frustration, the young lawman didn't want to be part of this mess, but it was his job so he turned to the men and spat out the words he didn't want to say. "All of you get out of the truck, turn around and put your hands on the hood."

The boys protested, "Ah man, don't try to blame us for that nigger git'n shot!"

His quick reply, "Well, my gun hasn't been fired — yet!" He drew his service revolver from his holster for the second time that night. "Now, I don't know who shot this man, but I aim to find out, so all of you turn around and put your hands on the hood of that truck and spread your feet apart."

Still protesting, one of the good ole boys said, "Have you

lost your mind? There are nine of us standing here. We could take you in a minute."

Again with a quick reply, "Maybe, but if you don't turn around and grab that truck, the first six that move toward me are going to have holes in their chests. Now you decide, I have to qualify every six months with this thing and I'm pretty damn good with it. I ain't never shot a man with it and I don't want to start tonight so now pick your poison. I believe we are all going to make the paper either way."

He pointed his .38 caliber snub at a man holding a pistol. "Drop your weapons, turn around and grab the truck, I ain't gonna ask you again."

After his last statement, one laid his pistol on the ground, one was pulled out of a back pocket and laid on the ground, two shotguns (one a pump with a sawed off barrel) were laid down and the last man with a rifle hesitated. The lawman pulled the hammer back and cocked his pistol then trained it on the rifleman. The rifle was laid on the ground and with an attitude, the last man turned and put his hands on the truck.

Seeking control of the situation, the man with the badge offered, "Now let's just all calm down. I called for help and I see his red light flashing from here. I'm nervous and if you run, I will shoot to stop you; hopefully it won't kill you!"

When I first heard the news of Willie's death, it didn't seem real. Roy Asholee had just pulled up in our driveway as the second deputy sheriff's car turned on the field road. As he stopped beside his partner, the flashes of red light allowed us to intermittently see the store bums standing with their hands on the side of their truck. Roy walked up to our porch and said, "I think that nigger that stutters is dead. I saw him lying limp in the yard with his old lady squalling, holding him. He wasn't moving at all."

My old man stepped off the porch to walk over to Roy's truck and my mother said, "That deputy said you were not to leave the porch."

The old man turned on her like a rabid dog. "Shut your

fucking mouth; ain't nobody gonna tell me I can't leave my own porch!"

With that scolding, she went back into the house. Roy and my father huddled near his truck and talked as Roy showed him his pistol. He put it back in his pocket and laughed as my old man patted him on the back and laughed with him. Another deputy arrived and the store bums were loaded into the three cruisers; Roy got in his truck and left. My father was back on the porch when the young deputy pulled into our driveway with a number of the rabble rousers in the seat behind him. He told my father that the coroner was on his way to pronounce Willie dead and determine the cause of death. The deputy went on to say he thought he had been shot.

Standing on his porch, my old man said, "Well, it's good enough for him if he's the one burning my houses!"

The deputy said, "His wife said he was trying to put the fire out when he was shot."

My old man asked, "And you believe that stupid nigger?"

The deputy simply said, "Yes."

From the porch, my father yelled to the lowlifes, "Don't worry boys, we'll be there to get you out as soon as you get there." With that pronouncement, the deputy pulled away and headed for Aiken.

The store slugs were booked and fingerprinted and the reporters took pictures to put in the Aiken Standard newspaper the next day. The headline read, *Arrested for Murder and Accessory to Murder* and their story, along with coverage of Dr. King's assassination filled the newspaper. There was a lot of violence going on around the country and our little part of the world fell in lock step with the evil. Of course, my father was telling the paper that he would personally see that the bums did not spend a night in jail. All they were doing was helping him protect his property, something the law in this county wouldn't help him do or let him do himself. The county fire department never did come to help, but near morning the US Forest Service bulldozer arrived and plowed fire lines around the burned down houses.

The deputy sheriff would not be interviewed and would not have his photo taken, but everybody knew him and the newspaper put his high school yearbook picture in the paper. After all the paperwork and statements to the higher-ups were given, he came home on Sunday morning to his wife sitting on their couch, crying. She stood up when he came in and put her arms around him as he stood exhausted and motionless. The young man held his wife close to his chest and said, "I had to do my job and I know it was the right thing to do."

She squeezed him and patted his broad back and tried to comfort him. "I know baby, I never doubted you'd do the right thing."
He replied, "I'll probably have to find a new job."

She rubbed her hand over his head and pulled it close to her face. Just before she kissed him she looked into his eyes and said, "I know honey — it'll be all right, you did the right thing! I love you."

All of the riffraff had their bail set at $25 each and were released Sunday before church. Roy Asholee gave one of their daddies the bond money for all of them. A reporter rode out to question Roy, the unofficial mayor of Salleys Kitchen. He told her the money for their bail came from some of their friends, but declined to name them.

While she stood under the wired-in shed writing notes in her tablet, Sully was leaning on one of the brick columns and he asked Mrs. Asholee if she knew a 3 letter word for heartbreak. She screwed up her ogre face, spit on the ground and yelled, "Hell no!"

The reporter, without looking up from her notes replied, "Cry."

Sully said, "No, my dear, the needed word has an 'o' in the middle, as if a tiny puncture."

Chapter Eight

It must have started raining in the wee hours of Sunday morning, for I awoke from a bad dream about Willie and Puddin. They were standing in a field during a rainstorm and my father was shooting at them and I couldn't stop him. He finally turned and shot me in the stomach. I awoke to thunder, lightning and pouring rain with a pain in my abdomen. Remembering the past night, I didn't want to get out of bed when I suddenly realized the rain meant an end to the drama-inducing drought and hopefully a reprieve from the old man's ill temper. As I stood and looked out my bedroom window the three piles of rubble, that were just a few hours ago homes of my friends, now steamed, releasing their last tragic gasp. I put on my Sunday clothes and got ready for church. The old man did not go to church that Sunday and Blackie and I didn't get to escape that afternoon. I lay in the glider on the porch all afternoon watching the rain drip off of the end of the tin roof. My heart was crying but I didn't let the tears come to my eyes; they would have chastised me. It was another crappy day.

Though gloomy, the rain brought with it a lessening of the racial tension, but the excitement of the shooting and the fires were the main topic Monday as I returned to school and a thousand questions. Everyone wanted to know about 'the dead nigger' and I didn't want to talk about it at all. My new seatmate sat mute as everyone prodded and pumped me for information. It was a hellish week and for once I was glad when Friday's school day came to a close. No one worked in the fields that entire week, but I cut and split firewood every day after school even though it was spring and we didn't need to heat the house.

When it rains, it pours! I don't know who said it first, but I certainly thought it to be true as I woke again to a rainy Saturday. I desperately wanted to avoid any torturous job my old man would dream up for me, so I cautiously looked around the house. It was obvious he was gone and my mother was working on her Sunday school lesson out on the porch. I immediately recognized my need for a hiding place, somewhere safe.

My out-of-sight, safe place since I was a little boy was the hayloft. Among the bales I had constructed a hideaway; a hay fort I called it. I needed to get there and secrecy was of highest importance. My clandestine movement through the gauntlet of my house was a tricky maneuver. If caught by the warden or his assistant, I would be sentenced to a dreary day of hard labor quicker than a duck on a June bug. While my mother had her nose in her Bible, I snuck into the kitchen. The rain clouds had turned the atmosphere of the usually bright, seldom quiet kitchen, into a dark and empty quarter. Quickly as possible, I filled an old pickle jar full of corn flakes then added milk and sugar. Just as fast, I grabbed the old man's peanut butter jar and made two sandwiches, then swiped a can of his Vienna Sausages, eased two of his Little Debbie Pecan Spins from the box and tossed them into an old A&P grocery bag. From the refrigerator I swiped an old piece of hoop cheese and the two last pieces of bologna, then filled an empty mayonnaise jar full of sweet tea. Putting all of my bounty into the brown paper bag along with a clean dish towel, my heart pounded as I prepared for my hiatus. At least I had a snack in case I got hungry. Needing a quick getaway, I cleaned up and grabbed both the Sears Roebuck and Montgomery Ward catalogues along with an old Field and Stream magazine. If I could make it to my hay bale fort I would have the morning to myself.

Stealthily scurrying for the tractor shed and scooting around the edge of the tool barn, I sprinted through the raindrops across the open prison yard all the way to the hallway of the mule barn. Climbing the board ladder in the first stable, with my package under one arm, I completed my successful escape to the dry loft. Blackie snorted as I walked over his stable, so I kicked some hay into his rack. Then making straight way to the secret bale, I moved it over and slid down the chute into the hay cavern. Then with a quick reach, I closed the secret entrance and felt for my battery powered lantern in the total darkness —

click, I was in seclusion, hopefully for the day. After eating all the food, I lay back on Blackie's blanket and started flipping through the catalogues. I couldn't stop thinking about Willie and Puddin. Trying to get them out of my mind, I dug out the Penthouse I got by trading a week's worth of ham sandwiches. Even that didn't change my mood, so I put my head back and started to think about all of the people who worked with me in the field and the beautiful girl that sat by me on the bus. Why did she want to sit by me? Falling asleep as I contemplated that crazy girl, I woke hours after arriving, hungrier than ever and needing to pee. Putting the two catalogues in the grocery bag, I turned off the now dim lantern and crawled out of the hay tunnel. The rain had stopped and there were puddles everywhere.

Tip-toeing back to the house I watched as Sully crawled down the puddle-filled paved road looking for a nine letter word that meant 'gloom'. With my eyes on that old blue Ford Fairlane, I ran right into the assistant warden, my mother, standing at the door.

She asked, "Where did you run off and hide? I haven't seen you all morning." I told her I was taking care of Blackie. She asked if I had been hiding in the hay loft all this time and I hesitated when I answered her. She coolly said, "Go brush all that loose hay off of your clothes before you come in my house."

Sunday after church it was raining again and gloomy boredom continued. I went back out to my hay fort with some fresh batteries for my lantern but I hated being alone in the hay cavern. Climbing out, I decided to give Blackie a good brushing and talk to him since we couldn't escape this Sunday. We discussed everything that had happened. He was always a good listener.

Chapter Nine

Monday on the bus, I listened as the events of Willie's death were recalled and rehashed. Everyone had a different theory, but they all blamed 'the crazy nigger'. Every planter in The Kitchen watched as Sully's cotton came out of the furrow after the rain in a perfect stand, reaching for the warm spring sun. By the end of the week, the stunned farmers of The Kitchen were full of resentment and their conversations were full of curses thrown at Sully. My old man was the only other farmer to have a decent stand of cotton as the mystery seeds germinated and grew. Sully was expressionless as he rode by our house pondering a seven letter word for lull.

Saturday morning, for the first time since Willie was killed, we stood together ready to work in the fields again. Without talking, we loitered under the enormous umbrella elm, Dagger, Albert, Della, Mary and me — Puddin and Wes were absent. The farm's monarch was taking his quick trip around the fields to see where we needed to work that day and all too soon he came wheeling back into the yard lickety-split. He slid to a stop at the back steps and ran in the house like he had diarrhea, but as we found later, it was just a loose mouth not his bowels. He ranted to my mother a while then picked up the phone and yelled in the receiver to another party. For some merciful reason our appointment in the hot morning sun and scorching sand had been postponed. With a curiosity that could have killed every cat hiding under the barn, I needed to know why.

Finally Albert, in a very low voice said, "Reckin he musta seed Mr. Sully disking under his'n cotton."

My head spun around and with shock on my face I said, "Say what!"

Albert continued looking at the ground, "I seed 'im dis mornan early, wid dat big ole "M" Farmall, a draggin' dat disk harrow down dem cotton rows. Had dat tractor throttle gap wide open pulling da disc wid black smoke shootin' outa dat ole piece of junk, but he was'n gwine so slow I coulda walk past 'em down dem rows. Had dat damn newspaper stuck up in his face and was justa turnin' all dat purfact cotton under da dirt hand wanted fors eberbody to sees."

As usual, I must have been the last to find out, for everyone else just looked at the ground. "Why in the hell is he doing that? He stood to make a killing on it this fall! Has he gone completely crazy?"

The answer made complete sense. "He dun had Willie attend to his'ns fields dis year. Dat ole fool dun tolded Willie and Puddin he wants forda sharecrop wid dem dis yar. Whats dey hadda mades he gwine split three ways, so's Willie coulda go back to college, hand Puddin coulda goed ta lib han works hin Orangeburg han keeps him gwine dis time. Hi guess he gwine spend da ress hone dem little bottles of Country Club Malt Liquor he drank all da time."

It was a scheme that only Mr. Sully could have dreamed up, but it all made sense. He was always busy trying weird experiments and needed someone to manage his cotton crop. Willie was just the man for the job and was just a few days from revealing himself in Sully's fields. The future looked bright for the young couple as they made plans. Having Willie to become an educated farmer and then come back in a few years so he and Puddin could farm as a family right beside my old man would have been the ultimate irony. Now I was beginning to understand and tears appeared in my eyes. Willie and Puddin deserved a break and received only despair. Mr. Sully must have been expressing his grief, too and I could not have thought of a better way for him to demonstrate his heartbreak to the community.

The tyrant I lived with had publicly threatened Wes and told the others if he saw him again he would kill him on the spot. After Willie's murder, a good number of the black residents of the community left; the rest cowered down to survive. Wes had to leave and I felt it my fault for shooting off my mouth. A sick feeling hung around my neck like a mule collar. I silently wondered why the evil in my life was so permanent and the few good things were so temporary. As my grief began to subside, I wanted to tell my father to shut his mouth and leave Wes alone, but Albert told me not to say anything in Wes' behalf because it was senseless to take a beating for something that couldn't be changed.

Sully put Wes and Puddin on the bus to Charleston. They had kinfolk there who were getting the refugees settled and on their feet. When Puddin started up the steps of the Trailways bus, she had turned to hug Sully for one last time, kissing his cheek then looking in his eye she said, "Dis hain't ober Mr. Sully, not bys a long shot, hit hain't ober!" Puddin would tell me later that she didn't know why she said that, but she meant it.

As Sully turned the magnificent stand of cotton back into the soil to break down and become nutrients for the next crop, we climbed out of the back of the truck to walk into the field across the fence. After we started down the rows of newly emerged plants, the old man left the field and was about to turn onto the main highway, when he looked back to see Sully had plowed across the field and was stopped at his fence talking to Della. It would have been hard to calculate the rage coming up from my father's red neck and covering his face as he slammed the truck into reverse, turned around and started back into the field with dirt flying everywhere.

We knew Sully was giving Della a message from Puddin and so did the fool flying down the end of the rows toward the stopped tractor. As he got to the fencerow, he jumped out and started walking down the edge of the field toward the couple talking. Maybe thirty yards away, Sully waved to him, then pulled the throttle down on the red tractor and started back to where he had stopped plowing. Politely, Sully had turned his back on my old man. Watching him drive away on his tractor, my father was furious and started yelling and screaming while shaking his fist in the air. When he got to Della he kept screaming, "What the hell were you talking to him about?"

Della was very collected and calm as she told him, "He wanted to know if you might want him to come over and turn your cotton over since his disk harrow was hooked up and ready to go."

Still with the red face, "That crazy son-of-a-bitch better not come across that fence, I'll blow his damn head off. He was talking a long time, what else did he say to you?"

Della couldn't hold it back any more, "He wanted to know if I knew a nine letter word for requite with an 'L' in the middle. Turning away from him, she calmly walked away and rejoined our group.

When chopping cotton, as the hoe hits the sand, it makes a skrich, skrich, skrich noise and that was the dominant sound heard as my father stomped and cussed his way back to the truck. The moment he was out of sight, we broke up with laughter.

In the midst of the fun, I had to ask, "Is that what he really said or were you just kicking sand in his face?"

She could hardly contain herself, "He did ask if I knew the…" she stopped in mid-sentence, then, with a grin from ear to ear, threw down her hoe and hugged Mary's neck. When she caught her breath she spilled the beans, "Puddin found out she's pregnant!" Then she and Mary squealed and jumped up and down for quite a while.

Chapter Ten

On Sunday morning the sun came out and by the time we got home from church, a perfect day was upon us. Hurrying into the house to change my clothes, I could finally feel the spring we had missed because of the drought and didn't want to be inside a minute longer than mandatory. As usual, I gulped down the Sunday dinner Mama had prepared and dashed out of the clapboard farmhouse with a wedge of pound cake in my hand, a buttered steak biscuit in my mouth and a big turnip under my arm for Blackie. He had pushed the staples holding the hog wire out of the fencepost and was sticking his head and long muscled neck out over the bulging wire. Displaying his impatience, he had pawed the ground bare where he was standing. We had missed our Sunday jaunt for the past two weeks and he thought it high time we got going.

Throwing open the gate, he trotted over to the corncrib where I kept his bridle and saddle and I grabbed his currycomb. As I was treating my faithful friend to a quick brush, he shook his head and snorted to remind me of his treat I had forgotten. I don't know if the turnip or the bag of sweet feed enticed him most, but I tossed the purple and white root onto the board floor of my improvised tack room and he began crunching it up with zeal. He devoured it in seconds and quickly began to lap the molasses coated oats and cracked corn in the bottom of his feed bucket.

Brushing his back to make sure there was nothing that would rub or irritate him under the saddle, I reached for the hoof pick Wes had fashioned for me from a big nail and a loop of metal rod. After making sure his oversized hooves were clean, I tossed the red saddle blanket over his wide black back followed by the small saddle that I was quickly outgrowing. Pulling the girth as tight as I possibly could, the sly old horse anticipated the tautness and inhaled to make sure I didn't pull it tighter than he wanted. This was his usual ploy resulting in the saddle being loose after he exhaled. He liked the front cinch to be loose, but on previous rides I had learned that a loose saddle and quick turns at a gallop would result in the saddle sliding sideways and my skinny butt landing hard on the ground. Making sure that didn't happen again, I pulled the cinch tight, then waited a few seconds until he exhaled. Once he exhaled I quickly snatched it tight before he could fill his huge lungs and swell his chest. He always grunted when I tricked him and I would pat his chest and say, "Oh no, big boy! I'll not end up in the sand on this ride!" He would snort in protest but keep gunning down his feed. Our ritual being complete, I climbed to the top of his back and we were off, away from the drudgery and unappreciated toil of that damn farm and into our world of freedom and adventure among the forest and fields scattered across the ancient sand dunes.

Our getaway gallop always took us to the sandy field road that meandered around the edge of the largest cotton field on our farm. It had been dotted with tenant houses until the recent debacle. As we sped past the burned out ruins, I looked away, refusing to think about Willie and Puddin. Poor Puddin, I knew she must have been heartbroken. My heart felt heavy knowing we would not be hearing Wes yell, "Ride'em cowboy!" as he always did when we galloped past his and Della's house. This day only a nasty burned smell came from the site. In usual fashion, I buried those bad thoughts down deep and forced my brain to think of something else.

Once Wes and Della's old house site was behind us, we turned and headed across the hayfield approaching a large forest on an old sandy wagon road that cut through the heart of the wood. To ensure good neighbors, as he insisted to my father, Sully had built a fence across the road to further define the property line, but in a rare act of defiance, I had cut the wire and transformed the section of fence across the road into a wire gap. Fastening a pole to the end of the wires, I made a wire loop at the bottom and top of the fence post making a passageway through the fence that I could open from my saddle. Though I had never had the nerve to ask, for some reason I felt ole Sully didn't mind my altering his fence or

Blackie and me riding on his farm. Today, however, my bladder was brimming with sweet tea so as I reined him in at the fence, I slid from my lofty seat to open the gap. Leading him through the opening, I patted him on his now sweaty shoulder and closed the make-shift gate. We were now on the Sullivan property as we had been many, many times before. Throwing his reins over a bush I walked past him and stepped just beyond the area where he could reach me with his nose. Another lesson I had learned from experience: a nudge at the wrong time could leave a fellow with wet underwear.

I should have taken care of this necessity before I mounted up, but I was so anxious to get away from that house, I figured I would stop at the first chance and take care of business. So standing at the edge of the road, I was well into the process and far beyond the 'letting it go' stage. In that sweet tea had been involved and since I had waited until I was about to wet my pants, I knew this might take a few more seconds than usual. With all that pressure being relieved I was naturally trying to see how far I could reach with my flowing stream.

Just as I reached peak distance, a female voice sounded off in close proximity, "Those bushes you are peeing on are not on your property!"

In a knee-jerk reaction, I spun around to see the 'who' and 'where' of the voice and to my shock, made quick eye contact with my beautiful seatmate from the school bus. Making such an abrupt about face without thinking, I exposed myself to the interloper. Just as quickly, I recognized my poor decision and turned back to face the now wet bushes. Her next words were even more alarming. "It's too late now, I've already seen it!"

Hoping she was not talking about what I thought she was talking about, I forcefully shut down the now waning process, made sure of placement and closed my fly. When I turned around, I'm sure my face was as red as a fox's butt at pokeberry time, but that loud-mouthed, sneaky female was already on the move toward the wire gap and quickly, as if she had done it before, opened it and walked through to the other side. She stepped over to the side of the sandy path, pulled her jeans and panties down with one swift motion and promptly peed on the grass. Her process involved squatting and was therefore much different than mine. After sufficient time, with a crumpled up Kleenex in her hand, she reached under and dried her drain. Then, with the same swift motion, she pulled up her jeans and panties, snapped the snap and walked away from the wet spot leaving the Kleenex on top. She came back through the gap, closed it, walked up to me without a hint of embarrassment, looked into my eyes and declared; "Now we're even!"

There are no words that can even come close to explaining how I felt at that instant. Her words and actions triggered my autonomic nervous system and made my fight or flight response kick into gear. I was very near the point of jumping on Blackie and galloping away as fast as I could. My heart rate increased, my eyes opened wide, my breathing sped up and had I not just emptied my bladder, I'm sure it would have gone on auto pilot also. As my decision-making process moved to emergency mode, conflicting thoughts flashed through my brain and in rapid order I contemplated, *I cannot believe this is really happening!* Immediately after that deliberation I wondered, *Am I having another one of those dreams?* Then finally, in a nanosecond of brain activity, my ever-present guilt chimed in with, *Have you no shame; this is Sunday, remember, and you're watching a girl pee!*

But even in my frozen state, I'm sure there was a smile lurking among the muscles in my face. In a blaze of cognitive activity, I considered a wide range of possibilities in rapid order.

I'm so lucky; I would have gladly given a year's worth of ham sandwiches to see that from any peep hole; did I pee on myself? I'm too embarrassed to look; oh no, she rides my bus and has that knife! Suddenly my heart pounded furiously as I supposed another scary notion: *Will she tell my father, or worse, will she tell her father? If you were to meet the Almighty right after you watched a girl pee and didn't try to look away and actually enjoyed the sight, would you go straight to Hell?* For more than just that reason I silently prayed, *Please, Lord, don't let me die now!*

All of these horrifying scenarios deluged my thinking process, mixed with a million other emotions, but the lasting aspect of the whole traumatic sequence was summed in my lingering thoughts:

My God, she's even gorgeous when she pees!

My brain's tachometer was well over the rpm red line and I wouldn't have been surprised if my head had exploded. But after that initial flurry of thought, I realized this was not a dream and SHE was standing just inches away from me.

Yes, she was the same girl that dressed like a fashion model and sashayed out to the school bus, but her clothes were not the same today. Sporting jeans with iron-on patches on both knees, that were starting to come off, she was wearing an old boy's t-shirt on which she – I guess it was her - had wiped her mouth on the front. Over that she wore a green and tan plaid shirt that I had seen Sully wearing, completely unbuttoned in front with the long sleeves unbuttoned and dangling around her hands. With worn out PF Flyers and no socks, I could see her painted toenails; she was not dressed to impress. But she was so beautiful, the same height as I was, her eyes were twin piercing pools of blue and outlined with long curled lashes and thick, long, eyebrows that narrowed as they moved across her eyes. Her skin the color of coffee with just a splash of cream added and her nose was perfectly set between her high cheek bones and slightly pouting lips. But her lips were dirty, she was chewing bubble gum and had obviously blown too big of a bubble. There were little black specks around her mouth and a little on the end of her nose. Standing less than a foot away from me, she was reading my face with those beautiful steel-blue eyes, waiting on a response.

There was no way I could have communicated intelligently

with anyone at that moment; thank goodness she was unflappable. Recognizing the panic in my eyes she said, "I walked up to the fence to see the burned houses. Did you know the man who was killed? He was Sully's friend."

Bringing up the subject of Willie and Puddin was just not fair. My emotions had taken a beating about Willie's death, but I could not tell anyone at home because they would think I was on the other side. Building my 'no, it didn't make any difference to me' façade I spoke my first word to her, "Naaah."

Still looking at my eyes she knew I lied. Now I had to repair my tough man image, so I walked over to the gap and told her that she could see the burned rubble from the fence. She replied almost too quickly, "Yeah, I know."

Asking if we could walk over to see the houses I said, "No!" in an instant.

She knew I was dodging something so I told her, "I don't want my father to see me - he might make me come home."

In a speedy reply she said, "I know what you mean. Sully would be out looking for me right now if I hadn't hidden his keys." She smiled and I smiled—a beginning.

Blackie had just about had enough of this chitchat and wanted to get back on the trail. He pawed and blew his nose with aggravation. "Where were you going?" she asked.

"We ride this way most every Sunday and cut through by the old Fant house, then across the Salley Road and over to Phil's Pond, then up to the store on the Old Tory Road and down the Brodie Road back to The Griddle. That's pretty much it."

Very interested, she continued to pry, "How far is that?"

Looking at the ground I offered, "Probably ten or fifteen miles; we know a bunch of shortcuts, too."

As she turned to pat the perturbed horse on his nose, he shook his head, then snorted and wouldn't let her touch him. It didn't bother her in the least, she reached over and grabbed his bridle and snatched his head back close to her. Blackie's ears stood up and his eyes cut to the girl in charge as she talked softly to him and patted his nose. "What's his name?" she inquired.

"This is Blackie," I proudly replied.

She kept patting his nose and politely said, "Hello, Blackie, I'm very glad to meet you."

Now there were two of us that didn't understand her. I grabbed the reins from over the bush and started a fake move to the gap. Quickly she told me I shouldn't go home just because of her. "Besides," she said, "Sully wouldn't care if you peed on every bush on his place."

I put my foot in the stirrup and swung up on the old draft horse. When I looked back down she was smiling and had her heart-grabbing eyes focused straight on mine. With all of my fears and inhibitions suddenly obliterated, I smiled back, kicked my foot out of the stirrup and offered her my hand.
"Go with us?"

As if practiced, she gave me her hand then jumped to put her foot in the stirrup and swung up behind me. Putting her arms around my waist, I nudged Blackie with my heels and he took off at a gallop. This was the first time a girl had ever put her arms around me and it felt so magnificent. Unlike the girls I observed at school, there was no silly screaming or squealing. She rode confidently behind me and it was immediately obvious she was at home on a horse as she rode in perfect balance with his gait. The big old horse didn't flinch at the extra weight and pounded down the sandy trail while we dodged low limbs and gave him plenty of rein.

After a little ways, I made Blackie slow to a walk so he could catch his wind and his usual protest didn't show. He never recognized his fatigue or let me know he was tiring and I loved him too much to hurt him. He was bred to pull a load and for me, he would do just that until he dropped.

Cresting one of the pine covered sandhills, I suggested we get off and walk a ways so Blackie could cool down. After just a few paces, a strange squeaking noise reverberated through the late spring air. Looking through the pines to the far hillside, we

94

spotted Sully's car creeping and bouncing down a rutted old log road in our direction. My walking partner let out a quick, "SHIT! He straight wired it." Disheartened, I sure didn't want this exciting afternoon to end. With a devilish smile she asked, "What are we going to do?"

Most willingly, I became her partner in crime and we jumped back on Blackie and rode to the bottom of the hill. Stopping in a creek that crossed the old log road, we jumped off and I led Blackie as we walked in the streambed as far as we could go into the brush. Standing ankle deep in the cool creek water, our excitement was fueled by adrenaline coursing in our veins. With her by my side, we stood facing a big sparkleberry bush that blocked our way. The thick undergrowth looked to be growing in the middle of the stream. Blackie and I knew better and as I handed her his reins, I wrestled my way into the thick brush, turned my back to the mass of branches and grabbed the biggest ones near the creek bed. Pushing as hard as I could with my legs and back, the massive sparkleberry moved and opened a walkway straight down the stream. After my partners scrambled through the passageway, I moved away from the thick mass of branches and joined them. The sparkleberry bush flopped back down in the brook as if it were a wall without any evidence of our entry.

That was just one of the titillating features of this spot on Sully's land. On the other side of the bush wall, a huge, old-growth, longleaf pine had been spreading its roots in the sandy streambed and growing toward the sky for centuries. Through the years an incredible grass-covered island had formed in the middle of the creek with the landmark tree holding the ground around its base. This was not just an old, old tree, but a very rare tree. All of the original longleaf pines that had once covered the landscape had long since been cut down, but this massive beauty had been miraculously spared. With the stream around its base feeding nutrients, the protection of the South Edisto River Swamp had prolonged and nurtured its growth, causing it to flourish.

The secluded half-acre isle was covered with soft pine needles around the base of the tree. Spreading out over the rest of the parcel was a bed of soft green grass, thick and squashy. On our many forays in and around the Sullivan place, Blackie and I had spotted the tall, solitary pine tree towering above the canopy of the rest of the trees. On our furtive forays through our neighbor's farm, I had searched many times for the base of the mammoth tree but could never find its exact location. On one particular ride, I stopped to let Blackie get a drink and decided to bushwhack into the swamp-like jungle to see if I could find it. After a long period of struggle, I fell into the stream on my knees and looked forward to see the tiny opening. I pried my way into the small space and found to my surprise, I could use my back to move the sizable bush to the side of the creek. Taking advantage of its flexibility, I forced my way in and discovered the fantastical tree and island. It was quite a struggle to get Blackie into the protected cove with me but once in, he loved the tender green grass. We returned a couple of times after our initial discovery, but I hadn't extended the energy to gain its access for quite a while, preferring to ride Blackie with the wind in my face.

Entering the magical cove, my fellow mischief-maker's mouth dropped open. Upon seeing the amazing and very private location, she twirled 360 degrees, soaking in the view. To let him rest and eat a while, I took Blackie's saddle and blanket off and pulled his bridle over his ears. He was so big he could never get out unless I held the bush back and besides, he loved the grass about as much as his sweet feed. Sitting down on the pine straw, I motioned for my new friend to join me. Side by side, we lay back on the soft brown needles as our eyes climbed up and up and up into the top of the centuries-old pine — an awesome view. Holding our breath, we listened as Sully drove by splashing through the creek and spinning his wheels in the soft sand as he climbed the hill. In a short while the squeaking sound returned and the old Ford splashed through the stream just before it climbed the other side of the sandhill and headed back toward the old mansion. Once his old jalopy was out of earshot, she sat up and turned to look down into my face with those mesmerizing eyes. Wondering what her next action or words would be, she once again took me by surprise. After a few moments of staring at me in silence, she leaned down and kissed me with her mouth open, her tongue searching for mine.

The truth was, the only other girl I had kissed was my cousin, Debbie. My mother had taken me to visit her sister during Christmas. Her oldest daughter, probably 20 or so, said she thought I was cute and snuck a kiss from me as I was coming out of the kitchen. It was a quickie and she smiled afterward and walked away. It was very exhilarating and with that experience, I thought I knew the correct way to kiss. Today, however, I was to receive my first in-depth lesson in the art of passionate kissing and the inevitable urges that follow.

On Blackie's deep red blanket, we began exploring the erotic uses of the lips. From deep, wet, French kisses to delicate petal-like brushes of lips over the eyes, to sexy, moist, licks of the ears, to long tongue strokes that tantalized the neck and below, we writhed with desire. Oblivious to the world, engulfed with passion, our fire of heavy petting blazed out of control as my hand rubbed across her stomach and gradually eased under a warm undershirt to find no bra. Suddenly the ante skyrocketed. My afternoon partner in passion sat up and pulled my hand from under her dirty t-shirt. Crossing her arms in front of her chest, she grabbed the bottom of the shirt and pulled it up and over her head, letting her long ebony hair cascade around her shoulders. To understate the moment, it was breathtaking! With her arms, she reached out and pulled my head to her breast as she lay back on Blackie's blanket. After clawing through my hair and pulling me ever closer to her, she reached down and under to pull her jeans and panties down for a second time that afternoon. She pushed my t-shirt up and unsnapped my jeans. Taking the initiative, I quickly pulled my shirt off and shoved my pants to my knees as she removed and tossed hers away. As she lay naked beside me on her back, I moved to embrace her once again and rolled onto a pinecone. God only knows how it had gotten on the blanket, but I yelped like a hit dog as I rose to my knees to grab the damn cone and throw it as far as I could from my position.

Giving light to exactly what I didn't want to be seen, my cry of pain caused her to raise up on her elbows and look directly at the most excited part of my anatomy. She looked a little amused and said, "It sure has changed." Not wanting conversation at this time, I repeated my move, this time without the yelp. Nature, I guess, guided us the rest of the way as it took several reference points to finally properly align. As I hovered just inches above her, I could see her eyes searching my face as she pulled my hips against hers and gave a little gasp. In a matter of seconds an impending crescendo climbed with each of my movements. Suddenly, a short circuit in my brain caused the most pleasurable shock wave I had ever experienced to throb through my body and with each heartbeat and movement, more and more of the pleasure surged through my body and exited at our union. My eyes didn't function properly, my breathing became strained, I couldn't swallow, and I was sweating profusely. My body trembled as my movement slowed and I emitted a low moan of pleasure. The world shook and I entered a surreal moment of complete ecstasy.

Slowly, I began to return to reality as my hormonal passion deflated like a slashed tire. Opening my eyes and looking down at my partner, it was quickly apparent she had endured - not enjoyed - what we had done. Suddenly, an avalanche of guilt swept over my being and I moved away from her and began pulling my jeans back to my waist. Flipping my t-shirt over my head, I put my sneakers on my feet. Sheepishly looking over, I noticed she was still undressed, sitting up with her arms wrapped around her knees holding them tight to her chest. Passion and adrenaline raced us down the slippery slope of first love, but once we reached bottom, they abandoned us, leaving us without a clue as to our next move. Having been deluged by lust, our virginity was washed away, leaving us with an immature relationship flooded with remorse. I assumed any chance of becoming friends had been ruined by my rush for satisfaction. Without knowing how to act, react or proceed, I was lost among the ashes of a once passionate fire.

Blackie remained unimpressed with the whole shebang and continued to chomp grass. He paid me no attention as I gathered her clothes and walked over beside her. They had been thrown helter-skelter around the area at the point caution was thrown to the wind. Standing beside her, holding her jeans and shirt, I didn't know what to do or say as she kept her head buried against her arms and knees. That beautiful hair was shining in the sun and I thought I would never again feel the magnificence of it sweeping over my face. With my heart pounding, she brought me to my knees - literally and figuratively - with the sound of her crying. Shame and blame combined as I earnestly spoke straight into her ear. I wanted to stroke her head but figured she would yell out and tell me not to touch her so I did what I had always done when people were angry at me and lashed out: beg for forgiveness. It didn't go so well at first.

"Please stop crying, I'm so sorry I hurt you and I know you hate me now but I sure didn't mean for that to happen and you have my promise I will never do it again." This was a statement I would regret making many times in the future. "Please don't cry; you don't even know me." (Another regrettable statement that made her sobs even louder.) "I mean, I don't know you either." (I was tanking) "But I sure would like to get to know you. You're beautiful; I mean I would be happy if you were my friend, I mean, a very close friend."

I paused for a long time trying to figure out what else I could say. "Since the first day I saw you, I wanted to know you. Remember, you sat by me on the bus?"

With her head still buried she sternly replied between sobs, "You didn't want me to!"

Trying to come up with a reasonable lie, "I just didn't know what to do, I've never been around girls before or sat with one on the bus, but I moved over and I was so scared to talk to you, I mean, you're beautiful and I'm, well, I mean, please sit up and talk to me. I'm not a bad person."

After a long pause, she put her chin on her arms and I could finally see her face again. The tears left streaks down her cheeks and after all we had done, she still had the bubble gum around her mouth and a little piece still stuck on her wonderful nose. Holding her clothes up so she could see them, she snapped at me, "What's the matter? You don't want to see me naked anymore?"

Now, how do you answer that? I felt guilty, but her nude body was a marvel and I would immensely enjoy eyeing it anytime. For the first time after the deed, I started to think a little and said softly, "I thought maybe you didn't want me to see you. I'm embarrassed when I'm naked. That's why I hate going to the doctor; they still treat me like a kid and make me sit naked on that damn paper covered table until the doctor decides to come in. And they open the door so wide that everybody in the hall can see you."

Finally she lifted her chin off her arms and said, "I hate going to the doctor, too. The last time he felt all over my boobs and you don't want to know what he did down there." She looked down in the direction of which she was talking and screamed out, "Oh my God! Get me something — a tissue, a towel or something!"

There was nothing. I look around but I knew there was nothing, and the problem was my responsibility. I pulled off my t-shirt and gave it to her and she cleaned up the mess I left and said, "My God, how much did you do?"

I was so ashamed and embarrassed. What could I say? 'I'm sorry' was getting old and she seemed to be getting frustrated with everything I said or did. Finally, after the cleanup, that I didn't watch, she put her clothes back on, but I did sneak a peek of her back as she raised her arms to pull her shirt over her head. Her body was simply magnificent.

She sat down near the base of the landmark tree and crossed

her legs like an Indian; I sat down and imitated her in silence. When the quiet was too much to bear, I asked if she hated me. Not quick to answer, she laid siege with those stunning azure eyes. If she did hate me, she would still be the most breathtakingly beautiful girl I had ever known.

Finally, "No, I don't hate you. I've wanted to know you since the first time I saw you, too."

I assumed she must have been talking about the bus, so I offered, "Everybody on the bus wanted to know what I did to attract you."

Before I could continue she said, "No! A year ago when I came to visit Sully, I was sitting in those wild plum bushes that grow on the fence line, watching you work up and down the rows. You were hot, and dripping with sweat and had your shirt off, like now; I watched you alone for a long time pulling weeds. Then I saw you with the others and how much fun you had with the men and how you teased the women. It was so weird because none of you had a thought of the others' color; no one living around here thinks that way. I wanted to meet you and hoped you wouldn't notice my color."

Feeling a little bolder, I crawled over beside her and put my arm around her shoulders, "But I did."

Her fabulous eyes met mine and she smiled, "I don't think you were looking at my color."

With no hesitation she launched into my biography and seemed to know more about me than I knew myself. I was no mystery to her, as she rattled off everything from my height, my weight, my age, my birthday, my graduating class, the college where I wanted to go, my parents' names, my church, my school, to my favorite car, and also added that I hated my father. The last one stung somewhat but I didn't deny it. She sounded pretty confident of my information which puzzled me for she had the whole kit and caboodle correct and I loved hearing her rattle on.

Suddenly, she stopped talking and pointed those steel blues straight at me. There was a silence and then, "Did you think I was a virgin before we… today?"

She had this way of reaching down in my psyche and making the truth comfortable. Anyway, I was captured by her eyes and trapped. A sheepish, "No" came out.

Ever the quick one to respond, she never broke her eyes from mine. "Well I was, but I didn't want you to think I was." She looked down then back up to my eyes again, "Were you?"

Damn, she was tearing my insides out, but she did level with me, so baa, baa, baa, the sheep spoke again, "Yes."

Predictably quick she yelled at me, "NO WAY! Then how did you know what to do? You didn't miss a move; you even closed your eyes and moaned just like in the magazine!"

Now, the truth is one thing, but I wasn't going to ruin her thinking me a stud just for honesty's sake! I shrugged my shoulders and smiled and she said, "Damn, I'm so naïve." as she looked at the ground.

Leaning close, my lips brushed her ear and as she turned to face me, our lips touched. This time I did the open mouth thing and searched for her tongue. I could feel her breath — warm, coming from her nostrils. She put her hands on both sides of my face and ever so slowly pushed my head back. Our lips were the last thing to part and made a smacking noise. My eyes opened, seconds later, hers; my God, those eyes, those wonderful blue eyes.

I guess the devil is always with me, even during intimate moments, because as I looked at her, an imp's smile spread across my face and made me say, "Did you know you had bubblegum all around your mouth and on your nose?"

She smiled while we were still embraced, and quietly said, "I know you're kidding me." I shook my head negatively and she screamed shoving me away from her and yelling, "MY GOD ALMIGHTY!"

With an immediate turn, she starts picking little black pieces of bubblegum from her nose and lips. Suddenly on her feet fuming she began walking in circles and I laughed out loud. My laughter drove her anger level up a notch and she screamed again. "You saw that and you still... With all that necking, you didn't think once that I might like to... cannot believe you would let me..."

Walking over, I grabbed her in a face-to-face bear hug, holding her arms and hands by her side. With our faces inches apart, I tried my best to kiss her, but she evaded my every move and swore at me like a sailor. In this case, the boy was stronger than the girl and finally she laughed and kissed me, then I let her go.

Just at that instant, we heard a distant sound that made us both silent. A car horn was honking a series of blasts. HONK – HONK – HONK then a pause and HONK –HONK –HONK again and again and again. Her radiant smile dropped as she turned to me, "I've got to go. That's Sully and he wants me to come home right now. I'm sorry."

My mood sank as I pleaded, "Are you sure you have to go now?"

She nodded her head affirmatively and walked over to hug me. Holding me tight against her body for a long time, I could feel her warm breasts on my chest. Then walking over to the bush wall, she waited for me to push it back so she could escape. Reluctantly, I stepped into the creek, gave the bush a heave with my back and we were exposed to the other world again. She stepped into the cool stream, heading for the opening.

My hopes were high and I was anticipating a long, wet, parting kiss. Instead, as she hurried by, she punched me in the gut. Not a slap or a light parting shot, I'm talking a full-fledged lick that pushed my stomach to my backbone, knocked my breath away, doubled me over and caused me to fall into the water with the sparkleberry bush engulfing me. Crawling out of the limbs and leaves, I struggled onto to dry land trying to get my breath back, flopped on the grass and rolled on my back.

As I lay gasping for air, I heard her yelling, "That's for letting that blonde hick smack me in the back of the head and I will get even with you later for not telling me about the bubblegum and making me kiss you! Don't talk to me on the bus tomorrow; I don't want them to know about us, they might try to hurt you."

While wheezing for air, I heard her running up the sandy hill.

***

Sully was sitting in the old blue Ford trash heap just behind the mansion with the door open and his feet on the ground. With the ever-present newspaper and pen in hand, he was concentrating on a puzzle but stopped every so often to honk the horn three times. When his daughter came in sight she yelled, "Stop blowing that damn horn; people are going to think you're crazy!"

Her words immediately grabbed his attention and he smiled as he said, "But my dear, most everyone around has concluded that I am most certainly insane!" As she walked closer, he noticed her exuberant smile and asked, "Would you perchance know an 8 letter word for encounter?" She grabbed his newspaper and tossed it into the air as she sat in his lap. Throwing her arms around his neck, she kissed him on the cheek and let out a devilish little squeal as she kicked her feet up and down.

Chapter Eleven

Dooney Cutter drove our school bus and he lived on the river past Roy Asholee's Store. His daddy, Boot Cutter, was a bootlegger and everyone knew he made rotgut liquor somewhere on the South Edisto River. He was also the meanest, most vile man in Salleys Kitchen. It was common knowledge that he and Roy Asholee were partners and with this fact ever present in my mind, I had avoided even the hint of a problem with Boot's boy. He never said much and was wearing his usual stone face as he made the second stop on his bus route to pick me up. Stepping up onto the bus Monday morning after our tryst, I had so many butterflies in my stomach, I felt it would have been easy for me to have fluttered away.

Taking my regular seat in the middle of the bus on the passenger side, I sat next to the aisle hoping I wouldn't puke. She was the third stop so I didn't have long to wait. Just like before, she sauntered down the lane like a beauty queen and stepped onto the bus. Honing in on me with those radar baby blues, I knew she would be sitting with me. What I didn't know, and the thing that scared the hell out of me, was what outlandish stunt she would pull this morning. As she approached, I moved over to the window and stared straight ahead. She sat down with her notebook and purse and I nervously turned to face her with fear popping out of my face like acne. Instinctively she turned to face me and flashed her practiced 'Miss America' smile.

Nothing was said but plenty was thought, on my side anyway. That beautiful creature held me in her arms, kissed me with passion and clawed, my hair then abundantly shared herself with me — me! — a nobody from nowhere. Why? Why in the hell did she want to sit next to me? My self-esteem had been obliterated from years of living with my old man and having been told so many times I was nothing until I thought I was nothing. Without one ounce of self-confidence in my body, I assumed she was thinking, *What a pitiful lover he turned out to be.*

Staring out the window, I let the familiar sights pass unseen in front of my eyes as she looked straight ahead and occasionally down at her nails. She moved to open her purse once and I flinched thinking the knife was about to appear, but she took out a sandpapered popsicle stick and worked on her nails with every eye on the bus, except mine, trained straight at her. She finished working on her nails and blew them off, then buffed them a couple of times on her shirt. Having heard the familiar sounds of the bus so often, they floated through my mind like any other morning and I didn't give them a thought. The squeal of the brake drums as Dooney pumped the brakes at yet another stop, the clicking of the hand brake as it was locked into place and a blast from the horn to tear someone away from a bowl of cornflakes were the regular sounds I ignored. The door handle being pulled open and the low idle of the engine as we waited for the next passenger to climb aboard were just sounds that flowed in and out of my head without notice.

As those commonplace sounds once again registered, I realized this stop was anything but routine. We were stopping to pick up Betty. She had not ridden the bus since 'the incident'. Betty walked from her house the few short steps to the bus and was blushing red, embarrassed as hell or angry as hell; either way, my butterflies returned with a vengeance. I wanted to let the window down for two reasons: in case I had to vomit and also, if the knife came out again I was going to jump.

Thank God for ole Burt, but I don't think his actions were for my benefit. Sitting on the third seat from the front, he moved over and Betty settled her swinging hips on the seat beside him. Burt was a master of exploiting the moment and I watched as he immediately began his reflex ogle.

The ride was uneventful from that point and my stomach settled somewhat, but I still had trepidations. Betty, on the other hand, seemed gripped by the fear of God. As soon as the bus came to a stop, she made a dash for the front, pulled the shiny chrome door handle and was off at a trot before Dooney could grab his welding book. Burt was still winding up his tongue when the blonde country girl entered the smoky restroom by the gym. The beautiful stranger sitting by me sat unperturbed as the bus cleared and we were, once more, the last two off. Without sharing a word between us, we parted ways and she walked to the front entrance. With purpose, I hurried to the end door and scooted down the hallway to hide behind a locker door and watch her enter the main hallway.

Approaching the big glass windows separating the main office from the hallway, she tapped on the glass with diamond shaped wire sealed in it. The secretary looked up and offered a smile then a wave as she turned to speak to the open door of the principal's office. He stuck his comb-over out and offered her a smile. Waving to them, she took a seat in their line of sight on the parent's bench just across from the office door. She worked on her fingernails with that sandpapered popsicle stick, smiling to her classmates as they smugly walked by. When the bell for homeroom stopped ringing, she kept her seat. Just a few seconds before late bell was to ring, she stepped into the room and took her seat in that desk that everyone dodged like the plague.

Sitting three or four seats behind her, I scrutinized her moves and waited for the first period bell to ring. She stayed seated until everyone left the room and only then, stepped into the hallway with just enough time to make it to the next class. It was her routine for the rest of the year and another of her idiosyncrasies that intrigued the hell out of me.

For the first time ever, I did not dread the end of the school week. Instead, I fulfilled my Saturday sentence with vim and vigor leading Mary, Della, Albert and Daggar to ask what had gotten into me. With a smile on my face, I started singing that old field song they usually sang when I asked too many questions. Della said, "Boy, you done got to be a Big Ike. You startn' to show too much of yo black side!"

I just smiled, said yes ma'am and kept singing. They knew something was up but as much as I wanted to spill my guts, I couldn't tell them about Salley.

After Wes had vanished, the old man pulled in some old trailer houses for Della and Mary to occupy. They refused to live in them and moved in with other friends. He hired some other men with families to work in the field, but as everyone knew, they didn't last very long listening to my father's mouth. In a week or two the new families disappeared and he had the nasty mobile homes pulled away. I kept my nose to the grindstone for I didn't want to be the next thing to disappear from the field. All I wanted was the company of that beautiful creature living on the farm next door. After supper and a bath, I headed to bed early on Saturday night.

On Sunday, church was torture and I tried to do the right thing, but I got the evil-eye twice from my mother. Sunday dinner was one large gulp as I sprinted for Blackie's gate. Even he was not moving fast enough for me today. No combing this week or sweet feed either. I threw on his saddle and hit the trail with sand kicking up behind us. Reaching the gap I stayed in the saddle, grabbed the flimsy post and threw it to the side. Then off like a barrel racer headed home, we galloped to the creek and the bush wall. Sliding off Blackie's back like a calf roper in a rodeo, I dove for that sparkleberry bush like I had a piggin' string in my mouth and wanted to pull three of its limbs together and tie a half hitch around them.

Wiggling for position to push back the heavy bush, I was ready to pry my way in, when an angelic voice from the heavens found my ears, "Hey Stupid, I'm over here." Pushing Blackie back out of the way, I looked around the trees and there she sat — on a magnificent Appaloosa like none I had ever seen.

When the excitement of love and lust takes control of your brain, the hormone adrenaline is released causing the neurotransmitter oxytocin to fire pleasure and reward seeking signals across an untold number of synapses attached to countless neurons in rapid order. Occurring during a nanosecond of time, this process is often experienced in close human relationships and is referred to as 'the rush of love'. It's that flash of time when exhilaration, anticipation and stimulation combine to make your breathing labored, your heart race and bullets of sweat pop out on your skin — a breath of time when your heart beats in your ears, your knees begin to buckle and desire assumes the driver's seat in your brain and stomps the accelerator. Some people are lucky enough to meet a soulmate who triggers this pleasurable sensation on a regular basis. I so hoped this girl was mine, for standing in that creek, hearing her voice berate me, looking around Blackie to see that fantastic female throwing me the finger, watching her spur that fine-looking animal and yell, "See you later Sucker" as she left me in her dust, made my neurotransmitters fire like a gazillion machine guns.

Luckily, my heart was young and could survive that sudden surge of adrenaline and rush of blood to my brain and other parts of my body. The chase to catch her kept me on that thrilling edge and had she known where she was going, Blackie and I would have never in a million years had a chance to catch her. But once she turned on Orange Gate Road there was nothing left but Orange Gate corral, a two acre lot where old man Fant kept his milk cow before he and the milk-maker met their maker. I pulled Blackie to a stop at the gate for there was only one way in and one way out, so when she realized her dilemma, I wanted to be waiting. It didn't take her long and when she got back to me she was as loud and mad as a wet setting hen.

She spat the words out of her mouth, "I hate it when I realize I've screwed up, especially when I've done something stupid."

My laughing didn't help, but my heart was still racing and I figured we needed a long walk so we could cool down. Both horses were winded and I wanted to know the story behind that superb animal she was riding. "So why didn't you tell me you had a horse?"

As soon as it came out of my mouth I knew what she was going to say and I mouthed the words in a mocking way as she said them, "You didn't ask me if I had a horse."

Aggravated, I shot back, "Cute, but it doesn't answer the how and where of that good looking piece of horse flesh under you."

To continue the sparring she sarcastically said, "Is it the body you always see first?"

In truth I answered, "Well, yeah." She kicked the sides of the spotted beauty and cantered toward the main dirt road as she sighed loudly with her eyes rolling back in her head. I caught up with her and she ignored me for a moment. "So where and how did you get that gelding?"

Finally, I must have pulled the right stick out of the beaver dam because it burst and she started rattling off the story.

"At Foxcroft, my last school, I had to participate in an outside activity each session, but most of the girls refused to play sports with me because things always 'happened' to people around me. The coaches said I was a little too exuberant… I don't know. Playing field hockey I broke a girl's nose, playing soccer, I kicked a girl's two front teeth out, playing basketball, dislocated a referee's shoulder - but she was a klutz. And the water polo thing was not really my fault, but I swear they were all wussies and every time it was just a freak accident. Anyway, the guy who worked with the equestrian team was my math teacher, Mr. Lloyd. He was also an ex-Army officer who trained for the U.S. Equestrian Team and went to the Olympics after WWII. He told the Dean that he had a filly once, that acted just like me and she ended up being one of the best horses he ever owned. Yes, he was an ass. So the Dean said I could try, but if anybody got hurt, that was it, nothing else. After class one day, he asked if I had a horse. My quick answer was – 'Are you kidding? I'm Lebanese on an international exchange program; that's the only reason they let me in this place. I can't afford a pony that Barbie could ride, much less a horse.' He told me not to be such a smart-ass and to come to the riding stables at seven Saturday morning.

"That morning it was real cold with snow everywhere and the horses' breath looked like smoke coming out of their nostrils. He put me on an old mare and sent me trotting around an inside arena. When I came back around to him he chewed me out and asked had I ever been on a horse before. I told him no, except on the merry-go-round. He grabbed my jacket by the sleeve near my shoulder, jerked me down to his face and said, 'I take horses seriously, do you understand, smart-ass?'

"From that moment forward, I just kept my mouth shut, did what he told me and made his team. It was a lot of fun and to my surprise I won a lot of trophies and ribbons that year. That summer, Sully asked me if I would like to have a horse of my own. 'Of course', I said and laughed. I didn't think he would buy me a horse, much less one ranked as an up and coming champion. The first Saturday back at school that fall, this big van pulls up to the stables and off walks Spot."

At this point I had to interrupt; I couldn't let that name pass without comment. "Wait a minute, did you say Spot? Was he already named when you got him?"

She turned her face and sarcastically said, "No, his registered name is Bentwood Downs Spotacular Bear. How about Blackie, did you name him?" She had a valid point and so I shut up and she continued.

"The first time I saw him I laughed at all the spots that covered his body. He was wild looking and I soon found out his spirit matched his looks. Mr. Lloyd said Sully had found him and mentioned him as a possible horse for me. After finding out about Spot's pedigree, he collaborated with his horse colleagues and pulled some strings for Sully to have the opportunity to purchase him and he wanted me to start riding him exclusively during practice and in the events that year.

"Bragging that Spot was ranked in the top five of that year's new comers to the circuit events, Mr. Lloyd went on to say the school and a lot of other people were watching to see if I deserved him and would exploit his potential to the fullest. I should have known after all of that gibberish, Spot was something special, but by this time, I was in love and just wanted to touch him. He was trying to munch some hay on the ground, so I walked over and scratched his head between his ears. I could have told you right then and there, they had doubled their trouble putting Spot and me together. When I touched him, he jerked his head up in the air, hitting Mr. Lloyd right in the nose and he fell back on the ground holding his face. Instinctively, I reached to grab the lead on his halter and Spot dragged me about fifty yards across the practice field. Every now and then he would pick me up off the ground with his head because I had grabbed his halter and was determined not to let go. He finally pissed me off so I took the end of the lead rope and started to flail the daylights out of him.

"About three quarters of the way across the field he decided he had had enough and stopped dragging me, so I stopped hitting him. He was out of breath and I was, too, so we had worked ourselves to a stalemate. Before he could do much thinking, I grabbed his mane and swung up on his back, then rode him to the back of the track. We fit together like peanut butter and jelly and he was following my commands as if I had been on his back since he was a colt. As I rode him around the field, I started to put him through his paces and then tried some of the compulsory exercises required at an equestrian event. Obviously he had been trained, for he was perfectly on stride, followed every leg command and held himself very erect and correct. Back at the barn, Mr. Lloyd was holding his nose and screaming to put him back on the truck. Ignoring his rants, I rode him around the practice field about an hour then cooled him down, gave him a comb, then put on his blanket. The stall nearest the office and tack room was open and I claimed it for him. He was perfect.

"Mr. Lloyd was out about half of the term for facial reconstruction and when he came back he demanded Spot be removed from the barn. He had been registered in my name and I had to be his owner in order to compete so he was my horse. There was no way I was giving him up. But Mr. Lloyd kept screaming he was too unpredictable for competition, potentially dangerous for the students on campus and a risk for the public at large. I had already ridden him in two events with reserved champion in one and grand champion in the other. He wouldn't let us compete in any other events that year so we took a lot of long rides with the Blue Ridge Mountains as our backdrop. Spot knew Mr. Lloyd hated him and every time he walked into the barn office he would start kicking the stable walls; it was funny. Finally, he made me move Spot out of the school stables. The barn manager at school owned a training facility and had a horse farm near the mountains. He offered to let me keep Spot there if I would work for his board. I had planned to bring him home with me after I left Foxcroft, but I was ushered out so quickly, I couldn't arrange it. I needed Sully to help me, but it was planting season so he had other things on his mind."

As the Spot saga came to a close, I remembered the other things Sully had on his mind during that time.

Spot and Blackie still had some run in them so we picked up the speed and galloped side by side. We cut across by Murdock's house and as we galloped by his mini junkyard, his old hound ran out from between two of the ancient cars as we passed and it spooked Spot. He shied very quickly and unexpectedly to one side of the dirt road. If I had been on his back when he made that maneuver, my butt would have been on the ground, but she moved like she was part of him and patted his side to calm him down. They were magnificent together and I had never seen anything like it. Stunned, I could not believe how well she handled that huge mass of muscles and spots.

On familiar terrain, I took the lead as we turned off the county dirt road and followed the two sandy ruts through a cathedral of tall longleaf pines. A controlled burn had removed the understory and we could easily see a distant doe bounce deeper into the forest. Stopping for a moment, I pointed to where the Red Cockaded Woodpeckers had pecked holes into the trees.

The pine tar oozed from their nest cavities like wax dripping down a candle. We kept following the sandy furrows and were soon surrounded by old live oaks with long limbs that grew down to the ground. Each was dripping with acorns and adorned with Spanish moss tendrils. This was always a noisy area, full of squirrels fussing about intruders in their domain. They were a selfish lot and didn't want to share the acorns that littered the ground. Fussing and flicking their fuzzy tails at us, we laughed at them, but kept moving along as the two sandy grooves merged into one sandy lane that curved its way toward the river. About a mile before the river, we arrived at my intended destination — the pond. I hopped down and took Blackie's saddle and blanket off while Salley was still sitting on Spot. Usually very reserved, I seldom took my clothes off in front of other people, but she had a flare for the dramatic and I wanted to show her I could be shocking too. For some insane reason, I quickly 'shucked to the buck' and jumped in the pond. It was so cold I just knew there had to be some ice somewhere about, but I wasn't about let her know I was freezing.

Sitting in her saddle, she smile and asked, "Well, Adam, how's the water?"

It took me a minute to figure out what she meant, then lying like a rug, I shot it right back, "Oh Eve, it's warm as bath water and twice as refreshing."

Then I gritted my teeth and swam a few strokes, dove under for a few seconds, then stuck my head above the water to see if she had taken the bait. When I looked to her horse, she had dismounted. Spot was tied to a tree and as I surveyed the area to find her, she stuck her fingers in her mouth and whistled so loud it reverberated across the pond. Standing on the rickety old dock, in only panties and bra, she yelled, "Here I come, Adam!"

Determined to 'get her goat' again, I yelled, "Oh no! This is a 'birthday suit only' pond. No chickens allowed!"

I knew calling her chicken would be a shot at her pride. Sticking her tongue out, she reached to her back and unsnapped her bra, then leaned over and pushed the tiny pink panties to

114

her ankles, stepped out of one leg-hole and kicked them on top of the bra already lying on the dock. In typical girl fashion, she held her nose and squealed as she ran off the dock. Quickly bobbing her head back up out of the brown tannin water, she saw me headed for the shore. It was too cold for me and I wanted to get back in my clothes, besides the cold water was making an important part of my body shrink out of sight and I certainly didn't want her to comment on that happening. She had proven to be brutal with few words.

By the time she quit yelling and calling me names, I was on the dock trying to pull my underwear up over my wet sticky legs. She swam for the dock as I pulled up my jeans and when she grabbed the gray board ladder she yelled, "Don't you look at me when I climb up!"

She knew, as did I, that wasn't even a consideration, so with that impish grin across my face, I yelled to my buddy, "Yes, Ma'um!" She climbed up that old ladder like a beauty queen coming out of a pool and my mouth dropped open as I saw her tiny black bush. She switched her demeanor to the fashion model that rode the bus as she stepped into her panties then hooked her bra in the front, spun it around and put her arms through the straps. I had no idea that's how it was done, but that wasn't the only thing I learned on that dock. As I sat there, she headed for the tree limbs that held her clothes, stepped in her jeans and buttoned her shirt. After she returned to where I sat, she took a swat at my head, sat down beside me and pulled on her boots. The sun had cooked the old boards so I lay back a while to warm up. As the birds continued to sing in the surrounding trees, she joined me and we lay side by side watching a turkey buzzard circle above us. My thoughts had been of her almost constantly since last Sunday and I had been tantalized by her sitting next to me on the bus for a week. After seeing her perfectly beautiful nude body, I was about to explode, so I leaned over to kiss her and she put her hand over my mouth and pushed me back.

"Oh no, buddy! We won't be doing that anymore! You

promised me you wouldn't ever do that again."

Suspended in air after she moved her hand, I watched her fish in her pocket and pull out a chap stick to coat those pouting lips. Afterward, she closed her magnificent eyes and faced the sun. I was deflated; my very own words had come back to haunt me. Yes, I meant them at the time, I think, but my God we knew each other better now - or did we? Dumbfounded, I lay back down beside her and didn't say a word. When curiosity finally overwhelmed me, I broke the silence.

Chapter Twelve

"Why did you go to school in Virginia?" I asked.

There was not the usual immediate response, but after a quiet few seconds she put her forearm on her forehead to shade the sun,"Because of 'who' I am and 'what' I am."

That statement did not answer the question so I persisted. "And just who do you think you are and what, for Pete's sake, do you *think* you are?"

This time the response was quick and quite matter of fact, "My full name is Salley Adsila Sullivan. Salley is from the wife of the first Sullivan who came to this area and owned a mill near here according to Sully. Adsila is a Cherokee name and means 'Blossom'. I never tell people about my middle name because they always say, 'Oh, are you a Cherokee Indian?' No, I'm an American. While I have been trained to act like a blue blood with a famous pedigree, I'm really just the opposite — a mixed-breed mongrel bitch."

There was no way I was going to reply to that statement, but she continued, "I am the third and only girl child produced out of wedlock by Polly Ahyoka Chapman and James Anthony Sullivan, V. My mother is part Negro and part Cherokee. Her ancestors were members of the group that hid deep in the mountains during the Removal and Trail of Tears. She was born on the plantation of a Cherokee slave owner and member of Thomas' Legion in the Army of the Confederacy. He had many Cherokee families living and working on his land, as well as slaves.

After the war his slaves were considered freemen but they continued to live on his farm and follow his leadership. Because smallpox brought in by Union troops during the war had decimated the tribes, the remaining Cherokee shunned the white man and kept them away from their farms. As far as the government and society were concerned, Negroes and Cherokees were considered 'colored' and as such they were forced to live among each other. The Cherokee women naturally formed relationships with the freemen, producing children. As

117

long as the mother was Cherokee, the children were considered Cherokee, also.

"When the Federal Government decided it inconvenient for the Cherokee to collectively own such a large tract of land, they divided it and gave parcels to individual Cherokees listed on the Baker Rolls and much of it was swindled away or stolen by white men. The Cherokee plantation owner was allowed to keep his land and he also claimed the land given to those who worked for him. Just after the turn of the century, he met a timberman at one of the Confederate reunions, a white officer from the Legion that talked him into swapping some of his Cherokee land for a farm twice the size just across the border in South Carolina. He took the deal and moved a group of women and children over the mountain to a quiet little valley in South Carolina. My mother knew little about her mother and nothing of her father. Her father was more than likely the son of a slave that became a freeman after the war and continued living on the farm. Her mother was probably one of many Cherokee girls that grew up in the tribal family."

Salley knew a lot about her mother's native culture and she continued to tell me about her heritage. The Cherokee society is matriarchal and women anchor the families. Female children and grandchildren often remained on the Cherokee farms for several generations. After Salley's grandmother died of tuberculosis, her mother was raised by an old Cherokee woman and was taught the old ways as a small girl.

"My mother lived in a beautiful mountain valley called Eastahee and met Sully during his college years. The depression had crippled the country and money was very scarce. Sully was always looking for a way to earn gas money for his forays into the mountains and trips home to Salleys Kitchen. As he was riding through the mountain valleys on a Sunday, driving his usual twenty mph, he saw my mother standing in the creek beside the road and stopped to ask what she was doing. She would not talk to him but showed him the oak strips she was soaking in the cold mountain water. He drove away with her face permanently etched in his memory. My daddy said the next week he returned to find her in the same spot, so he stopped again but his time she was prepared and held up a woven basket. He didn't really want or need the basket but he nodded and said a few words, indicating he would purchase it. Pointing to an area of trees across a meadow, at the foot of a mountain, a thin trail of smoke was rising above the canopy. She smiled, then turned and hurried toward it. Driving down the valley a ways he found the pig trail of a road leading to the smoke. Driving as far as he could on the narrow wagon road, he stopped when it turned into a path and began following it into the woods on foot. Soon he approached an opening in the forest and discovered a three-house complex with more than a dozen women and children."

Still lying on our backs, she stopped talking and turned to face me. I saw her somber and heartfelt expression and though she was smiling, she looked as if she was about to cry. Looking back up at the sky, she continued to tell me about her mother's family.

"One weekend, a few years back, Sully came to our home he built for us in the mountains and while I was sitting in his lap, he told me this story. He said the first time he entered the little open area in the woods where the houses were grouped, it was as if he had walked back into another century and had come upon a Cherokee village. When he told this story to me, his eyes lit up and I could tell it was one of his most cherished memories.

"My mother motioned for him to follow her as everyone in the compound stopped to look at him. Not knowing where she was leading him, he followed her to a log building that looked like a corn crib. When she pulled the door open, it revealed two or three dozen split oak baskets of every size imaginable, hanging on the walls. Sully doesn't smile or talk often, but when he told me how my mother turned to him and said, 'I'm Polly' while poking her chest with her index finger, he had a dreamy look in his eyes."

Stopping for a moment, Salley looked out across the pond before she turned back to me and continued her tale.

"Sully told me he pointed to his chest and said his name hoping she understood him. Even though my daddy has an exceptional vocabulary, he said he struggled to communicate with the beautiful girl from the woods. He tried to explain why he was riding through the valley and realized he didn't know, himself, but they continued to smile at one another. With his hands and few words, he let her know he was attending school on the far side of the mountains."

It was easy to see Salley adored Sully and I envied her. The relationship she had with her father was so different from mine. She continued her story. "An old woman appeared from somewhere in the village and wanted Sully to buy a nice big basket but he didn't have but one dollar to his name so she took his money and gave him a tiny basket. My mother quickly snatched it out of his hands, replacing it with a larger more complex basket she was holding. The smiling continued and she followed him back to his car, waving to him as he backed down the narrow trail.

"Though smitten, Sully has always been an entrepreneur, so he returned the following weekend to find the pretty bronze colored woman in the same spot of the creek waiting for him. When she saw him she took off running. Again, he followed the pig trail to the little village, but this time he asked the old woman how much for all the baskets in the log building. She shrugged her shoulders and called another woman to the building who promptly did the same thing. He had returned with twenty dollars borrowed, scraped from penny stashes and cajoled from friends. He had also pawned everything he had of value. It was an enormous amount in that day and he was taking a huge chance. Putting it in my mother's hand, he told the old woman he wanted twenty dollars' worth of baskets. They emptied all the baskets from the crude log building and stacked them in the back of Sully's Fordor. For the next week, he peddled baskets to every little general store in the mountains and during every spare moment, he offered baskets to his teachers and anyone else he could corner. He told me each basket he sold brought a smile to his face as he remembered my mother."

Lying beside me on the dock, Salley turned to read my face and could easily see I was hungry for more.

"The following Saturday, he bumped and bounced down into the little valley on the worn-out two rut road again, to find my mother waiting near the stream beside the road. This time, along with the ear to ear smile, she offered a 'hello' as he stopped. Opening the door and motioning for her to get in, she didn't hesitate. Sully told me this time, he beat the bushes and limbs back and drove all the way into the pristine area in front of the houses. The site was hidden under the trees and not visible from the road. Never having had a vehicle in the compound before, all the inhabitants poured out of the lodge style houses, as the couple climbed out of the car together.

"Standing with his foot on the bumper of his red Ford, he counted out sixty dollars into the hand of the old woman that was obviously the matriarch. When the last green bill was counted into her palm, he closed her hand around it, bowed his head and said thank you. Then he looked to the old woman's face and said, 'Again?'"

Salley was proud to tell me her father was quite a business man. "He had already reclaimed his pawned items and taken out his investment. Most of the college boys that loaned him money wanted baskets for their mothers; even the old man at the pawn shop bought a number of baskets and asked if he could get more. Sully was convinced he could sell even more baskets.

"With a stunned look on her brown shriveled face, the old woman nodded her head yes and my mother reached to take Sully's hand in front of everyone. Sully admitted that was what he had wanted all along. But he didn't know that by holding his hand and returning his smile, she was virtually announcing their engagement. Smiling and walking on clouds, Sully was pulled and pushed by the children of the village to another outbuilding where the door was thrown open to reveal another stash of baskets just as large.

"After another successful week of peddling, Sully returned with more cash. Obviously feeling he could be trusted, they were out of baskets, but loaded his car with other things made from split oak strips, including all sizes of fish traps, swings, stools, chairs, and household items. He even took two tanned deer hides along on this trip and as expected, sold everything."

Chapter Thirteen

With the sun baking our faces, we rolled on our sides and faced each other just inches apart. I wanted so desperately to hold her in my arms and feel her warm body, but she wasn't through talking. She seemed as if she needed to tell someone this story and I was overjoyed she chose me to hear it.

"For the rest of Sully's college career, most every Friday after class he maneuvered the mountain roads to Eastahee, gathered baskets and he and my mother then traveled about selling them. They always returned with food, clothes and things from the towns below the mountains.

"As his graduation neared, Sully and Polly were considered man and wife by her people and had their own lodge in the compound. They also had twin boy babies, my brothers, and showered them with affection. My father said he labored long and hard trying to decide if he should encourage them to cast off their primitive living conditions and traditional ways of life. Even though his little boys were part of the backwoods community, he decided it was not his decision to make and he visited the elders of the Eastern Bands of Cherokee that had organized themselves in a very modern way in the North Carolina Mountains. Eventually he persuaded a tribal leader from the Keetoowah Band to visit the tiny village and soon the group was extended an invitation to join with those living on the reservation near the North Carolina-Tennessee border. Most of the women visited the reservation, met men and melded into the hill tribes with federal recognition and assistance, but with Sully and Polly providing a steady income, the old woman refused to leave and stayed behind in the valley. My mother had never known her mother and considered the elder woman as such. By the time Sully graduated, he had persuaded the old woman to accept a few more modern conveniences and he built them a nice modern home just across the meadow near the creek and road."

We walked off of the dock and over to the horses to check them. Blackie was eating grass but Spot was tied to a tree and

Salley pulled two shiny apples from a pouch tied to her saddle and fed them to him. He seemed perfectly content in the shade and she pulled his saddle off and began to rub him with a cloth from the pouch. She told me it made his coat shine. As she rubbed his spots and muscles she continued her story. "Sully joined the Army during WWII and stayed in Europe for three and a half years. He wrote my mother a ton of letters. She told me his letters were the main reason she learned to read and write. When he returned from Europe, he went back to graduate school on the GI Bill. I know he only went to graduate school because it was paid for and he could be near my mother. He graduated with a master's degree in economics, and then promptly returned home to be with his Grandma Lou during her final years. That is when he started buying stocks and planting other crops than cotton. He spent most of his time in Salleys Kitchen but made the three hour trip to visit my mother and us as often as possible. Grandma Lou died before I was born and Sully buried her beside her beloved Trip in the cemetery at your church. After her death, Sully began drinking and soon had a problem. He has battled alcohol dependency since her death.

"I was born in the spring of the year, just before Sully planted his cotton. He had traveled to the mountains with a pocket full of money the previous fall and made my mother leave my brothers at home while they went away together. He took her to a college football game, after which they spent the night at a small roadside motel near the Seneca River. My mother told me it was one of the most wonderful weekends she and Sully spent together and she had no doubt that I was conceived in that little motor lodge near the border of Anderson and Oconee counties in the upstate of South Carolina. Sully just smiled when I asked him about it, but he didn't disagree with my mother."

After she had rubbed every inch of her beloved Spot, she put the cloth back in the pouch and walked with me to the edge of the pond. I picked up a pebble and skipped it across the water.

"That little house in the valley that Sully built us was my home and I lived there as a young girl. We were never wealthy but survived happily while Sully traveled back and forth, never letting go of his home and cotton farm in Salleys Kitchen. He made frequent visits to the mountains and even brought us here a few times."

Sitting cross legged in the grass, we watched a bluebird pluck a grasshopper from the tall weeds and take it to a hollow in a tree. Little mouths snatched it from her and she hurried away for another.

Salley smiled at me and continued her tale. "This is kind of weird but my whole life has been weird — so what! When I was a little girl, the old woman I considered my grandmother, died. As she was slowly dying, she made Sully promise to have her remains buried beside her old lodge in the little village. This was about 15 years ago and it caused a lot of trouble for Sully. He had to hire a lawyer and threaten to sue the county for her to have a traditional Cherokee burial. The day after she died, with the help of a government official that represented the Cherokee Mountain Tribes, he was finally able to keep his promise. With political pressure, the county officials looked the other way and the old ones from over the mountains came to perform the ceremony. I was a little girl, but I remember her body being placed in a shallow grave beside the old dirt floor house, then covered and molded over with clay. A fire was built in the grave and an all-night bonfire baked the clay and cremated her remains. Afterward, they placed all of her personal things in the grave beside the clay caste of her body and it was carefully covered over with soil and a tree planted on top. Our little village was the site of dancing and chanting around that fire throughout the ceremony. Some people wanted to film it, but Sully told them he would have them arrested if they came anywhere near the village. It was one of the last traditional Cherokee burial ceremonies occurring off of the reservation. That huge hot fire is one of my forever memories."

Salley kept talking and I listened. "After my Cherokee

grandmother died, Sully decided to move the family to Salleys Kitchen to live with him. Once there, my mother took me to your elementary school to be enrolled. When the lady in the office saw my mother and heard her Cherokee name, she called the principal into the room. He looked at my mother and told her,'We would really rather not have to explain why your little 'burnt biscuit' is not the color of the other boys and girls. They are not old enough to understand that sometimes accidents happen. We know you would rather have her attend a different school.'" Salley stopped momentarily to see my reaction and then continued.

"When we got home and told Sully what the principal said, he got real drunk. The next morning, he got on the phone, made some arrangements and I have been in different boarding schools since. He moved my mother and brothers back to Eastahee and my brothers finished school in the mountains where I guess the children understood. At first I came home to the mountains every summer and Sully came up to see us on the weekends. As I got older I came home to the mountains some, but when I was invited, I went home with friends from school. I told people my parents were Lebanese but I was born and raised in America. I bet I know more about Lebanon than the people who live there. I almost made it through their haughty school and graduated but this year for some reason, I don't know why, I got in trouble a lot. Finally, they called and told Sully to come get me. To transfer my credits here I had to take a lot of tests at your school over the holidays and that's how I got to know Mr. Rawls and his secretary. He went to graduate school with Sully and was very impressed with how well I did on the tests. The school board agreed to let me finish high school here and Mr. Rawls didn't tell them I had been involved in a lot of... let's just say 'altercations'. I'm trying not to get in trouble because Sully has already said I would finish in reform school next year if I messed up again. The private schools drilled and instilled the 'act and dress as a lady at all times' routine, and Sully said I had to wear my 'adult disguise' for the rest of the school year, but I hate being fake. Since the first day of boarding school I have been buried in that 'holier-than-thou', 'you must act lady-like at all times' crap. It's all I have ever known so it's kind of automatic when I'm in my school mode, besides when I act like 'myself', I get in soooo much trouble."

Suddenly, I felt I needed to tell her something that might ruin my life, but I couldn't stop the words from pouring from my mouth. "My life is divided into two worlds, too," I admitted. "Only my black friends know the real me and I always feel like such a fake at school and church, but if I didn't pretend to be white, I wouldn't last long in Salleys Kitchen and I have nowhere else to go. Besides, I've never been in a fight. I'm afraid to get in a fight!"

I looked up to see her reaction to my confession but she didn't react. I didn't have to ask her the type of 'altercations' in which she had been involved. I had seen her in action. Without thinking too much I asked, "Why do you have that knife if you know you need to stay out of trouble?"

We lay quiet for a while watching the fluffy white clouds float above our heads. Then she started to cry. Her crying was something I just could not take and I wiped one of the tears from her cheek and said, "Please don't cry. I'm sorry I said anything. It's your knife and you can do as you please." That made her cry even harder and I thought for a minute I had hurt her feelings again. Suddenly, she stood up and reached into her pocket and produced the knife. Every muscle in my body tensed as I knew she handled it so well. Pulling back her arm, she tossed it into the middle of the pond. It made a 'ploop' sound and sent ripples out in all directions.

"I don't know why I had that knife. I guess it made me feel big and tough and safe, but I don't want to be big and tough around you and I don't know why, but I feel so safe when it's just you and me. I don't know why I act so crazy."

I had no idea how to answer. Having just confessed to being afraid to defend myself, I didn't know why she felt safe around me. She was crying and that alone tore me to shreds so I

127

just put my arms around her and held her. When the crying started to subside, I told her how I felt in my hay fort in the barn. No matter what was happening outside, I could escape among the bales of hay and dream of things to come and feel okay inside. She said, "I want to see your hay fort sometime."

That sent a shock wave through my heart. I didn't want her anywhere near my parents, but I said, "Sure, we'll go there together and you will feel safe, too."

The truth was I hadn't felt safe since I met her. Being with her kept me on the spine-tingling edge, like throwing rocks at a hornets' nest; a daring act no doubt, but if you were successful, you'd better be ready to run for your life.

As we stood to leave, she kissed me, ever so lightly on my lips and smiled weakly. Clopping back in silence through the woods toward the dirt road, we stopped our horses under the old water oaks. She looked like she was about to cry again and it gave me a troubled feeling. I had a habit of making her cry and needed to figure out how to stop upsetting her. But this time she didn't cry. Instead, she pierced my heart with those dazzling eyes and said, "I don't know why I told you all of those things; I've never told anyone. Please don't repeat what I said."

She didn't realize how I felt about her and I thought it time she knew my feelings. "I've never been a very brave person, but I will tell you this, from the bottom of my heart—I would probably lose my life before I would betray you."

Now she did start crying, and I felt it impossible to figure out what she wanted from me. She looked so sad and I knew that feeling. Suddenly I decided she needed to see my happy places, the places that made me feel better and the places that helped me forget my double life!

Chapter Fourteen

With a big smile on my face I said, "For fifty cents I'll give you the whole tour."

Wiping her tears and snubbing, she smiled a little and said, "How good's my credit? I don't have fifty cents."

Kicking Blackie in his sides, I blurted out, "I'll send you a bill — come on, you won't believe this stuff."

First was the honey bee nest built on a window in the old Fant House. From inside, safe from the stinging workers, you could observe the operations of the honey factory. Built against the window, the glass bisected the hive. Someone had shot the glass with a BB gun and there was a small hole near the bottom. Carefully, I took a piece of broom sage and stuck it through the hole to retrieve a taste of the honey. Her smile made me want to break the glass and face the bees so she could have it all, but I thought better.

"Come on, there's lots more," I said and we left for more adventure. After a little ways, we turned off the main road, quietly slipping behind a thicket of pines and rode down into a sandy gully as I put my finger to my mouth. On a previous ride, Blackie and I had watched a grey fox, with a mouse in her mouth, sneak into a well-hidden den on the side of the ravine. As we slowly approached, the mama fox and her five pups were playing in a sand bed washed up by the last rain. She seemed patient with them as they jumped and snapped at each other and climbed all over her. Mama finally caught our scent and jumped up in alarm. She disappeared into the woods as the pups ran for the den, but they stuck their little noses out to see what was going on. On the way back to the county road I told her about the Sunday I saw her nursing six pups.

She asked, "What happened to the other pup?" I shrugged my shoulders and motioned for her to follow me.

About 50 yards from the pups, I pointed to a spot under a limb on an oak tree. There on the ground was a half dozen or more owl pellets scattered about. I slid down from my saddle and picked one up, then climbed back up to show it to her.

When I broke it open it revealed little bones and fur tightly packed into the pellet. She didn't think it was nasty like most girls would have. Pointing to the other pellets, I told her, "One of those probably has the bones and fur of a fox pup. He was too far away from the den when the owl swooped down. Wes says that's the way of the wild."

Tossing the pellet back under the tree, I watched her wipe a tear with the bandana around her neck. I didn't want her to be sad so I said, "Come on, this next crowd will make you smile."

Riding back out to the dirt road, we followed it to John Rich's Watkins Store. He sold Watkins Products and kept them in a small outbuilding. Behind it I knew we would find the stooges of the local animal world — a pack of thieving raccoons trying to get into Mr. Rich's trash. It was an on-going war between the Watkins man and the coons; today it looked like the old peddler was winning the battle. The gray bandits, with masks across their eyes and chain gang stripes on their fluffy tails, were trying their best to crack Mr. Rich's trash stash, but having no luck. Fighting with each other, pushing and shoving and generally acting like Larry, Moe, and Curley, they hissed a warning as we rode up and surprised them, but they knew we weren't John's wife. Kora Rich was always packing heat, even at church, and when she caught the black eyed bandits even near the trash cans, she'd unload her .32 caliber pistol at them, but I had never heard of her hitting one. They never hissed at her, rather ran for their lives and scattered like a covey of quail when she showed up. After a few minutes of laughing at their fighting and fussing, we headed across the highway.

The road we were following ended at The Griddle, a frying pan shaped, 200-acre farm that looked like someone had ironed it flat and leveled it in every direction. When the cotton was planted, the rows made it look like a griddle pan. As was my father's farm, The Griddle was part of the Sullivan place in decades past. The narrow pan handle of this plot of land extended west, all the way to the border of my old man's farm and was bisected north to south by a paved farm-to-market road referred to as the Salleys Kitchen Airport. Crop dusters and sprayers used the long, hard-surfaced road to land their planes, take on their payloads and refuel. Once cotton had lapped in the middle of the row, a tractor could not be used to spray the DDT that killed the evil boll weevil and bollworm, so during that stage of the growing season, there was always a good chance an airplane was parked on the sandy pad near the road. I loved to stop and give them the once over and even sit in the pilot's seat to see what it was like. Today there was a two-seater parked there. We tied our horses to a small tree and sat in the plane for a while, pretending we were flying over the countryside. She was smiling and put her arms around my neck as I helped her out of the smelly plane. Blackie never liked to stop here for he hated the smell of the poison, so we didn't stay very long.

As we crossed the back side of my old man's farm, she asked me if I wanted to farm cotton when I got older. Without looking at her I said, "I couldn't farm here even if I wanted; my father would never allow me to use anything that belonged to him, especially his land. I have always told myself, at my first chance, I'm getting as far away from this place as possible and never coming back."
She smiled and said in return, "Would you take me with you?"

I answered, "You better believe it!" As I laughed with her, an exhilarating sensation washed over my being and I wondered to myself, *If this is what love feels like, I want to be in love forever.*

Each wonder I had shared with her was an expression of me. They were things I had never shown anyone else and each remarkable phenomenon offered me a happiness I found nowhere else. By giving me the courage to share the secluded places of my heart, she had become the greatest phenomenon of all, filling my cup to overflowing with a happiness for which I had searched for so long.

She was smiling, but her eyes were expressing something

much more intense, something that mirrored the way I was feeling. She was such a puzzle to me, with so many components in the makeup of her life; I was wonderfully dazzled by each and every one.

Once across the far side of my old man's farm, we ended up back at our starting point where we let the horses have their heads so they could drink from the little stream that flowed through our secret world. Out of our saddles, we splashed water on ourselves to wash off some of the dust and sand. I knew it was getting late and nearing the time for her to ride up the hill home.

As we stood ankle deep in the flowing water, she looked at me and moved closer, but I was no fool this time. Ready for any sucker punch she tried, I held my hands out in front of my gut in a defensive posture as she moved to within inches of my face. Capturing me with those heart-breaking eyes, she grabbed the back of my head and pulled my mouth to hers. Kissing me so passionately I thought my knees were going to buckle, she roughly put her tongue in my mouth and moved her lips all over mine as if she were trying to suck every bit of moisture from my mouth. As the sand and dust on our lips got smeared all around our mouths, I tried to pull her so close that she would become part of my body. Every second of that grating clench was ecstasy for me. When she finally broke the embrace our lips were extra wet and I stuck my tongue out to feel mine and make sure they were still there. With those eyes staring at me, she wiped her mouth with her forearm as I stood in shock. Quickly, she climbed up on Spot and he spun in a circle while she tried to keep her eyes on me. She pointed Spot up the hill and his hooves dug into the sugar-like sand. Suddenly, she reined him in and stopped, turned her torso and propped her arm on the horse's rump. Her beautiful hair was streaked with dust as it fell across her face and she left me with a question that burned my soul for a week. "Are you the kind of person that breaks your promise?"

There was no understanding her! Staring at me for a

second or two, she quickly turned around, clucked to Spot and he immediately lunged forward and darted up the hill. Thinking quickly to myself, *What promise was she talking about, I don't break promises. Oh shit! That promise!*

***

Once she brushed Spot down and put him in the stable with his food, she patted him on the withers and asked, "Have you ever been in love Spot ole boy?" After she paused for a minute, she answered, "Me neither, but if this is what it feels like, I want more."

Leaving the barn she followed the cobblestone path to the mansion and was walking past the century-old wisteria vine that encased the arbor in back of the house. Sully was sitting in an old aluminum lawn chair that had two or three broken webbing straps hanging down. He asked her as she walked by covered in dust, "Any idea of an eight letter word for significant other? It has an "L" and an "M" in the middle of it."

She never looked his way, just clomped by in her boots and said, "NO!"

Chapter Fifteen

The next week I could hardly wait to get on the bus each morning. The queasiness in my stomach was still there, but that girl was now my total world. Still mute on the bus ride, her resounding silence kept me on edge, but she seemed unperturbed. She continued her routine of being last off the bus, waving to the secretary and principal and sitting on the parent's bench under their gaze. She appeared in each of the classrooms seconds before the tardy bell as I admired her from afar. The atmosphere returned to the usual loud and boisterous settings on the bus and before homeroom.

Allowed to rejoin the roughhousing and jocularity, I still felt a lingering awkwardness from that clique and I sensed they felt uneasy around me. Burt met me at our regular school haunts including PE, Study Hall, and lunch, but we didn't talk on the bus anymore. Lunch was usually prime time for coaxing Burt into revealing titillating tidbits about his older brother's dating exploits. As we passed in the hall, he mentioned two different girls on the same couch this past weekend, which meant he would have some great stuff to tell me. Sitting on a retaining wall in front of the gym, I was all ears and could hardly wait to hear of the Casanova's couch conquest. This time, however, he had a beginning 'show and tell' session planned and pulled an object from his pocket saying, "Look at this!"

He dropped something in my hand. At first I thought it was just a piece of chocolate candy wrapped in gold foil, but when I flipped it over, the label read 'Trojan'. Under the label a slogan advertized, 'Safe, lubricated, extra sensitive', then under the slogan in tiny type it read, 'contains one latex prophylactic with nonirritating mineral oil lubrication.' None of those words made total sense to me so I looked at my instructor and asked, "What is it?"

With a leer on his face he proudly announced, "It's a fucking rubber."

Shocked, I asked, "A what?"

The sex instructor repeated his words for the slow learner, "It's a fucking rubber. You know, you put it over your thing when you're fucking."

Next question, "Why?"

And the honest reply, "I don't know - I just know how it works. It's like a rubber glove for your thing, I guess to keep you clean, I don't know. There must be something that can get on you, like when you paint and put on gloves. I don't know what girls have in them."

Things were beginning to make sense, but I was still a little confused, "I've seen those before, but they didn't look like that. They were long like a balloon and had a tip on the end like a nipple on a baby bottle." He explained, "This is the same thing, but it's rolled up."

Again, I asked, "Why?"

A simple answer, "So you can put it on. It's easier that way. I watched my brother put one on with one hand, and in a hurry, too. You don't have to open the plastic or anything, just squeeze each side and it falls out of the foil and drops into your hand, then you just put it on top of your thing and roll it down like a sock."

This lesson was an eye opening experience and a monumental moment in my sexual education. While I would never have shared my Sunday afternoon experiences with Burt, I was beginning to put the puzzle pieces together. If Burt was anything, he was generous and he looked at me and said, "You want it?"

Shocked at his benevolence, I said, "Sure, where'd you get it?"

Always resourceful, he said, "My dad has a whole box of them in his sock and underwear drawer. My brother gets them all the time so I figured I'd better grab a few — you know, just in case."

I flipped it over and over then stuck it in my jacket pocket as the bell rang. While grabbing our books, my schoolmate said, "Hey, you want to come over and spend the night this weekend? We haven't been getting together much since you got stuck sitting by that tall nigger girl on the bus."

I winced when I heard that word, but I wouldn't let it filter down to the thinking part of my brain. I just brushed it off and said, "I don't think so because my dad's going to make me work and I'm going to ride Blackie Sunday."

We rushed off to study hall and sat across from each other at one of the library tables with our books in front of us pretending to study. His words stuck in my mind, like a song or a tune you can't stop whistling over and over: *since you got stuck sitting by that tall nigger girl, since you got stuck sitting by that tall nigger girl, since you got stuck sitting by that tall nigger girl.* Trying not to appear upset, I smiled and kept my nose in a book. After a while, I felt my buddy nudge me under the table with his foot. When I looked over, he had drawn a picture of a school bus with two stick figures sitting beside each other, one with big lips and frizzy hair and the caption read "you and your nigger.'

Suddenly my rage hit overflow level and I reached over and grabbed it, wadded it up, then threw it in his face. I could have probably gotten by with that if I had just laughed, but my anger zoomed out of control. With all the force I could muster in a sitting position, I kicked him under the table and he yelled out, "Ouchhhhh!" With a 'what the hell' look on his face, he retaliated to my shin. The next thing I remember was grabbing him in a headlock after he hit me in the nose and falling to the library floor with chairs, tables and books flying everywhere.

Sitting in Mr. Rawls' office, we glared at each other and listened to his phone conversation in the outer office. He was talking with the bus maintenance shop about a student bus driver who had been clocked at 63 miles per hour by the town cop while he was manning his regular speed trap. Speaking into the receiver he said, "Those buses are supposed to have governors that won't allow a speed of over 35 miles per hour; this is the third time Raymond has caught him with his radar gun and the last time he was traveling over 73 mph. How is he doing it? You told me you've checked the bus engine three times, so check it again and please figure out how he's doing it! The next thing, they will be drag racing down Main Street!"

When we heard the phone receiver hit the holder we knew he was in a foul mood and as luck would have it, just as our time of reckoning was at hand. There was a moment or two before he opened the door when we heard him talking in a low voice to the school secretary. He walked in and rubbed his face with his hands, pushing his glasses up on his forehead and giving his eyes an extra grind or two.

Face flushed, he turned his attention to us. "Why were you two fighting in the library? Last time I checked, you were bosom buddies. What's going on?"

Neither of us said a word. As an experienced disciplinarian, he wasted no time on chitchat and moved straight to his strength. "I guess we'll just call your parents and let them come in to discuss this tomorrow."

With that he took out his pen and starting writing a note on a pad. That scenario was totally unacceptable for me. I wasn't going to get my butt beaten twice for Burt so I jumped in first, "He drew a picture of me."

The head man looked at my former friend, "Well?"

Not looking up, my sparring partner said, "I didn't mean no harm by it; I was just trying to be funny."

A little upset might understate the big guy's disposition at that point. "Is that what this is about — a picture that one of you drew of the other?" We both nodded our heads yes and hoped it would seal the deal. "Stand up both of you!"

I had always wondered why there was a towel rod on the back of his office door. He reached over to a shelf beside his desk and grabbed a piece of wood that looked like it was a short boat paddle only thicker with holes drilled in a pattern near the business end. He looked at Burt and said, "Grab hold of that towel rod with both hands!"

When the first lick hit his butt I felt weak in the knees as my ex-chum grimaced and squeezed the rod, for I knew I was next. Four more butt numbing and cheek blistering licks met his behind and each time it seemed as if the force picked his feet up off the floor. This was my fault and I hadn't been fair to him. Burt was through and told to wait at the front counter. I grabbed the bar with visions flashing through my head and a buzz in my ears, but when the first lick smacked my behind, it left a feeling and memory that remains to this day. But I wasn't to get the quick treatment like my cohort.

After the first lick he paused for a question. "He must have drawn a pretty nasty picture of you." Then another lick and another after which he paused again and said, "If you need to tell me something about what he drew now is the time."

I remained silent so he gave the last two in rapid order without near the previous force. He opened the door and I spilled into the outer office and in front of the counter.

"You two get back to class and if I see either of you in here again there will be some parents in my office, too." With that, Burt threw open the door and headed out. The secretary pushed a hall pass in front of me and I grabbed it, then followed Burt at a distance back to study hall.

Sitting on opposite sides of the library for the rest of study hall, I felt guilty about getting Burt's ass burned. He and I had been buddies since first grade and I had heard him use that word hundreds of times. This time 'that word' severed our long-standing relationship and if I knew Burt, revenge was being considered as he sat glaring at me across the room. Reflecting on what had happened, I decided it was stupid to have attacked him. I would hear that word used hundreds of times in the future and if I attacked everyone who said it, I would have my ass kicked on a regular basis. Burt shouldn't have said that word, but he didn't know any better. It was part of the vernacular in our everyday lives. I shouldn't have waited until now to let him know not use it around me, but that would have ruined the camouflage under which I hid in my black and white world.

Suddenly I realized, I had just torn a hole in my façade and the world was about to know my true feelings. From this point forward, the people at school, the people at church and my parents were sure to find out I had chosen to side with the enemy. Feeling sick to my stomach, as I became conscious of the ramifications of losing my temper, I wondered why I had chosen now to ruin my comfortable life. Soon thoughts of Salley reminded me of the reward and erased my concern, for I knew I would fight - even if my life was at stake - to be with her.

Chapter Sixteen

We continued to act as if we knew nothing about each other on our daily bus ride, but on Friday afternoon she opened her purse and pulled out a pencil and a piece of gum and didn't offer me a piece. Out of the corner of my eye, I watched her push the thin sugared stick between her lips and lick the paper side of the foil wrapper. The sight of her tongue set off a surge in my body, but I stifled the scream that was reverberating in my head. She opened the colored outer wrapper and wrote something on the inside, then tossed it on the seat between us. At her stop, she gathered her things and got off the bus, leaving the wrapper on the seat. While all eyes were on her every move, I pocketed the clandestine note and read it as I walked to my house, *Go Mount wknd – see ya Mon.*

Not wanting to believe the message, I tried to make the words mean something else, *Let's mount up this weekend, see you man*, but I knew what it meant.

I rode up and down the sandy road at the bottom of the hill below her house on Sunday afternoon while Blackie protested and wanted to know why the weird route. Finally I got up my nerve and rode to the top of the hill in back of her house. There was no one around and to my surprise, Blackie wasn't acting nearly as spooky as I expected. We rode through a neglected grove of pecan trees and slowly approached the huge dilapidated old barn. Acting much more confident, my ride seemed to share my curiosity as we cautiously entered the dark passageway that ran the length of the structure. As soon as we moved from the sunlight into the cool dark hallway, Spot nickered and welcomed us to his new home. The hallway was open on both ends with stables on each side. In the middle of the barn there was passageway that crossed the long hallway. Above the middle passageway facing the mansion was a huge dormer that opened to a cavernous hayloft running the length of the barn. Spot was in one of the stables near where the hallways crossed and he was as glad to see us as we were to see him. This was a whopper of a barn with 20 stables in each quadrant of the building. Trying to imagine what it must have been like to have 80 mules and horses in this building at once was breathtaking. Jumping from my saddle, we quickly found Spot in a very clean stable with an orderly feed room next to it. There were four English style saddles and one western saddle hung on the wall along with the rest of his tack and care items. On the far side of the room was a huge wooden bin full of pelleted horse chow and bales of alfalfa hay stacked floor to ceiling in the back. The smell of the alfalfa was a new aroma and not the regular smell of Coastal Bermuda hay. There was a desk with two chairs, a file cabinet, clipboards holding papers and a blackboard with dates of vet appointments and vaccinations scribbled on it. She was quite the horsewoman and that was just another element of her life I adored.

I tried to think of this place during its heyday. It must have been a hub of activity when it was full of animals that had to be cared for and fed. It was stunning to consider the number of slaves that would have been necessary to keep this storehouse of horsepower operating. The strength of the cotton plantation lay solely on the shoulders of slaves and their care for the animals that worked in the fields. It was hard for me to imagine the mindset of the rich white planters as they callously wielded complete control over such a massive workforce. The enslaved human beings, the horses and the mules were all considered animals they owned. They must have felt like medieval kings with absolute supremacy over their subjects, having the ability to end a life at the snap of their fingers without any consequence to themselves. I could not conceive of such power.

Nosing around a little, I noticed some old tubs stacked near the feed room and in the dusky light I could see numbers stamped in the sides and realized immediately they were identical the ones my mother found in the station wagon. I think we knew all along that Sully was the anonymous donor of the cotton seed. The more I came to know this old man, the more I liked him. I began to see Sully in a totally new light, much like my friends of the field.

Grabbing a handful of the store-bought feed, I tossed it on the feed room floor for Blackie, and left him with his friend. The depths of the old mule repository beckoned me and I moseyed to the far end for a more detailed look. The view out the end of the old fortress overlooked Sully's largest cotton field and brought to mind the majestic view that Salley's great-great grandfather must have seen a century earlier. He must have thought he was a very successful man to own such a vast domain. I wondered what he would think if he saw it today.

After looking back to check on Blackie, I walked over to the first of three small barns that were shaded under a huge live oak with limbs reaching out in all directions. Peeping through the doors of one of the outbuildings, it was obviously a blacksmith shop and probably where everything metal for the plantation was fabricated. Spider webs hung from the rotted old bellows that once pumped air onto the hot coals of the forge. Taking care to watch where I stepped, I bushwhacked to the next long building. It wasn't as long as the mule barn but close and had the largest collection of horse and mule drawn farm equipment I had ever seen, most in disrepair or suffering from rust and rot. These ancient implements were used in cotton production, but there were other antique implements just as interesting, such as earth moving, logging, haying, threshers, including a group of wagons rotting away at the far end. Sully's old M model Farmall tractor seemed out of place among the mule powered equipment as did the modern implements around it. Remembering Blackie, I thought I should return to the barn. As I stepped through the tall grass, I came upon a neatly laid cobblestone path that curved its way from the massive barn to the huge antebellum house. Looking at the mansion, it was deserted and I knew the girl for whom I longed had gone away, at least for a while. My only option, it seemed, was to patiently wait for her return.

Leading Blackie from the barn, Spot whinnied as his best friend and I clopped out. Climbing on his back, we slowly trudged down the hill and stopped at the creek. With an urge to scream, I felt Blackie expressing his sentiments, too, as he shook his head and snorted in frustration. He was a creature of habit that I had manufactured and without the ability to understand, he was puzzled as to why we were burning daylight. He pawed the ground then began slinging his head side to side and chomping his metal bit. I patted his side and talked soothingly to him. We had been together for almost ten years and our communication was a mixture of my words and his actions, with neither of us hesitating to express our aggravation. So, on his insistence, we took the long way home and ended up on the near side of The Griddle with the wind at almost a standstill.

We crossed the flat field at a gallop and rode through the low ditches, hoping to startle a deer and watch it effortlessly dash across the field and glide over the fences. Stopping to check a creek where a beaver dam was under construction, I was amazed at how much they had built since our last visit. Glancing back toward Roy Asholee's Store, I caught a glimpse of a figure crossing the road headed in the direction of the store.

The store was closed because South Carolina law prohibited the sale of alcohol on Sunday. A law preventing beer from being obtained on Sunday was not something disagreeable to Boot. It was a win-win situation for him in that his rotgut liquor sales increased, plus his advocating no alcohol sales on Sunday kept him in good standing with my mother. Those milk jugs she sold were always needed, not to mention those who blasphemed the Lord's Day were sure to encounter her public wrath and could spark a visit from the ABC man.

As a child of the Great Depression, my mother saved everything, including the newfangled plastic milk jugs. Collecting all of the unbreakable jugs in her reach, she stored them in our old smokehouse throughout the year. To stay in her good graces, store bums, field hands and kinfolks alike, tossed their empty milk jugs in the back of my old man's pickup and reminded him to tell my mother of their generosity. Usually around the time of the Lottie Moon Christmas Offering, an annual offering taken up each year to save the heathen souls of the hordes in China, my mother would pull them out and sell them to increase her contribution to the missionary fund.

Roy Asholee always gave my mother a generous five cents for each of the reusable containers and she believed his money to be a blessing for items that would otherwise be destined for the trash dump. She knew very well he used them to sell his illegal and deadly bootleg. The evidence of the poison he peddled was made clear by the growing number of alcoholics in the black community. In my short time, I had seen three men die a slow, maddening death. He sold his booze on credit and the debts of those addicted could be sold to farmers. It was part of a community business that greatly benefited Roy Asholee. My mother could always legitimize her contribution to the slow agonizing death of other human beings and make it right with the Lord, for the heathens in China needed to know Jesus and take Him as their Savior.

With my curiosity piqued, I wanted to see what person was lurking around the store on a Sunday. It looked like a familiar gait and as it disappeared into the trees, I put my heels into Blackie's side. We took off toward the nasty commissary and stopped in the woods just away from the outhouses to watch for the mysterious figure. The store was in plain sight and my mouth dropped open when Wes appeared momentarily behind the store with four gallon milk jugs of clear liquid then disappeared in the bushes near the far side of the store. I tied Blackie to one of the trees near the outhouse and quietly made my way closer. Easing up near the store, I watched him open a door on the side, concealed from view by some shrubbery. After unlocking it he stepped through and down some steps. This was brand new to me for I never knew there was a basement under the store. Closer to the opening, it was easy to see everything he was doing. There must have been 300 to 400 plastic milk jugs stacked on forklift pallets. Who knew there was that much room under that trash dump they called a store? Easing up to the door, I pushed it open and the squeak made Wes turn quickly to face me with a look of horror on his face. He didn't say anything at first and he really didn't need to give a reason.

Finally I asked, "You work for Roy or Boot?" He told me he was working for both of them, which sent shivers down my spine, for I quickly understood that my being in this place could easily result in a hasty and unexpected disappearance.

"What are they going to do with all of this rotgut? Has it already been cut?"

My old friend nodded his head and said, "Hits cut han ready ta go on da truck, almost $6,000 worths of rotgut liquor."

Realizing I was alone, he told me more than I wanted to know. They were selling that much about two times a month. It was all brought to the store to be cut, after which Boot let Roy know it was ready and the buyers would be alerted. The liquor brought from the still was very high proof and they watered it down before selling it. A white man in a box truck came and paid with cash.

He said, "Deys gib me bout $50 two-shree times a month, but deys always takes out whats I owe dem so hit don't leb much."

Knowing better than to ask, I couldn't stop myself, "Why do you owe them money?"

He shrugged his shoulders. That wasn't even half the money that he could make in the field. He said, "I runs dey still in da swamp hind yo house mos nights when we's working hit off. Dat's how I's gots in da yard widout yo daddy see'in me."

I really didn't need to ask, I could tell by looking at his eyes, but I asked anyway, "Are you still drinking this stuff?" He swore he wasn't but his bleary eyes and smell of rotgut on his breath told me he was lying. He didn't act the least bit drunk.

Wes was usually a functional alcoholic, appearing sober as a judge, though thoroughly plowed. I asked if he was going to stay here, maybe work for the old man again. He shook his head and told me he could never work for him again. He explained he was between a rock and a hard place: if he didn't do what they told him, they would tell my old man he was responsible for burning his houses and for killing Willie and he'd be killed on the spot. The law would thank them for solving their case. But worst of all, they threatened Puddin and told him she would disappear if there was any trouble. I stood transfixed looking at a man I would have given my life to help just a few weeks earlier. There were so many questions I needed to ask.

"Wes, did you kill Willie?" Like a man up to his neck in a quicksand bog, hopelessness oozed from his eyes. Maybe it was the rotgut or maybe it was emotions but he did something I had never seen him do before - he cried as he told me the long, horrible tale.

It seems Roy Asholee was giddy with delight when he heard Wes had been by to warn me about the trouble. I started in on an apology but he wiped his nose and said for me to hush because I did the right thing and 'hit was water done long gone unner da bridge' anyway. He said he came to warn me so I wouldn't get hurt because a man who had once worked for my old man was mad cause he didn't get paid and told everybody he was going to set something on fire. He said some folks were just looking for a reason to get revenge for Dr. King's death. When that black boy that shot his mouth off heard about the white boys getting together, he left the county in a hurry. At the time my old man was stirring up the store bums, Wes was locked up down in the basement, but he heard the entire conversation. As he continued, he said after my father left, Roy told him to get three bottles of kerosene ready cause he was going to set my daddy's three tenant houses on fire. He managed to get Della, Mary and Puddin a message and they were supposed to get their belongings out and be gone by nightfall.

Trying to hold his composure, he said Roy made him get in his truck that night with the three fire bombs, but when they drove up Willie had refused to leave and told them, "It ain't right to burn a body's house down just to start trouble."

Wes continued, "Mr. Roy had dat pistol and shook hit hat me — said burn hit down, so I lit the rag on the drank bottle of

146

kerosene and tried to throw hit under the house. It hit the side of de house and broke hand de fire spreaded all round. Willie run for the woods and I thought he was leaving for good. But he was ust a runnin to breaks a pine limb to beat the fire out. We droves on to Mary's house and coutched it afire and when the fire got up pretty high, we's moved on to me and Della's house."

Wes told me Della had gotten everything out of the house she deemed valuable so he set it on fire and watched his home become a blazing inferno. Roy was still driving the truck as they rode through the woods behind all of the houses and stopped out of sight behind Willie and Puddin's house.

"Dem boys from da sto had ust pulled up and was a whooping and hollering and shooting dey guns up in de air so Mr. Roy said, 'Where's Willie?' I didn't say no word and he pointed dat lil' pistol hat me, so's I tolds em last I seen, he was running for da woods."

He said the nasty storekeeper was laughing as he looked at the fire, when suddenly, Willie stood up. With his back to them, his silhouette was illuminated by the fire. Roy cussed and leveled that .22 pistol at Willie and pulled the trigger three times. Wes said his heart cried out but his mouth didn't make no sound as he was shooting. Willie fell dead; only one bullet hit him—in the heart.

Afterward Roy looked at Wes and said, "You belong to me now nigger. If anything happens, your black ass will be the next one to go."

"A few nights later, I runned off and found Mr. Sully. He put me and Puddin on dat bus headed ta Charleston to some our kin folks. Puddin saw ebertang dat happen'd from de woods hand told Mr. Sully afore we's lefts for Charleston. Hin a day or so, Mr. Boot come to Rutledge Street in Charleston to find me. He'd done beat Daggar wid dat lil' pistol hand made him tell where we had goed. Next night, he rode up 'n down the road in front of de house real slow-like wid his arm slung out the window. After ha while, he stopped and hollered out my name so's I just comes out and ax him what he wants. He said, 'Get your black ass in dis car or I'll kill both of you'n whiles you sleep.'"

Wes told me he didn't want Puddin to have any more trouble so he got in the car. As they pulled off, Boot blew the horn and waved to Puddin who was looking out the window. He was laughing as they left the city. Wes was afraid and trapped with nowhere to turn. He asked me, "Yous gonna tell Mr. Sully 'bout me being back?"

Looking in his weary eyes I told him about Puddin and the baby and he said, "If Mr. Sully's watching out fors dem, den he knows I back. He's'll do what right hand take care of boths dem womens. Dem twos won't be part long, they's need each other to makes it.

A few days after Wes left Charleston, Puddin' called to tell Sully about Boot coming down. He already knew Roy was responsible for shooting Willie in the back so now he had the police watching Puddin in Charleston. I figured Sully had told the police about Roy killing Willie and I realized why he was scared to have me around him, especially with the chance that Roy or Boot might show up at any moment. He told me it was time for me to go, but I sat looking at him as tears came to my eyes.

Wes and I had always guarded against getting too close. I knew he loved me and I loved him, but our situation didn't allow us to physically express that to each other. The closest physical contact I had had with Wes was him touching my face once and a slap on the back a few times. But as he saw the tears appear in the corners of my eyes, he did something he had never done before. He hugged me and held me close to his chest. Throwing my arms around him, I cried like a baby as he embraced me and wondered how things had gone so wrong for him. Then quickly, he pushed me back and said, "Yous and Blackie needs to go on from outa here now, go on! Dis ain't no place for ya'lls to be, too much trouble hea. Go on!"

Slowly I walked back to Blackie and rode away from the

store. Several times I wanted to look back, but I didn't. It had been a very dismal Sunday and I just wanted to go home and let the day end.

Chapter Seventeen

On Monday I held my breath as the bus screeched to a stop and all eyes turned toward the old mansion. With that elegant gait and her hips gently swaying, the girl who owned my heart moved purposefully down the lane like a model on a catwalk. Staring straight ahead, with a profound look on her face, she seemed to be in serious thought. Wearing a mini-dress that was at least eight inches above her knees, she had the shoulder straps of her dress pushed out on her shoulders and the neckline was scooped seductively low. With a purse hung around her neck that rode on the side of her hip, she held her notebook, as usual, close to her chest. Her hair glimmered in the sun as she had it rakishly pulled to one side of her face. A picture of poise and grace with every step she took, I wondered if the girl that almost sucked my lips off and hit me in the gut with a sucker punch was hidden under all of that modern attire. My self-worth soared and made my spirit whirr like a hummingbird, for I knew the real person inside that beautiful body. It made me swell with pride to know in her eyes I was head and shoulders above every other person on the bus. As she stepped aboard the bus and again took her usual place beside me, I showed absolutely no emotion outwardly, but inside, I was screaming and shouting, *She chose me, you assholes, ME!*

With my cup overflowing but not a word being said, we uneventfully traveled to school.

Following her usual routine, she entered the classroom just before the bell and remained until everyone left the room. If perchance I was to pass her in the hall, she did not speak or smile but blew by me as if I didn't exist. But when near her, I kept her in my peripheral view.

All week Burt stared at me but would not speak and I knew him well enough to know he was sharpening a knife that was destined for my back. Time seemed to crawl to a standstill that week and as it came to a close, I got the worst news by way of my father. He told my mother, "The weatherman says rain Sunday, if you believe him. We'll have to get all of the hay out of the field Saturday."

This meant eight hours in the sun picking up 35 pound bales with dust and hay sticking to every part of my sweaty body, then 4 or 5 hours tossing the bales from the truck into the hayloft. That little tidbit of information seemed to cover me with an irritable veil that thickened as the weekend approached. Saturday was a bright sunny day without the hint of rain as we moved over 300 bales of hay to the loft in 90° heat, but as Sunday arrived, the weather report proved accurate.

I prayed during church for God to stop the rain. Promising better behavior, no more bad language or thoughts, I gave my full attention to the preacher, and as the service ended I prayed for a miracle, maybe a small miracle, just enough to make it stop raining after we ate Sunday dinner. The deluge stopped as we drove home, so I whispered a little thank you prayer to the Lord for granting my wish and promised better behavior in church.

As I swallowed the strawberry shortcake in two gulps, and was putting my plate in the sink, thunder boomed and lightning struck nearby. In seconds it was pouring down with no sign of stopping and a blue sock of low-down funk was pulled over my world. Feeling trapped in the house, I had to escape to somewhere safe and there was only one option. Running the usual route to avoid a cold drip of water down my back, I had my snacks and reading material stashed under my arm as I ran into the first stable where the board ladder took me up to the hay loft. I knew Blackie would be in the stable out of the rain and I could fill his hayrack from an opening in the loft floor. As I started up the ladder I heard him snort and smiled for even he sounded blue.

Knowing he hated the rain too, I thought Blackie would like some of the fresh new hay to munch during the rainy afternoon. Before I climbed into my 'hay hole' to sulk, I grabbed an armful from one of the bales that had burst and walked over to the hole above his hay rack only to find it full. Oh well, Albert must have filled it before he left the loft yesterday. I heard him moving about in the stall below, but with the rack full, I couldn't see him. Oh well, I climbed over the new stack of hay and moved the secret bale. Quickly, I tossed the goodies down the hay chute, then put my feet in and slid down to a shock that almost made me wet my pants. I let out a yelp when I saw her and she coolly said, "If you do that again this place is not going to be a secret."

She already had the lantern on and quickly grabbed the bag to see what there was to eat. Skipping lunch, she had barely made it to the barn before the second downpour. In the lantern light, I could see her shivering so I gave her my jacket and she leaned back on Blackie's red blanket and began devouring a chicken leg. Taking everything out of the brown paper bag from the Red and White grocery store, I folded it flat as a makeshift table. As I placed the contents on top of the bag, she dropped the chicken bone on it and grabbed one of the recycled margarine containers. With the only spoon, she began wolfing down the potato salad and wasted no time starting in on the strawberry shortcake. Grinning from ear to ear, I watched her every move. Elated, scared, excited and aroused all at the same time, I was in heaven.

Yes, I had been taught it was impolite to stare at someone, especially while they're eating — so shoot me, I forgot. She reminded me with a swift kick and said, "Don't stare at me while I'm eating, that's what those redneck hicks do to me at school!"

I graciously apologized and then shoved her over so I could lay back on part of the blanket. She seemed a little pissed off about something, but I figured it was the rain. This was a great thing that had happened and my happiness continued to radiate out of my face in the form of a giant smile.

Seeing my pleasure she demanded, "What are you grinning about? I thought you would be mad about not getting to ride."

I continued to beam, and without thinking said, "This might be better than riding."

My smile quickly evaporated as I noticed my dog-eared

Penthouse lying at her feet. I had hidden it in the hay and somehow she had found it. Now I was sure she thought me a pervert or something and I reached for it, but with her mouth still full, she snatched it away from me and said, "I was reading that!"

Reading? What the hell was there to read in that magazine? She let the centerfold flop down and held it up with one hand and chewed on an apple with the other.

"I don't see what's so great about these mags; they don't show anything but nipples and a tuft of hair. Boys have both, what's the big deal?"

I wasn't about to venture an answer to that one, because frankly she was right, but the pics sure did arouse your imagination as well as other things. She flipped the mag to me and I quickly hid it away and leaned back on the blanket beside her. Upon finishing the apple, she wanted to save the core for Spot and dropped it back into the bag. Still cold I guess, she stuck both of her hands in my jacket pockets and made a funny face. Curious as to what I had in my coat pocket, she pulled out the gold foil wrapped condom that Burt gave me and I grimaced. She had a way of uncovering all of my secrets and making me feel extremely awkward.

Examining it closely, she stared at it for a while, then flipped it over and stuck it to her nose for a smell before she tossed it to me. "What's that?"

She was being honest and I thought, for once, I had the upper ground, so with confidence I volunteered, "It's a fucking rubber."

She wrinkled up her face and asked again, "A what?"

I repeated my answer with further explanation, "A fucking rubber — you put it over your thing and it keeps it clean when, you know — you do it."

In a blink, she took my know-it-all status away from me, "That's not what you call it. It's called a condom."

I offered my child-like rebuttal, "No it's not."

She stuck out her hand and said, "Let me see it again, I've

153

never seen one like that." I put it back in her hand feeling defeated and she looked at the label and read the words out loud. I had read those words at least a thousand times, and knew them by heart. As she read them I repeated them in my mind, *Trojan - safe, lubricated, extra sensitive, contains one latex prophylactic with nonirritating mineral oil lubrication.* Then she confidently said, "I've never seen one like this before but I know it's a condom. They showed us these things in Sex Ed at Foxcroft. It's to keep from getting pregnant. They gave us all one and we blew them up like balloons. The ones we had were in plastic packs stuck together and the teacher tore them off and gave us each one."

I had seen those, too, so this was my chance to regain the high ground, "This is a one-hander for when you are in a hurry. You squeeze the sides and it pops out in your hand then you put it on top and just roll it down."

She interrogated me further, "I thought you said you had never done it before we did it. Sounds like you know what you're doing."

With a little stuttering I finally said, "Burt told me that's how he saw his brother do it in the dark on the couch with one of his girlfriends."

Not understanding Burt, she said, "You mean his brother lets him watch?" I told her no, that Burt was sneaky and was outside peeking in the window where he had pulled back the curtains for the occasion. In silent contemplation she held it for a while then flipped it back to me. "Well you won't be using it for a while unless you break your promise, besides I'm having my period."

I mulled over her words. *That damn promise thing again and what the hell was she having — her period?* I didn't have a clue. With those steel blues, she could read me like a book.

"You don't know about periods? Have you never heard of a girl being on the rag?" Now that was something I had heard before and Burt and I had teased girls on the bus by saying that to them, but I thought it meant they had diarrhea. Man, was I in

154

for a shock.

With the thoroughness of a veteran teacher she told me about everything from sperm to egg to menstrual cycle to babies and where each was located, what came out and how to correctly address the situation. I knew she was smart, but I didn't know she knew everything. Completely overwhelmed would be the best way to describe my brain at that moment. In my hay fort in 15 minutes I had learned more about the birds and bees than from four years of listening to Burt. My mood had gone from 'very stimulated' to 'no longer aroused' during her detailed description of procreation. With all of that scientific talk about fluids and blood and babies coming out, no way, I didn't even want to kiss.

Lying together on Blackie's blanket, with her stomach finally full, I was tired of talking. She curled next to me and felt warm so I snuggled as close to her as I could get. Decades later I would become familiar with this ruse and recognize it as her approach to topics she knew I did not want to discuss, but this was my first time and I felt warm and fuzzy. While I braided some hay into a bracelet to put around her arm, we listened to her transistor radio as she faked sleep and lay beside me with her eyes closed. Out of the blue, she said, "Why did you and Burt get in a fight?"

Now she was out of bounds with that and I was silent so she followed up with another question. "What did he draw that made you mad enough to hit him?" She was way out of bounds and I was not answering. Besides, she had her eyes closed. And as I would also figure out later, persistence was her strong suit. "Did he say or draw something about me?"

That did it, she broke the dam and I lashed out at her, "Why don't you just shut up? It's none of your business so shut up and leave me alone!" I moved off of the blanket and leaned against the hay bales opposite her. In the silence, she sat up and looked at me with the face of a sad puppy. With everything in me I tried not to look at her face but the truth pulled me to her eyes.

"Okay, okay, he drew a picture of you and me on the bus — you had big fat lips and curly hair."

She wanted the whole dark truth, "But my lips aren't big and my hair is straight as an arrow."

Spilling more, I continued, "He wrote something under it too — he wrote 'you and your tall nigger' and he called you that when he gave me the condom, too." Holding on hard to keep my emotions back I decided to take my own advice and shut up.

We sat in silence for an eternity before she asked, "You mean you would give up your best friend because he called me a nigger? You, a person that is afraid to fight and even shies away from an argument, tried to punch his face in because he used a word that you have heard a million times before and drew a funny picture of us that didn't even look like us?"

I spat back at her, "He has never been my friend; we just knew each other and talked about things together." I crossed my arms on my chest and thought, *That is it; I'm not talking about it anymore; even if she didn't understand, no more talking!* Again we sat in silence for an eternity until she blew the lid off my conscience.

"You know what I think? I think you felt guilty and were mad at yourself and took it out on your friend. Have you ever said the word nigger talking to him? Have you ever written it under a funny picture you drew and shown it to him? I know you have done it, you would have had to have done it at some time going to that school or they would have figured you out by now! You've probably said that word plenty of times when you knew there were no black people around. Now suddenly that word makes you do something you have avoided all your life?"

I was humiliated! She was right and I knew it. At the point of tears, she stared at me in silence. Then she did something that sealed my fate forever. She crawled over the hay to me and passionately kissed me on the lips then pulled me over to the red blanket beside her. As she lay with her head in my lap, I stroked her hair and we were silent. Then she said, "It's hard to

156

live in two worlds. Everybody wants you to choose sides."

I wanted to tell her that I had decided on which side I had to stand, that my life would be forever changed, but I didn't at the time. Later I would realize she knew exactly what I had done and why.

We sat listening to the rain peck the tin roof of the barn and occasionally heard Spot or Blackie snort and stomp. They seemed as blue as we were about the weather and the thought of her words and what I had done sent cold chills down my back. She was obviously more at ease with the situation than I because she fell asleep and drooled on my jeans. Finally opening her eyes, she automatically slurped and looked down at my pants. Wiping the spot with the arm of my jacket she said, "Oh crap! I'm so sorry!"

She kept apologizing, so I finally put my finger to her lips and smiled. "It's okay, now we're even."

Smiling and capturing my heart with those eyes, she pulled my face to hers. Moving slowly, I positioned myself on top of her and we practiced open mouth kissing. It had become an enjoyable habit and we practiced every chance we could afford. Ever so slightly, I moved my hand under her coat and she stopped kissing for a moment and gave me the most devilish smile for about ten seconds then said, "You do remember what I told you?"

Then she put her tongue right back in my mouth and started to suck my lips off. I guess I got too stimulated and all the blood left my brain for other areas; anyway there was that delay between her statement and my comprehension. She allowed me to caress her breasts and I was super ecstatic to find she didn't have on a bra. But suddenly, it dawned on me what she meant, that menstrual thing and the blood and all that. As her explanation of sex bobbed around in my head like a pinball, I became a little less aroused and moved my hand from under the coat to her face. Sure, I wanted more, but kissing her was wonderful and I was thrilled to be doing that at the moment. I wondered to myself, *Do all girls have this much control?*

157

Chapter Eighteen

We broke for air and she told me it was time for her to go. As we climbed down out of the loft, I felt the moment was fleeting and I needed to say something prophetic about her questions. When she pulled the cinch tight on Spot's saddle and pulled the stirrup down into place, she turned to me for what I knew was going to be one last wet, heart throbbing, weak-in-the-knees, well appreciated, long, open mouth kiss — but boy howdy, did I muck that up.

Wes told me once, "The road to hell is paved with good intentions." That statement, I was to find out, is very true, for I was to visit hell that rainy day standing in the hallway of that barn.

Once again I fell under the spell of those arresting eyes accompanied by that mesmerizing smile and they evidently stopped my brain from working and made my mouth utter one of the most foolish statements I would ever make in my life. Looking into her eyes I said, "Are you a nigger?"

Don't ask what I was thinking and don't ask what I was trying to say. There is no sane rationale for my words, but as soon as they came out of my mouth, I felt my world collapse. Her bright eyes and loving smile blazed into a demonic stare that made me hiccup with fright. I remember thinking, *I don't think I'll get to kiss her goodbye this time.*

I had no idea of what I was about to receive. In the nanosecond before it happened, I remembered her volatility, but again, I didn't think to protect myself. With all of her fury, she slapped my face with the Muhammad Ali of all slaps. It knocked my face to the side, put the taste of blood on my tongue and made me see stars for a few seconds during which she jumped on Spot. When my focus came back I looked up to see fire in her eyes as she held the reins tight and Spotacular rearing his front legs high in the air. I was afraid this would be the end of us if I didn't say something quick. In the fraction of a second that she was staring at me, I wanted to say I was sorry, but I had already said those words too many times. From a deep 'self-dug' hole of desperation, I managed to get out, "If you are, then I'm a nigger lover!"

Her horse spun in a circle and upon reaching the 360-degree mark, no one can tell me different, I know I saw her crack a half-way smile as she kicked that beautiful Appaloosa in his ribs and they rode off like Roy Rogers on Trigger after the bad guys. Watching her disappear into the rainy dusk, I rubbed the side of my face and ran my tongue over the cut place inside my cheek and thought to myself, *You fool, you fool, you fool!*

***

The next morning I had a perfect red handprint on the side of my face along with a sore, puffy, indentation on the inside of my cheek, but I was able to hide it from my mother. When Salley got on the bus, as usual, she sat down and never looked my way. Since the print was on the right side of my face next to the window, she couldn't see it and I had managed to disguise it from the others by holding my cheek on or near the window. When the bus pulled to a shrill stop in the parking lot, I forgot about the handprint on my face and turned to face the aisle as people exited.

A boy in the seat in front of us saw my face and yelled, "What the hell happened to your face? You say something stupid to your old man again?" Everyone on the bus looked and laughed. It had only happened once, but they never forget something like that. I turned before my seatmate could see the calling card she left but this was the first time at school that confidence did not radiate from her face.

As I entered homeroom, the teacher told me that Mr. Rawls wanted to see me in the office. Panic filled my mind as I tried to think of what I might have done. Briefly, I wondered if Burt had set me up as an act of revenge. My heart was racing as I walked toward the parent bench and saw the slugger already seated there. Her eyes told me she was horror struck when she saw my face but as usual, said nothing to me in public. As the eyes of the school fell upon us, I knew Mr. Rawls was not one to miss something going on behind the scenes, so it was a given he and his secretary were part of that audience. Finally, 'the man' called both of us into his office and sat us in his paddling chairs. Keenly aware of my surroundings, my butt crack tightened remembering the licks I took at his hand last time.

He went through the face rubbing thing and then lit up a Salem and spoke, "We've got graduation coming up in a week or so and I'm sensing trouble. Either one of you want to tell me what's going on?"

With innocent eyes she looked at him and said, "I'm afraid I don't know what you're talking about. I haven't been here long enough to know what the 'in crowd' is doing."

After her perfectly placed statement, that he swallowed hook line and sinker, he turned his attention to me. "Did your father put that handprint on your face?"

Quickly I told him, "No, I said something to my cousin and she got a little mad at me." It was all I could think of at the spur of the moment. My cousin had been the only other girl to slap me and she had a pretty good reason. My mother had taken me to her family reunion at the State Park and while we were swimming she jumped off the diving board and lost the top of her two piece swimsuit. I quickly swam out to retrieve it and told her I wouldn't give it back to her unless she showed me her budding little boobies. I was just kidding and relented, giving it back to her with a devilish smile. She had the same reaction that Salley had in the barn hallway, but my cousin didn't leave a mark.

There's no way you could persuade me that her heart wasn't racing as fast as mine. Evidently, though, we were both pretty good liars because he sat and stared at us for a long time. Waving his hand, he told us to get to homeroom, but stopped us before we could get out the door. "Wait, we need to talk. Sit back down."

This time it was serious because he took out a Salem and put it between his lips, then suddenly looked at Salley while snatching the menthol butt out of his mouth. "I'm sorry. You're allergic to cigarette smoke aren't you?"

She smiled that million dollar smile and said nothing but it was obvious she had planted that seed when they first met. Now, straightening his comb-over, he sat down and hesitated again. I wondered, *What in the world is going on?* This was starting to get serious. Stuttering and stammering he finally said, "Well, um, I know this might be none of my business, but I don't want either of you to have problems. We don't have too many graduates that qualify for college, much less, have students with a real opportunity to become college graduates, so we are proud that both of you are in our graduating class."

Pausing again, he was hesitant but finally continued, "This will be the 23rd time I have given out diplomas to a graduating class at this school and I know pretty darn well how seniors act just before they graduate. This year is different, however, because there are a lot of changes coming to this school in the next few years. I need to think of the community, the school and the future after this class is gone." Now I really began to worry. He was hem and hawing around like he'd been caught with his britches down. She looked at me puzzled and I gave her the same look back.

Nervously, the principal tried to nonchalantly mix his concern in with his babble, but it came out like a red letter, bold print, banner, "We've never had an interracial relationship here at the school and I don't know what the reaction might be, but I lay awake at night thinking of what could happen."

All this time he had been looking everywhere except at us but once he got the words out, he looked up for a reaction. There was shock on our side of the desk and I was not about to be first to take on this subject, no matter how much practice I had had deceiving people. But I should have known my partner had a lot of experience handling this topic and she coolly launched her rebuttal like a seasoned attorney.

"Mr. Rawls, has someone said something about us?

Certainly I know of nothing we've done to indicate we have any type of relationship other than sitting beside each other on the school bus." Then quickly she took the high ground from him with, "I hope you don't think this is anything other than a rumor being circulated because of the color of my skin."

Realizing he was standing on the edge of a cliff, teetering toward an abyss, he decided to join her on the high ground, "That is exactly what I figured this to be since first I heard of it, a vicious rumor. But I was concerned when I found out that some of our students had planned a cruel prank." Very upset, his face reddened, but he forged ahead, "We were having watermelon for lunch today and it came to our attention that some students, actually most of the students, were planning to throw that watermelon at the two of you and shout something hurtful."

The dam burst, the flood was released and he could not stop his thoughts or fears from coming out of his mouth, "Before you ask, I cannot tell you how we found out, but it will not happen nor will anything else of this nature. It is just the sort of thing I do not want to happen at graduation. We will eventually have to merge the black and white schools in a year or so and I want it to go as smoothly as possible. There will be no overt actions against any student white or colored that may lead to racial problems. They haven't had one single problem over at the nigger school and we're not going to have any here."

With the suddenness of a heart attack, he sat frozen with a stunned look of horror on his face. A Freudian slip from the subconscious had suddenly burst out! This was very understandable given the burden of stress inflicted by the momentous topic. Having finally expressed his racial concerns in a tactful manner and having that ordeal behind him, he seemed to relax. It also caused the careful scrutiny of his words to be lax and therefore caused the utterance of the word he had tried so valiantly to avoid in her presence. The degree of horror that struck him after his poor choice of words was immediately revealed by the look on his face. Knowing the pain that word had inflicted upon me, I felt his agony, but he was on his own as I sat in frozen silence. He knew as well as we did that nothing he said from here forward would make us believe that word was not one of his everyday words.

In 1968 the word nigger was deeply ingrained in the language of the South and was an often used colloquial expression in all of the former Confederate states. A denigrating term for Negros, it was acceptable and unavoidable in a regular conversation among whites during that period of time. Ironically, I had heard it used often by my black friends of the field as a self-deprecating term. Still having the results on my face from the use of that word in her presence, I was not about to look at my partner.

I could feel for Mr. Rawls, but I could not reach him. I too, had allowed it to become part of my daily vocabulary and used it without a thought as to the deep-seated prejudice it epitomized. But he was an educator, a man with a master's degree and *some of his best friends were black.* What had happened? Nothing had happened — the prejudice and bigotry were hidden there just under the surface all along and like a fart, it slipped out at an inopportune time. He had been forced to promote the appearance of equality in the public school where he was principal, but the actual acceptance of all races being equal was an idea he, along with all other Southern whites, just could not make their subconscious accept. His attempt at 'self-behavior modification' had not been fully realized and his true nature that he had tried so nobly to suppress popped to the surface like a milk jug on a trotline. With seven years until retirement, he was confident he could keep his resentments, his dislikes and his aversions hidden just under the surface long enough for him and his family to claim the state retirement he felt he had earned. He had followed the rules of the game so well, jumped through every hoop and put on a dog and pony show each time the State Board of Education had visited. But now, in the fourth quarter of the game, they were changing not only the rules but the playing field as well. In his eyes, it was unreasonable, unjust and just plain wrong! But now he sat with fear oozing from his pores.

After his lingo-lapse, Mr. Rawls fell apart. His apology was hollow and in fact everything he said following the poor choice of words was gibberish. I personally believe he saw himself standing on the handrail at the Niagara Falls holding his retirement over the churning waters with a sewing thread. In a quick, apologetic panic, he ushered the two of us out of the office and into the hallway so he could sit down, smoke a Salem, and consider his preferred choice of suicide.

Entering the hallway, Salley grabbed me by the collar and pulled me into the water fountain alcove and covered her mouth to muffle our conversation. Touching the red handprint on my face, her eyes said it first, and then she spoke the words, "I'm sorry I slapped you; I should never have done that. It was very mean of me, do you hate me?"
I smiled and said, "I let you sit by me on the bus, didn't I?"

She smiled and gently touched the red marks on my face. After a moment, she looked toward the office and said, "He deserved a slap, not you. I guess it's good to know where you stand with your so-called friends. Who told him about you and me? Have you said anything to anyone?"

With assured confidence I said, "I haven't said a word to anyone so that leaves you, Blackie or Spot."

Always quick with the wit, she stated unequivocally, "Don't be silly, Blackie and Spot would never rat us out."

As we contemplated our next move, I wondered if Burt had a hand in the watermelon plan. He was not one to forget being wronged and that kind of prank had his name written all over it. He was also brainless enough to somehow let it slip out to the principal.

Chapter Nineteen

Unbeknownst to us, we had been stabbed in the back by none other than that pack of black-eyed bandits — those trash-loving raccoons. Kora Rich heard the noise at the trash stash behind her husband's store and looked out her window to see if she could maybe get off a few shots at the bandits when what did she see, but a long black-haired nigger girl and that boy who stares at Betty's legs in church riding horses together. That very day, Betty's next-door neighbor stopped by to buy some Watkins Tonic and the pistol packing motor mouth spilled her guts. Having heard of the knife incident from her neighbor, she was well aware of that nigger gal and from that moment on, we became the number one topic on the community gossip hit parade. Everyone was very familiar with the idiom used to describe John Rich's wife, 'Telephone, telegraph, and tell Kora Rich!'

Her exact words were, "They came out of the woods together then rode down the road and back in the woods again! There's no telling what they're doing in those woods. It's a shame and disgrace to see that sort of thing in our community." This of course meant everyone knew except my parents. No one had the guts to mention it around my hot tempered old man or my sanctimonious mother.

You could attach many labels to Salley, but 'faint of heart' was not one that fit her. She was a master of using a person's weakness to her advantage and I watched in wonder as she demonstrated her skill. Faking menstrual cramps, she waltzed back in the office and told the secretary of her problem and asked to use the phone to call Sully. Her wish was granted on the spot and she instructed me to meet her and Sully on the dirt road behind the school before first period. Leaving my books in my locker, I asked to go to the bathroom five minutes after arriving in homeroom, then walked out of the unmonitored back door and dashed across the track to the patch of pines that separated the back road from the school property.

Sully walked into the school and signed his daughter out

as his friend tried to apologize for letting the 'N' word slip out in front of her. Sully laughed at him and said, "A wise man once said it is better to keep your mouth shut and be thought a fool than to open it and remove all doubt."

With that pronouncement, he asked his old friend if he perhaps knew a 10 letter word that meant intolerant, but he was too upset to answer. He and Salley walked to the 'ole slow blue' and drove away from the school. Once out of sight, they made a turn onto the dirt road down which I stood and came poking down the alleyway, stopping beside me. As I opened the door, a handful of papers fell out and while I scrambled to pick them up I heard the first period bell ring.

Once in the car, Salley told Sully and me she overheard the secretary telling Mr. Rawls about her phone call. "As I walked out of the office, I noticed he had one Salem burning in an ashtray on the counter, one burning in an ashtray on his desk, one burning in his mouth and one burning in his hand. He finally noticed he had four cigarettes going at once and he threw the one in his hand and mouth out the window. Sitting at that old desk, his comb-over fell over his face and he started rubbing his eyes like he was trying to push them out of his head!"

That was one of the first and few times I ever heard Sully laugh out loud. I was scared silly to be cutting school for the first time, but I had to smile at her description. We rode the few miles back to Salleys Kitchen going twenty mph or less all the way with Salley fussing that he go faster. The only thing he said during the excruciating ride was, "I need a seven letter word for nightmare with a 'B' in it."

Taking the backroads, we arrived at the Sullivan farm and he drove around to the back of the mansion. Stopping the car in a large sandy area between the arbor and the small outbarns, Sully did not shut off the old heap while we got out. I had only seen this part of the house from a distance, so I was plowing new ground. As soon as we were out, he drove away. She took my hand and said, "Come on," as she pulled me in the direction of the spooky old dwelling.

She retrieved a key from under one of the cobblestones that formed the ancient patio and it looked just like the one on *The Andy Griffith Show* that hung on the nail outside of the jail cells. Unlocking a door twice the size of a normal one, she squeaked it open a little and then ran to put the key back in its place. Hurrying back up the stone steps to join me, she grabbed my arm and pulled me into a cavernous kitchen. It had to have been built over a century ago and as I looked around with an open mouth, she banged the huge back door shut with her hip.

At the far end of the kitchen was an enormous brick fireplace, probably large enough to have cooked a whole hog, with a wrought iron crane that swung in and out of the fire area. The floor and the fireplace were made of the same type of brick and they spread out from the huge hearth across the entire room. In the middle was a large table made of stone. The black slate table top was held up by four carved granite columns. Stained glass accented the doors on the long white cabinets along walls. A three compartment sink that was the size of a bathtub and carved from a single slab of slate matched the countertops and huge table. It was the kitchen of a castle and in perfect order. At the opposite end of the room, near the middle of the mansion, was a narrow set of back stairs. As I stared at everything in the unique kitchen, she continued to pull me across the brick floor up the narrow black wrought iron stairway. The treads had been worn to a concave shape from millions of steps. I could only assume they were worn down by slaves serving the master and mistress of the house. We arrived on a landing area with a fancy wrought iron rail. She pushed open two louver doors and we entered a broad hallway that ran the width of the house on the second floor. Along each side of this mammoth hall were doors to rooms with a sitting area at each end. In the middle of the golden wood-grain thoroughfare was an intersection where it met the most magnificent formal stairway climbing from the floor below. It was in the middle of a 25 foot tall open foyer with an elaborate crystal chandelier that sparkled above the shiny steps and rails. Just across the wide hallway at the top of the formal stairs was a semicircle-shaped parlor with floor to ceiling windows that opened onto a balcony with a breathtaking view of all of the main fields and other buildings. It was easy to imagine the Lord of the Manor standing on this balcony with brandy and cigar in hand surveying his vast holdings with pleasure.

Once in the second story hallway, she continued to pull me past the huge parlor and stairway to the sitting area at the east end of the house. She had taken me to her room and with her hands full with her notebook and purse she turned the fancy doorknob and kicked the door open with her foot. Throwing open the heavy door she ushered me into a gigantic bedroom suite with several other doors that led to even more areas. Pulling me into her boudoir, she closed the door with a swing of her hips.

It was as if we had stepped into a different world. Totally out of character from the stately antebellum home, the décor of her room was modern and, as she described it, groovy. It was a frilly pink polka dot room that looked to have come straight from Teen Magazine with a white canopy princess bed and matching polka dot bedspread. There was a record player and Beatles posters all around with an Elvis album cover on the floor joined by the Everly Brothers and Jerry Lee Lewis. She threw her notebook and purse to the middle of the big fluffy bed and started taking off her earrings and her shoes at the same time. She turned her back to me and asked me to unzip her dress and it dropped to the floor. The next thing she pulled off was something I had never seen before — panty hose. The only ones I had ever seen were the ones my mother wore that fastened to straps hanging down from a garter belt. These went to her waist like long underwear and she pulled them down to her ankles then tossed them with her foot to a nearby chair. Standing in front of me in just panties and a bra, she laughed at my nervousness and shook her hips to tease me.

Walking over to the chair, she grabbed a t-shirt and pulled

it over her head; then, she picked up a pair of jeans from the floor. Pulling them over her hips, she zipped them up and snapped the snap at her navel. Reaching under the back of her tee shirt, she unhooked her bra, then stuck her hand in each sleeve and pulled the straps off her shoulders, pulling her arm through each to free herself from it. Easing it from under her shirt, she gave me a devilish smile, then pulled it back like a slingshot and shot it at my head. Catching it, I could feel her warmth on the undergarment as I watched her pull a navy blue sweatshirt over her head. It had white block letters on the front that spelled out Foxcroft.

Like a doe from a ditch, she leaped across the room and landed in the middle of the polka dot bed with a flop, sitting with her legs crossed Indian style and motioning for me to sit beside her. This was not happening. I was so nervous and the cheeks of my behind were precariously clamped together like a vise. With one wrong move I could have uncontrollably farted like a trombone; besides, the bulge in my britches could not have grown much larger without an explosion. There was no way humanly possible for me to join her on that bed in a comfortable posture that would not have embarrassed me in some way.

Resisting her tempting offer, I walked to the window and asked with a nervous voice, "Where was Sully going?"

She quickly answered back, "I don't know, wherever he goes during the day. Why?"

To myself I thought, *Why? Did you say WHY? How about... Because I'm in his daughter's bedroom and she's taking her clothes off and trying to get me onto her bed. Why you ask; because I'm scared shitless you brainiac!* But instead, I excitedly said, "Show me the rest of your house. I've never seen anything like this."

With a bounce she was off the bed shrugging her shoulders and giving me an, "Okay, come on."

Following her down the grand stairway my hand slid along

the shiny rail that gradually curved into a seashell spiral on the floor below and her voice echoed throughout the cathedral-like entrance hall. The walls, she said, were covered with French wallpaper that Grandma Lou ordered during the Depression and paid for with gold. The one piece mahogany rails were original to the 1830 construction of the house and the chandelier was made of cut crystal from Russia and came from Salley's adopted great-great-great grandfather's house in Charleston. He was a ship's captain and slave trader in the lucrative Triangle Trade between the colonies, England and Africa. In giving the specifics of each part of the ornate house, my guide's attitude was not a prideful effort to demonstrate her home, rather a memorized sleep-walk through an ancestral past of which she begrudgingly was part.

Passing through the imposing entrance hall, she flipped on a spotlight and it shined on the chandelier, sending shards of light around the massive foyer and stairway. I realized the huge decorative light was not electrified but made to be lit by candles. Leading me to the left side of the impressive vestibule we entered a large dining room with a 16-foot ceiling that filled the front corner of the house. She continued her monotone soliloquy describing a young boy who was shot by Union soldiers and died on the magnificent dining table. Telling of her great-great grandmother Clara Ruth Rutledge Sullivan nursing him, she added that after he died his ghost was trapped and still haunts the room. Cutting her beautiful eyes at me, she looked for my reaction. I acted cool outwardly; inside, it only added to my growing fear.

Crossing through the impressive reception area again, we entered the other large room that filled the right front of the mansion and she mundanely announced it was the meeting room. This was where the brutal General Sherman planned the burning of Columbia and was confronted by her great-great-grandmother. She flipped back the rug to show a long gouge that the Yankee soldiers made in the otherwise perfect pine floor. Then she continued by telling how the Yankee General spared the house from being ransacked and burned, causing it to become a cursed house that the people of the community hated. None of this made sense to me at that time.

In the rear of the formal room, nearer the center of this castle, we walked through an ornate mahogany archway and into an area she called the library. Also with 16-foot ceilings, there was a balcony around the room with near empty bookshelves above and below. A spiral stairway led to an enclosed room that made up the fourth wall below the balcony. She referred to it as the reading area, which was now Sully's office. She said it was supposed to be the help's quarters but ended up being a farm office. It had doors leading to the kitchen and back hallway. The decor resembled his car in that it was covered with pieces of paper and empty beer bottles. A mountain of debris had consumed his desk and spilled over onto most of the floor. Also in the dim space was a leather chair and couch on each side of a mahogany table. A pillow, looking to have been regularly used, lay on the couch with newspapers scattered about all folded with the crossword puzzle filled in with ink. Behind the large ornate desk was a small table with a machine spitting out a paper tape with letters I could not read. The tape from the machine was everywhere. When I asked her what the ticking and clicking contraption was doing, she said it was recording stock information for Sully. She said that was how Sully really made his living, but he didn't want anyone to know; he wanted to be known as a cotton farmer.

Bored with the tour she quickly concluded that all the rooms upstairs were bedroom suites that weren't used and held an assortment of antique this and heirloom that. The ornate furniture on the front veranda was made from teak wood and a favorite place for the male dinner guests to sit and smoke cigars as they sipped blackberry brandy.

After the extended tour, she announced, "I'm hungry! Come on, let's go to the kitchen."

I was certainly not staying in this part of the house alone with ghosts of dead people and a machine ticking and spewing out paper tape everywhere. Just to satisfy my nervousness, I walked over to one of the tall floor-to-ceiling windows in the dining room to check and make sure Sully's worn out old car was not coming up the sandy drive. Just as I timidly pulled the sheer curtain over to peer out, the devil in blue jeans decided it would be cute to goose me. She grabbed my behind and I jumped, then spun around and grabbed her shoulders and pulled her toward me in an embrace that I thought might lead to something. I fell back against the wall with both of us smiling. I knew from her sly smile she was thinking the same thing and I moved my lips to within inches of hers. Less than a second before our lips united, she screamed, "Ouch, ouch, ouch!"

My first reaction was to keep going and ignore whatever it was, but she pulled her foot up and kneed me in the groin. Thank goodness it was not a serious attempt to harm, but just a reaction to the pain she felt in her big toe. Pushing me back, she flopped onto the floor and grasped her foot. I immediately noticed the tip of her white sock had a quarter-size spot of blood on it. In her typical language she said, "Holy shit! What did I stick in my toe?"

As she sat on her behind among the shiny floor boards, the sock was snatched off and I do believe if I hadn't been present, she would have stuck that big toe in her mouth. Trying to fan the leftover embers from the fire we had burning, I offered to kiss it and make it better.

Laughingly she took a swing at me and said, "I'm really hurt, you ass; is that all you ever think about?"

Realizing she wanted some sympathy, I figured it was a small price to pay for the possibility of better relations later. Sitting down beside her, I pulled her toe to within inches of my eye and plainly saw the cut she had received. She insisted we find the weapon that had injured her biggest little piggy so I joined in and we searched the floor. There was nothing to be seen by our four keen eyes or felt by four hands rubbing the floor. So, what's a little pain when there is so much pleasure to be had? "Let's just let it go and we'll fix your toe and…"

I was abruptly interrupted with her demand. "No, I want to see what stabbed my toe."

With renewed apathy, I joined her to search again. Frustrated, she kicked the molding with her good toe, where the wall met the floor. By mere chance I happened to be looking at the area when her foot hit the piece of trim work. A momentary flash of gold appeared then disappeared and captured my curiosity, so I moved closer, wondering if my eyes had deceived me. There was nothing to see but this intrigued me and in a room with a ghost, I wanted to find out what I saw. Falling back to the scientific methods of high school physical science I told Salley to recreate the conditions that caused me to see the flash. Without hesitation, she whacked the molding again with her sock foot and as if on cue, the flash occurred again, but this time I pinpointed the exact location and zeroed in to solve the mystery.

First, with our noses inches apart I pushed the fancy baseboard molding that covered the bottom of the wall and saw nothing. Then pushing and holding the quarter-round wooden strip at the bottom of the baseboard, I made the little gold switchblade appear and disappear but it was still a mystery as to what it was or how it got there. Like a cat after a mouse my wounded cohort darted to the kitchen and I heard her rummaging through a drawer. Returning in a flash with screwdriver and pliers in hand, Miss Handywoman pried the molding up from the floor a little and I grabbed the sharp tip of gold, squeezed hard and pulled. Suddenly, we were gawking at a tarnished old gold star with one shiny tip. Completely hidden from the world, only one of the five tips could be seen and that tip was only visible when the molding was pushed against the wall. That tip had been polished each time a floor mop pushed against the wooden finishing strip.

Holding it with the pliers, I turned it around and noticed it seemed to have had something attached to the back and we agreed it was probably a pin that attached it to clothing.

With the most serious face, Nancy Drew said, "I've got it!"

She paused just to tick me off so I said, "What?"

As if waiting for me to take the bait she began singing, "You can trust your car to the man who wears the star—the big, bright Texaco Starrrrrrrrr!"

Without giving her a chance to escape, I dropped the tool and seized her in a bear hug. I had learned that controlling her hands and arms was crucial when trying to steal a kiss from her. We rolled over the ancient floors that had so many stories to tell.

As we rolled, we laughed and I was trying my best to steal a kiss, but she wouldn't let me near her lips and kept laughing until our rolling took an abrupt halt as my back hit Sully's shins. Briefly pausing in my attempt to smooch I glanced up to see what had stopped us. Honestly, I almost choked to death on my spit as I jumped up coughing. Putting on a useless act of innocence, I came face to face with Sully. Of course this made Miss Jocularity go completely hysterical, laughing so hard it caused her to gasp for air like she was crying.

Talking to myself, I kept saying over and over, *Just keep your mouth shut and be ready to run.*

Finally, she calmed down somewhat and was only breaking into laughter every minute or so instead of constantly pointing to me laughing. Still infected with the titters, she got up and walked over and kissed Sully on the cheek. He never spoke but she started talking and was doing enough for all three of us. Picking up the star she put it in his hand while she explained how we found it under the molding near the floor. She even produced her stabbed big toe as evidence.

The rumpled old man with a five o'clock shadow from yesterday, just stared at the star as she flipped it over to show him the back, where something had been torn away. Acting as if he held a million dollar diamond, he never looked away from his hand as he wandered, seemingly stunned, into the mess he called his office and pushed the door closed. Still laughing, she skipped toward the kitchen singing, "You can trust your car to the man who wears the star…" I followed, not sure of what had just happened.

As I sat at the stone table in the kitchen, Salley was oblivious to my worry. It would have been impossible to explain the war being waged among my emotions. As my black-white façade eroded, guilt and fear had combined in a portion of my brain. This forced me into an out-of-body experience at times and I often felt as if tragedy was about to consume my being. By casting my lot with these exiled and vilified people, my fate among the whites of Salleys Kitchen was now certain. I would soon join this loving father and daughter in being treated as a pariah and like watching from a window as a horrible event occurred, I saw my demise as if it were happening to someone else. I had found love and as a moth is drawn to a flame, even the fear of death could not stop me from giving my heart and soul to Salley Sullivan.

I was terrified in that I was going against everything I had been taught in the ruling white world. Blaspheming God and dishonoring my parents seemed to be the lowest form of sin and I was engaging in both of these iniquities on a fulltime basis. My soul would be damned to eternal Hell and my mother would see that I occupied the hottest and most excruciating part of the Devil's underworld. How low I had fallen from the pedestal she had constructed for others to see me upon!

To my peers, my parents and every other white person with whom I had contact, the love of my life was a nigger girl to be scorned and abused like every other black person in our community. But to me, the sight of Salley Sullivan took my breath and each time I was in her presence I felt like the luckiest boy in the world. How marvelous I felt, just being near her and watching her smile. I believed with all my being, she was my soulmate and I wanted to make this dream last for the rest of our lives. Helplessly engulfed in the eye of a storm, I was doomed.

And even though I hoped against hope, I felt terror would soon overcome the euphoria. No longer having the ability to move from the black world to the white world with anonymity,

I was now blissfully attached to this wonderful paradox and I readied myself for the coming onslaught. With an overwhelming exuberance, I was scared out of my mind.

There were many firsts for me during the summer of 1968, and eating a frozen TV dinner in an aluminum foil plate was one. Still on high alert just in case Sully came to his senses and launched into a fit of rage, I was looking over my shoulder as I watched Salley move about the antique kitchen. She walked to the refrigerator and I noticed her taking two frozen blocks of foil from the freezer on top. A red plastic radio was blaring out, *A one-eyed, one-horned, flying purple people eater, shore looked strange to me!* It was obviously elevating her mood to silly.

She put a little wiggle in her walk that I had never seen before as she headed to the oven, popped the blocks in and turned the dial for heat. With the same wiggle, she made her way back to the ice box and poured two glasses of iced tea and put them on the table. Reaching in an old wooden box with a hinged top, she kept her eyes on me as she pulled out two packs of orange peanut butter nabs and some pork rinds. Continuing to stare, she pulled two stools to the table. Made from seats taken from mule implements and bolted to the top of an old bar stool, they were certainly comfortable and unique. She continued to wiggle her bottom as she sat down and put her elbows on the tabletop.

I was sitting beside her in the other mule seat, but still alert and concerned about Sully's return. Thirsty, I automatically grabbed the iced tea glass and took a big gulp. Expecting the sweet almost syrup-like tea that my mother made, I gagged as I swallowed the cold, bitter brew, never suspecting anyone would serve iced tea without sugar.

"What in the crap is that?" I coughed.

Without expression and still staring she said, "Yankee tea. I can't stand sweet tea. Sorry, we don't keep sugar around."

I thought for a moment then remembered, "You liked it in the hayloft!"

176

She shot back, "It was all you had!"

Needing sugar I asked, "Well, do you have a Coke or something?"

Still with the stare, she deadpanned, "Sully keeps some prune juice in the fridge, but I think it's pretty old."

Giving up, I poured my tea in her glass and walked to the ancient carved out sink to fill my glass with water. As I approached the table, she stood up and grabbed my glass of water and set it quickly on the table, then engulfed my entire mouth in a wet, exciting, passionate kiss all the while grinding her body against mine. As quickly as she grabbed me, she pulled away and began dragging me toward the back stairs. Trying to keep up with her pace, she ordered, "Come on!"

Up the stairs we flew like a flash, all the while I was saying, "What about the stuff in the oven?"

Still on the move, she replied, "Sully'll get it."

As the door to her room got closer, "Do you think he'll mind if he sees us in your room together?"

The answer was a huge sigh as she jerked me into the pink polka dot room and pushed me onto the bed and started to unsnap my jeans. "Wait, he's right down stairs under us!"

She huffed out another huge sigh and she began to take her clothes off. About half way naked, she reached in her bedside drawer and grabbed something. Turning to me, she dropped a gold foil wrapped condom in my hand. "Put that on!"

Startled I tried to ask, "But I thought you were having your... you know."

Finally at the point of frustration she shot, "It's over; just shut up and put it on!"

I was to experience another first in '68! My Levis and underwear hit the floor as I squeezed the sides of the shiny package and presto, just like Burt said, a rolled up oily condom fell in my hand. Proceeding as Burt instructed, I put on my first condom and it fit like a glove. Trying to admire my handiwork, I was snatched into her arms and onto her naked body. My feet

177

hung off of the pink polka dot bed with my trousers around my ankles. Much more adept this time, we again raced forward in passion. Again, as she held me, I had that devilish urge and said, "What about my promise?"

Frustrated with desire she said nothing and covered my mouth with her mouth and darted her tongue between my lips. As before, the same incredible, sensational, heart stopping, head pounding, waves of pleasure pulsed through my body, but this time she moved with me and I watched her incredible eyes as they urged me on and on. Arching her back, she exposed her neck and drove me on as I began to kiss and brush my lips down her throat. Her body insisted we continue the pursuit and I wanted to please her with every fiber of my being, when suddenly she gasped for air. Her body shuddered beneath me and she huffed and huffed as I slowed to a barely discernible pace. No longer tense with urgency, that beautiful body relaxed and seem to melt as she wrapped her arms around me, kissing me, gasping and saying over and over, "Oh Wow!, Oh Wow!, Oh my — Wow!"

Everything had gone so well this time, I felt we had found perfection together. The physical pleasure was intense, but short lived. The best detail of the whole encounter, the phenomenon that lingered and filled me with complete and blissful satisfaction, was lying beside her, knowing I had given her such pleasure. I was on cloud nine simply because she was ecstatic. She giggled, she kissed me, she squealed, she shook and squeaked then hugged my neck and finally rolled me over and put her long shiny black hair across my chest and lay her head on my racing heart. We didn't move for a while then she softly asked, "Do you want to do it again?"

Man, what a question! I didn't know if I had the energy to pull my jeans up and she wanted to go again. Leaning up slightly to kiss the top of her head, I sheepishly said, "I don't think I can."

With typical quickness she lifted her head and pulled that silk-like hair across my face then captured my eyes with her eyes and said, "Maybe later and it's probably best because your thing has lost his attention."

No quicker than she had spoken, she jumped up and walked naked into the bathroom and turned on the water. I saw her peep around the corner of the bathroom door and take a glance at my 'thing'. She smiled and said "Wait just a minute." She emerged with a steaming hot wet washcloth, tossed it over my inattentive area and flopped back on the bed beside me. I gathered myself and held the washcloth in place while doing the 'pants-around-your-ankles' shuffle into her pink bathroom. During my clumsy move to the toilet, she was up on her elbows looking at my butt and gave the following report: "Did you know you had dimples on both cheeks of your ass?"

I thought - *Take a cheap shot at a man when he's vulnerable.* Deciding not to say anything, I was sure there would be an appropriate time to get her back.

As I was taking care of business she yelled into the bathroom, "I am really about to starve. Let's go eat lunch!"

My immediate thought was, *Oh no, the food is in the oven!*

I looked out of the bathroom door and she knew what I was thinking. "I'm sure Sully heard the bell and took it out of the oven; he always does that for me."

But I was thinking, *Does he know what we've been doing up here before lunch? He'll read my guilty face like a book!*

I walked out of the pink potty with my jeans and shirt restored to their proper position, with a look of horror on my face. "I can't go out there and face him! He'll know exactly what we've been doing!"

She was back in her jeans, sweatshirt and sock feet and nonchalantly said, "I'm sure he has probably figured it out by now. Who do you think bought me the condoms?"

Wild eyed I yelled, "Who bought you WHAT?"

Again, completely at ease and heading for the door, she casually said, "It was no big deal; they weren't that expensive. I thought I needed some tampons last night and he drove me to

Shuler's Drugstore to get them. After finding what I needed, we went to pay. Behind the counter there was a display of condoms just like the one you had in the hayloft. I asked the druggist if he would grab a box of those condoms for me. He looked at me and then looked at Sully. I didn't know what he was thinking so I said, "Daddy, could I get a box of those Gold Trojans?"

Totally bonkers, I implored, "You just saw them and asked him to get you a box of Trojans and he got them and paid for them without any conversation?"

With the door open and wanting to eat, she said, "He stared at me a minute then told the man to put a box of them in the bag."

Flabbergasted I asked, "You mean you have a whole box of condoms in your dresser drawer?"

Motioning for me to come out the door she said, "No, Sully kept them and told me I had to ask him for one or two when I needed them."

My head was spinning in disbelief and I was thinking to myself, *Holy Fucking Shit! What have I gotten myself into?* Walking down the enormous hall past the formal stairway I was trying to figure the implications and what all this meant. I started to say something, "You mean..."

She cut me off at the pass and said, "I love Sully with all my heart and he knows everything I do, because I tell him everything I do. He's the only man on earth I love unconditionally... so far."

Reaching the ornate back stairs to the kitchen I asked, "You tell him everything?"

She confirmed, "Everything!"

In a state of stunned disbelief, I followed her down the steps to the black, white, and brick kitchen where waiting on the table were two cooked TV dinners with forks and knives on top of a paper napkin and a glass of ice water for me. With the wiggle still in her walk she scooted in her sock feet over to the refrigerator and poured more of the bitter tea in a new glass with ice.

She pulled the top off my foil contained dinner as the steam rose up to the wrought iron pot rack above. Pulling the top from her dinner she was quiet, but after a few seconds she looked over with those beautiful steel blue eyes and made me tremble when she asked, "Have you ever been in love?"

I couldn't answer so I shook my head no.

She softly said, "Me neither."

Curious as to how this meal would taste, I waited to see if she wanted to say grace. When she didn't, I joined her and began to cut up what was called Salisbury steak—a hamburger patty floating in a compartment of gravy. Two other foil pockets held wax-like green peas and mashed potatoes with a crusty brown shell over them. Surprisingly, it was edible but the peas tasted like chinaberries. Mysteriously the radio volume had been turned down, when suddenly she heard Steppenwolf being introduced by the fast talking DJ and weird sounds sprang from the radio.

"Oooo! Oooo! I love this song!"

She dropped her fork and bolted for the counter. Turning the volume up near maximum, she started dancing as *Magic Carpet Ride* belted from the radio. Just to show her I had a move or two I joined her on the brick dance floor. My friends from the field were the best dancers in the world and they often tried to instill a little rhythm in me. They always laughed and said I danced like a white boy but I tried my best to hold my own with them. Just as I started to groove, the kitchen hallway door flew open and the slouchy old man himself came shuffling into the dance hall. She ran over and grabbed him around the neck, kissed him on the cheek and announced, "I feel groovy, man! Dance with me, Sully!"

Unperturbed, he continued to the wide door leading to the porch. He stopped just before heading out and said something. Automatically, I turned the music down to hear what he said.

"Do either of you know a three letter word for 'in thing'?"

She jerked my hand away from the volume knob and jacked

the music back up. She blew Sully a kiss and yelled, "RAD, MAN, RAD."

With my heart in my throat I decided I had had enough dancing and sat out the rest of the song, amid her taunting and pleading with me to dance with her.

At 3:30, we were looking down the black ribbon-like paved road as it meandered up and down over the ancient dunes. A yellow school bus popped up on the furthest sandhill, so I gave Salley a quick kiss and ran down their driveway to stand in the middle of the main road. There was no one on the bus with Dooney and of course, he acted like he was not going to stop. I had played chicken before while Daggar was driving the truck in the hayfield and found the secret to be, just don't flinch and hold your ground. I hoped Dooney would, like Daggar, decide not to run me over, but he misjudged his braking ability a little and slid the bus to a stop over the top of me while I held onto the black bumper for dear life. He never got out of his seat to see if I was hurt, just opened the door and waited for me to get up and on the bus.

Of course, Salley had watched the whole thing and came running to my aid. I dusted off and stood in the bus doorway sandwiched between the two of them. She started in on the raw-boned redneck with a tongue lashing that would have cowed most, but the old river rat gave as good as he got and I was glad I was between them. Finally he said, "Get the fuck out of the way!"

Dropping the clutch, he started off. She screamed at the top of her voice for him to stop. I don't know what possessed him, but he stopped. She climbed up one step to where I was standing holding the door handle and shot a mean stare at the bus driver, then turned to grab my head and lay a lip lock on me like you see in the movies. She ground her mouth into mine and cleaned my tonsils with her tongue for at least a minute while Dooney watched. Leaving me gasping for air and weak-kneed she hopped off the bus, crossed in front and gave the greasy haired young man the finger. He looked at me and I shrugged my shoulders. This time he dropped the clutch and floored the accelerator with no intention of stopping, but a disguised smile snuck across his face.

I didn't sit down because I figured he wasn't going to stop at my house and I would probably have to jump, but to his credit, he did slow down a little as he neared my driveway. Closing my eyes, I jumped and rolled. My smile returned after opening them and realizing I hadn't killed myself. I stopped by the faucet in the middle of the yard to clean up a little and drank some water, then walked in the house as if nothing had happened.

My mother coldly said, "Get your clothes changed then take the Farmall over next to The Griddle and plow those short rows that your daddy left this morning." It didn't seem right for the last quarter of the day to end in such an ordinary humdrum way because the first three quarters had been the most exciting school day ever!

***

The next morning, as she got on the bus, Salley tossed three Hershey Bars tied together with a red ribbon in Dooney's lap as she walked back to sit by me as usual. He looked at the chocolate, then in the big mirror at her, trying to decide. About half way to school he tore one open and began to chomp it down. I looked at her and she looked at me then Dooney shot a glance at us as he broke off another piece of the chocolate and worked it into his mouth. As usual, we got off the bus last and walked straight to the back of the track, through the little thicket of pines and got into the trash-filled car with Sully. We did that for three days and no one from the school said a word.

Sully knew his daughter had already completed the qualifications for her high school graduation and was only going through the motions to get her diploma. He also knew his friend, the principal, had committed an egregious faux pas and now, did not want to make trouble in any way. Neither Sully's daughter's nor my absence presented a problem for the school administration. They gladly looked the other way. In fact, having the despised couple away from the school gave them a measure of relief.

Never one to follow convention, Sully was a pragmatic man who loved his daughter immensely. Having noticed an improvement in her behavior since our meeting, he was hoping it was a sign of maturity and her moving away from the vexing mischief that had gotten her into so much trouble. Though he knew nothing about raising children, he wanted his little girl to be happy as she approached womanhood. He had watched me grow up and heard Wes and others in the Black community speak of me. Though I never knew of it, he had often wondered aloud to Wes how a man and woman so filled with hatred and bigotry could have produced a son like me. They agreed it had been good for me to grow up in the cotton field with kindhearted folks around me. Though he never displayed it, he was overjoyed that his troubled daughter and I had found one another and he considered our relationship to be fortuitous and wanted it to continue. Once on the ride from school to Salleys Kitchen, his daughter was telling him how much fun we had had together. With a deadpan face, he looked straight at me and raised his eyebrows, then asked if I knew a word for happily opportune. I quickly said, "No sir!" But he knew the inevitabilities our hormones would produce and his practicality led him to do some things others might think inappropriate. Later in life, I would have a greater understanding of the honest and practical love he had for his daughter and greatly admire his forward thinking.

Salley brought a big purse on Wednesday and opened it to show me a carton of Lucky Strike cigarettes with a red ribbon tied around it. When we got off the bus, she left them in the driver's seat before we headed for the alley behind the school. As we climbed into Sully's old Ford, he was, as usual, working a crossword puzzle and asked if we knew a five letter word for AWOL. Back at the Sullivan farm, we had to unload a truckload of alfalfa hay that Sully had picked up in Aiken from the folks that furnish the thoroughbred training track. This was one time I didn't mind throwing hay bales into the loft. She couldn't get his old truck to crank so we could put it back under the equipment shed. Having been around Wes and pieced together equipment all my life, I quickly taught her how to roll it off and pop the clutch to crank it. She was thrilled and afterward made it sound like I was a genius. I basked in her praise and soaked up her kind words like a sponge. After lunch we showered together and wasted gallons upon gallons of water, but had pleasure beyond measure. When Dooney stopped the bus in front of the mansion, I really thought about not getting on it, but quickly realized the peril it would cause and reluctantly kissed her goodbye. Knowing it would only be for the afternoon and night, I climbed aboard for the short ride to purgatory.

Once home I was quickly reminded of why I hated that farm. My father announced that I would be staying home from school on Thursday and Friday to help him get some things done around the farm. He said he would call the school and tell them I had to stay home, but I told him there was no need because I was a senior and they didn't care if I missed. That night I contemplated taking a few of my belongings and walking to Salley's house but I could not summon the courage and I dared not use the phone. I had no way to tell her my father wouldn't let me go to school on Thursday or Friday. When the bus slowed down at my house on Thursday morning, I was sitting on a tractor at the end of the driveway. I motioned for Dooney to go on by my stop with a lump in my throat. There were some jeers and laughs thrown out the windows at me but I heard Dooney yell, "Sit down and shut up!" That crazy river rat made me smile for the only time that day. On Friday I was disking around the end of the field beside the road when Dooney passed; he didn't slow down or wave.

Chapter Twenty

I spent Saturday morning side dressing my father's cotton and that afternoon pulling any weeds that had jumped up along the long green rows. Salley's day was a little less arduous, in that Sully took his little girl for a pedicure and some shopping in Aiken. Still horrified about her telling her father of our carnal get-together, I wondered how he could act so reserved at the news of his daughter having sex with the boy next door. It was completely opposite from what my father's reaction would have been to the same news. Being that honest with either of my parents was mind-boggling. A relationship that loving and honest sounded like the greatest gift that could be given from parent to child and I envied Salley and Sully. I would have been elated just to have had a conversation with my mother or father, never mind being open and honest.

The next morning I was impatient and forced myself through the compulsories of church on autopilot and returned home with one thought in my mind. Inhaling my Sunday dinner, I saddled Blackie and we flew to the creek. Three and a half days without seeing or touching Salley had driven me near insane. On the edge, I promised myself if anybody or anything tried to stop me from seeing her today I would destroy them. The moment I saw her standing beside Spot, my heart began beating furiously and I couldn't get to her fast enough. Jumping off Blackie before he stopped, I fell and my head hit the sand. It only made me more furious and I stood up ready to beat Blackie with a stick, then she called my name and time stopped. Running to me, she brushed the sand from the side of my head then wrapped her arms around my neck and kissed me with a fiery passion. Pulling back from our kiss, she was grinning like a mule eating briars. I noticed she was wearing a backpack as she grabbed Blackie's and Spot's reins and walked into the creek without saying a word. Once in the cool water she turned to face me with one of the Gold Trojans she had gotten from Sully between her teeth. In scant seconds, I was holding the ole sparkleberry bush back out of her way as she led both horses down the stream. With that cunning little mischievous smile, she stopped for a moment to give me a passionate kiss as I strained to hold the mass of limbs out of her way. Finally I had to pull my head back and stop the kiss to say, "If you don't get past this bush soon, I'm going to collapse and these brambles are going to devour us." With a sexy little smile, she slowly sauntered onto the island just as my strength was exhausted and I could hold it back no longer. The weight of the bush pushed me across the creek and to my knees on the far bank. Watching me climb out of the sparkleberry brambles like Brer Rabbit, she was tickled silly.

"Why are you so cruel?" I asked. She could tell her latest mean joke was taking a toll on me. Quickly, she pulled me onto the blanket she had spread and began to undress me as she rubbed my aching muscles and kissed me all over my body. Each time I would start to say something, she would put her finger on my lips, so I finally gave in, relaxed and let her lead. Then standing, she slowly took off her clothes and took charge as we lost ourselves in a passion for which I had longed for days. Afterward, with my head in her lap, she soothed my anger and petted my ego.

She told me Dooney stared at her all the way to school on Thursday and hung around the bus acting like he was checking the tires until she got off. Quietly, without looking her way, he said, "I saw James on a tractor when I passed his house this morning; I think his daddy is making him stay home and work." He must have known, under her tough cover, she was upset when she saw I was not on the bus. Without any further conversation, he turned and walked away.

She smiled and said, "Sometimes the most unexpected people can help you."

As I dozed in the sun, she pulled her version of a picnic from that little backpack of hers. She proudly presented me with a mason jar of sweet iced tea and I told her it was the best tea I had ever tasted. She immediately called me a liar and I began my appeasement exercises which made her even more suspect.

"It's very good tea, maybe not the best I've ever had, but close."

I didn't want to do anything to hurt her feelings and I wanted her to know I was sorry for the way I acted when I arrived. My life at home was pushing me to the edge and I felt like I was about to explode until she cut my fuse. As we lay beside each other on the soft pine straw, we began to talk about life. I don't think either of us intended to have such a serious discourse, but our island offered us such a sense of comfort and security that our talk became an intimate discussion of our hopes and dreams for the future. Homes, places, people, schools, religions, death, children, careers, cars - even clothes were discussed as for the first time we opened up and laid bare our true feelings and thoughts.

After a lifetime of letting others dictate my every move, she wanted to know my honest point of view and demanded I be completely truthful. Using my ability to maneuver around tough subjects, she knew immediately when I said something just to please her and would scold me. Our conversation turned into a truth session, something that was out of my comfort zone. As the afternoon progressed our discussion became more open and profound and ended up being the most intelligent, thoughtful and fulfilling dialogue I had ever had with another person. Salley had a way of unlocking my heart, my mind and my soul to pull the real me out of a lifetime of mute darkness. Having an opinion and offering it without fear of repercussion was a new and exciting responsibility, for my truth coach made me defend my way of thinking and tell her why I believed in certain principles.

No one had ever allowed me to express my true beliefs and suddenly having to defend them was a challenge. When she asked me if I believed in God, my answer was a repetition of the words I had heard in church. She would not let me off with such a contrived answer and demanded I tell her what I really believed. When I told her I believed in a being that helped guard and guide our lives, but didn't necessarily believe that much of the Bible, she smiled and accepted my answer without an ounce of judgment or criticism. Feeling more comfortable about letting her see the real me, I was ready to tell her everything I felt. Then she asked me if I believed all people were created equal and I quickly said, "Yes, everyone — male, female, black, white, red, yellow, brown — no matter who or why or where or what they chose to be, they should be treated equally."

After saying all of that, she looked me in the eye and said. "Do you think it is right for two women to love each other and live together as a married couple? What about two men? Should they be allowed to love each other and live together as a married couple? The Bible says it's a sin and people who do that are going to hell."

Boxed in, I swallowed hard, because I didn't want her to think I was weird or perverted, or an atheist, but I knew she would make me tell the truth so I bared my soul. "No one can tell someone who they love, be it a man and a woman, two women or two men. It doesn't work that way. You are given one half of a certain type of love at creation along with the desire to find someone else that has a half love that perfectly matches your love. When matching loves are found they can be combined to create a perfect love. Life is a search to find that perfect match and no one knows with whom it will be found. Most often it is found between a man and a woman, but it can be found between two women or two men and there is nothing that anyone can do to change that fact. If you try, you will make life miserable for those with perfect matches and I hate people that make life miserable for other people."

She smiled and said, "Wow! You are a free thinker. That's the kind of thinking that can get you labeled a queer."

Very concerned, I urgently asked her, "You mean you think that's wrong? Only a man and woman should be allowed to love and live with each other?"

I assumed my truthfulness had given her reason to push me away. I was thinking to myself, *Damn, Damn, Damn! Why did I open my mouth? I always say the wrong thing at the wrong time!*

From where she sat beside me, she turned with tears in her eyes and put her arms around my neck. With her head on my shoulder and her warm breath on my neck, she said, "I believe everyone should be allowed to love and be with whomever they choose. It's just that Sully is the only other person I know that has that belief. I've never met anyone else who believes the same as us. It's just a little overwhelming to know I have been lucky enough to find someone who is a perfect match to my love."

Speechless with relief, I knew this girl was wonderful, but now my soul was telling me I had found that once in a lifetime, perfect match. We were creating our world on our island and we would separate ourselves from the narrow-minded people of the world. Salley Sullivan renewed my spirit and for the first time ever, gave me reason to believe there was a wonderful life waiting out there for us. I was starting to believe there was true goodness in the universe.

Staring at me with those sparking pools of blue, she told me, "I believe our coming together was predestined; that the power you believed in guarded and guided us and brought us together for a definite reason." As I held her in my arms and stared into her eyes, she said, "I love you with all of my heart and I want to be with you forever."

With my heart over the moon, I told her, "I love you with every fiber in my body and want nothing more than to be with you until the end of the world." Admitting for the first time that we loved each other was a momentous point in both of our lives.

In our budding relationship, the newness of sex was great and always exciting when we were together, but I now began to believe it was just a small part of a huge and thrilling life that was unfolding before us. As we melded our hearts and lives together, the possibilities that beckoned us were infinite and we so wanted to be together in whatever was ahead. More so than any of our previous rendezvouses, that afternoon forged in us an undying desire to spend the rest of our lives as one. Unaware of the future we faced, this Sunday afternoon became an anchoring point to which we would each cling in the years ahead. It was an unforgettable experience that took place while Spot and Blackie enjoyed the tender grass.

***

Time seemed to be speeding away and significant events were racing into our world. After 12 long years of public schooling, a long awaited, culminating event was almost upon us. Graduation was one week away and scheduled for the next Sunday. Qualifying seniors would march, wearing caps and gowns, into the school gymnasium and receive their official diplomas. This formal procedure was only a part of the ritual celebration.

Traditionally, the last 10 days of school were considered, unofficially, optional for graduating seniors. This last charade of public education was usually divided into 3 periods: a few days of hell-raising around town, to include painting the water tower with Class of 'the appropriate year', then a 5 hour journey to Myrtle Beach for participation in a 2 to 3 day drunken stupor/orgy and finally, the long ride home followed by a few days to sober and mend from the excesses. This rite of passage would include most every male and female walking across the stage on Sunday.

Hungover, fighting diarrhea, with bandages covering self-inflicted wounds and sporting the occasional black eye or missing tooth, most seniors that would walk across that stage in the gymnasium planned this rowdy interlude of debauchery for years in advance. Staying in legendary motels that graduates from previous years had passed on in oral tradition, most hoped to have tales of their own to tell from their vague recollections of the semiconscious 3 day period. This was a co-ed time of release from normal inhibitions and with the help of much alcohol, a time of wantonness and sexual fantasy was brought to center stage. It often led to some strange bedfellows as the sun rose over the Grand Strand the morning after. Many times, discoveries were made of secret crushes and desires that had never been known. Sometimes inebriated blunders caused friends never to speak to one another again; other times, life mates were discovered, with the impetuous quickie marriage on the way home to be announced at graduation. But mostly nausea, headache, and sick silence occurred over the 5 hour ride home along with a few exchanges such as the realization: "Oh my God, I don't have on any underwear!" then a flash of memory and "I can't believe I did that!" or "You did what?... With who? Oh my God!" and "How was it — did you talk afterward?"

In keeping with tradition, the sojourn to Myrtle Beach could be made any time during the last two weeks of school but the optimal day to start the decadence and depravity was Wednesday. Most everyone who had not arrived at the beach earlier, planned to arrive around lunch on Wednesday, allowing for a warm up to the festivities. That afternoon, the search for rooms and friends began along with the consumption of copious amounts of beer. That night, brews were traded for real alcohol as trash cans, kitchen sinks and bath tubs were filled with gallons of fruit juice and quarts of grain alcohol with Dixie cups placed at the ready. Thus began a period of sporadic memory loss which was to continue through the day and night of Thursday.

Friday was the day for sobering up and rounding up all inebriated, incarcerated and infatuated friends. With luck and bail money, most were able to leave the jurisdiction of Myrtle Beach after lunch Friday with hopes of arriving home before midnight. Stopping for the usual poop, pee and puke in Columbia, some didn't drag back into town until the wee hours or later Saturday morning. This schedule always left about 24 hours for gossip to be fully disseminated and further sobering up before Sunday's graduation. Also, the motel rates were cheaper on weekdays.

When Salley told me of the seniors on the bus talking about

going to Myrtle Beach, it suddenly reminded me of the trip Burt and I had planned and the deposit I had paid him. Since 10th grade, we had planned to go Myrtle Beach together and watch out for each other, but all of that was off now. He had thrown in with a group of town boys right after our fight, but I never told my parents that we were no longer friends. News of Burt's and my friendship ending never got back to my parents; I assumed because he wanted to keep the deposit money I had given him. This beach trip was still going to be a blast!

Sunday night I told my parents that Burt and I were leaving for Myrtle Beach after school Monday and I would return Friday afternoon. I would call them from Roy Asholee's Store when I got back. A group of boys were going together and if we were going with them, we had to leave Monday afternoon. Our plans had been made a long time back and the memory of the money I had to beg from them for the deposit had been eclipsed by the turmoil during planting season. They had not remembered my trip either, until I sprang it on them Sunday night. I knew the old man would launch into his usual cussing, 'you sorry little worthless shit' routine and tell me I was leaving when he most needed me. He didn't have Wes any longer and bad things had been happening in a pretty regular sequence on the farm. I had already heard him talking about hiring a mechanical cotton picker to make the harvest this year. He was on edge and now I wasn't going to be around as his whipping boy!

He would have really blown a gasket if he had known that for three days last week I had been riding the bus to school then walking to Sully's waiting car and spending the day at the Sullivan Mansion. On this Monday, as I waited for Dooney to pick me up, I had my suitcase with me and was in a dream world. I was not due home that afternoon and was supposedly headed for Myrtle Beach with Burt, to return on Friday afternoon.

I was standing just inside the front door waiting that morning waiting to leave for school when my old man walked up and said, "Don't you get locked up down there," then he laughed and said with a sneer, "and watch out for the 'clap' from them strange women at the beach." Not wanting to hear any more of his advice, I opened the door and began to walk out, when he said, "Here!" and threw a fifty dollar bill on the sideboard. I knew my mother made him give me the money; no one else could have persuaded him to do it. She did not want people to think our family was poor. I grabbed it and jammed it into my jeans pocket as I picked up my bag and walked out to meet the bus. Nothing else was said.

Once at school, Salley and I made our usual departure and met Sully on the familiar old road behind the school. Pulling around back of the mansion, we rushed onto the sprawling back porch, then traipsed through the kitchen and up the now familiar back stairs to her room. Sully was parked under the equipment shed finishing a puzzle. He needed just one last word to complete it— a nine letter word that meant suitor. Though I was still apprehensive, his presence was not nearly as scary as before. The neat part of this visit was the fact that I would be staying all night. We had dreamed and longed to sleep with each other for the entire night and often said how wonderful it would be to wake up in each other's arms. I had only spent the night away from home a few times, so butterflies once again hummed in my stomach.

Salley had never learned to drive and we spent the day in Sully's old rattletrap truck with Salley trying to drive it around the edge of the fields at the back of the farm. She didn't have a clue of how to change gears so her driving lesson was a ridiculous 2 person effort with me in charge of the clutch and gearshift while she concentrated on the accelerator and steering wheel. We didn't tell him, but a good bit of Sully's latest bizarre crop, the yellow flowered canola, got squashed around the edge of the field more than once. Late that afternoon we parked the suffering old truck under the equipment shed and together we took care of her few chores.

We had a supper of frozen TV dinners because Salley's cooking was equal to, if not worse than, her driving. Afterward, we went upstairs for our long awaited night together.

The sleeping arrangements began awkwardly as I sat stiffly on her fluffy bed. She finally made me take my shoes off and I gradually relaxed and lounged with her on top of the polka dot bedspread. We watched *Perry Mason* on a little portable black and white TV from her bed while she ate Ritz Crackers from the box and kept saying, "He did it, look at his eyes! He's guilty! I know he did it!"

Turns out, she was wrong, but she said she thought Della, Perry Mason's secretary, was a very sexy woman. I couldn't let that go unchallenged, so I said, "Are you crazy? She's old!"

Of course an argument ensued over what was really sexy and she ended up throwing crackers at me after which, Matt Dillon and *Gunsmoke* came on. As Miss Kitty appeared on the grayscale screen, I said "Now there's a sexy woman!"

She huffed, got up and walked into the bathroom and returned wearing pajamas. She looked at me and said, "Put your PJs on so we can get under the covers." To which I replied, "I don't wear pajamas in the summer. I sleep in my underwear." She replied, "But you'll be almost naked!" With a smile my reply was, "Almost!"

She put her hair in a ponytail and put Noxzema all over her face, wiped it off, then brushed her teeth. Before she got into bed she dug through my suitcase to find my toothbrush and with a smile put it beside hers in the bathroom. Once under the covers, she stuck her cold feet on my butt and fell asleep in two minutes. I watched the end of *Gunsmoke*, turned the tiny TV off and climbed under the covers with her. It was the craziest thing, but the overwhelming sex thing had taken a short break and I lay beside her and enjoyed immensely the sound of her breathing.

On Tuesday we walked down to the island and got naked.

My excitement at the sight of her nude body was evident and she thought it the funniest thing but her giggling and the cold tannin water soon deflated my... ego! With my urges postponed, we lay on towels in the soft grass to let the sun suck the water from our bodies. Like the afternoon on the dock, the sun seemed to make her want to talk about her family. She began telling me about her older twin brothers who lived near her mother in the mountains. Describing them as 'very Indian', she said they were very big into the ways of the Cherokee culture and though she loved them, she had never had a close relationship with them. They had homes, families and children of their own and when she and Sully visited her mother, there was always a family get-together outside around a huge fire. With a little sorrow in her voice, she wondered aloud what her life would have been like if she had stayed in the valley and grown up with her mother. With what she told me, I knew she loved her mother, but Sully was the light of her world and she worshiped him.

After lunch, we helped Sully unload some bags of soybean seeds into one of the barns behind the house. In his professor-like voice, he told me that the unpretentious soybean could solve many of the problems of the world if planted and grown in large quantities then distributed at low cost. He felt it was the crop of the future and he wanted to become as familiar with soybeans as he was with cotton. I laughed inside, but did not say anything; that would be a world changing event!

That night we couldn't keep our hands off of each other as we washed the few dishes after supper. While I finished up at the sink, she darted upstairs and left me alone in that big old kitchen. I wasn't a scaredy-cat, but I sure didn't like being left alone in that rambling castle full of ghosts. Drying my hands, I put it in high gear and darted up the steps just a few seconds behind her. When I walked into her room, she was wearing a tiny camisole as she sat on her bed looking down at one of the gold condoms she was flipping over and over in her hand. My clothes were coming off the minute the door closed and when I jumped on the bed beside her, I noticed she seemed to be in a melancholy mood. Selfishly, I thought immediately, *I bet her period started, damn, she always acts funny when that happens!* Leaning over to kiss me, she licked my lips and then moved her head back. Holding out the condom she said, "Do you want this?" I quickly grabbed it and started to open it when she said, "You know we don't HAVE to use it."

I froze for a minute and looked into her eyes. *Was she saying what I thought she was saying? No way! We couldn't do that now… but… it would be pretty cool.* Looking at me in silence, she was waiting on my response and I knew I had to tread lightly on this subject.

Finally, with the seriousness of a heart attack, she said, "There's nothing that would make me happier than to have your baby."

"What?" I said in a state of shock and fear. "Have you gone crazy? We're not old enough to have a baby and I don't have any way to provide for us. What are you talking about?"

With a serious face she said, "Sully would let us live right here and farm with him." I was now terrified!

Without one thought I shot back, "I'm not living in this place and around these people! And I'm certainly not going to raise my children here in this redneck snake pit!"

"But I thought you loved me and wanted to spend the rest of your life with me!"

Completely speechless, I sat in stunned silence trying to figure the best way out of this mess into which I had stumbled. I loved her with all my heart, but I wasn't daddy material yet and especially not here!

When she couldn't control herself any longer, she broke out in hysterical laughter and between gasps for air she pointed to me and said, "When you get really worried you have the funniest look on your face! It cracks me up! You nut, relax, we're not going to have a baby! I just love to see you get all roiled up. I'm sorry, but you are so funny! I guess that's why I love you!"

Looking down my body, she noticed her little joke had again caused my excitement to wane. Standing, she twirled around in her little negligée then pushed me down on the bed and started kissing me like she was going to suck my face off. Sliding her hand down my stomach, she made my excitement return almost immediately and I felt her putting on the condom. She stopped and smiled at me, "Well, I'll be damned; you *can* put them on with one hand!" I grabbed her naked body and flipped her on her back.

Later, as we huffed and puffed for our breath, she said, "Wow! I should always make you a little mad before we do it; that was fantastic!" Then she cuddled next to me and we fell asleep deep in her soft comforter among the pink polka dots.

Wednesday, we spent the day in the mammoth old barn fixing and cleaning things. After lunch she insisted we clean out a stable for Blackie when he visited and make it horse-comfortable to her standards. We hauled all of the old bedding and a century's worth of dried manure out of the enclosure next to Spot as he pawed and whinnied, wanting our attention. Spot remembered well the box of apples she had persuaded Sully to buy her from the produce stand in Aiken. His nickering and persistence at getting her attention finally paid off as she stopped to show him some attention and give him an apple. When the guest stable was finally up to her standards, she sprayed the entire stable with bug spray, then sprayed a light mist of water on the dirt floor to keep the dust down. Finally, she put wheat straw down for bedding, alfalfa hay in the rack and tossed a coffee can of horse chow in the rubber feed bucket hanging on the wall. Blackie would think he was in high cotton when he stayed here overnight.

That evening we sat on the 130-year-old brick hearth in the kitchen and drank Nehi grape drinks while roasting hot dogs over a little fire. Sully brought us graham crackers, Hershey bars and marshmallows to make these things called S'mores. Salley could not believe I did not know what they were or how to make them — another first in '68. After the sticky, gooey, chocolate delights, we used the neatest thing — an ancient long handled little skillet with a wire basket over the top to pop popcorn. We ate until we were about to burst, then waddled upstairs to watch TV and do some heavy petting. Lost in our passions, we heard the phone ring downstairs. Sully must have answered it and we sat in silence for a minute, wondering who had called, then fell asleep like fat little pigs.

When I felt the sun on my face in the morning, the sound of voices outside the door got me out of the frilly bed in a hurry. As I threw on my jeans and a shirt, my sleeping partner came back in the room with a big cup of coffee in her hand and offered it to me.

I turned up my nose and said, "Oh no, coffee tastes like mistreated stump water!"

With a condescending smile she pecked me on the cheek and said, "You can put cream and sugar in it if you like. Oh, that's right, we don't have any!"

She sipped the black liquid with delight. Walking in the bathroom she coldly said, "That phone call last night was from your parents looking for you. Sully told them he hadn't seen you."

There was a long pause and then she stuck her head around the door with a toothbrush and white foam coming out of her mouth. "I guess we'll just have to run away together." I wasn't falling for that story again. Showing her sad face, she quickly took the brush out of her mouth and yelled, "HA! I'd never run away with you, you sleep in your underwear! Anyway, that call was from Dr. Carr. He wants me to bring Spot in for a vaccination and while he's there I'm going to get them to fix his left hind shoe, it's loose. Think you could drive Sully's old rattle trap truck and pull Spot's trailer into Aiken?"

My answer was, "Well, since it's a fact that you can't, I guess I'll have to do it!" She stuck out her white tongue then returned to the running water. When she came out, she wanted to kiss me with fresh toothpaste breath, but I quickly recoiled, remembering I needed to do the same.

When I walked down the steps into the kitchen, she had on a big floppy hat and looked like a tomboy hippie I had seen on TV. With her pink Foxcroft T-shirt, jeans, boots and that wild hat, she looked a little crazy, but the craziest thing was that truck to which Spot's trailer was hitched. It was her driver's training vehicle, that old rusted-out fertilizer truck that Sully had owned since before I was born. Whenever we saw him driving it to the field, Wes always said, "He out ust leave dat ole heap long de edge o dey field an' lets hit rust in peace."

There was nothing on it that didn't rattle, smoke or make a weird sound. The seats were worn down to the springs with burlap fertilizer sacks now employed as seat covers and the clutch was almost completely worn out, so you had to kind of jam it in gear. The passenger's side door had been a casuality of one of Sully's dreadful driving deeds and was wired shut, forcing driver and passengers to get in through the driver's side. But hitched to the back was one of the nicest two-horse trailers I had ever seen. It had a room in front for Spot's tack along with feed and hay. She said it was where she changed into her riding habit when she went to competitions. Spot might be pulled by a junk heap, but he was riding in style.

She walked to the barn to get Spot as I kept the truck running and wondered if we would make it to Aiken. She loaded him up and we pulled out of the sandy yard as Sully sat in his car with the newspaper inches from his face trying to remember a word that meant gypsies with a b in it.

In an effort to disguise me, she put her big floppy hat on my head and gave me a pair of Sully's old glasses with the lenses removed. We did not want to be recognized by the locals but, I felt really stupid. Stopping twice, once at Warner's flowing well and once at a flowing well at Shaw's Creek, we had to refill the steaming radiator. Arriving at Dr. Carr's office, she ran in to tell the Doc we could not shut the engine down. I backed over to the side and they unhooked the trailer. Then with a smile, he shook his head telling me to go across the street and back the smoking heap up on a little hill so we could roll it off to get it started later. I think he just didn't want people to see that thing in his parking lot. Leaving the hat and glasses in the heap, I walked back across the road and looked at Salley standing beside the vet. She had a beaded headband around her forehead and looked like a beautiful Cherokee princess. She introduced me to the Doc and told him I was her friend. With a smile he shook my hand and asked if I was from Virginia.

I said, "No, I live next door to Salley."

With another smile he offered, "How convenient."

Backing Spot off the trailer, we found out it would be well after lunch before the farrier could come by to fix his shoe. The old vet saw our concern and told us about a polo practice on Whitney Field. Having long wanted to see that high-brow equestrian sport in person, I thought this would be a neat opportunity and Salley readily agreed. With some of my beach money, we bought bologna, bread, potato chips, candy bars and Nehi drinks at the Jockey Commissary near the railroad track where they unloaded horses in the old days. Supplied with a picnic extraordinaire, we walked down South Boundary through the green tunnel of live oaks growing over the avenue. Cutting through by the Standardbred stables and track where they train horses for harness racing, we watched some of the high stepping potentials in action. Then following one of the many unpaved 'horse ways', we passed the Aiken Training Track as some beautiful thoroughbreds were making their way back to the stables. Laughing and joking, the exercise riders sat atop the tall, sleek animals wet with sweat from their workout. Dancing and jumping, they wanted to run, but were being made to walk and cool down. Traveling further along the sandy loam lane, we passed a number of beautiful homes shaded by old oak trees with stables nearby and soon knew we were close when we heard the shouts of riders and thundering hooves. Finding the polo practice field near Whiskey Road, we watched from the rail for a while before I spread out one of Spot's blankets on a nice grassy area near the end of the playing field. With my hippy-looking girl beside me, we picnicked in the sun while watching the pros practice. Every horse was a muscled, athletic beauty with its mane roached and tail braided into a net-like cover to keep the mallet from getting tangled.

One of the men on the field was particularly loud and had a foul mouth. Each time the white wooden ball jumped the rail and there was a break in the action near our area of the field, he kept staring at Salley. Changing horses several times, he cursed and chastised the grooms constantly telling them what they were doing wrong and how he wanted things done. He rode each animal with reckless abandon, spurring them to full speed then snatching the reins, bringing them to a sudden full stop. Over and over he drove the horses until they heaved for breath and as each tired he would switch to another. As he himself seemed to be tiring, he swatted one of the balls in our direction and it hopped over the short wooden barrier. I grabbed the beat up ball and tossed it back on the field, but he twirled his mallet in a circle like a baton and smacked it back to us.

Snatching the reins, he wacked his sweaty horse on the rump with his mallet and made him trot over to us. As he approached us, he smiled and said, "That's for your lady friend. I think I know her."

We stood up as he approached the low rail and climbed off the beautiful lathered up gelding. He took his helmet off then offered his hand to me. "Hello, I'm Jon Chesterfield." Then he turned away from me and focused solely on Salley. He kind of tipped his head to her and said, "Did you ride with the Foxcroft Equestrian Team? I saw your shirt from the field and thought I recognized you. You rode that Appaloosa, Spotacular, didn't you?"

She smiled that Miss America smile and offered him her hand, "Yes sir. I'm Salley Sullivan; we're in town today to get one of his shoes fixed."

The sweaty man was short, with dyed black hair on each side of his head and bald on top. He was wearing tall black riding boots almost to his knees with menacing looking stud spurs protruding from the back of the heels. He was dressed in a red-trimmed polo getup and stood beside his horse holding his mallet and helmet as he beamed when he realized his memory was exactly right. Then Salley tried to introduce me. "This is my friend James," she offered with her hand on my shoulder. With a momentary glance at me, he didn't offer his hand again and quickly returned his focus to Salley. Acting kind of cocky, the middle aged man continued to stare at her then pointed with his mallet to a magnificent house across the street with an equally impressive barn just to the rear.

"That's my house over there. Please come by and have some lunch with us. Jonathan is there; do you remember him riding with Evansdale Academy?"

She nodded yes and they chatted about what a shame it was that she didn't participate in any competitions last season. He kept insisting she come to his house so she looked at me and I shrugged my shoulders. She finally accepted his invitation and he quickly jumped on the massive animal and galloped to his house. I didn't know what we were walking into, but I followed her into the yard of his compound.

Between the stables and huge home there stood a massive white tent with three spires sticking up among the overhanging trees. In and around were landscaped terraces with all manner of wicker furniture and tables. Under the tent, on the lush grass, were a number of tables and chairs along with a convenient masonry bar. An outdoor fireplace stood just outside the tent and all around there were black men wearing white jackets, standing at the ready waiting to serve him and his guests.

He gave his horse to a man at the barn and hurried up to the tent saying, "Have a seat and I'll send some drinks out in a jiffy. The other guys will be coming by to join us after their horses are put away." His offer was made as he hurried on his way into the mansion.

I could have told him we had some Nehi grape drinks in the bag, but I don't think he was talking about that kind of drink. Taking a seat, we looked around at the opulence and smiled at each other. In just a few minutes, a preppie boy our age walked out wearing sunglasses and told me he was Jonathan Chesterfield, Jr. He then turned and hugged his former opponent. Like his father, he ignored my presence and steered Salley and their conversation away from me. They talked while I stood around like a third wheel. Eventually I moved to one of the many tables and took a seat. Almost instantly, a maid brought out a tray with a crystal pitcher of fancy lemonade, several glasses, two or three dozen little sandwiches and a large lump of something that looked like potted meat. She placed the silver tray on the table in front of me and filled one of the goblets. Taking a small silver plate from a large stack, she placed on it some weird looking crackers and pieces of the thinly sliced potted meat. After she left, I put one of the thin slivers on a cracker and found it tasty in a strange way.

While I munched on the crackers and whatever, I watched Salley talking with her friend and it became obvious she wanted to leave. I listened as she tried to end her conversation with 'Little Jon' and kept saying we needed to start back to the vet's office and pick up Spot. Finally, she just told him we had to go. He insisted on driving us in his Jeep and would not accept 'no' as an answer. Reaching in his pocket, he pulled out a key and pressed a fob on the key ring. Immediately, one of the eight garage doors across the landscaped yard began to open. Disappearing into the mammoth garage, he backed out a Jeep that was painted like a rainbow. I jumped in the back, holding the wet paper bag and, of course, she sat by him in the front. Arriving back at Dr. Carr's office, he asked how we were getting the trailer home and she pointed across the road to the heap parked on the little hill and smiled. He laughed out loud but quickly regained his composure and offered to tow the trailer to Salleys Kitchen with his Jeep. She told him no again, but he kept insisting.

Feeling meager, I walked over to the wreck of a truck and let it roll down the hill a little before popping the clutch to fire it up. Sounding like a stock car at Darlington and steaming like a locomotive, the old heap came to life. I watched from the seat of the rattletrap as Salley pointed to me and shook her head no, before giving him a half-hearted hug. Writing his phone number on the wooden polo ball his father gave Salley, he handed it to her with a big grin on his face. As he pulled away, she flashed her Miss America smile again and waved to him. While she sat with her foot on the gas pedal and kept the piece of junk running, I hooked the trailer to the old truck and loaded Spot. With his shoe fixed and vaccination complete, we headed back to the sandhill crossroads.

As we were leaving town on Old Tory Road, she dug around in the wet paper bag to find the church key and opened the last Nehi saying, "He thinks his shit doesn't stink. When you went across the road to crank the truck, he told me he would take me to dinner one night, somewhere nice for a change. Didn't ask if I wanted to go or anything! What an ass! I told him you were my fiancé." That news kind of stunned me for a moment.

After riding without talking for a while, I broke the silence by asking, "Does that mean we're engaged to be married?"

Smiling from ear to ear, she coolly said, "I don't have an engagement ring and I know you haven't asked Sully for his permission, yet!" My smile beamed from ear to ear as I began thinking of a way to get a ring and approach Sully.

Looking in my direction, she asked if I liked the crackers and foie gras I was eating at the Chesterfield house.

Taking a sip of the grape drink, I passed it back to her and said, "You mean that potted meat stuff? Yeah, it was pretty good."

She smiled and said, "He told me it was pâté de foie gras with fresh French black truffles."

Scrunching my face I said, "What?"

Still smiling she said, "It wasn't potted meat, it was goose liver and black mushrooms from France."

She handed the grape soda back and I took a gulp and let it linger in my mouth before I passed it back and said, "You're kidding! Is that how goose liver tastes?"

Continuing to smile she nodded her head yes and said, "That stuff is $150 per pound and there was probably a pound on that serving tray."

I shot back, "It wasn't that good!"

She guzzled the last of the grape elixir then burped loudly with a devilish smile. As I struggled to keep the old heap on the road while we crossed over the South Edisto River Bridge, she leaned out the window and tossed the polo ball into the black water. Moving back to my side, she kissed me on the cheek, then stuck her tongue in my ear and nibbled my earlobe. It's a wonder we made it back to the mansion.

Chapter Twenty-one

Arriving home, we unloaded Spot and Salley rode him around a little to see if he was comfortable with his new shoe. All seemed well, so we decided to give him a bath before she put him back in the barn. Knowing it was coming, but not really caring, I knew she could not be trusted with the hose and sure enough, she tried to drown me several times before I could get it away from her. Erupting with hysterical laughter, she loved taking advantage of anyone and reveled in the pleasure of seeing them look stupid.

After putting Spot in the barn we headed back to the house, soaking wet. Suddenly she slipped in one of the puddles and faked a sprained ankle. Boy was I an easy mark for her. Hurrying to her side, she grabbed my arm and pulled me down into the mud then proceeded to cover my head and face with globs of dark wet dirt. Knowing retaliation was at hand, she squealed as I coated her with mud, leaving both of us looking like two pigs in a puddle. It was kind of fun to go crazy for a while, but cleaning up was going to be a pain and I started by turning the hose on myself to get most of the mud off.

Taking control of the hose, my fellow mud-hog tried to wash off the black dirt and get most of it out of her hair. In two seconds she was out of her clothes and standing naked in the mud. She hosed herself off again with her nipples shrinking to pebble size then she said, "Strip off! You're not going up to my room dripping mud all the way. Who do you think will have to clean it up?"

I hesitated trying to think of an alternative and without giving careful thought to things such as, *Is the door unlocked? Is anyone else home? Will she do something mean?* and of course, *Where's Sully?* But she kept telling me to hurry up and quickly we were both buck naked.

With me following her, she made a dash for the brick floor of the mammoth kitchen. But we didn't make it that far because the door was locked! She said the key was not under the cobblestone, but not to worry, "I'll run around to the front and use that key and then come through the house and let you in."

With a desperate look of panic on my face I begged her to be quick. "Hurry please!"

I waited and waited and waited then I heard her running up the steps to her room, so I banged on the door and in a last ditch effort yelled, "Open the door, damn it! OPEN THE GODDAMN DOOR!"

But no such luck and yep, you guessed it, Sully turned into the driveway and tooled around to the back of the house in his mobile trash can with a crossword puzzle under his nose. While he was wracking his brain for a nine letter word that meant humiliated, I was in panic mode. In desperation I ducked behind a ladder back rocking chair which didn't cover much at all, especially in the most important area. Maybe if I had been a couple of inches shorter or a couple of inches higher, but as it was, I ended up right in between with just my hands to cover specifics.

Sully was definitely in deep thought as he put one foot in front of the other and pulled the rails to climb the steps at a snail's pace. As the rail ran out and he stepped on the floor of the wide back porch, his eyes followed the wet footsteps across the floor to the bottom of the see-through rocking chair and my bare feet. Raising his eyes slowly, he finally leveled his face on mine so that we were in the proverbial situation of eyeball to eyeball. Of course, this was the moment Miss Funny Bunny decided to open the door, fully clothed and act as if she had been home all along.

"Hey Daddy, we've been back a while. I've been waiting on you, where have you been?"

The old man was having none of her foolishness. He glanced to my spot behind the useless chair as the prankster began to spread it on even thicker. Looking at me she kept up the charade.

"What are you doing here? I thought you had gone home; oh

my God — you're naked!"

Slowly turning his head back to his daughter, she finally lost her composure and doubled over in hysterical laughter and pointed at me in frenzied glee. Throughout her caper, Sully never said one word and finally, fed up with her hurtful joke, walked passed his uproarious daughter and into the house. Still delighted with her prank, she reached inside the door and threw me a towel. She continued to laugh and saying, "Your face — you should have seen your face! It was so funny!" I never saw a damn thing funny about the whole affair.

I was still not speaking to her after my shower and if I had had a place to go I would have gone there. Her pranks at my expense were getting a little out of hand and while I sat watching TV on her girly bed with my back leaning on the iron headboard, I was fuming. As daylight began to fade, the door opened very slowly and my friend, who had exposed me to such humiliation, the girl who had stolen my heart, the girl who had changed my whole life, the girl who I had been with for the last week, sheepishly came into the room and quietly eased up to the bed as if she were trying not to wake me. Standing in a little girl pose with her tummy protruding as she bit on her thumbnail, the quiet words came from her mouth, "I'm sorry."

There was a long silence because I wasn't about to let her off that easy. I stared at my crossed feet and held my tongue. Finally, she had to say something and the words came out softly again. "Do you remember asking me why I got into so much trouble at Foxcroft?" It's always my curiosity that pulls me into the tomb of doom and this was no exception as I turned my head to face her. "Well, that's the kind of thing I did."

As she spoke, two tears appeared in those glorious steel blue eyes and slid down her cheeks like wax dripping down a candle. Snubbing followed, then as she sniffed her nose and hiccupped she said, "I ruined all my friendships and made most of the teachers hate me doing things like I did to you. I don't know why I can't stop trying to make people look stupid, and it always ends up with me looking stupid."

By this time she was really squalling and I took her in my arms. Holding her close, I whispered in her ear, "It's okay, it's okay. I was hurt a little but I'm getting over it because the whole thing was pretty funny."

She snubbed with her face still buried on my shoulder, "Do you really mean you don't hate me?"

Like the sucker I am I answered, "I don't hate you, I love you."

Without so much as a wet spot on my shirt or a tear in her eyes, she pushed me away and said, "Good because Sully is fixing us steaks tonight and I'm going to try to talk him into letting us have some wine. Come on, let's go downstairs."

I stood frozen, saying over and over in my head, *You fool, you fool, you fool…*

As we clumped down the back stairs and into the grand kitchen, Sully had placed a wide cast iron grill on the cooking crane with three huge steaks on top. As we arrived he was just pushing it over a bed of red hot coals in the bottom of the fireplace. In just a few minutes the smell in the room was intoxicating. He had three crystal wine snifters on the coal black table beside an old bottle of wine that looked as if he had dug it out of the ground somewhere. After wiping the dust off of the bottle, he wrapped it in a white towel and used a corkscrew to open it. Carefully and deliberately, he poured about two sips into two of the glasses and filled the other glass three quarters full, then sat the old bottle on the slate table. He picked up the glass with the most wine and motioned for us to each take one. Carefully placing the goblet to his nose, he inhaled the aroma of the amber liquid then held it in front of his forehead and said, "To my family and their triumphs and tragedies." After his pronouncement he took a sip of the wine and kept it in his mouth, sloshing it around like it was the last gulp of a cold grape Nehi on hot summer day.

That was one of the few times I had heard him say something that wasn't pertaining to a crossword puzzle. We put the glasses to our noses, smelled and looked at each other, then slowly placed the edge of the glass on our lips. Very cautiously we tilted it to let the liquid ease its way over our lips and onto our tongues. Holding it there for a moment we both swallowed and tasted the wine which quickly caused us to gasp for air, as the burning, dreadful-tasting liquid slid down our throats. I knew she was thinking the same thing I was thinking, *Holy crap! Is that what wine tastes like?*

Sully held his glass up again and said, "To those that through adversity follow a moral law."

I appreciated the sentiment of his words and thought them to be profound, but it was a little too soon for me to burn my throat again. Salley must have agreed because we both put our glasses on the slate table without tasting the wine a second time.

Setting his glass on the table, too, Sully walked over to the grate and turned the steaks, making them sound off with a sizzle and drip liquid fat into the cherry coals below with a spit and momentary flash of flames.

The girl that had infuriated me moved to her father and put her arm around his waist as she looked at his eyes with that gaze that always took my breath. This was the first time I had seen them close together and I became fully aware of the family resemblance. Though her skin was a much darker bronze, their facial features were identical and the shape of their smiles was interchangeable. But more, they had the same eyes. How could her beautiful eyes in such a spectacular setting be the same as those of that wrinkled and stubble-darkened face? As they say in The Kitchen, he had marked his pup well.

Still looking deep into his eyes she asked, "Are you going to talk to us tonight?" He didn't answer, but smiled and quietly asked her to set the table in the dining room. She objected, wanting to eat in the kitchen by the fire. She told him she didn't want to eat with a ghost and frankly, I didn't either. He smiled and nodded his head in agreement. Pulling a starched white table cloth from one of the multitude of drawers, she stretched it across the end section of the black stone table, and then dashed out of the room, returning with a silver candelabrum that held three long milky white candles. Disappearing again, she returned with an old wooden box and placed it on the counter near the sink. Opening the case, it revealed its green velvet lining with silver spoons, forks, and knives stacked together in order. From another of the bank of drawers, she produced three linen napkins then once again dashed out of the kitchen and returned with a rectangular basket full of matching china all monogrammed with a silver "S" in the center. Effortlessly, she set the century-old table in simple, but breathtaking elegance. She lit two oil lamps near the rear of the room, turned off all of the electric lights then set the candelabrum in the middle of the tablecloth and lit the three candles.

Her father flipped the steaks for the final time, waited a second or two and carefully placed each one in the middle of a white china plate. Then to my surprise, he used the fire tongs to remove three rosin coated potatoes from a three-legged cast iron pot nestled in a bed of glowing fire coals. Placing each on a square of brown paper, he let them cool a bit, and then opened them with a putty knife to reveal the steaming insides. He took a huge metal spoon and removed the flaky white goodness from each with one fell scoop. Placing two mounds of the steaming spuds on each plate beside the sizzling steaks, he quickly plopped a spoonful of butter and sour cream along with a toss of salt and pepper in a manner that indicated he seemed to know what he was doing. Finally, he pulled a lettuce lined bowl with pieces of cantaloupe and watermelon from the refrigerator. I was more than impressed as we sat down together, he on one side of the table and the two of us straight across from him. She quickly crossed her heart and repeated a prayer and Sully began to carve his steak. I made a mental note to ask her about crossing her heart before praying.

The steaks were perfect, tender and juicy with a little pink and the potato was something I was obligated to put on my list of wonderful firsts in '68. It was very tasty with a rosin flavor that one might think distasteful, but amazingly delicious. The melon was cold and sweet and Salley enjoyed it as much as I did. It was a memorable meal, but I had no idea of the memory Sully was about to make.

Every so often he would refill his glass with wine, but he didn't offer - nor did we ask - for more. Cautiously I sipped the iced tea. To my surprise it was sweet tea and she smiled with pride. We ate in silence until Sully finished his meal and refilled his glass with the last of the amber liquid. He took a swallow with all the motions of before and looked up to the ornate tin- tiled ceiling. As our eyes met we shared a smile, then Sully began to talk.

"This land, among these sandhills and pine trees, has been owned by my family since 1783. It was a time just after the great upheaval of the Revolutionary War and though the people of the area were happy to be free, devastation had visited most every person in the region. Many loved ones were lost during the war. Others, neighbors and friends, were lost because they had remained loyal to the king and were now outcasts in the new nation.

"The prominent men of South Carolina joined with other colony leaders in Philadelphia to draft a constitution that would guide the radical new democratic style of government being proposed. Here, near the South Edisto River, where the Tory Road forked away from the Charleston-Augusta Road, a young man decided this to be the place for his new beginning.

"Wandering into the sandy crossroad to rest during his travels, he followed the familiar sound of millstones grinding grain and soon found fate smiling on him. With the help of the kind people who had brought him to this new world, he was able to purchase this confiscated British land and a mill. On this property, James Anthony Sullivan started over.

"Serendipitously meeting a beautiful 16-year-old girl named Salley Kontén Galphin, they fell in love and worked together to carve out their new life. With resilience, practicality and hard work, they became role models to all who harvested the great

213

bounty of this frontier's edge. On this land they created a hub around which other men and women would gather and join in their efforts to form a free society that welcomed all. The honesty and integrity that permeated their lives made everyone admire them and seek their friendship as a community grew around them.

"James Anthony, as Salley called him, detested slavery and thought it a fatal flaw in the United States Constitution. Though Salley was manumitted by her grandfather, her mulatto mother remained a slave and she understood well the brutality and degradation of human bondage. As a couple, they detested the institution and never missed an opportunity to speak their minds on the subject. This was not thought odd in the backcountry where most Scots-Irish men worked by the sweat of their brow to survive and owed no man. But in the low country, where the gentry did not work or sweat at all, it was almost heresy.

"Each new generation is saddled with a tremendous burden of responsibility, an obligation to take the reins and decide the path of the future. It was the dream of my great-great grandparents, James Anthony Sullivan and Salley Galphin Sullivan, to not only carve out a life here on the edge of the wilderness, but to build a life that followed a virtuous and moral path that their descendants would follow. They taught their son to follow the Golden Rule and reminded him that only by the grace of God had he been allowed to inherit such a gracious and prosperous life. But as all parents learn, modeling good behavior and teaching morality are only influences they can share. Ultimately, their children would have to decide the path of their future. It could only be hoped that their offspring would remember their teachings and choose the right path."

Sully paused and looked into the fire as he continued, "Unfortunately, their son, my great- grandfather, James Anthony Sullivan, Jr. (AKA 'Lil Sully), was pulled by the love of a woman and the gleam of gold onto a path that he knew to

214

be wrong and allowed slavery to become part of this land. His decision ultimately cost him his life, but worse, his actions perpetuated an atrocity and heaped unspeakable turmoil upon the lives of every generation to follow. Some of my ancestors, in the generations afterward, recognized the catastrophe he orchestrated and worked to right the wrong, but others, as he did, allowed the lure of riches and power to pull them away from their civic responsibility and denigrate the virtues of their heritage. They allowed an evil to continue and the darkness and woe of their decision still affects us to this day. Through the years, vindictiveness and bigotry have ballooned to horrible proportions amidst the people that live in this once caring community that my great-great-grandfather built. His blood runs in my veins and that is why I live on this land and try, through all my frailties, to make change happen and right the wrong."

Sully stopped talking and walked over to the fireplace and began to poke the coals. We looked at each other with solemn faces and pondered the story he had begun to tell. After a few minutes he came back to the table, finished his glass of wine and began a story that has lived in my mind to this day.

"My grandfather and grandmother tried desperately to change the mindset of the community and bring it back to the hardworking and vibrant hub of cooperation it was in the beginning. But Trip (James Anthony Sullivan, III) and Lou Sullivan could not inspire in their children the desire to continue the efforts that were needed to bring about change.

"Grandma Lou gave birth to 2 girls, Sarah and Anda, during Reconstruction. Her final child was born well after the middle years of my grandfather's life — a boy that was, of course, named James Anthony Sullivan, IV, but called Jay by most. He was raised in this house and grew up, like his older sisters, hating the time he spent here. Most of the people alive at that time had vivid memories of the Civil War and the Reconstruction period of occupation. It was still an unhealed wound and the people in the community harbored resentments and did not speak highly of the mansion or the Sullivan family.

It was said their teenage years were hell, but I don't allow them that excuse. For some reason, they did not inherit the kindness of my great-great grandfather, nor was his sense of civic duty passed to them. Early in the gay '90s, Jay met a pretty young girl from Aiken. As seems to be the pattern with most members of the Sullivan family, after a stormy romance, they were married and my two older sisters, Harri and Abbi were born soon after. While my grandfather Trip was alive, the family grew cotton and my parents lived here in the mansion with my sisters. There was plenty of room and while the cotton didn't make them rich, it provided an adequate living for the family and those that would help them.

"I am Trip Sullivan's last grandchild and the only male child born to Jay Sullivan. I am the last of the five James Anthony Sullivans to live on this land. Unfortunately, I came into this world a few years after my Grandfather Trip died and never had the honor of knowing him. At his death, my father and his two sisters divided the money made from Trip Sullivan's last cotton crop and made plans to leave Salleys Kitchen. Wanting to sell the Sullivan farm, my Grandma Lou stopped that effort when she reminded them that everything Trip Sullivan owned was left to her upon his death and she would not agree to it being sold while she was alive. Frustrated, her daughters pitched a fit and in an attempt to reconcile, Grandma Lou agreed to sell two parts of the farm that Clara Sullivan, the second James Anthony Sullivan's wife, had purchased and were not originally Sullivan land. The girls took the money and moved away from the community with their husbands and families. My father, Jay Sullivan, also packed up in preparation to leave. Telling his mother she could come with him or stay and live alone, my Grandma Lou said she made the worst decision of her life. Just after the turn of the century, she begrudgingly joined her son and his young family as they left the sandhills of South Carolina for the promise of the golden hills of southern California.

"First finding employment as a farm manager in the San

Joaquin Valley, Jay Sullivan found all that glittered was not necessarily gold. He became disillusioned sharecropping alfalfa on someone else's land and fighting for the precious water. As wealthy and powerful men began to buy up land and water rights, Jay Sullivan moved to west Los Angeles in hopes of finding a new way to make a living for his family. His version of the story tells of him meeting a man peddling a modern way of life soon to be in every household. As bountiful amounts of water loomed in the city's future, it seemed his new business was a sure bet. He felt sure every family would soon have one of the new-fangled water closets in their house.

"My father soon made indoor plumbing his obsession, which allowed our family to have the most up-to-date and well-advertised toilet in the area. He seldom spoke of the mansion in Salleys Kitchen while I was growing up because it belonged to my Grandma Lou. He focused his life on selling water closets and making money and we enjoyed a comfortable high middle class life in west Los Angeles."

After that mesmerizing soliloquy we sat staring at Sully with our mouths agape as he turned the empty glass in his hand. Finally, he sat the glass down on the white tablecloth, took a deep breath and continued.

"I became an adolescent during the Roaring 20s, listening to the music of flappers as my older sisters danced and partied in the warm breezes of the California coast. Their dresses were hemmed almost to their knees with my mother having a hissy fit, but still sewing them as they wanted. It was a time of new cars, fancy clothes and posh people adorned with expensive jewels. Our family enjoyed a very comfortable life while I lived at home, but just after I started college, the stock market crashed and water closets were suddenly not a must-have item anymore. My father told me I had to come home and get a job because he could not afford to pay for school. Deciding to stay in South Carolina, I was suddenly on my own and had to pay for school the best way I could.

"During the decade of the 20s, my father bought gold bars

that he kept in our living room in a safe disguised as an ottoman. It was so heavy it started to separate the living room floorboards from the walls and he had to have workmen pour a new concrete floor and put the hardwood boards on top. Never showing them the safe, he told the workman what he needed and they built a wooden box for him. Covering it with material that matched his favorite chair, he fastened the box over the safe so only he could remove it and the wheels on it allowed him to roll it around on the reinforced floor. He opened it late at night while everyone was asleep and held the shiny bars, stroking them before putting them safely away. His obsession kept us from appearing wealthy, but unlike our middle class neighbors, he was financially comfortable before the crash. We lived frugally, not from a lack of money, but so he wouldn't have to liquidate any of his precious bars."

It was obvious Sully disliked his father. I knew how he felt, but I didn't say a word and kept listening as did Salley.

As a 12-year-old girl, Grandma Lou came to live in this house just after my Grandfather Trip returned home from the war and she became his wife at age 16. He was 36 years old and she said she loved him more than life itself."

Under the table my hand moved to Salley's leg and she covered it with her hand as my heart palpitated under my shirt.

"She told me that my Granddaddy Trip wouldn't sleep with her for almost three years after they married, so finally on Christmas Eve when she couldn't take it any longer, she walked into his room naked and climbed into his bed and slept with him every night after that until he died. They tried in every way to help the newly freed black folks in the area and even gave part of their family farm to the freed slaves who had worked there. The community people resented their empathy and tried in every way to run them out of the community.

"My Grandma Lou's mother-in-law, Clara Sullivan, my great-grandmother, despised everything they did to help the slaves she had once owned. She built this mansion and lived

218

here with her son Trip and his wife Lou until she died of tuberculosis. She brought a slave girl, Lou-Dell, to live here from her home in Charleston and Lou-Dell waited on her hand and foot until the day she died. Having confronted General Sherman and his men as they marched toward Columbia and watching the destruction they left in their wake, Clara was filled with uncontrollable rage toward anyone or anything from the North."

Sully paused and again picked up the empty wine goblet. Holding it and turning it in his hand, he continued, "The first battle of the war had taken her husband who had been her balance. A very headstrong woman, he evened her out and kept her from the extreme episodes of anger that could take her over. The news of his death at First Bull Run stunned her, but as did most of the southern women who lost their men, she became a stalwart supporter of the Confederate Cause and rallied all to defend the beloved homeland of the South.

"Her son, my grandfather, Trip, was taken prisoner during the same battle in which his father was killed and he was confined at Johnson's Island in Sandusky Bay, along the Lake Erie coast in Ohio. A prison for captured Confederate officers, he faced starvation and hypothermia during most of his captivity. He always told Grandma Lou his POW time was punishment for fighting for a cause he knew to be wrong. His story of coming home after the war was shrouded with mystery and he refused to talk about or discuss the hardships of his long journey back to Salleys Kitchen. It was only a few years ago that I found out he had also been a 'Galvanized Yankee' and fought in the Dakota Territory. He took that secret to his grave.

"Grandma Lou told me about my mother and father's hurry up wedding held privately on the farm in the middle of the creek that fed the millpond. She told me she would remember to her grave Delores wearing that white wedding dress and her mama and papa smiling like no one knew the truth. She told me she gazed up at the huge pine tree behind them in the middle of the creek during that ceremony and lost herself in wondering how the virgin longleaf had been spared to live so long."

Salley squeezed my hand and I almost swallowed my tongue. He was talking about our secret place. She looked at me with wide-eyed wonder and I knew she realized the same thing. Wow, if that tree could talk, what a tale it would have to tell.

Sully went on, "My Grandmother Lou always had resentment in her words when she spoke of her son, my father. She said Jay's wedding was only the tip of the iceberg of trouble he caused the Sullivan family."

It was obvious that Sully's grandmother was his role model and it was also obvious she was the reason he returned to South Carolina and his ancestral home. He continued his story while we listened intently.

"Of my two sisters born before me, Harri the oldest, was on the way a little before the nuptials and my other sister Abbi, was born only a year later. A few years later, I became the third 'oops' baby for Jay and Delores and in frustration, they gave me to Grandma Lou to raise. I consider that the greatest gift of my life. She instilled in me her virtues and gave me a longing to come home to South Carolina. With a true belief in the things that were honorable, just and righteous, she was never very religious and usually raised her nose to those who, as she described them, 'wore their religion like a new suit of clothes.' Never above cutting corners to reach her definition of 'fair and just' she infuriated many with her methods, doing something we refer to today as 'leveling the playing field'. With a multicultural troop of friends, she coerced and cajoled neighborhood folks into hiring her menagerie of Asian, Mexican, Black, and down-and-out people as domestics. She them then kept close tabs on them to ensure they were being treated properly. In our area of west Los Angeles, she was a force with which to be reckoned and a constant embarrassment for her son who was striving to climb the social ladder.

"During a formal political function for which my father had maneuvered for months to get invitations, Grandma Lou's surprise arrival floored him. She was adorned in one of

Delores' finest dresses with an elderly Chinese gentleman in tow wearing one of Jay Sullivan's old black tuxedos. The only hint of their social class was their sandals which they promptly removed at the door, promenading barefoot to the front of the ballroom to be seated with the mayor and some other very well-to-do folks. The table was engulfed in laughter and excitement the entire evening as my Grandma Lou and her friend entertained the group by tucking and twisting the table napkins into animals and spinning yarns to everyone's delight.

"As the evening came to a close she walked to the back of the room and put her arm around her son to ask if she and her friend could ride home with them. Furious, my father refused until his mother said she would tell the mayor of his refusing her a ride and ask him for a ride home. He quickly reneged. Returning to her table, the Oriental gentleman rose to take her arm as she announced to the table that her friend Mr. Woo was the finest Bonsai expert on this side of the Pacific. Then waving to Jay, she told the table of VIPs that her son - back there - was a toilet expert. She told them he had been full of it all of his life, but at least now he could get rid of some of it properly. Laughter erupted and as it subsided, she announced if any were to need Mr. Woo's or her son's service, their call would be greatly appreciated. After one final roar of laughter from the table, Grandma Lou and Mr. Woo graciously retreated and joined the embarrassed son and daughter-in-law as they made their exit. Needless to say, my father never got over that night, but his business grew larger with the city purchases from the mayor's office, so he was forced to contain his anger and she loved every moment of his annoyance. She and Mr. Woo often sat for hours telling each other of their homes far away."

Salley and I were totally engrossed in the story Sully was telling. I could see by Salley's expression, she was hearing it for the first time. I don't think either of us had any idea of the scope the Sullivan family saga encompassed. Neither of us knew the complete story or where it might end.

Chapter Twenty-two

Sully turned his seat to face the fire and barely audible, seemed to be talking to himself. He twittled with his napkin and touched it to his eyes at times, but then, as he stared into the fire, he continued as if he felt obligated to finish the story.

"On August 15, 1927 Grandma Lou and I left west Los Angeles in a Windsor Maroon 1926 Model T Fordor Sedan that she bought for $200. A gentleman who employed one of her friends as a domestic had dramatically increased his wealth during the stock market boom of 1926. Her friend, Renata, told her that since her boss had become richer, he bought a brand new Cadillac for himself and his wife. It seemed his old Ford did not have the aura of prestige needed for his new status in the community.

Having spent years planning her 'escape', the possibility of the out-of-vogue Ford being available was just the news she wanted to hear. Arriving at the well-heeled gentleman's house with her friend the housekeeper, she sat down at his breakfast table and was waiting when he came down for coffee.

Demanding to know her identity, she politely but frankly told him her name was Lou Sullivan, a close friend of Roy Cryer and she was there to purchase his old Fordor.

He laughed at my Grandma Lou and said, 'YOU are a friend of the mayor?'

She laughed at his disbelief along with him and said it was good to see he was in such a jovial mood because she much preferred to conduct business in a happy and cordial atmosphere. Becoming annoyed, the man in his pajamas and robe asked how she got into his house. She told him his housekeeper was a close friend and kind enough to let her wait inside until the gentleman got up.

The homeowner screamed for his housekeeper and demanded to know why she let this woman in his house and added, "Roy Cryer doesn't even know this woman exists!"

As her friend arrived with his morning coffee on a tray, Grandma Lou smiled at her and asked her if it would it be possible to bring the telephone over to the table. Pulling the long cord, she brought the phone to the table and set it in front of my grandmother. Grabbing the earpiece, she clicked the cradle up and down until an operator answered. Speaking into the funnel-shaped mouthpiece, she asked the operator to please ring Mayor Cryer's office. As she listened, she held the earpiece at an angle so the gentleman could hear the conversation. Not laughing as hardily as before, he listened as the lady at the city hall switchboard answered and announced, 'Mayor Cryer's office, how may I help you?'

"My Grandma Lou asked if George was in his office and said Lou Sullivan was calling. The owner of the Ford looked at my grandmother and wondered who this woman was. There was no sound for a few moments, then as he leaned his ear to the earpiece, he heard the mayor say, 'Hello Lou, how the hell are you doing and why are you calling so early in the morning?' She told him she was calling to make sure he was on the job and not sleeping in. My Grandma said you could hear his laughter booming from the phone and as it subsided she quickly said she was with one of the mayor's friends and wanted to buy his car. She told him the man's name and said he didn't know her and she figured the mayor might explain to him she was no crook. Laughter again boomed from the phone and finally the mayor said, 'Tell him you are my good friend and he better give you a good deal!' Then he asked if she wanted him to talk to the man. She said with a chuckle that she thought he got the mayor's message after which his laughter again sounded from the phone and he told her to come see him soon."

Salley's great grandmother sounded like quite a woman and I wished she was still alive. She would have been a great friend to have on your side. After a pause, Sully continued. "She used money saved over her 25 years of 'captivity' as she called it from selling eggs to the neighbors and taking in mending. Her cottage industry infuriated my father. He hated having a chicken coop at the edge of his backyard and loathed

223

having the clothes of strangers in his house, but she refused to stop her entrepreneurial efforts and always put her money away in a jar hidden in the ground somewhere behind the chickens. I tried my best to talk her out of buying the beautiful car. My father had purchased me a 'one-way' ticket to South Carolina for college and I knew he would gladly buy her a ticket, also. I didn't think she needed to waste her money on the car when she could just ride with me on the train. To say the least about my Grandma Lou, she was headstrong.

"After weeks of planning and saying goodbye to her friends, my grandmother announced we would be leaving at daylight the next morning. I packed my few things and put them among an assortment of items she had insisted we take. As we pulled out of the big city on our first leg of the cross-country trip, my Grandma Lou yelled out the passenger window to my sisters and parents with a huge smile on her face, "Goodbye and good riddance!" As perky as a spring chick, Grandma Lou had planned to set up camp and cook each night, but she didn't let me stop driving for 18 hours. She told me she wanted to make sure we were far enough away that no one could stop us and make us go back. I didn't know what she was talking about at the time, but I knew my Grandma Lou well enough to know we'd better not stop for a while. We traveled toward San Diego and hoped to use Highway 80 on our journey to South Carolina.

Newly designated the Dixie Overland Highway, our chosen route was purported to be the most efficient cross-continent auto trail available. Just after we turned onto Highway 80, we stopped for our first night and I set up our makeshift shelter. I pulled out the heavy portable stove and almost hurt my back. Grandma Lou opened the door to the small fire box and said, 'Get that out.' Looking in the sooty iron cooker, my eyes fell upon six ash covered rectangular blocks and as I reached to grab them I soon realized why she was in such a hurry to get out of town. Under the camouflage of soot and ash were hidden six of my father's precious gold bars. I remember saying, Grandma Lou, you didn't!

She returned, 'Like hell I didn't, he'll never miss it until it's too late. Mr. Woo fashioned me some brass bars that were identical and I swapped them. By the time he figures it out, I'll be in Salleys Kitchen and he can't touch me there! I don't care how mad he gets, it's my compensation for being force to live in exile for 25 years.'

Grandma Lou had her own justice system and though I was stunned at her bold and clever heist, I ultimately had to agree with her fair and just reasoning. She referred to her having the gold as a 'transfer of ownership', and I never heard my father mention the missing gold on the rare occasions I talked to him later in life. As she washed the pots and dishes that first night, she told me the details of the gold procurement. I wanted to know how she got the safe open.

Grandma Lou proudly said it took her years to arrange everything and she had the brass bars hidden under some of her flowerpots. My father was never careful taking the hassock off of the safe and she had figured out exactly how he did it. Figuring out the combination to the safe was the part of the caper for which she was most proud. She laughed out loud after she told me, "It was his damn fool birthday! He always did think it was the most special day ever." On an evening when he and my mother went out for a night with the bigwigs, she opened the safe and replaced three of the gold bars with her brass ones. She told me it was so easy she had Mr. Woo make her three more and did the same thing again. Deciding not to push her luck, she didn't try again but she said it was like picking pears off of a tree. She hid the bars in the old stove and waited for her time to escape. While drying the pots and dishes she had washed that first night, I finally understood why she wanted to buy the car. How does an old lady hide that many gold bars in her luggage without getting hemorrhoids and possibly a hernia?

My grandmother was quite a character. When the folks at the bank asked her, 'Where did you get a gold bar, Mrs.

Sullivan?'

With the boldness she exhibited all of her life, she said, 'I stole it!' Then with a laugh, she would say, 'Not really, you know in California the streets are paved with gold. You should go there and get you some of the riches.'

They thought she was a crazy old lady, but when the rumors got back to Salleys Kitchen, tales of stolen Confederate gold began to circulate. The old people of the community still hated the mansion and they kept the hate-fires burning by embellishing the old stories. They had heard the tales all of their lives and gladly added any new snippet that might come along. My grandmother laughed at the rumors and told me about the hatred of the Sullivan family during Reconstruction. She said the KKK burned so many crosses in their yard that people traveling through thought it might be a cemetery in front of the house. I loved to hear her laugh. So in a way, my father, Jay Sullivan, financed the renovations to his old home whether he wanted to or not. We had only one problem — we had to use the gold for so many things for the farm and pay for my school that it finally ran out. We never got to finish the outside and I figured since I was going to be the last person to live in it, there was no use to waste the money."

With a 'wait-a-minute' look on her face, Salley chimed in to say, "But I'm living in it now and I want to fix it back like it was when it was built."

Sully gave her some reassuring words. "I know you do sweetheart and I've made arrangements, so don't worry. Not only will it look almost like it did when it was built in the 1830s, it will also be on the National Register of Historic Places and wholly owned by you."

She ran around the table and kissed him while hugging his neck. Then quickly she ran back to give me the same treatment and sat hungrily waiting for more of the Sullivan family history.

He stopped talking as though he were finished and got up from his seat. Unsteadily, he walked toward the small door under the back steps that led to the basement. As he flipped on the light he said, "I put that light in so I wouldn't kill myself going down these steps." We followed close behind, just in case the wine in him did produce a tumble.

Shifting from one foot to the other, he jarred the stairway as he took each deliberate step moving down into the dank earthen room. The concentrated spotlight he had rigged was shining toward the back of the subterranean cavity but spilled over into the other areas enough to where we could see furniture, cabinets, bottles and other debris being stored. We followed him closely and constantly looked around the spooky cellar with cobblestone floor and walls.

As he passed several holes gouged out of the stone wall, he rubbed his hand over them and said, "My granddaddy Trip knew about the metal loops that had been put in this wall when it was built. He remembered them as a boy and hated them for they were used to chain up some of the house servants during the time of a slave revolt. He and his sister Ruth chipped them out with a hammer and chisel soon after he returned from the war. Grandma Lou said Clara, their mother, cursed them with every lick of the hammer, but they wouldn't stop until every metal loop was removed". Peering closely as we passed, it was eerie knowing humans had been chained in this basement.

There was a clear trail going to a large cabinet against the back wall. Once there, Sully opened one of the cabinet doors and put his hand on a handle-looking piece of metal. He turned it clockwise then pulled the cabinet and it opened like a door to reveal a room full of barrels and bottles.

"This was my great-granddaddy's wine cellar and he had it dug out and constructed before the house was built over it."

One wall had shelves divided into diamond-shaped compartments and it cornered into another wall where heavy racks held wooden barrels, some stacked on top of each other. Each section of bottles or group of barrels had yellow disintegrating paper attached with the vintage year and notes of climate, harvest, and other information about the aging process.

Sully reached for one of the dirty, dusty old bottles and as we turned to leave he said, "I was told all of this brandy was bottled by the slaves before the war. I would have never known it was here if my Grandma Lou hadn't brought me down here. I think all of it is blackberry brandy and I assume James Anthony Sullivan, Jr. made it or had it made before the Civil War. I didn't come down here much while Grandma Lou was alive, but after her death I have enjoyed it too much through the years."

Following Salley and her father, I was cautiously walking with them toward the stairway when we were engulfed by a strange draft of air and it was obviously felt by all. We were surrounded simultaneously by a cold and hot sensation that eerily consumed our little group. As the two of them stood at the foot of the stairs looking around, I bolted past them and hurried up the steps, taking them two at a time to quickly return to the safe brick floor of the kitchen. But the waft followed and kept us immersed in a cool and warm sensation. This sent chill bumps up my spine, basically spooking the hell out of me.

As the father and daughter reappeared from the bowels of the mansion, I blurted out, "What the heck was that feeling?"

There was a quiet pause as Sully used a knife to scrape the green wax from around the neck of the bottle and uncorked the brandy. Holding the opened bottle he said, "That was the boy next door," as he poured the brandy into our glasses. Then abruptly, he turned to face me with a stare of consternation. His words seemed to hijack his train of thought and stop him cold in his tracks. Looking to his daughter, there was an awkward pause before he turned to me and said, "But that's who you are, aren't you?"

I turned to Salley and begged for help with my eyes. I was apprehensive about the strange thing that had just happened and his tying me to the apparition was a little nerve-racking, not to mention eerily true. He looked back to the glasses and poured a finger's depth into ours, then filled his goblet almost full.

Quivering a little, I eyed the brandy in my glass. Remembering the cowboys on TV throwing back a whiskey at the bar for bravery, I thought I needed the same at the moment. Though my knees were knocking, I wanted to look tough. Recalling the first taste of the dark liquid Sully had poured in our glasses, I didn't want to be slowly tortured again. Acting without thinking, as I so often did when I was around Salley, I picked up the crystal glass and tossed the homemade brandy to the back of my throat and gulped it down all at once. Almost instantly, I knew exactly how it felt to swallow a piece of hot molten lava. It seared my mouth, throat, esophagus and stomach leaving a smoldering ash-like taste that reminded me of the aroma left in the air after a flash fire burns through a pine forest. Sully calmly reached over and took the glass from my hand as I coughed and choked from the after effects. My buddy patted me on the back and asked me if I was all right. What kind of question was that to ask a fellow who had just burned his guts out?

As if to say 'that's enough brandy for you tonight', Sully put my glass in the sink and walked over to sit down opposite us. Still trying to regain my composure, I steadied myself on the table and slowly sat down.

Holding his glass, Sully offered another revelation that floored us. With the effects of the brandy slurring his speech he told of his returning to the farm after meeting Salley's mother and encountering a young black man about his age. He said the local boy insisted on helping him with work on the farm and together they cleared the large overgrown field behind the mansion once it was tillable again, his new friend taught him the ins and outs of cotton production in the Kitchen.

Sully then said it was during that first year's cotton crop that he found out Wes' father was the son of a slave that had worked on the Sullivan farm. Though the brandy was affecting his motor functions, it didn't seem to have affected his thinking for he looked straight at me after revealing Wes as his longtime friend. With his eyes looking deep into my mine, he said Wes told him he had been born on the land that had been given to his grandfather by Mr. Trip Sullivan. His grandfather died after being free for only two decades, but was so proud to leave his son a farm. Trip Sullivan mentored Wes' father and watched after him until his death. As a little boy, Wes had played on a cotton sheet at the end of the rows while his mother and father worked the cotton on their farm. As he got older, he helped his father as they struggled to hold onto the farm and make a living.

As had eventually happened to all of the other freedmen that were given part of the Sullivan farm, other white men of the community swindled and stole the land away from them after the patriarch died. Wes told Sully of having an indelible memory of him standing under a big elm tree and crying as his family was forced to leave their home and walk away from the farm they had worked so hard to keep. There was only one elm tree that I knew of in Salleys Kitchen and I knew it well for I had stood under it many times and cursed my father. Sully said Wes was the reason he had been able to keep the Sullivan farm producing cotton and his Grandma Lou thought the sun rose and set on that young man's head.

Sully continued, "My grandmother was the source of much of the Sullivan history passed to me and my research has proven everything she told me to be true. Her stories told of the deep resentment the community showed Grandpa Trip. She said of her husband, 'I never knew a man to work so hard to help his neighbors only to be treated like a cur dog with mange.' Apparently most all of the white people of Salleys Kitchen hated him and his beloved horse. Each time he rode him through the community they sneered and turned their noses up. Some even threw things. Eventually he sacrificed his treasured horse in an effort to help the community."

With labored words, Sully continued, "A well-to-do farmer in Virginia had died and word found its way to my Grandfather Trip that his son had taken over the farm and no longer had a

230

use for the new-fangled engine his father had used. The Sullivan farm desperately needed a new source of power since the millpond dam had been wiped out when Sherman's men came through. He decided to trade his prized horse for the new power source. Grandma Lou said he tossed and turned quite a few nights trying to decide if it was the right thing to do. Finally, he made the long trip to Virginia to complete the deal. She said each time he used the engine here on the farm she knew he was thinking of his beautiful spotted stallion, Two Bears, that he was riding when they met."

Salley sat contemplating what her father had just said when suddenly her beautiful blue eyes opened to their maximum. She breathlessly said, "Daddy, do you mean my great-grandfather's horse was an Appaloosa?"

Sully methodically ignored his daughter to continue the family history. "Before Grandma Lou died, Wes and I were cleaning out one of the barns when we ran across that old engine. It was bolted to the same crate that it had been shipped in from Virginia to Salleys Kitchen. The board with the town in Virginia had been pulled off but the board above it had 'entwood Farm' still painted on it. It was many years after Grandma Lou died that I finally figured out the town and name of the farm. After a long search and investigation, I found out Bentwood Farms still existed and they were famous for producing Appaloosa champions. When I talked with the owner, he said in his family's oral history, passed down through the years, his grandfather had traded a useless engine for the first Appaloosa stallion that came to the farm. That's the reason I went straight to him when you said you wanted a horse of your own."

Jumping up from her seat Salley screamed, "You mean my great-grandfather's horse was Spot's great-grandfather?"

Sully quietly said, "There is no way to prove that fact, because Appaloosa pedigrees were not recorded before 1938, but the present owner of Bentwood Farms told me that it sure sounded reasonable to him.

Shrieking with delight and jumping up and down, Salley said, "It's true, I know it's true, Spot's ancestor was part of my family history, it has to be true, there's no other explanation!" Sully shrugged his shoulders as his daughter hugged his neck and kissed him repeatedly on his stubbled cheek. Finally, she gave one last shriek and sat back beside me, trembling.

I didn't even know this man could carry on an intelligent conversation until a few hours ago and now he wouldn't stop talking. It may have been the brandy, but his propensity to use big words seemed to have subsided somewhat. He continued the family legacy going back to the first Sullivan coming to America as an indentured servant. The tone of his voice changed as he told of the first slaves to come on the property and the drive for wealth that continued the scourge. It was obvious he was unsettled by that period of family history.

As he wound down from an excess of brandy, he said, "Wes and I were like brothers in our early years together and we grew the best and most cotton in this land. I loved him like family but we had a habit of crawling into a bottle together and drinking our way to trouble. It's a wonder we lived through those first ten years together. We had big plans to change this community and run the sons of bitches out that are ruining Salleys Kitchen, but here it is twenty years later and neither one of our sorry asses has done one goddamn thing to stop them. Hell, we're probably helping them stay, if the truth is known." His daughter ran around the table to comfort him, but I knew the truth of his words. With the brandy gone, his night was over and as Salley walked him to the couch in the office, I made my way up to her room for the last night of my Myrtle Beach escape.

When she came in the room I was still dressed and lay on her bed, toying with some of the frills on the comforter. It was obvious, the moment she entered, she was crying as she walked straight to the bathroom and closed the door behind her. Kind of disappointed, I slowly pulled my white t-shirt over my head then pulled my blue jeans off and turned off the lights except for the lamp on her side of the bed. As I crawled under the covers I wondered if I should have tapped on the door and asked if she was all right. I lay back and put my hands under my head with my elbows sticking out on each side. The week had been remarkable, starting with driver training in the rusted heap and ending with Sully being escorted to his couch. As I lay dozing in and out of sleep, I really thought her face was a wonderful sleepy dream until her lips touched mine and she passionately kissed me. As she pushed her hands under my shoulders and laid her head on my chest, the heat of her body permeated my heart and we breathed as one. After a moment, she raised her head and again and looked into my eyes as her impassioned expression took complete control of my life. In the short time we had known each other, our worlds had merged to become a dream-like time of ecstasy. Having no idea what the future had in store, we simply wanted to be together, forever in this moment.

With the stamina of youth we made love through the night. Deliriously exhausted, sleep finally prevailed with our bodies and beings intertwined. As the sun peeped over the horizon it shot bright rays through the sheer curtains and they danced in the breeze as we awoke, consumed in the morning air of first love.

There is nothing more exhilarating than waking to remember the rapture of love and realizing its reality. As she lay with her head on my chest, I gazed at her bronze body and raven-colored hair — truly Venus was lying in my arms. I refused to move and lay stunned, wondering why I had been so fortunate to meet her and have my life changed so dramatically for the better. Her hair cascaded over my torso like long black ribbons as the cadence of her breathing sent pulses of emotion through my spirit. My fate was sealed, no matter the sacrifice — no matter the personal loss; I had to be with this beautiful woman.

Opening her eyes, she slurped and said, "Crap, did I drool on you again?" Wrapping my arms around her in the morning's gentleness, I couldn't have been happier with the wet spot she left over my heart. After a few passionate moments, we regrettably climbed out of the tousled bed and stumbled to the bathroom with giggles and laughs. While we were showering she said, "I'm going to have to ask Sully to get us some more condoms." I really could not believe this girl and her father. Their relationship was beyond anything I could comprehend, and I envied them so! But now, I had to return to my world.

Chapter Twenty-three

When Burt and I originally planned the Myrtle Beach trip, on our return, I was to be dropped off at Roy Asholee's Store and I would call for my father to come pick me up. To keep up our charade, I didn't want anyone to see Sully and Salley drop me off at the store. Instead, they left me in town behind the Tire and Oil Filling Station and I looked around for a person I could trust to keep his mouth shut and take me to Asholee's store. Some of my classmates were there but I knew they were Burt's new friends and would stab me in the back in a minute. Without letting them see me, I walked into the grease pit where Possom was changing the oil in a canary yellow Chevy II. Squatting down, to see him in the pit under the car I said, "Possom, are you going out my way anytime soon?"

He looked up and gave his trademark grin as he held a light in one hand with an oil plug in the other. "I hadn't planned on it." As he turned back to the oil pan at hand, he stopped and turned back to me. "But you know I do need to take this chicken shit yellow Chevy out to make sure it's running right. I could go out that way if you want."

Possum was not the brightest star in the class and I had let him cheat off my paper many times while he was in school. Though he was not the smartest person I knew, he was the most loyal and would never say a word if I asked him not to mention he saw me. He was also a devout Ford man and took every opportunity available to degrade GM products, especially hot rods like the box-shaped Chevy II he was lubing. Screwing the plug back in the oil pan, he deftly threw the required number of quarts of oil in the top of the engine and in just a few minutes climbed out of the oily cavity and pulled off his coveralls. After backing the bright lemon colored car from the garage, he pulled down the garage door and locked up the bay. Then grabbing his keys from the counter and locking the cash register he pulled the station door closed and said to those sitting around outside, "I'll be back in a few minutes."

Maneuvering the quasi-racecar around to the side of the

building, he yelled out the window above the rumble of the engine, "Git in!"

With a devilish smile he revved the 396 cubic inch engine, making the red tachometer needle jump, then jammed the four-speed stick into first gear and popped the clutch. All of the 375 horsepower created by the motor was transferred to the wide, almost slick rear tires and smoke began to boil out of the rear wheel wells. A loud squeal shot from under the back of the yellow speedster and rudely entered my ears as my body was nailed to the back of the bucket seat like metal on a magnet. Looking over at Possum with a terrified smile, I held on to whatever I could grab. He was clutching and shifting gears as we fishtailed out of town trailing a bluish white smoke. Making excellent time, we reached the back road to Roy Asholee's Store and I was more than ready to get out of that dragster. Yelling at the top of my voice, I screamed, "Stop Possum! This is where I need to get out!"

Slamming on the brakes, the speedy Chevrolet skidded to a stop as a cloud of smoke and dust swallowed us. I asked him not to tell anyone he had seen me and explained I needed to walk the rest of the way.

He said, "Gotcha man!" as he repeatedly revved the engine and worked the four-speed shifter. I grabbed my bag and thanked the grinning driver, then quickly stepped back and away from what I knew would be a hunk of metal making a semi-controlled about-face. As the engine in the Super Sport Chevy roared back to life, the tires squalled and the little yellow speedster pirouetted 180 degrees in the road and Possum headed back to town shifting and smoking the tires with every gear change.

Feeling none the worse for wear, I swung my clothes bag over my shoulder and pulled my underwear out of my crack as I walked toward the back of the store. Like a green tunnel, trees on each side of the dirt road leaned toward the middle, shedding their spring flowers and dropping them as if they were honoring me with a ticker-tape parade. The chirping birds would have to do for a screaming crowd and I couldn't help but smile and wave to the cheering throng. The smell of freshly plowed soil indicated cotton was now tall enough to plow and the ritual of the cotton cycle was well underway. Happy in knowing I was the luckiest person in the world, I jumped and kicked the ground like Blackie on a perfect Sunday afternoon. Feeling as though I was walking on air, my thoughts did not dwell on the drudgery and toil I would face tomorrow. Instead, I reeked with the joy of being alive and overflowed with excitement about the future. On Sunday I didn't have to go to church because I would be graduating from high school and finally have the turmoil of being among that crowd of white supremacist bigots behind me. The relief of finishing that hate-filled gauntlet was fantastic, and if I could just get past graduation, I could be with Salley and my world would be complete. Like a Pentecostal dancing at tent a revival, jubilation pulsed through my soul and mere words could never have expressed the feeling. For once, I may have understood the rapture felt by those who the Holy Spirit led to speak in tongues. I was walking in high cotton.

The putrid smell of hog pens, outhouses, and rotting trash uncouthly invaded my nostrils and snatched me back to reality like a roped calf. Nearing the back of Roy Asholee's Store, I was hoping to get through this last part of my hidden agenda without misfortune and quietly get home without a confrontation. However, I felt invincible at the moment and disregarded my own better thoughts; I had to look for any sign of my friend, especially having just found out his connection to Sully. No one else would have known anything was going on, but I knew where and what to look for from behind the smelly latrines. My heart rate picked up quickly as I barely made out Wes' image hidden behind the jungle-like shrubs concealing the basement entrance. He was unloading plastic milk jugs from a narrow riverboat on a trailer, moving fast and looking over his shoulder so I knew he was unloading rotgut liquor. Not meaning to be sneaky I made my way to the shrubs and stepped through their camouflaging limbs behind him and said, "Hey ugly!" The sudden voice scared him something fierce and he dropped one of the plastic containers splattering the illegal liquid all over the floor of the cellar.

Suddenly Boot Cutter appeared from the dark recesses of the spider web encrusted vault and shouted at Wes, "What the hell you doing, you clumsy black bastard?"

As he eyed me standing close to Wes, he pulled a long machete out of his rubber swamp boot and moved toward me.

Wes quickly stepped in front of me and said, "No Mr. Boot, please sir, he ain't meant nut'n and ain't giwne say nut'n. You ain't gots to worry wid him."

With a backhanded swipe he hit Wes near his ear using the flat part of the long knife and knocked him to the ground continuing his advance toward me. I was frozen in place and the huge ogre grabbed the front of my t-shirt pulling me close to his filthy face. Wes dove for his ankles and wrapped his arms around them begging him not to hurt me but Boot kicked him away and sneered at me.

When he screamed at me, brown saliva flew from his mouth, along with a noxious odor that made me cringe in fear. "Boy, you mus wanta die or dos I's need to make that sorry nigger right there cut yo nuts out and stick 'em down yo throat? Wat dey hell you coming back hea for? I bleve yo little white ass don bited off'n mor dan you can chew!"

Wes was on his knees begging him not to hurt me and he kicked him in the face. "Git yo nosey ass out from heah for sumpin bad hapn's and you has a accident and disappears. If'n I's hea you been talkn' bout dis place or catch you near hea again, you'll die, you understand me boy?"

He shoved me to the ground and I pushed with my feet to slide on my butt backwards away from him. I was dragging my clothes bag with me. Once out of his grabbing range I jumped up and ran to the front of the store.

Having faced the devil himself and lived through it, I was rattled as I entered the relative safety of the front area of the store, but eerily, there was no one around. Dusting myself off and checking the skinned place on my arm, I looked around trying to locate the usual store bums. With none in sight, I thought it best not to tempt fate a second time, so I hurried along to take care of my business and get the hell out of this place before something else happened.

As I walked through the wire-enclosed shed area, I put my clothes bag on a stack of drink bottle crates before going into the store. There was a peculiarly strong odor of rotgut liquor hovering about that I had never noticed before and it added to my nervousness. Obviously shaken by what had happened, I approached the grimy counter near the back of the store. Roy had evidently seen and heard my encounter with Boot and he quickly recognized the fear on my face. Never one to miss an opportunity to reinforce his power and control over a person, he decided it would be fun to humiliate me.

Sheepishly I asked him, "May I use your phone to call my father?"

Usually the mention of my father reminded him of the consequences he faced from harassing me. But with the latest bit of gossip he had obtained, the threat of my mentioning him to my father was nil. Showing his rotten brown teeth, he grinned at me, "Sure, sure you can. Come around behind the counter so you can dial the number." As I walked around the rack of Lance crackers and peanuts, the filthy troll of a man said, "Where've you been? Looks like you're feeling a little rough."

Grabbing the slick black phone receiver I held it to my ear and immediately heard the voice of Mammy Steeple. She, Roy Asholee, and JD Staley were on the same party line, which meant I would have to wait until she stopped talking to use the phone. I hung up the phone and timidly looked over my shoulder to tell the brown-toothed storekeeper I had just gotten back from Myrtle Beach. He laughed and swapped the half eaten cigar to the opposite side of his mouth with his yellow tongue and said, "That ain't what I heared. I heared you been heah in The Kitchen all along, staying at the Sullivan place."

239

Laughing loudly this time, he opened his mouth and wheezed like a hyena. With my fear renewed I reached for the phone staring at the nasty man and to my relief I heard the needed dial tone. Dialing my home phone, it rang three times before my mother said, "Hello?"

I quickly said, "Hi, I'm home. Can you come get me?"

In a very matter of fact voice she said, "I'll tell your father." Then the dial tone returned.

As I put the receiver back on its cradle, Roy grabbed my wrist and said, "You been fucking that little nigger gal of Sully's ain't you? You been git'n dat pussy right reg'lr ain't you?"

I jerked my arm out of his hand wondering how he had found out and boiling inside with anger I shouted back at him, "Shut your filthy mouth!"

Realizing he had touched a nerve, his laughter grew louder as brown drool poured out of the corners of his mouth. Continuing his barrage, he uttered more, "I'd like to have a little cut of dat pussy too, reck'n we could work outs a deal to let me fuck'er too?"

Horror stabbed my heart as a loud buzz hummed in my ears and my eyes focused solely on the fiend laughing at me. Suddenly visions of Roy Asholee grabbing Salley, like he had just done me, shot through my head. I could hear her scream while he was laughing and my rage grew beyond control. With my teeth grinding together, a guttural sound came out of my mouth as my hands grabbed each side of the storekeeper's greasy head and my fingernails sunk into the skin of his ears and scalp. Using every ounce of force in my arms and upper body I shoved his face down onto the keys of the old cash register and heard a crunching sound coming from his nose. Unable to stop as he recoiled I repeated the same action two more times before he fell behind the counter reaching into his pants pocket. He pulled out a little silver pistol but couldn't get his finger through the trigger guard, giving me enough time to stomp his hand and wrist multiple times. When the gun fell to the floor, I kicked it and sent it skidding behind the counter to the front of the store. Lying in the floor with blood spurting from his head and nose in several places, he strained to say, "You gonna pay sonny boy. I'll see that you get hurt real bad for this, you little son-of-a-bitch."

With his last statement I drew back my foot to kick him in the head a few times, but stopped before I did it. He mumbled something as he spit blood into his hand, but I just stared at his bloody pulp of a face. A horn blew and I heard one of the just arriving bums say, "Hey boy, yo daddy's heah."

Suddenly, the sight of him made me sick and the contents of my stomach surged up my throat as I puked all over Roy and the floor around him. I gagged and spit then wiped my mouth on my shirt as I turned to hurry out the door. Grabbing my bag of clothes I stepped outside and got sick again, puking on the asphalt between the store and my father's truck. The store bum under the shed let out a rebel yell and screamed, "YE HAWWWW, MYRTLE BEACH! MAKES ME WANT TO BE YOUNG AGAIN!"

I got in the pickup wiping my mouth on my t-shirt as my old man laughed and slapped me on the back. "Keep yo head out dat winder if you gonna do dat again."

I stuck my head out the window all the way home, just trying to get air back into my lungs. Stopping in the sandy driveway, I got out without saying a word and walked up the steps into the house.

Once inside, my mother said, "Welcome home stranger; haven't seen you in a while."

Dropping my clothes bag in the kitchen, I hurried into my room and shut the door behind me. My father was laughing as he spoke to my mother, "Just leave him alone until morning, he'll be all right. He may have a headache but he'll get over it." Falling on my bed, I heard him laughing as he went back outside.

Welcome home, indeed!

Chapter Twenty-four

Saturday was a time of great anxiety. I had had people say and even do mean things to me all my life and I had never reacted the way I did Friday afternoon. All day I tried to analyze what had happened and why I had done something so alien to me. It was more than the 'N' word. I was scared when Boot grabbed me and I tried to get away from him, but the mere mention of Salley's name in a threating way caused me to lose all fear and I was barely able to stop myself from killing Roy Asholee. That thought filled me with horror. Was I capable of killing someone?

After doing every nit-picking job my father dreamed up for me, I was exhausted at sundown. Lying in my bed after going through the motions of supper and my bath, the drone of my old window fan and the almost cool breeze it offered lulled me into a catatonic-like state. Salley Sullivan was the only thing on my mind and I could not focus on anything else. In that in-between world just before exhaustion pushed me into REM sleep, I vowed over and over I would kill or be killed before I would let anyone or anything harm Salley. In my sleep, I killed them all, time and time again. As I awakened, I realized that fact. Without a shadow of a doubt I would not hesitate to kill if it meant protecting the girl I loved.

Sunday was Graduation Day and as was tradition at our small rural school, all churches participated in the occasion and suspended their morning and evening worship services. A local preacher, chosen each year on a rotating basis, would make one last attempt to 'put the fear of God' in the students, fill the parents with spiritual fervor and generally bore the hell out of all the hungover students in their hot robes. This would count as Sunday worship for those seeking the perfect attendance pin at their local church.

As I lay in bed that morning, I could only wonder what would happen next when the knob on my door turned and I heard it squeak open. My mother stuck her head in and demanded to know if I intended to eat breakfast. I nodded yes and she said, "Well, wash the crackers out of your eyes and come to the table."

As I sat down, the old man was reading a *Progressive Farmer* magazine. He was expecting me to lie and my mother did not want to hear what happened at the beach. She wanted to continue the charade of concern for her little boy so she could hold her head high at church. Continuing the farce, she asked what made me sick and I told her, with a straight face, we ate at a juke joint on the way home and I must have gotten a burger with spoiled mayonnaise. My old man pulled his magazine away from his face and said, "Man, you have to watch out for that kind of thing!" He chuckled as he returned to drool over the color pictures of the latest model of John Deere cotton pickers on the back cover.

As I finished my eggs, my mother said to her husband, "Isn't there something you want to tell your son about this afternoon?"

Without moving he looked over the top of his magazine and said, "Oh, yeah… you can drive the pickup to the school this afternoon and we'll come later in the station wagon. We thought you might want to go get a burger after graduation, but you better be careful and not get one with spoiled mayonnaise; and you be careful with my truck!"

Then my mother added, "And please don't let that demon alcohol enter your body and ruin your mind. Keep Jesus in your heart and the devil behind you!" I nodded my head and went back to my room to wait on the next bell to toll.

At 3:00 I dressed and gave my mother her mandatory peck on the cheek before leaving in the pickup for the school. I still had money in my pocket from the $50 bill, so I drove to Sonny Boy's, the local hangout. At the burger joint, I walked in to the strange sound of people talking, pool balls colliding and pinball machines dinging. Everyone stopped what they were doing to stare at me; I was not a regular but they knew me from school. There was only one person in the place that I felt comfortable about asking a few questions. Pretending not to hear the comments uttered in the corners, I walked up to the counter and asked Sonny Boy why everything got so quiet. He laughed and said, "You and me both know why these cats hate your guts. You hanging with a girl that's the wrong color." I winced and said, "Does everybody know?"

He laughed again and said, "Let me put it this way — there's only two people in Salleys Kitchen that don't know - your mama and daddy and the only reason they don't know is because ain't nobody got the balls to tell either one of them."

Sonny Boy was Greek and had come to my church on the invitation of the girl that had played the organ. His brother was the expectant father of the talented church musician-in-exile's child. Before the news of the pregnancy broke he and his brother were happily accepted, but when the news hit, everyone started treating them as outcasts. Once, when he was standing all by himself after church waiting on his brother, I walked up and befriended him. He was nervous and chain smoking cigarettes until we started talking and made friends. He was happy that someone was nice to him. I didn't see him but once after that, when Burt took me to the burger joint. He had become the short order cook and the locals had gradually accepted him as they enjoyed his cooking and he worked hard to make friends. He told me that he had bypassed their hearts and brains and gone straight to their stomachs for acceptance. Understanding the good ole boy atmosphere, he was friendly to me, but not so friendly as to make the regulars turn against him. He had to live and work among this crowd and I had made my own bed hard.

Looking at the floor, I turned to walk away when he called to me. He was smiling under that thick, coal black, hair slicked flat on his head and said, "Hey wait a minute. I've got something I want to show you." He pulled a box mixed with cherry bombs and M-80s from under the counter.

Since Burt had gotten his driving license, he enjoyed tremendously riding around and tossing those huge firecrackers in the yards of teachers and other people he considered buttholes. I had been on one of his booming forays on one rare Saturday night when I spent the night with him. My mother and father had gone to an all-day farm equipment auction and I was allowed to go to his house after I finished work. We had stopped by Sonny Boy's to get some fireworks.

During the last year, cherry bombs and M-80s had been outlawed and most people could not get them anymore. Leave it to Sonny Boy- he had a connection in the fireworks underworld and could get most anything. He reached into the box and grabbed a handful, putting them in one of his white burger bags saying, "Here, celebrate tonight, and here, I've got something else you need to try." He pulled two quart bottles of Boone's Farm Wine from the cooler and smiled. "You need this too, if you going to celebrate right."

He winked with a smile, so I gave him ten bucks out of my pocket and walked away with the bag under my arm and a bottle of wine in each hand. I assumed this would be a solitary celebration and I guess he did too. Something told me this was going to be a strange night.

At 4:00 I parked behind the Agriculture shop and walked to the gym where we were supposed to meet. As I passed people I knew, not close friends or anything, just people with whom I was acquainted, they looked away and some even snickered. Reaching the gym door, where the seniors were gathering, I looked for someone, anyone, to hang out with while waiting, but no such luck. The throng parted leaving a narrow path for me to enter the gym, so I walked onto the familiar hardwood floor where, during PE, I had ogled many of the girls who were graduating with me tonight. This evening, however, everyone was fully clothed and folding chairs covered every inch of the shiny floor. A portable stage stood in front of the chairs with green plants and a podium, behind which was hung a green banner that read 'The Class of '68 Will Always Be Great.' A nervous Mr. Rawls, having been warily monitoring the door, spotted my entry and rushed over like he wanted to sell me a life insurance policy. Shaking my hand, repeating the agenda, rubbing his hands together and generally acting beleaguered, I felt somewhat sorry for him. His last question seemed to come out in a measured way with great caution, "Are your mother and father coming tonight?" Nodding yes, he quickly and intently asked, "How about Sully and Salley, are they coming?"

I gave him the old teenage shoulder shrug and looked around to see if anyone else was in the building. There were little cliques here and there, but as I approached they scattered like flushed quail. The message was plain and I understood the implications, but I hoped there was at least one person in the whole damn school with the gumption to talk with me face to face and not whisper behind my back. As time for the ceremony drew nigh, I was filled with a feeling I had missed something, then Burt entered the gym and walked in my direction. Not getting too close he yelled, "Come outside, they're handing out the caps and gowns!"

Quickly turning his back to me, he hurried outside. In his haste, he almost ran over the girl that owned my heart. She moved to the side to avoid him as my pulse sped up and I moved toward her. Wanting to plant a big wet juicy kiss on those glossy lips, I didn't, because it was more than obvious she was in her no nonsense mode and I greeted her with only words. "Hi, what are you doing here? You didn't have to come."

She quickly snapped, "Man, I wouldn't miss this groovy event for anything in the world."

We both turned for the door to collect our caps and gowns when Sully walked in and passed his daughter a note as he kissed her on the cheek. He walked to some chairs on the back wall, away from the crowd now gathering on the gym bleachers. She read the note then held it so I could read it. In big letters, he had written, DO NOT GO OUTSIDE. We looked at each other then walked over and sat down in the folding chairs beside him. Soon my curiosity got the best of me and amidst the protest Salley was making with her eyes, I slipped behind the fake Palmetto trees, and exited through the utility tunnel connecting the gym to the school. The janitor hid the key over the door, so it was an easy and hidden way out. From the overgrown shrubs near the school building, I peeped through the leaves to see the front of the brick gymnasium and I could plainly see a group of rowdy town boys gathered at the end of the sidewalk. Up on top of the metal cover over the sidewalk leading to the gym, stood Burt and one of his Myrtle Beach cronies. Holding a five gallon bucket of black paint tipped to pour on some unsuspecting person coming out of the gym, they stood in wait. The rest of my fellow graduates were gathered around two cap and gown sets hanging on a rack in plain view.

This stunt was so typical of something planned by Burt and it made me smile to have so easily found out his method of revenge. Burt was not a rocket scientist and I was amused at his lame attempt, but too quickly remembered his intended targets. Thinking fast, I ran to the pickup and grabbed a cherry bomb from the white bag and hurried back to my spying spot. As I peeped around the corner, Mr. Rawls stood under the covered walkway, unaware of the paint bucket above him. He was talking to the robed senior class, "Okay folks, let's line up alphabetically like we did at rehearsal." He then turned to go back inside and alert the lady playing the piano.

With a collective moan, everyone shuffled closer to the door as Burt and his partner prepared to hand the sloshing bucket of black paint down to their buddies. Striking a match and letting the flame settle on the end, I held the firecracker fuse in the fire and watched it spark and fizzle, burning its way down to the plum-sized red ball filled with an outlawed amount of explosive powder. Just as the oversized paint container was on its way down, I lobbed the small bomb and it landed at the feet of those helping bring it to the ground. The explosion reverberated through the area sending a concussion wave back to my face. The bucket, being held out over the sidewalk cover, was jerked back by Burt's partner and they were both doused with black paint. Recognizing their disaster, the bucket was dropped. While falling the eight feet to the sidewalk below, it hit a metal pole sending a perfect spray of black, sticky paint over most of the gowns and caps gathered about. As I ran for the utility room door, the screams and cursing reached crescendo. Ducking like a rabbit into a hole, I disappeared into the wire and pipe repository then reappearing in the seat beside the puzzled father and daughter.

The crowd on the bleachers had risen to their feet, with some heading for the door to find out the reason for the explosion. Having seen the debacle, Mr. Rawls moved back inside and stood at the door as he yelled, "It's okay folks, it's okay, just a premature celebration firecracker. If everybody will have a seat we'll get started in just a few minutes."

There was a chuckling kind of rumble through the crowd as everyone returned to the folding chairs and hard bleacher seats. True to his word, Pomp and Circumstance began pouring out of the old piano and after a short delay, the Senior Class of 1968 marched into the transformed basketball arena.

Without caps and gowns, most of the graduation candidates had obvious splotches of black paint on their faces and hands. White collars were now smeared where attempts had been made to remove it. The entire senior class had a 'pissed off' look on their faces and as they lined up across the stage with every eye glaring at the three of us sitting against the back wall. A puzzled murmur swept through the crowd as the graduates took their seats. The two obviously empty seats caused everyone to quickly follow their finger down the names in the program to those missing. Almost in unison, the eyes of the spectators fell on us as a most troubling hum passed through the crowd. I'm sure the most extenuating aspect of the whole affair was my grinning from ear to ear.

As the local Methodist preacher gave the customary 'Always Put Christ First' sermon to the fuming students, they were still wiping black paint off their faces and hands as the mothers and fathers mumbled to each other. The Right Reverend could have danced a buck dance naked on the stage and no one would have noticed. My parents were sitting prominently on the bottom bleacher with perplexed looks on their faces. Wondering how I would explain the recent happenings to them, I avoided making eye contact as a flurry of speakers bored the gathered and word of what had happened slowly spread.

Finally the un-gowned class stood, preparing to walk to the front of the stage, receive their diplomas, and smile for the camera snapping their picture. As graduates' names were called, they filed across the stage, shook the superintendent's hand as they received their credentials and returned to their seats. Our names had been skipped, but Mr. Rawls quickly announced, the next group would be presented diplomas and receive awards for outstanding achievement. As the group dwindled, Salley's name became next on the list. She made eye contact with me, kissed Sully and calmly walked like a lady up on the stage to receive her sheepskin. As with the others, it was announced she received scholarship offers from the following universities and she smiled with only two people applauding in the entire gym.

There was complete silence from everyone else as Mr. Rawl's blood pressure reached stroke level. Several other students received their diplomas and awards before he called my name and I nervously walked onto the stage. The school leader, with a look of uneasiness on his face, presented my diploma as he leaned to the microphone saying, "And now a surprise for this lucky young man. He has won an agriculture scholarship including a 'Get Started Early' award and will be attending a summer session at the University. He'll be leaving in a few short days."

Mr. Rawls handed me an envelope and I stared at it bewildered. The Master of Ceremonies gave great effort to start a round of applause by clapping enthusiastically, but quickly aborted his efforts realizing my mother and father were the only ones joining the congratulatory response. As I looked toward the two farm folks trying to understand the odd response, my shoes clopping and the squealing reverb of the microphone were the only sounds being made. A wave of guilt hastily crashed on the shore of my conscience, for I never meant to embarrass them. Making contact with my mother's eyes, she coldly stared me down as I walked past and returned to my seat at the back of the other graduates. I sat in a fog as my beautiful friend sat like a queen on a throne and ignored my presence. Alone at that moment, I felt the world wanted me dead as countless misgivings flooded my strength of mind.

As the recessional began, Sully took her hand and made for the door with me following close behind. As they hurried to the jalopy she kept saying over her shoulder, "Go home, don't hang around and get hurt. Go home, please go home."

I stood in silence for a moment, then sadly walked to the pickup and left for home, deciding at the last moment to go back by Sonny Boy's. It was the hangout of all the popular people and I had only experienced it that one time when I spent the night with Burt. I at least wanted to thank Sonny Boy and see what I had missed all through my high school years.

Driving the old man's pickup, everyone knew exactly who was behind the wheel as I circled through the u-shaped line of cars pulled into the many slots to order shakes and burgers. With my window down, the jeers and taunts began as soon as I passed behind the first car. As horns sounded off, Danny Dolen's canary yellow Chevy Nova backed out of the slot in front of me. Stopping quickly, I glimpsed in the rearview mirror to see someone backing out behind me. I was trapped.

Smiling from the driver's seat, Ray's perfectly-combed, Brylcreemed hair shined as he turned to face me, "Why, hey there, little nigger lover. I heard you messed up graduation for everybody tonight." His girlfriend was a Class of '68 graduate. "We think it's only fair for you to get a little payback!"

Caught in their blocking maneuver it was evident my window needed to be rolled up post haste. Reaching for the driver's side window handle, I rolled it up as fast as I could and reached for the handle of the passenger window across the entire truck cab. As Danny and his buddy got out of the Chevy,

I conceded the far window and went for broke. Shifting the old F-100 into reverse I began moving backward to gain a little room for a maneuver that I hoped would get me the hell out of this mess. Salley's advice to go home reverberated in my mind as I stopped less than an inch from Bobby Barvin's shiny blue Oldsmobile 442. Shifting to first gear, I held the brake pedal with my heel and pushed the accelerator with my toe, then popped the clutch. As the back tires spun on the concrete they squealed and smoked as their motion sent the back of the empty truck bed sliding left toward the pushbutton microphones where food orders were placed and bumped to a stop against the concrete curb. Pushing in the clutch, I immediately turned the steering wheel all the way right, then dropped the clutch again with the brake held and the accelerator on the floor. For the second time the front of the truck swung to the right, as half-eaten burgers, milkshakes and French fries pelted the windows and cab. I jumped the curb to enter the empty sandy lot next door. Used as overflow parking for the drive-in, it was a mere sandpit. After narrowly missing a number of shiny hotrods, I spun the old farm truck in several donuts and covered the area in a thick cloud of dirt and dust, then headed out of the area as quickly as possible. Just as I hit the asphalt highway in front of the burger joint, about six beer bottle missiles were launched my way. Three found their mark bursting on the back glass and side of the truck but one came through the open passenger window, exploding as it hit the steering wheel, covering me with beer and glass. With that, the game was on, as the hotrod boys fired up their pampered autos to give chase, however, I knew their weakness. The secret was dirt roads, for none of the foul mouthed motor-heads would follow me if dirt and dust were being thrown on their shiny hand-waxed show cars. Hitting the first dirt road out of town, I watched the headlights behind me grow smaller and disappear. Having my hackles up, I swung back by the hangout in the opposite direction, just to taunt the assholes and flip them the finger. No one chased this time.

251

Not wanting to face my parents and go through the abusive ordeal on the horizon, I decided to take a tour of the familiar dirt roads of Salleys Kitchen. Blackie and I had traveled many of the sandy lanes on our Sunday jaunts, but tonight, I ended up way back in the middle of nowhere, at the pond where we started our 'fifty cent tour'. As I turned around to leave I stopped and backed the banged-up old truck to the water's edge, let down the tailgate and sat staring at the moon while gulping the Boone's Farm wine. Every now and then I would light one of the firecrackers, hold it as long as I safely could, then toss it into the air trying to time the explosion to occur just above the water. The blast would light up the black water and the concussion would send ripples across the way. After finishing one bottle of the wine, I lit the fuse of an M-80 and dropped it into the bottle. After watching the fuse burn down, I threw it at the last minute as far across the pond as I could. It exploded and sent shards of glass in every direction. Uncapping the second bottle, I lit more of the firecrackers and tossed them high over the water. After each blast, the water rippled and smoke lingered in the air just before it curled, rose and floated away from the water. I wanted to follow the smoke up from this place with her by my side. With each swig of wine my timing grew worse, finally one of the small bombs exploded under the water. I knew what I had done, but hoped to be wrong, when one, two and finally, three fish floated to the top of the water in the moonlight, belly up. If you're not careful, fireworks can hurt or kill you, even the innocent ones around you. Seeing the dead fish float to the surface was omen enough and I quit playing with the little killers.

About 2 AM, as I staggered to the truck door, a black hand covered my hand, pulled it away from the handle and caused me to stumble and fall flat on my butt. In my stupor, I squinted to make out the person that caused my fall.

I yelled out, "Hey Wes, you a lay late and a lollar short cau' I just dranked the lass squol'r of Mr. Boone, so tuff shiiiiiiit!"

He squatted down beside me and said, "I ain't never

thought I'd see da day I'd be takin' care of yo drunk ass wid me stone cold sober."

We both laughed and I started to fall over on the ground but he grabbed me and held me in a sitting position. Laughing, he slapped me several times hard on both cheeks. Of course I didn't feel much pain, but I spouted, "Aaa, whacha do dat fors?"

He said, "Cause I needs you to hair me and understands." I must have had a few lucid moments because I remember him telling me Boot and Roy wanted to kill me and were planning to do it soon. With the world spinning, I vaguely remembered him saying, "I think I's talked 'em outa hit. I's told 'em hit was sumthin yous would hate worser'n any thang else and yous was lebing for college pertty soon anyhows."

Still slurring my words I asked, "Wor'sn dy'n? Wha da hell is dey wor'sn dy'n?"

I vaguely remember seeing tears in his eyes as he said, "I ain't gwine bees able to a tell yous dat rat now, but I wants yous to know I love you wid ever bit o my heart. My times is short on dis here earth, but, don't you ever worrys none for me, I do the right thang and I ain't bout to lets dem hurt you!"

He put his arm around me and stood me up half dragging me to the back of the truck, rolling me onto the tailgate, then into the bed. I remember looking up at the moon and stars as he cranked the truck and we started moving. Suddenly I felt sick and there was a rumbling in my bloated stomach as I lurched for the side of the truck bed and executed a perfect arch of wine colored projectile vomit on the driver's side of the truck. He looked out the back window and said the last thing I remember, "I'm glad you ain't sit'n up heah wid me cause I couldn't put up wid dat smell. You'd ust had'a got home on yo own."

About 4:30 or 5 in the morning I woke up lying on the tailgate of the pickup smelling like a well-used Monday morning beer-joint trash can that wasn't emptied Saturday night. I felt as if someone had repeatedly kicked me in the stomach and then let Blackie take a dump in my mouth. Thirsty wouldn't cover my need for water. I was parched and stumbled to the faucet by the pump house in the middle of the yard. It tasted like the best water I had ever had, so I naturally drank too much, making the sick drunk feeling return. Upon a gigantic burp, I felt some better, but not much.

Trying to slip into the house and make it to my room undetected, I tip-toed past my parents' room only to hear, "Boy where you been? Ain't no use you getting in bed; your ass is gone soon as I get up outa this bed." I heard him but didn't listen, pulled off my smelly clothes, turned on the window fan and fell asleep across the bed in my underwear.

I awoke to the sting of a belt slapped across my butt and turned to see my father swinging the leather strap again. Still in a sleepy daze I grabbed the black blur and held on so he couldn't swing it again. He yelled, "Take your hands off that belt. I'm going to leave some strips that'll teach you not to be fucking a nigger gal. You ain't going to forget this beatin' for a while!"

The feeling that consumed me at Roy Asholee's Store returned and I lost any fear I had. He tried to jerk the belt from my hands, but just the opposite occurred as I yanked it from his hands then threw it back behind my bed and the wall. Exhausted, hung-over, and fighting the urge to heave, I stood up in my underwear and shoved him with both hands into the doorway where my mother was standing with her arms crossed in judgmental agreement. She quickly retreated as my mind made out exactly what he had said and my rage pushed me forward. Trying a roundhouse punch to my head I easily blocked his arm by raising mine then I shoved him away from me again with a lot more force making him stumble backward to the floor. He tried to kick my legs from his position on the floor but I hopped backward and stared at his face. It's uncanny how restrained anger can build up until it turns a usually compliant person into a fighting fury in a moment's notice.

Stepping back from him, I let him get back on his feet. Because my head was throbbing like a bass drum at a high school football game, I spoke in a very restrained but convincing voice with my finger pointing in his face, "You might not think much of me and I don't care what you say about me, but if you call her that again, I will try to kill you. Do you understand me?"

Turning to walk away from me, he spat back, "What, you think you can sucker me like you did Roy? You think I'm going to let you tear up my face and break my nose? You better think twice sonny boy. I'll kick your ass from here to Georgia." At this point I gave no consideration to any possible consequences and if he had called her that name again, one of us would have been arrested in connection with a death.

He spouted at me one last time before he left, "You're a fucking idiot. You hear me? And from now on you ain't no son of mine!"

As I turned to go back in my room I said, "If only that was true."

Chapter Twenty-five

Pulling open the drawer and picking up a pair of clean jeans with a t-shirt, I grabbed a pair of white socks along with my sneakers as I walked past the blitz of noise coming from both of my parents and into the bathroom. While they screamed at me, I heard my old man say I had better be in the field when he got back or he would have me arrested. Shutting and locking the door before I got in the shower, my head was throbbing and I felt sick.

Della, Albert and Mary were walking out of the yard as I left the house and I followed them to the field. Working all morning hung over, with the back-door trots so bad I was afraid to fart, he caught Albert at the opposite end of the field and told him to tell me to start plowing the edges of the cotton fields. It was a hell of a Monday and I skipped lunch for obvious reasons and stopped working at a sensible time of five o'clock. Driving the tractor from the field back to the house, I parked it under the shed and put the keys where they always hung and noticed the pickup truck keys hanging beside them. It was to be a quick shower for me and I was headed to the Sullivan Mansion to see her. After dressing, I started to brush my teeth when I heard a timid knock at the door. Unlocking and opening the door my mother was standing with her arms crossed ready to rebuke me. I returned to brushing my teeth as she talked.

"I should have listened to your father when he said he needed you this summer in the field. We paid a lot of money for you to have a chance to go to that summer session of college and I had to beg him to let you go. Now you're treating us like dirt. I have already tried to get the money back but they said it was too late. We'll just lose it if you don't go. Are you going to waste the money or what?"

Spitting and wiping my mouth I returned, "I don't know."

She then told me, "There's a group of boys coming through here Friday at 2:00 and I arranged with their mothers to let you ride to the college with them. Are you going to ride with them or just waste the money and…"

I gave her a quick harsh stare then said, "I DON'T KNOW!" I splashed some Brut on my face and walked past her to the kitchen.

Grabbing my wallet and the keys to the station wagon from their customary peg on the wall, I heard my mother yell from the door as I cranked up the Country Squire, "Where are you going?"

Backing up so I could drive out the driveway, I yelled back, "I DON'T KNOW!"

It was a little over a mile from our driveway to Salley's tree-lined lane. About three quarters of that distance the road was straight and flat, but just before her driveway, the roadbed makes a rather sharp turn to the right on a high, somewhat banked curve. This stretch of the road had been the sight of many wrecks and a few deaths. For ten or twelve miles, the road is straight as an arrow and only rises and falls over the ancient sand dunes. Late at night, the boredom of the long straight road had a tendency to put some drivers to sleep, making them miss the curve and plunge 25 feet into a waste area.

As I pulled to the edge of the asphalt, I glanced to my left to see the familiar squiggly waves of heat rising from the blacktop. Turning right to check for traffic, a car appeared over the little hill just past our house and as it came closer in view, there was something odd about its appearance.

My attention perked up as I noticed the familiar dented and bug blackened grill of Sully's snail-mobile closing at an unexpected speed. Having never seen the old heap traveling that fast, I kept my focus and noticed Boot's beat up station wagon following close behind. As they passed in front of me, I saw Sully's face squinted in fear as he tried to control the speeding old car while it bounced and swerved from the middle of the road to the edge of the grass shoulder. Less than the length of a car behind, the bootlegger's station wagon was speeding ever closer to the old Ford. Just beyond the end of our driveway Boot held his hand out the window and fired a pistol at the old car swerving in front of him. Then he floored his vehicle and rammed Sully's car in the rear, making the tires squeal as it swerved violently from side to side. The usually slow driving old man was fighting to keep his car under control. I heard Boot fire at Sully again just as they reached the high banked curve then watched as he rammed Sully's car once more. The sound of squealing tires and crunching metal made my stomach contract as I floored the accelerator of our station wagon to follow. Nearing the notorious curve, a huge cloud of dust and smoke appeared over the side as my eyes caught a glimpse of blue smoke pouring from Boot's old wagon speeding away. Stomping the brakes and squealing to a stop, I rammed the wagon into park, jumped out and ran over to the edge to see the bottom of Sully's car with the wheels still spinning and papers floating in the air amid the dust and smoke.

Not knowing whether the smoke from under the hood was a fire or steam spewing out of the radiator, I quickly slid down the bank and tore through the bushes to find Sully. He was nowhere in the car and my panic doubled when I heard the woof of a fire starting under the hood. After being pushed over the bank, the car must have rolled two or three times, ejecting Sully and I prayed to God he wasn't under the now burning heap. The station wagon I was driving now blocked the road. A trucker stopped to help and followed the black marks and broken glass to the smoke coming up from the ravine. After sliding down the bank, he ran to me asking what had happened. Trying to tell him in as few words as possible, I yelled out, "PLEASE HELP ME FIND SULLY!"

He ran to the far side with no luck. I crawled on my hands and knees as close to the flaming car as the heat would allow me and finally spotted Sully's dirty socks protruding from under the hood of the car. I yelled, "HERE HE IS!"

The robust trucker fell to the ground and crawled to me. Pointing to Sully's feet, I saw the Good Samaritan turn his back to the flames shooting from under the hood and grab one of Sully's legs. Following his lead, I took a deep breath and reached through the fire, grabbing the other leg and we were able to pull him away from the fully engulfed car. As soon as we had him safely away from the danger, the guy who's name I never knew, ran to his truck and returned with a fire extinguisher to spray the flames. Keeping my body between Sully and the wreck, I wiped the dirt from his face and prayed for him to be alive.

By this time, passersby had stopped at my house to ask my mother to call an ambulance. It seemed like hours passed as I squatted on my knees beside Sully's body, before I heard the scream of the siren, and finally saw the blinking red light. Not knowing what to do, I left him lying on his back without moving him. He was not bleeding and I knew he was alive because I saw his face grimace a few times, but he didn't seem to be breathing. Finally, the ambulance drivers arrived along with people to gawk at the horrific scene. Sliding down the bank, they took my place as I moved back and let them assume control. After pulling him up the bank on a stretcher, they loaded him in the rear of the emergency vehicle and one of the white clad ambulance men yelled to me, "Get in, we need to go right now!"

Pulling my mother's car onto the side of the road, I left the keys in the ignition and climbed into the jump seat. The medic riding on the other side was pumping Sully's chest as we left the scene with the siren wailing its horrible sound.

An anonymous person called, laughing, to tell Salley of the wreck and we met her running toward us as we left the scene. I screamed for them stop, but they refused. As I opened the door to jump out the driver finally stopped. Running up to us, I saw the horror on her face and felt helpless.

I jumped out, pushed her into the seat beside her dad and ran around to the front. We left again for the hospital with my heart and soul screaming as the medic worked to keep Sully alive. Holding her in the waiting area of the emergency room while she cried hysterically, I listened as she cursed the people of Salleys Kitchen. Every now and then she would stare at me with a look of disbelief and I would hold her trembling body against mine.

She kept repeating, "I hate this place. I hate this goddamn place and everybody in it." Shoving me away, she would return seconds later for me to hold her again as I helplessly tried to console her. Finally, a young man, in a doctor's coat came out of the closed doors to ask the nurse at the station a question. She sadly looked our way and pointed. The very young looking man walked toward us as Salley hurried to him. Escorting us into a room just away from the public area, we sat down as she asked in a trembling voice, "Is he still alive?"

This guy was barely older than we were and he was acting very fatherly saying, "Now young lady, this is a time that you're going to have to be strong."

The minute I heard his patronizing tone, I wanted to tell him; *You might not want to speak to her as if she were a child because...* I never got to finish the thought, as she backed him into a corner and exploded, "Goddamn it, I asked you a question; is he alive?"

He changed into his doctor mode quickly and cowered under her finger as he said, "Mr. Sullivan is paralyzed from the neck down. He suffered severe trauma to his third and fourth vertebra resulting in damage to the spinal column from that point down. He has no movement in his arms or legs and we are assisting him in breathing. We don't know if there is brain damage, but it doesn't appear so. The ambulance folks did a great job just to get him here alive." She caught the full brunt of the situation and it stunned her. She turned to me with her face begging for an answer, but I didn't know what to say.

I held her again as she cried with the doctor persisting with his questions. Putting my hand up in the universal sign of stop, I once again wanted to warn him about pushing her at this moment, but like a fool he didn't take the hint, "Miss, I need to know if you are of legal age or I need for you to tell me his next of kin that is of legal age. We need to decide if he is to stay on thebreather or be taken off supported breathing altogether."

This guy was holding a burning match as he peered into a

can of gasoline. Unable or unwilling to learn from his first mistake, she turned on him with brutal efficiency and again backed him into a corner with her long beautiful index finger under his chin. Remembering the knife situation, I prayed she didn't grab him by the hair, but I didn't think she needed to be that rough with this guy.

In a clear and distinct voice, with her body straight and taut, she spoke unequivocally. "You will do everything humanly possible to keep him alive and you will never again ask me or anyone else that question. Do you understand me? Legalities are to be the least of your worries at this moment and if the time comes that we need legal authority, I'll cover your ass up with so many lawyers you'll wish you had kept you smart remarks to yourself."

I had been privileged to see this side of her on the first day we met and knew well she was not to be treated or spoken to in an abrasive manner. The immature doc was getting his first lesson on proper decorum while interacting with Salley Sullivan. He cowered and quickly backed away while she burned holes in his face with those blue-steel eyes. Scurrying like a rat in a corn crib, he disappeared behind a pair of swinging doors as we stared at them flapping back and forth.

Almost immediately a much older gentleman, dressed in the same type of white coat with a stethoscope around his neck, walked out of the still moving doors and hurried over to her. As he looked straight into her eyes, she began to cry. Lovingly, he put his arms around her and held her close to his chest. He patted her back and gave no indication of wanting to hurry her grieving. We stood in the middle of the waiting area for quite a while and he just held her as I looked on helplessly. Looking down at the floor I noticed he had a spot of blood on the toe of his white shoe and I wondered if it was Sully's.

After a time her sobs subsided and she faced the gentleman as he said, "I'm Dr. Baughman, your dad's physician and I have known him since he came here from California in the late '20s. He is a fine human being and I'm proud to call him my friend.

You're the light of his life, I know because I watched his eyes light up when I asked about you. He has even shown me pictures of you on an Appaloosa named Spot." She smiled weakly and he hugged her again.

"I'm going to get you back to see him in just a few minutes, but I don't want you to let his situation or the equipment scare you. He's having trouble breathing and we've got him on a machine that helps him, but he's talking more than I've ever heard him talk before."

The old doctor chuckled as he said, "The last thing he asked before I came out here, was did I know a seven letter word for sanatorium."

Neither of us had ever seen a person in an iron lung. Seeing only the head of the person you love sticking out of the huge noisy cylinder the size of a refrigerator. It is not unlike seeing a person that has been transformed to one-eighth human and seven-eighths machine. As we inched toward the coffin-like apparatus, we could hear the regular swooshing sound it made each time it helped Sully take a breath. He was lying on his back at our waist, with the machine closed and sealed around his neck. His head was supported by a small shelf with a pillow and there was a mirror at an angle above his head so he could see someone standing behind him. If you wanted to talk to him the nurse had to adjust the reflecting glass to your angle, but if you needed to make eye contact with him, you had to almost hug the machine and peer down the end of the device from which his head protruded. It seemed like a scene from an unbelievable science fiction movie. I couldn't really tell you what Salley was thinking, but I could see the despair on her face as her trembling hands flew to her mouth and she gasped. Quickly, she composed herself as much as possible, moving close enough to brush his mop-like hair from his forehead and lean down to kiss him. The touch of her lips brought a smile to his face and he began to speak.

"A rather inglorious way to come upon your latter years, but the old 'sawbones' says I have an excellent chance of garnering a few more birthdays, as long as this hydraulic metal object continues to inflate my diaphragm. It would never be my wish to burden you, my dear, with something this indecorous, but I was selfish enough to want to see you just a little bit longer, sweetheart. Are you okay?"

She nodded her head and snuffed as one of her tears landed on his cheek. Wiping it ever so lightly with her pinky finger she said, "You've never been a burden for me and you are the most unselfish person I have ever known. You know I love you and as long as you're still alive I'll put up with anything."

Sully's face exuded frustration as it became obvious he wanted to touch her and couldn't. Placing her cheek on his forehead, she caressed his face and said, "Don't worry, I'll take good care of you; no matter what happens, I'll take care of you." As they talked, I was trying to slowly and methodically exit by backing out of the room, but Sully made me halt in my tracks.

"Your beau observed my predicament just prior to Boot setting my near demise into motion. As I approached home, it became abundantly clear my unfamiliarity with maneuvering at such a high rate of travel was becoming problematic. My trusty old Ford seemed to surmise, as did I, Boot was not discharging those lead projectiles at us in a sense of love. I was able to circumvent their impact, however his callous insistence that we be removed from the thoroughfare and descend 25 feet at a rapid velocity proved the most damaging."

The people in the room chuckled as he continued, "Sweetheart, please inform your suitor of my desire to have a word with him at his earliest convenience. I should like to proffer my profound appreciation in person."

My face felt as if it was a bright red beacon flashing from my shoulders as everyone looked at me and he figured out I was in the room. Sully continued to rattle on, "Obviously he has made his way to this infirmary just to be in your company? That young man is totally enchanted with your being; of course I think that's reciprocal. Is he nearby?"

She sheepishly smiled, made eye contact with me and

said, "He was standing about ten feet behind you trying to sneak out the door, but he stopped and now I think he's about to pee in his pants."

Sully laughed out loud and told his daughter, "You need to show a higher regard for that young man lest he lose his infatuation for you. He alone, my dear, had the intestinal fortitude to return after tasting your rogue humor."

Now she flushed and said, "Sully, please! He's standing right behind you."

With his eyes rolling back in his head as he tried to look back at me, he said, "Ask him if he would move closer so I might see him."

Slowly, with my head down, I moved to their side. As his eyes danced in his otherwise frozen head he searched for my eyes. Once in his full line of vision, his eyes locked on mine. He stared at me in silence for what seemed like a hundred years then said, "Did you observe all involved in my quandary this afternoon?"

Sheepishly I nodded yes and said, "Boot Cutter rammed you several times and fired a pistol at your car several times. I saw everything."

Again he stared in silence and finally said, "It is a tough decision that confronts you my dear young man and I don't envy your dilemma. I trust you and Salley will give it proper consideration for the consequences are grave. I have no doubt as to your moral courage and I trust your decision with utmost assurance, however, I would urge you to give thought to your and my daughter's future together as you deliberate."

The frustration in his eyes was more than evident as he came to the understanding that his quiet and well contemplated life was no more. His fate now rested in the hands of others as he reconciled himself to being helplessly paralyzed, enveloped by a huge hissing, pumping, machine that would rhythmically suck the breath of life into his lungs until his dying day.

Sully's eyes moved to Salley's face. I was completely

befuddled and as I backed away from the breathing apparatus I inadvertently backed into the South Carolina Highway Patrolman working the wreck. He looked into my eyes and in a solemn voice said, "Did you see everything like you told him?"

Speechless, in shock, and scared out of my mind, I ran from the emergency room and crouched outside in the darkness under the spreading limbs of a Magnolia tree. The familiar and heavy smell of its blossoms brought back memories of lying under a similar tree in my front yard. During lunch on a hot and sultry day, I would lie down in its cool, fragrant shade and wish my father would not make me return to the hot cotton fields but let me lie in peace the whole afternoon. Just as I knew then, I knew now the inevitable moment was near and I would be pulled away from its luxury into the hell of my life very soon. Glancing back to the emergency room door, I saw the patrolman step toward me, but just as quickly, I saw Sully's doctor catch his arm and tell him something. The highway cop stared at me for a second and then walked back into the hospital. Squatting under the tree, trembling with a sickening nausea bubbling in my stomach, I retched in pain and began to sweat profusely.

Alone with my fate, I was overwhelmed by the here and now and began to hyperventilate. My family had rebuked me, my friends had scorned me, and Wes, the one man I thought would help the most, was in cahoots with the two men I feared most, Boot Cutter and Roy Asholee.

There was nowhere to run and no one who could help me; I sat alone in the dark, heaving for breath and shaking with fear when suddenly I felt the comforting sensation of her warm body engulf my back. Putting her arms around me, I turned to find her tear-filled eyes and comforting breath on my face. We said nothing but held each other for a long, long, time.

"Did you see everything that happened?" I nodded yes and welled up with tears, but she kissed me and asked, "Are you going to tell the patrolman what you saw?"

With fear and trepidation pulsing through my body, I didn't

know what to say, but she knew my horror. "If you tell them the truth, you can't stay here; they'll kill you and probably me, too. If you don't tell the truth, they will go free for paralyzing Sully, but we might be able to stay together. We can take care of Sully, but we would be looking over our shoulders for the rest of our lives." With her father's practicality, she summed up our checkmate; our game was over and we had lost.

I could never let Boot get away with what he had done, but the truth would untie the Gordian Knot that united our souls. Tragically, I knew deep in my inner being, if we were separated, we would never be able to find our way back together again. My body felt akin to being drawn and quartered in some medieval dungeon as spasms of pain surged outward from the pit of my soul. Without speaking, we slowly and sadly began to comprehend the only wretched option available. Holding each other, we trembled and slumped to the ground, hoping to awaken from the dark, insane nightmare our love had created.

Chapter Twenty-six

After I gave my statement to the highway patrolman, he drove me home. As I got out of his patrol car, my old man was standing on the back steps and he yelled, "You should have just kept him in jail, because I ain't going to have him in my house!"

Ignoring his threats I walked up the steps, pushed him out of the doorway and walked in the house to find my mother standing with her arms crossed in condemnation. Without fight left in my body I lumbered back to my room and shut the door. I heard the patrolman talking to them but I was too tired to listen.

The next morning after showering and dressing, I intended to take the pickup and drive to the hospital, but the keys had been removed from the peg where they usually hung. Asking for the keys produced silence, so I left the house and began walking to the hospital. Passing the curve where Sully had crashed, I saw his car still at the bottom of the ravine with its bottom side up. With cold chills climbing my back, I walked by the scene and wondered what I would do if Boot Cutter were to ride by in his old station wagon. Having resigned myself to the fact of having a price on my head, I was not afraid and actually looked forward to a confrontation with either him or Roy Asholee.

Knowing my situation, I turned to look at the sound of each car approaching from my rear and soon began sticking my thumb out to try and get a ride. Hitchhiking most of the morning to the hospital, I arrived to find Salley still sitting beside the machine with her hand on Sully's head. Touching her arm, she was trembling so I sat beside her and she put her head on my shoulder. We sat silent and listened to the machine's rhythmic pumping and hissing until her mother and brothers arrived. Her mom took her place and we were sent home with her older brother to rest.

On the ride to Salleys Kitchen, she talked in a delirious way from not having slept for over 30 hours. With her head in my lap she told me Sully had not said a word since he talked with me and she was worried he might lose his will to live. Rambling on for a while, she finally succumbed to sleep and drooled on my jeans as we made our way to the mansion. Her brother watched me in the rearview mirror and seemed relieved I was there with her. The fear of impending doom rode along in my mind, like a sharp stick constantly jabbing my brain with the thought of having to leave her. My life had become hers and I did not know if I wanted to live without her.

Once back at the mansion, I put my arm around her waist while she was sleepwalking up the well-known back stairs to her polka dotted room. Pulling off her sneakers and jeans, I put her to bed and kissed her brow. She did not want me to leave and refused to let go of my hand, so I sat on the edge of her bed for a few minutes until she fell asleep.

My mood was somber as I walked away from the mansion. Trudging through the sand, I crossed the cobblestone culvert and headed toward the hell waiting for me on the farm next door. Arriving home just at sundown, I expected to be greeted by my sanctimonious mother, but instead found the house to be locked up tight and no one around. I had forgotten it was Wednesday, so my mother was at church and my old man was down at Asholee's Store, probably discussing my demise. Without the least thought, I walked around to the outside of my room and removed the electric window fan, stepped in the window and put the dependable old breeze-maker back in place. Knowing my parents well, I wedged a chair under the door knob to slow their irate entry when they arrived and found me in their house.

Sleep was slow to come, but the cool air blowing over my sweaty body and the drone of the old fan motor finally lulled me into a slumber I would regret. In my dreams, Roy Asholee was holding her and tearing at her shirt while I watched helpless to stop him. He laughed with his evil smile and rubbed her breasts as I screamed and cursed him and all the while I could see her steel blue eyes filled with terror.

Boot Cutter then entered the scene and began to hack me with his machete as I finally awoke in a cold sweat to the sound of my old man banging on the door cursing me in real life. The bed sheets were damp with my sweat and I was shivering in a daze until my father, the raving lunatic, began pounding on the door and threatening to call the police to arrest me.

In the morning, I had no way to get back to the hospital, so I began walking again and at the sight of the wreck, the patrolman that took my statement, was investigating the scene. He yelled to me and asked where I was going. I told him to see Salley and he said she and her brother were already at the hospital. He asked if I'd like for him to take me there in his patrol car; I gladly accepted. Salley and I spent the day together sitting with Sully while her mother and brothers slept on cots the nurses provided. That night we were sent back to the mansion again with one of her brothers. As soon as she fell asleep, I went home to find all windows and doors closed and locked. I walked to the hay loft and fell asleep on the hay. Waking in the night, I suddenly felt I had to see her and at least try to find a way to be with her. I did not want to live if I could not feel her touch, if I could not smell her hair or taste her kiss. If giving up everything in my life were the cost, I would pay that price to be with her. She was the only person I had ever loved and the only person who had ever loved me. I could not face the bad without her beside me. Having yearned for love all of my life, it finally filled me to overflowing and if it was to be ripped away, I didn't want to live. I was determined to see her and be with her, no matter what may be ahead.

Climbing down from the loft, I intended to walk to the mansion, but as I stepped into the humid night air, Blackie whinnied and for the first time in quite a while, I smiled. Walking over to rub his nose, I could tell he wanted to go with me and who could blame him? Quickly I grabbed a snap lead and hooked it onto his halter then jumped on his back and we raced from the yard like so many times before. His old metal shoes clicked as we crossed the paved road and headed for the gap beyond the rubble of Della and Wes' old house.

As we approached the barbed wire gate, Blackie did not slow to his usual gait. Instead, I could feel him gathering speed and hear his breathing as he sucked air through his nostrils. At the point of no return, I urged him on, suddenly, the gap was upon us. Like a thoroughbred on a steeplechase course, the big footed old draft horse folded his front legs and thrust mightily with his powerful back legs. Together, in the magic of the cool night air, boy and horse soared over the fence wire to the opposite side without losing stride. Wide-eyed and adrenaline fueled, we galloped through the creek near the ancient longleaf pine, splashing water in our wake as Blackie dug hard to keep his pace. I hugged his thick neck as we climbed up the hill to the huge old mule barn behind the mansion. Sharing a feeling of elation, we heard Spot whinny an excited welcome as we approached. Ducking my head, I rode Blackie into the hallway of the barn and stopped just at the spotted horse's stall. Opening the stall door next to him I led my panting and lathered up steed into the enclosure and struck out for the lighted mansion. I should have given Blackie some water and walked him so he could cool down, but my urgency didn't let me think of him at that moment.

Racing to the mansion, I flew up the back steps and knocked on the enormous kitchen door. Her oldest brother was drinking coffee near the fireplace with a look of worry on his face. Seeing me, he smiled and walked over to let me in. Unaccustomed to another male showing love and concern, I was stunned when he hugged me as I stepped onto the brick floor. He thanked me for coming back and I immediately thought of Salley, asking if she was okay.

With the same striking features as his sister, the brother was a tall dark man with long black hair and a muscled physique. He was wearing a leather necklace with some type of claw around his neck. He told me he had not heard a peep from her since I put her to bed early in the afternoon and asked me if I would go up and check. He told me to ask if she wanted something to eat because he was worried. She had not eaten since she left home yesterday.

Bounding up the back steps from the kitchen, I quietly approached the door and tapped lightly. There was no sound so I opened the door and saw her sleeping soundly among the covers. Unable to stop myself, I joined her under the polka dot comforter and she drowsily opened her eyes and smiled a weak smile.
She spoke softly as she asked, "What are we going to do?"

Stroking her raven hair I replied in earnest, "Don't worry, sweetheart, we're going to be together. No matter what, we're going to be together. We'll have to figure a way to make it work. I can't be away from you."

She wrapped her arms around me and pulled me close, spreading her warmth to my chilled body. My heart throbbed as her essence surrounded me and like a drop of brightly colored dye spreading through a clear glass of water, our souls merged. Her lips hungrily met mine and our bodies united as my heart pounded in my head. With passion our only refuge, we made love with reckless abandon and as our need was filled and our bodies entwined, we vowed over and over to stay together no matter what was ahead. As if this were our last embrace, we were trembling as we held each other and let our exhaustion lull us to a state of semi-sleep.

She heard Spot first and sat bolt upright with panic running through her head. "Did you hear Spot whinnying?"

Joining her in the sitting position I answered, "No."

But seconds later we both heard his blood-curdling scream and ran from the room down the back stairs. Reaching the cobblestone we heard his frantic call again along with the sound of him kicking the side of the barn like he was tearing it apart. Sprinting to the barn, I fumbled for the light switch and finally lit the hallway. Spot was in panic whinnying to the top of his voice and kicking his stall with both back feet so hard it shook the barn. Peering in his stable there was nothing apparent that would spook him this much. But a heartbeat later she let out a

271

death scream and yelled, "NO!"

She was staring horrified in the stall where I left Blackie. The stall door was still closed but I could smell the pungent odor as I fought with the hasp. Finally getting the door to open, I saw Blackie lying on his side gasping for air. He was gurgling down deep inside and his tongue hung from his mouth coated yellow from the radiator antifreeze he drank. Someone had cut the top from a plastic milk jug (the kind that usually holds rotgut whiskey) and mixed the sweet tasting deadly poison with water and put it in his stall. He was hot from our ride, I didn't give him water; I left him thirsty and now he was dying.

My old man had once left some antifreeze and water mixed in a bucket after he had drained the radiator of a tractor. At that time, I had been watching a stray dog steal food from our farm dog's food pan for several months, but figured we had plenty to share and had let him continue with his theft. Over the months the stolen food had allowed him to gain weight and he was beginning to look like he belonged to someone. The drained radiator fluid my old man left uncovered was quickly found by the scavenging dog. The scene of his agonizing and slow death had haunted me for quite some time as I watched him convulse and writhe in pain for two days before he died. Later I felt great guilt for not putting him out of his misery sooner.

My best friend was not going to suffer that agonizing fate. Salley's image was blurry as I looked at her through the tears streaming from my eyes. She said, "Let's get a vet here quick!"

Knowing the reality of the poison, nothing was going to save him and I knew that fact too well! Sobbing I told her, "He's already dead."

As if someone turned my head and made me focus, I saw a pick-axe leaning against the side of the barn left from cleaning the stable. There was not an alternate route, no avenue of avoidance, no way around what I had to do. Without hesitation, for I knew I couldn't do it if I stopped to think, I grabbed the pick and swung it high into the air and with all my might I buried the long rusty spike into Blackie's temple just above his shiny black eyes. The old draft horse kicked his back feet once in automatic reflex and then settled comfortably to die a quick death. Slowly and carefully removing the point from his head, I squatted to touch my friend that had helped me escape my captivity so many times through the years. He was the reason I met Salley and now his joy was gone from my life.

As she put her arms around me and placed her head on my shoulder, we stood frozen in anguish as we heard the squeal of tires and the unmistakable sound of Boot's old station wagon gunning down the road. Staring in disbelief as Blackie's blood drained from his body and pooled on the stall floor, the loss I felt was immeasurable.

During all of this, Spot continued to whinny and kick the walls of his stall. Salley finally opened his stable to try and calm him down, leading him away from the barn. There on the floor of his stall was another container of antifreeze waiting for him. Frantic, she grabbed his lips and pried his mouth open to realize he had not drunk any of the poison. Relieved, her eyes met mine and it became obvious they were leaving a message for both of us. My conversation with the highway patrolman had sealed our fate. Wes was right; there were some things worse than dying and if we stayed in Salleys Kitchen, more of those unspeakable horrors awaited us. Sitting in the doorway of the century and half old stable, I stared at Blackie's shiny body and cried until I had no more tears.

As morning broke and the dew began to steam, my father rode toward the mansion on one of his tractors. He backed up to the barn and hooked a chain to Blackie's front legs and pulled his stiff body out. Without saying a word, he shot callous glances at me every now and then. Devoid of any feeling, he dragged Blackie's body down the sandy lane. His head bounced over the cobblestones and his yellow tongue hung from his mouth as that bastard coldly pulled his remains down the highway. I knew he wouldn't bury him and I knew he would not let me use the tractor to do it either. Instead, he would drag him down near the swamp and let the buzzards pick his bones until he gradually rotted and became part of the cold black soil.

After he was out of sight, Salley and her brother loaded Spot to take him to Dr. Carr's for a check over and he would be kept there for the foreseeable future. The trailer was hooked to her brother's pickup truck and he was in a hurry to get his little sister away from the dangers of Salleys Kitchen. Rushing her into the truck, they left the mansion pulling Spot's trailer toward town without a word of goodbye or a farewell wave.

I sat alone under the arbor in Sully's old chair with a hole in my heart. It was at this point that my attitude toward life changed. My mind and body became void of all fear and concern. Unfamiliar with such a release, I was a little disoriented but was soon rinsed with a sense of calm that swept over me. I was not sad or mad; neither was I happy or glad. An inner need to step up and face death urged me ahead with confidence. I supposed facing my deadly foe was the only method of burning away my pain. That folly often accompanies heartache when thoughts of the future are obscured by agony.

Chapter Twenty-seven

Hearing the sand crunch under car tires, I immediately assumed Boot was returning to finish me off. Having manufactured a need to face my demons, I waited for him to appear, resigned to the fact that either he or I would soon cause a death.

Fate, however, steered me in an unexpected direction as my mother drove around the corner of the mansion and stopped her station wagon next to the arbor where I sat. Still languishing in the fog and shock of utter devastation, my face must have revealed my agony.

Without getting out of the car, the woman that gave me life, stared in silence for some time before she said, "Get in! You're not going to waste our money. Your father and I paid for that college summer school and you're going. If you stay around here they're going to kill you and I'm not going to have people talking about me because of your stupidity."

Frozen by her cold remarks, I sat motionless with a fixed and penetrating stare at her face. Finally she got out and opened the door to the back seat and said again, "Get in, I ain't going to have you living in my house and this is the best way to get you out of here." Slowly I got up and got in the back seat.

When she stopped under the giant umbrella-like limbs of the elm in our backyard, I saw my father sitting in his pickup truck. It seemed odd for him to be sitting in the heat of the sun and he ignored our arrival as if he knew we were coming. He never gave a look in our direction, but continued to clean his fingernails with his pocketknife. As I stepped out of the station wagon my mother said, "Go get my old suitcase from the dining room closet and put the clothes you want in it. Get everything you want now, because you probably ain't going to get to come back."

Moving like a sleepwalker, I went into the house and did as she said. Opening the closet door, I reached in and pulled the old beat-up satchel from under a stack of quilts and blankets. I was surprised to see a Daisy BB gun box fall from the corner where it had been hidden. It had to be the BB gun sent to me by my cousin. It was no big deal, but I had waited for it to come in the mail and I couldn't understand why they would hide it from me. Opening the box I could see the air rifle was almost new, still shiny with a box of brass BBs on the floor beside it. Holding it in my hands I turned it over and over. Placing it back in the box, I left it in the closet.

In my room I put my jeans, socks and underwear in the bottom of the suitcase and stuffed as many shirts as I could on top before I pulled the torn zipper closed. There was some change I left on top of my dresser along with a chapstick, my pocketknife and two of the leftover M-80s from graduation night. Without a thought, I raked the pile of junk into my hand and stuck it in my jeans pocket. My coat was stuffed into an A&P shopping bag along with my penny loafers and my stuff from the bathroom. Walking back through the kitchen, my mother stopped me for her parting shot.

"As hard as we tried to teach you right and wrong, you let a little nigger gal mess up your life. Now you've made your own bed hard and you will just have to lie in it."

Teetering on the edge of rationality, that word, again, set off an explosive charge within my inner being. The guilt I felt from years of denying my feelings and even using that very word myself ripped my conscience to pieces. Dropping my belongings I walked back to the closet, took the Daisy air rifle from the box and held it by the barrel as I returned to the kitchen. Like clockwork, I swung the rifle butt across her precious tea cup collection and smashed as many as I could with a forehand swing, then with my backhand, I broke as many of her mother's china plates, cups and serving pieces as were handy. As a little boy, I had stood up in a chair to see the fancy cups and saucers, only to be caught by my mother and whipped with a wire flyswatter. Having been punished without so much as touching them, I thought I might as well get my money's worth for the punishment I received. To cap off my fury, I broke the BB gun over my knee and threw it on the floor. As I picked up my belongings I spat the words, "Keep Jesus in your heart, Mother!"

That would be the next to last conversation I would ever have with the woman that birthed me. The old man was oblivious to everything that had happened in the kitchen as he was listening to the weather and farm report on the pickup radio. I put my things in the back of the truck and sat down on the seat beside him. Nonchalantly without a glance my way, he cranked the pickup and pulled the shifter into low gear, easing the truck through the sandy driveway toward Roy Asholee's Store. Looking through the bug-spattered windshield, my stomach was already in an uproar and a lump rose up and stopped momentarily at the back of my throat. A flock of turkey buzzards were circling low over the edge of the woods near the swamp. There was no doubt in my mind that the most dominant of the vultures were on the ground pecking Blackie's eyeballs out of their sockets. They had probably already torn the soft flesh from his nose and held strips of his soft ears in their beaks. From having seen them in action on the carcass of a neighbor's cow that died giving birth, I knew they were not far from ripping open his belly and pulling his guts out while fighting each other for the opportunity to tear his huge heart into shreds.

The image made me sick and the lump proceeded up my throat. Hanging my head out the window I retched and vomited while dizzily watching the sand disappear as we reached the paved road in front of the house. Once I set back upright in the seat, I heard my old man chuckle. Looking over at him after I wiped my face with the tail of my T-shirt, I caught full sight of him picking his teeth and making an obnoxious sucking sound as he tried to remove a piece of meat from his last meal. Immediately, I stuck my head back out the window and dry heaved once or twice more.

When he turned the key to shut off the truck in front of the filthy store, his hand moved to his shirt pocket and pulled out a twenty dollar bill. Flipping it on the seat between us he said, "Your Mama said them boys wanted $5 for your part of the gas. I

277

told her it was a waste of money but she wants you out of here. You can have the rest for food when you get there, but that's it. I ain't sending another dime for you to throw away on some nigger. You can go in there and get change from Roy."

I heard the word but my rage had subsided. In his case, ignorance was bliss for he would never realize how close he came to dying in that truck. Wadding the money in my fist, I climbed out of the old pickup for the last time and grabbed my things from the back. Walking away from the truck, I didn't want to get near that store. Instead, I walked slowly to the middle of the intersection and stood where everyone could see me. The old man pulled the truck closer to the side of the store and parked with me in full view like he was waiting for a drive-in movie to start. After four or five cars passed and curiously stared at me in the intersection, a sputtering old gray Plymouth Valiant popped up through the heat waves rising from the hot asphalt. With the brakes squealing like a stuck pig, it slowed to a stop beside me and the driver asked my name. Telling him, he asked if I was the farm boy who wanted to ride to college with them. Nodding my head yes, he pulled the old car over and all three boys got out. The trio wore dark dress pants and short sleeve white shirts with narrow black ties and all three had pocket-protectors in their shirt pockets stuffed with pens and pencils.

The driver was pimply faced and the only one of the three not wearing black horn-rimmed glasses. He was their spokesman. Rubbing his hand over his oily black hair he spoke in a high pitched voice and said, "The trunk is full so you'll just have to sit on your suitcase and hold that bag in your lap." Without my saying a word he continued, "Marvin bought the gas when we left and we calculated your part to be $3.83."

With that pronouncement, Marvin stuck out his pasty white hand for his money. Speaking for the first time I said, "I don't have change right now, but I'll give you this twenty and we can stop later and get change."

The three stood like statues staring at me after my

explanation and Marvin continued to hold his hand out to dun me. Their spokesman again gave reason for their weird actions. "When my Grandma decided to give me this car, instead of my sister, it was because I told her I would always do what she taught me and she always reminded me, 'Neither a borrower nor a lender be,' so as long as we are riding in the car she gave me we're going to do as she said. Now you can go right over there to that old store and ask for change while we wait."

I stood for the longest time trying to make sense of his declaration. I finally realized it didn't matter how ridiculous they may be acting, I wasn't getting in the car without paying $3.83, cash on the barrel head. Smiling, I put my bags down and started for Roy's store. "What the heck?" I mumbled to myself. "$3.83 was as good a reason to die as any other."

Taking my life in my hands, I headed for the nasty store. My eyes had to adjust from the bright sun to the dim light inside. Refocusing, I saw Roy leaning against the bird-shit door in the back. There was a nasty bandage on his nose between two black eyes and that ever-present, nasty cigar was in his mouth. He was puffing smoke nervously turning the tip red under the ashes. His right hand was down by his side and I knew from his posture and the smirk on his face he was holding his finger on the trigger of his pistol. Walking slowly to the counter, I assumed at any moment he'd raise it and squeeze off a couple of rounds at me, but he held his fire and waited for me to speak.

"I need to get some change," I said cautiously and added, "Please."

In the squeaky patronizing voice of a perverted weasel he spoke, "Well, it sure is a surprise to see you back in here. Only thing is, I don't think there's anybody here that you can sucker punch now, boy. You can try but you'll die this time."

Remembering the reason I was forced to come in the store, I thought to myself, *I bet that weirdo's Grandma told him to kill his enemies with kindness, too!* Looking at the floor I noticed the old Prince Albert can had been kicked up on one side so I rotated it with my toe to expose the hole that I now knew went to the basement. Still looking at the floor I said, "I'm sorry all that happened. I shouldn't have done it. It was wrong and it taught me a big lesson. I guess that's the real reason I came in here, to say I'm sorry."

I kept my face toward the floor with his silhouette in the corner of my eye. He took the advantage I offered and shouted, "You damn right it was wrong you little bastard. You lucky I didn't cut your nuts out, you little shit. I still might do it - now git the fuck out of my store!"

Still taking the humble position, I told him, "I'm leaving for good right now, but I have to pay those boys out there so I can get a ride. I need to get some change."

I held up the twenty and neither of us moved or spoke for a while. Finally he said, "Lay it on the counter and move back."

I did what he said and moved back about ten feet to the middle of the store. He walked slowly toward the counter with his eyes dead on me. Once behind the counter he brandished the .22 caliber pistol and pointed it at my head. Then he laughed and put it on the counter in easy reach, pulling the cigar from his mouth and putting it also on the counter with the burning end hanging off the edge. Reaching in his shirt pocket, he counted out some bills and laid them beside the gun. He picked up the twenty, added it to his wad and with a smirk, stuck it back in his pocket. I moved forward to get the change and startled him.

Grabbing the gun he yelled, "Hold it right there you little pecker head or I'll shoot your nuts off before I plant one between your eyes."

I froze in place and he recognized the fear on my face. Realizing his power over me, his courage grew. Laughing out loud he suddenly leaned forward to spit in the direction of my face. His saliva wad hit me in the neck and I quickly wiped it with my hand and looked him in the eye. Realizing he had pushed me to the limit of civility, he began to back away from the counter keeping the pistol aimed in my direction. When he reached what he thought was relative safety, he waved the gun for me to pick up the change. As I moved forward, the Lance cracker rack blocked his view from my chest down. Reaching for the money, I stuck it in my jeans pocket without counting it.

Wanting to get the last laugh, he said, "Ain't you gonna count it? I might'a cheated you."

As I started to remove my hand from my pocket, I felt the two M-80s left from graduation and pulled them out. Staring at the mini-bombs in my hand, he assumed I was counting the money, but quickly, I twisted the fuses together with my eye on the smoking butt he left on the counter. Carefully reaching for the burning remains of his cigar, I broke off the chewed end and I slid the nonsmoking end over both fuses and dropped everything to the floor.

Looking back at him I knew he was clueless when he said, "There's a fifteen dollar charge for changing money. That's okay with you, ain't it?"

He laughed like a hyena. With my toe I guided the smoking little package to the uncovered hole in the floor and it vanished out of sight below. Hurrying out of the store I heard the shiny myna bird saying, "Wat kin I's hep yous wid?" and then the sound of spit hitting the coffee can.

In a court of law it is called premeditated murder. With malice and forethought, I had attempted to kill four people. I knew Roy, his wife, Boot and Wes were more than likely in that store and if those powerful firecrackers ignited, the explosion and resulting fire would leave little chance of any of them surviving. But the only twinge of guilt I felt was for Wes. He had been my teacher, my counselor, and my friend as I moved from boy to man. From those years of learning and listening, I knew- if he had been standing beside me as I dropped those firecrackers to the floor and had known they would end his life and the lives of Boot, Roy and his wife, he would have pushed them in that hole with his own foot. My prayer was for him to meet a forgiving God at the gates of Heaven; a God that understood the tragedy of his life and realized that a community of bigotry and hatred had refused the gift of Wes that He sent. Our community, our country and our world had not been allowed to enjoy the benefits this talented man could have offered. I wished my friend a quick death and joyful meeting with his maker.

Wasting no time, I reached the dun colored Valiant and plopped the four ones in Marvin's sweaty little hand, threw my suitcase in the back and jumped in with the grocery bag on my lap. With my head crooked over like a giraffe in a cage, I left Salleys Kitchen with the three prospective engineers arguing whether to give me change or figure how much the overage would lower each of their parts. Putting my arm around the white shirt in the back seat beside me, I good naturedly patted him on the back to assure him I was fine with the three of them owing me seventeen cents. Actually, I was wiping the slimy chewed tobacco from Roy's cigar stump off my hands and onto the back of his shirt while he smiled in friendship and adjusted his glasses to better see his slide rule.

When Roy Asholee's Store had faded from sight and we had puttered over a few of the sandhills that hid it from view, I looked back in dissolution. Though I had never planned for things to go so haywire, I had hoped, for Sully's sake, to play at least a small role in the destruction of the evil that had scorned and ridiculed him for decades. My love for his daughter would never die and my deep-seated hatred for those who were trying to end our relationship would remain with me for a large portion of my life. Neither seeing nor hearing any evidence, I assumed I had risked my life with harmless duds and my hope for a coup de grâce had failed. Staring out the back window I longed for her touch, I yearned for the taste of her lips and I could feel her penetrating eyes searching my soul and asking why. My first love was gone and I had an unbearable feeling it was forever.

With Salleys Kitchen growing smaller behind us, I continued to stare out the back window as the old gray Plymouth chugged up the last ancient sand dune from which I would be able to see the crossroad. On the horizon I saw a small plume of black smoke shoot up toward the white clouds and I smiled. *Maybe!*

I hadn't smiled since Blackie begged me to ride him to her house and it felt good to remember my friend. As we reached the top of the last sandhill, a sudden and violent, pyrotechnic display belched into the summer sky and like a fountain of flames, curled and grew among the clouds. First one, then two and finally three huge columns of bright orange silently penetrated the horizon with only my eyes seeing the inferno from the rear window. My fellow travelers were intent on solving the gas money problem and I saw no reason to spoil their fun.

May God have mercy on my soul.

Sully's Search

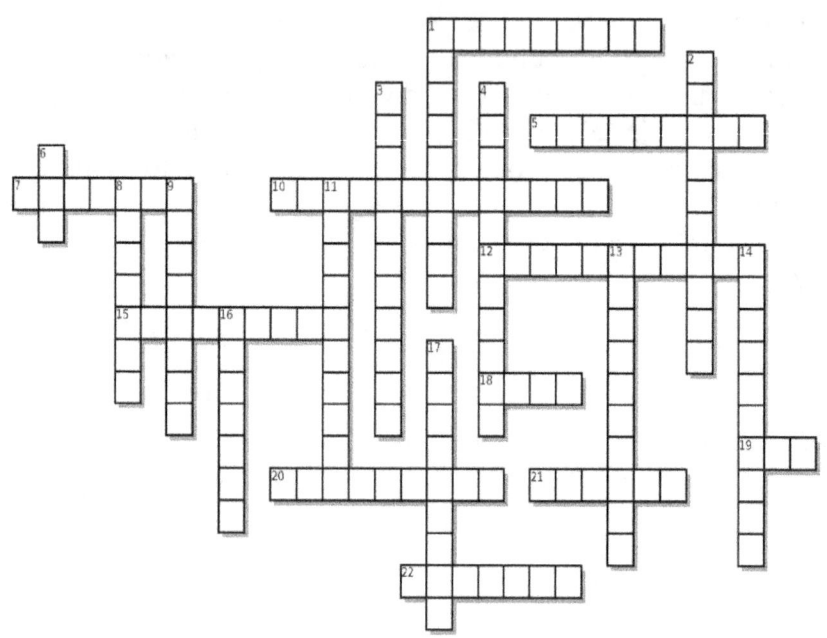

ACROSS

1 to seed
5 gypsies
7 ignorant in actions
10 happily opportune
12 misguided
15 confuse
18 hello
19 in thing
20 gloom
21 AWOL
22 lull

DOWN

1 suitor
2 intolerant
3 unconventional
4 benevolence
8 nightmare
9 significant other
11 encounter
13 explosive
14 hospice
16 eccentric
17 humiliated

Sully's Search

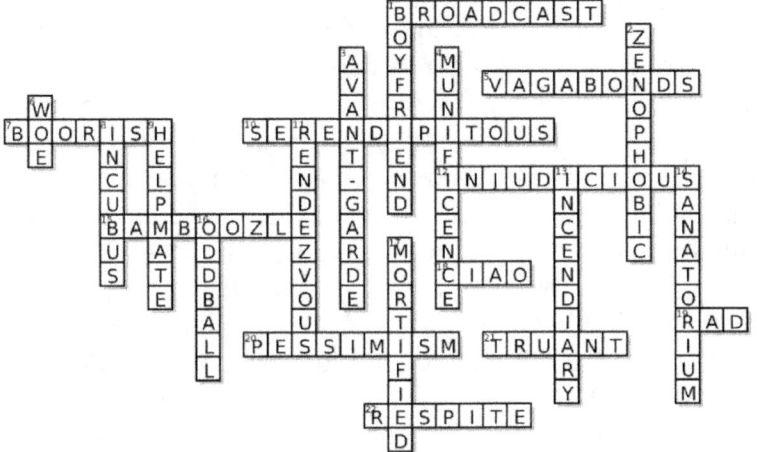

ABOUT THE AUTHOR

Bruce Weeks was born in 1954, the year of the Supreme Court Decision, Brown vs Board of Education and reared in the sandhills region of western South Carolina. Growing up on his father's cotton farm in the community of Kitchings Mill in eastern Aiken County, he entered the cotton fields at an early age and worked alongside the African Americans that toiled on his father's farm. Attending Salley Elementary School then Wagener-Salley High School, he left the area in 1972 to attend Clemson University. In 1976 he began working in research for Clemson University. In 1993 he went back to college at age 40 and received a Bachelor of Science Degree in Elementary Education. After 5 years in the elementary classroom, he became certified as 'Highly Qualified' in secondary History and taught in high school and middle school until his retirement in 2012. An avid fan of the Appalachian Trail, he has section hiked the trail from Springer Mountain, Georgia to Damascus, Virginia. He is now working on a hiker rest area near the trail and his cabin in the mountains of Virginia. A resident of Townville, SC, he and his wife, Jan, also a retired school teacher, have lived there for 40 years. They have two children and three grandchildren that they spoil as much as possible. Owners of two Boykin Spaniels they have found good homes for many little golden eyed puppies. When not writing, Mr. Weeks works on an extended list of honey-dos.

In stinging realism, Mr. Weeks' fictional story offers an authentic and vivid depiction of the brutal racism that gripped his home in Aiken County and most of South Carolina during the late 1960s. It is a must read given the drama that presently grips our nation. It's a timely reminder of a past to which we must never return.